"*Where the devil are you going?*"

"I wonder if I can hear ..." She threw open the window and the wild music drifted up to her from the glen below. "Yes, I can. Do you?"

"The bagpipes?" He nodded. "Have you suddenly developed a liking for them?"

She nodded dreamily as her gaze traveled over the men, women, and children still moving about in the torchlit glen. "They're part of Craighdhu." She looked at him over her shoulder.

And Robert was all of Craighdhu. He was the silences and the mysteries, the passions that excited her and the cozy fires that warmed her. She felt a surge of love for him so strong it almost took her breath away. "Can't you see that this is how it should be?"

He didn't answer and she turned to face him, a touch of defiance in her stance. "I tell you, I was right to do this."

He smiled slowly and held out his hand. "Then come and do it again."

He would not admit this passion he had for her was not a mistake. Well, she mustn't ask for too much. She had only begun and already won a great deal tonight.

She smiled happily as she started toward him.

The Magnificent Rogue

IRIS JOHANSEN

Bantam Books
New York Toronto London Sydney Auckland

THE MAGNIFICENT ROGUE
A Bantam Book / September 1993

ISBN 0-553-29944-1

Published simultaneously in the United States and Canada

Bantam Books are published by Bantam Books, a division of Bantam
Doubleday Dell Publishing Group, Inc. Its trademark, consisting of the
words "Bantam Books" and the portrayal of a rooster, is Registered in
U.S. Patent and Trademark Office and in other countries. Marca Reg-
istrada. Bantam Books, 1540 Broadway, New York, New York 10036.

PRINTED IN THE UNITED STATES OF AMERICA

RAD 0 9 8 7 6 5 4 3 2 1

*This book is dedicated to the Atlanta Braves,
who, through triumph and defeat, always
remain the most valiant of magnificent rogues.*

*M*ermaid!

Kate bolted upright in bed, chest rising and falling as she tried to still the panic tearing through her.

Had she screamed out the word? Dear God, let it not have happened. Yet her throat felt so raw, she knew she had betrayed herself.

She scrambled back against the headboard, wiping the tears from her cheeks as her gaze fixed fearfully on the door.

If she had screamed, they would soon come. She would hear the footsteps, and then the door would open. . . .

No sound yet. Perhaps she had not cried out, and if she had, maybe she had not awakened them. Perhaps God would be merciful, and she would be allowed to—

Footsteps.

Her eyes shut as terror closed around her. She braced herself, trying to smother the fear. She would not let them see her weakness, she thought fiercely. They would deny it, but she knew they liked to see her afraid. It was a weapon in the battle they waged against her. She was not usually so lacking in strength, but after the dream she always felt so frightened and lost that—

"Ah, my child. The dream again?"

Her lids flicked open, and she saw Sebastian Landfield standing in the doorway, illuminated by the single candle in the pewter holder he carried. His nightshirt and frayed gray robe clung to his thin body, making it appear frail. His rumpled white hair formed a shining halo about his lined face, and his gray eyes glittered with moisture as he looked at her. "I prayed it would not come. How it hurts me to see you suffer."

"I'm not suffering." She couldn't resist the small defiance, though she knew she would pay for it.

He came forward to stand beside her bed and put the candle on the nightstand. "How can you say that when you woke us from deep sleep with your torment?" He reached out and gently touched a lock of hair on her forehead. "And, look, your thrashing about has loosened your hair from your nightcap."

Blast it, she should have remembered to put on the cap. She carefully avoided darting a guilty glance at the despised night bonnet she had tossed impatiently on the bedside table before she went to sleep.

Sebastian's glance shifted to the cap. "It appears suspiciously tidy for having undergone such punishment, doesn't it?" He looked back at her. "But I know you would not have disobeyed me and left your hair unconfined. You have been so good of late."

She quickly changed the subject. "I'm sorry I disturbed you, sir. I would not have—"

"It is no disturbance to be called to my duty," he interrupted. "It is God's will. His fingers traced the path of tears down her cheek. "Though Martha was not overpleased to have her rest broken."

She wished he would not caress her cheek with those long, cold fingers. It seemed he was touching her more of late. She turned her head to avoid it. "I will give her my apologies. Where is she?"

"She will be here soon." He smiled sadly. "And I think you know where I had to send her."

To the top drawer of the cabinet in the scullery downstairs.

Kate shivered as she visualized Sebastian's stocky wife moving down the steps, a grim smile of pleasure on her face.

"Martha thinks you're too old to be having these dreams," Sebastian said softly. "She believes it's only pretense, that you woke us out of spite."

She looked at him in bewilderment. "Why would I be so stupid as to do such a thing?"

"Oh, I do not think you would. Martha is not always clever about people." His hand moved down to caress her throat. "And sixteen is not such a great age. There is still time to chasten and form you. Now why do you suppose you had the dream tonight?"

She didn't answer.

"Silence? Meekness is a virtue, but I don't think this lack of words is caused by meekness. Tell me of the dream. Was it the same?"

He knew it was always the same. She had cursed herself a hundred times for telling him about the mermaid, but she had only been a child when the dream started. She had not realized how powerful a weapon it would prove to him.

"Tell me," he repeated softly. "You know it is for the best. Confess your sin, my child."

She could lie to him and tell him the dream was not about the mermaid. He might believe her.

Anger flared through her. She would *not* lie. It wasn't fair. *He* wasn't fair. "You're wrong. It wasn't a sin." Her voice trembled with rage. "It was only a dream. How could a dream be a sin?"

"Ah, here it comes," he murmured. "Those golden eyes are blazing at me. All my efforts these long years, and you've learned so little. You pretend docility, but no matter how I try to tame your bold ways, there comes a time when you turn and rend me."

"Because it's not true! I did not sin." Did he think

she didn't know the difference? Sin was what she felt when she wanted to pull his hair out and kick his chicken-thin legs. Sin was what she felt when rage blackened within her at one of Martha's spiteful remarks.

"I've explained all this to you before," he said patiently. "Your soul flies free when you slumber and wallows in corruption. Why do you not understand?" He leaned forward, his eyes glittering with the fanaticism of his conviction. "You know how sinful you are. How could you not be depraved? You're the seed of a libertine planted in the womb of the greatest harlot born to man. The only way you may be saved from eternal damnation is through me. Now, confess. You dreamed of the mermaid?"

The resistance suddenly seeped out of her. It would do no good to deny it, she thought wearily. "Yes."

He relaxed slightly. "Very good. Now we must determine what led to this sin." His gaze narrowed on her face. "What did you do today?"

"I studied with Master Gywnth. I helped madam make candles."

"Is that all?"

She bit her lower lip. "After I finished my chores, I went for a ride on Caird."

"Ah. To the village?"

"No, the path through the forest." Memories flowed back to her, soothing her: cool, verdant foliage, the smell of earth dampened from the recent rains, the smooth slide of Caird's muscles beneath her, the velvet feel of his muzzle beneath her palm as she had patted him while leading him to the brook to drink.

"You would not tell me an untruth? You spoke to no one?"

"No one." She met his gaze and burst out, "No one, I tell you. Even if I had gone to the village, you know they will not speak to me. Not since you—"

"Then it must have been the ride itself." He frowned. "I never approved of letting you learn to ride. Such freedom is not good for one as weak in spirit as you. It encourages all sorts of—"

Fear ripped through her. He must not take Caird away from her. She could bear anything but that. "No! The lady said I could do it. You said the lady wants me to ride well."

"Hush! You see what impertinence these indulgences breed?"

"She is being troublesome?" Martha stood in the doorway. "Did I not tell you she was getting worse?" She crossed the room and handed Sebastian the small whip she carried. "If you would let me use this on her at my own discretion, she would soon be properly schooled."

He shook his head. "How many times must I tell you? It is my duty alone. You may go back to bed."

She looked at him, surprised. "You do not wish me to stay and bear witness?"

"You may go," he repeated.

Kate was as surprised as the woman. Her punishment was usually performed as a ritual ceremony with the woman digesting every facet of Kate's pain with supreme satisfaction.

"I want to stay," Martha protested. "Why make me leave?"

"It has come to my attention that you enjoy her suffering too much. We do not scourge her body for our pleasure, but to purify her soul."

A flush mottled his wife's cheeks. "I admit I have no liking for this strumpet's-leavings but you have no call to shut me away."

"It is my duty to protect as well as chasten her."

The color deepened with anger. "You lie to yourself," she hissed. "Do you think I don't know? That I haven't seen how you look at her now? I did not want to believe it, but you are—" She broke off as Sebastian's gaze burned.

Kate knew that look that seemed to devour everything in its path, but she had never seen it turned on Martha before.

"What am I?" he prodded with soft menace.

Martha moistened her lips. "Nothing. Nothing. Satan twisted my tongue." She hurried from the chamber.

Sebastian turned back to Kate. "It is time."

She knew what was coming. Her hands nervously clenched the sheet. During the confrontation with his wife there was a chance he might have forgotten about Caird. She must make sure his attention remained on the offense and not what he thought caused it. "It was only a dream," she whispered.

"The dream is a sin. Can you not see how it leads you to willfulness?" He stepped away from the bed. "Go position yourself."

She stood up and moved toward the whipping stool across the room. It would be over soon. He was always careful not to leave scars, and he seldom gave her more than a taste of the whip for such a small infraction. If she feigned remorse . . . Sweet heaven, the thought of groveling stuck in her throat. Still she would not only show remorse but beg him on her knees to keep Caird and the little parcel of freedom permitted her.

"Bare your back."

She quickly slipped her gown from her shoulders and let it fall to her waist as she knelt beside the stool. She could feel the cold floorboards through the thin cotton of her gown. She spread out her arms as he had taught her from childhood and waited for the first blow.

It did not come.

She glanced over her shoulder. He stood there with the whip in his hand, his gaze on her back. His cheeks were curiously flushed; his hand loosened and tightened on the whip in an odd rhythmic movement.

"How easily you shed your clothing. Are you completely lost to shame?" he asked hoarsely. "Is that how you behaved in your dream?"

She stared at him in bewilderment. He had never found fault with her in this way before. "I told you . . . the dreams are never like that." Why did he not start? She wanted it over. Trying to keep the impatience from her tone, she said, "You told me to ready myself. I only obeyed."

"With no modesty or decorum." His gaze was fixed on the hollow of her spine where it joined the soft swelling of her buttocks. "I have noticed how you flaunt yourself of late. I feared it would come to this as childhood left you. The bad blood is too strong for you to fight. You must try to tempt every man who comes near you."

"No!"

"Yes." His lips tightened as if he were in pain. "I have seen how you look at men beneath your lashes and smile with that pouty whore's mouth. I know that smile. I have watched her passing through this village, weaving her magic for nearly twenty years. Did you think I would not recognize the signs?"

"I'm not her. I'm not my mother." Her voice shook with anger. "I'm me. I swear I have no wish to tempt any man. I only want to be left alone."

"You lie. All strumpets lie," he hissed. "Even in your sleep you dream of sin. Admit it."

"I do not dream of—" Her hands clenched into fists. "Please do it and get it over with."

"So that you can go back to sleep and lose yourself in lust?" He drew his arm back to strike. "For the good of your soul I must make sure you are not able to indulge yourself this night."

Fire touched her back as the lash struck.

She bit her lip to keep from crying out.

"And I think we will have to rid you of that stallion."

"No!" She screamed at his words as she had not at the lash.

Another blow.

She desperately tried to think through the haze of pain.

The lady. If Sebastian feared anything in the world, it was the wrath of the lady. "The lady will not . . . like it. She will—"

"It is not always wise to tell the lady everything. The horse is old. He will fall ill and die." The lash struck again. "We will merely neglect to get you another."

Sickness moved through her. "You would kill him?"

"What is the life of a beast when it comes to saving a soul? I should have gotten rid of him when you fled three months ago."

The lash struck again.

And again.

And then again.

She had never seen him in such a frenzy. She did not know how many times the lash fell before the blows finally ceased.

She was barely clinging to awareness when he picked her up and carried her to bed. He laid her down with great gentleness. "Now you will sleep well," he murmured. "Though you should not have forced me to chastise you so severely."

"Please . . . not Caird . . ."

"We will talk tomorrow about the horse." He tucked the covers around her. "And then you will watch the act and know it is done only for your sake."

The devil she would. Her nails dug into her palms beneath the covers. She loved Caird. He was the only thing in the world she cared about, and she would not let him be destroyed. She would master this weakness and fight again.

He picked up the candle and moved toward the door. "Good night, Kathryn."

The door had scarcely closed behind him when she threw off the covers and staggered to her feet.

She could not let him kill Caird. Not Caird . . .

Greenwich Palace

"Black Robert . . ." the queen murmured. "You have him? You're sure, Percy?"

"Quite sure, Your Majesty," Percy Montgrave said. "I could hardly be more certain. I have two dead men and one wounded to testify to the fact. The earl of Craighdhu is awaiting your pleasure in the Tower."

"Excellent." Elizabeth's beringed hand slapped down on the arm of her chair. "Though God knows it took you long enough. I told you I wanted him six months ago." Her gaze went to the document on the desk across the room. "It's very nearly too late."

Percy's brow wrinkled in puzzlement. The entire court knew how distraught Elizabeth was about the contents of that order, but as far as he could determine, that order had nothing to do with the earl. "He's not an overly obliging gentleman. For a while I wasn't sure if the Spaniards would get him before he returned to Scotland."

Elizabeth shook her head. "He's too clever for them. You took him at Craighdhu?"

Percy shook his head. "Edinburgh. Craighdhu would have been impossible. Those barbarian clansmen of his would not have been amenable to seeing their chief in chains. His Majesty, your kinsman James, how-

ever, was all too eager to turn a blind eye while I removed an irritating thorn from his side."

"How impossible?"

"I beg your pardon?"

"How impossible is it to break Craighdhu's defenses?"

"Perhaps not entirely impossible." His lips twisted.
"If attacked by a fleet the size of the armada Philip of
Spain is building to put to sea against Your Majesty."

"That strong . . ." The news did not seem to dis-
please the Queen. "No weakness?"

"Craighdhu is an island off the western coast of
Scotland. I understand it's a barren, dark place of
mountains and mists. The castle is well fortified and
has only one harbor that can be broached from the sea.
That port is extremely well guarded." He paused. "May
I ask if there's a reason why we should be concerned
about the strength of his lordship's holdings?"

Elizabeth didn't appear to hear him. "What manner of man is he?"

"Deadly."

She waved an impatient hand. "I have no problem
with that. A man who is lacking in dangerous qualities
is no man at all. What other impressions can you give
me?"

God's blood, what did she want from him now?
More than a year ago she had demanded and received
the most detailed report on the scoundrel he had ever
compiled for her. He had been ordered to bring her
many such secret reports on various gentlemen during
the past three years, but something about the earl of
Craighdhu had caught her interest. He could not understand her obsession with this Scot. Robert
MacDarren held no power in James's court in Scotland,
nor in Elizabeth's in England. Of course, the possibility
existed that his pirating of Spanish ships had won her
approval. Elizabeth had always expressed a fondness to-

ward her buccaneers, but Robert MacDarren did not fly under her flag.

"Well?" she prompted.

He tried to ignore his own dislike of the fellow and give her what she wanted. "Intelligent."

"Brilliant," she corrected.

He inclined his head. "Perhaps."

"Don't quibble. He took four of Philip's galleons in six months."

"Which may mean he has excellent warrior instincts. That doesn't necessarily mean he's—"

"Brilliant," she reiterated.

"May I remind Your Majesty, he also took one of your ships?"

"I believe he had a purpose in that."

"Gold."

She gazed at him thoughtfully. "He's raised your hackles. You bristle when you speak of him. Why?"

Percy hesitated. "He . . . annoys me."

She was silent, waiting.

"I do not like these wild Highlanders."

"Particularly *this* wild Highlander?"

"He's nothing but an outlandish rogue," he burst out. "He has the tongue of a viper, no respect for any authority but his own, and . . . he laughs too much."

She raised her brow. "Laughs?"

"He finds humor in the most inappropriate subjects."

"Such as?"

He was not about to confess how MacDarren had mocked the turned-up toes of his fashionable puce-colored shoes. "Anything that is out of his realm of barbarism," he said tartly.

"Why won't you . . ." She trailed off, studying him for a moment, her gaze traveling from his scarlet-feathered velvet cap to the white doublet puffed to almost feminine fullness at his hips and then down to his fine purple hose and silver-embroidered garters. She suddenly chuckled. "He made fun of your attire?"

He flushed. Elizabeth's instinct was uncanny, and she never hesitated to tear aside barriers best left intact. "I did not say that."

"But a brilliant man who has been left without weapons would probe until he found a suitable one."

"Are you saying you find my attire—"

"Entirely suitable," she said soothingly. "You're the envy of all my courtiers, and I like a bit of gaud. But as you say, a man of MacDarren's barbarian upbringing would not appreciate the niceties of court dress." She changed the subject. "He was alone when you took him?"

"A chief of a clan is seldom alone. The clan demands a henchman to accompany the chief at all times for his protection. We were forced to take his cousin, Gavin Gordon, as well." He shrugged. "The man was surprisingly inadequate at his duty. My captain of the guard said it was MacDarren who was forced to protect both himself and the henchman. Gordon was wounded in the fray."

"But he lives?"

"He lost a good deal of blood, but he's on the mend."

"Good. We may be able to use him."

"For what?"

"Even rogues have loyalties, and from what you've reported, the earl is prone to be as extravagant with his friends as he is with his enemies." She stood up with a flurry of amber velvet skirts and adjusted the stiff pleated ruff that framed her throat. "As we shall soon see. Let's get to it. You shall accompany me to the Tower."

"Now?" His eyes widened in surprise. "But it is nearly midnight, Your Majesty."

"All the better. I do not want my visit to be

shouted from every street corner in London. Go tell them to summon my barge."

"Would not tomorrow do as well?"

"No, it would not," she snapped. "Thanks to your laggardness, time has almost run out. Do as I bade you."

Percy's lids lowered to hide his anger. By God, it went against the grain to stand here and take her abuse. Queen or not, she was only a woman, and her behavior in this matter went entirely beyond the bounds of reason. First, he had been insulted by that impudent rogue, and now he was being accused of laggardness. What was he supposed to have done? Gone sailing after that barbarian while he raided Spanish galleons?

He took a deep breath and then said through clenched teeth, "Immediately, Your Majesty." He bowed low and backed from the room.

By all that was holy, the man was growing pompous. Elizabeth watched the door close behind Percy before she strolled over to the window to stare out into the darkness. But though a fop and a trifle above his station, Percy was evidently no fool. He had gotten her MacDarren!

She glanced back at the document on her desk and felt the muscles in her back and shoulders tense. It was there, waiting for her signature. Dear God, was there no way out?

She knew the answer.

But she did not have to face it yet. In spite of the pleadings of those bloodthirsty leeches in Parliament, she would not give in.

Not yet.

Not before she set her plans in motion.

How had it come to this? she thought wearily. She had only wished to protect and guard, but lies had a habit of begetting lies until the entire world seemed webbed with falsehood.

She tore her gaze away from the document and immediately felt better. There was no way for her to win that battle. Her coming confrontation with MacDarren was much more to her liking. From what she had heard he was a man worthy of her steel, and there was nothing she liked better than proving to a clever man how much more clever a woman could be.

She turned away from the window and moved briskly toward her dressing room. "Margaret! My cloak."

"I failed you." Gavin glanced gloomily around the small cell and then looked at Robert, who was on the other cot across the room. "We would not be here if I had done my duty."

Robert yawned. "You're entirely right. You're an abysmal henchman. You handle a sword as if it were a broomstick and are as clumsy as a pregnant sea lion."

Gavin wrinkled his nose. "The rest is true enough, but I resent being compared to a sea lion. Besides, how could a lion be pregnant? It would have to be a lioness to— You're not listening."

"I'm listening. You were berating yourself for putting us in this predicament. Go on, I'm sure it's very good for you."

"It's true, you know. I should never have been the one to accompany you. Jock wouldn't have let you be taken."

"We were outnumbered."

"You've been outnumbered before. If I hadn't been wounded, you would have managed to get away."

"Gavin."

"Yes?"

"You're boring me. I agree you're a terrible henchman, but you've always had one saving grace. You were never a bore."

"Just a jester in your hall," Gavin said glumly. "You

should have left me at— My God, it's hot in here." He sniffed. "And it smells."

"That's probably me." Robert sniffed. "No, I believe it's you."

Gavin sat up in his cot and swung his legs to the floor. "Next you'll say I smell like a sea lion too."

"I've never gotten close enough to one to smell its scent."

"I have." Gavin's face suddenly lit up with eagerness as he remembered that golden day. "Once I camped out on the barrens and watched them. They were frightened at first, and then they got used to me and let me come close."

"Really? You never told me."

"It was when I was a boy." He frowned, trying to remember. He and Robert, who was five years older, had grown up together on Craighdhu. He had trailed behind him all over the island, and they had shared a multitude of experiences. That day had been so special to Gavin that surely he would have told Robert about it. "It must have been when you were in Spain."

"Perhaps."

Gavin couldn't see Robert's expression in the dim cell, but he heard the sudden reserve in Robert's tone that hadn't been there before. He had blundered again. He knew Robert didn't like to talk about that time. He wasn't usually so stupid; it must be this damn fever. "Well, anyway, I know I don't smell like a sea lion."

"I'll accept your word on it. Are you thirsty?"

"A little." More than a little in truth, but he didn't know if he had the strength to get up and fetch water from the pitcher on the table across the room, and he didn't want to ask Robert for anything more. He had done too much already. He had cared for Gavin as if he were a helpless bairn on the long journey from Edinburgh, binding his wound, bathing his head when the fever struck.

"Lie back down. I'll get you some water."

"No, I can—"

Robert was already moving. Gavin watched as he poured water from the pitcher into a goblet.

"Why did you take me to sea with you this time instead of Jock?"

"You wanted to come."

"I thought I did. All those stories of gold and glory . . ."

"Well, there was gold aplenty." Robert brought the goblet to Gavin. "But no glory."

Gavin drank thirstily. "I didn't like the blood. I didn't think there would be so much of it."

"You can't take ships without shedding blood, and Craighdhu needs the gold."

Gavin knew that was true. Craighdhu was not fertile enough to feed her people, and Robert had done only what was necessary.

He took another drink. "Are they going to hang us, Robert?"

"I don't think so."

"Then why are we here?"

"You heard Montgrave. The queen wants to see me."

"I told you that you shouldn't have raided her ship."

"I doubt if that's why we're occupying this cell. Everyone knows Montgrave handles the queen's more confidential assignments."

"Then why?"

"I have a few ideas. More water?"

Gavin shook his head.

"Then lie down again." Robert gently pushed him back and covered him with the blanket.

He had never known Robert could be gentle until he had fallen ill, Gavin thought. No, that was not true. He could dimly remember that gentleness when they were younger. But since Robert had been back from Spain, he had known only the hard, mocking man they called Black Robert of Craighdhu. The chief who distanced himself from everyone and let no one come too close, the leader who dealt in blood and force as easily as he executed the decisions of the clan. Not like himself, Gavin thought ruefully, remembering how he had hung his head over the rail and been sick after his first battle.

Robert sat back down on his own cot and leaned against the wall. He didn't seem worried, but then Robert seldom showed his feelings. Gavin had watched him sit that way a hundred times, outwardly at ease but drawing silence and strength around him like a cloak of power.

Gavin said, "If she does intend to hang us—"

"Then we'll find a way to escape."

"You'll have to go without me."

"No."

Gavin had known that would be his answer, but he felt honor-bound to pursue it. "I'm not strong enough to be any good to you."

"You're stronger than you think." Robert's tone was final, and Gavin felt a tiny rush of relief. It was all very well to offer to sacrifice your life, but it was infinitely better to have that offer refused. Not that he had expected anything else. Gavin belonged to Craighdhu, and to Robert that meant he must be protected against all enemies. Besides, why should he be worried? Robert would manage to get them out of here. Robert was more clever than anyone he knew. If it became necessary, he would find a way to escape. and take Gavin with him.

"You're probably right." Gavin's tone became light as he settled himself into a more comfortable position. "I've always found I rise splendidly to any occasion."

"That doesn't involve blood," Robert added dryly.

"Well, then you'll just have to think of some way to get us out of here that meets that condition, won't you?"

• • •

The cell was dank, dark, and unpleasant, Elizabeth noticed, as Percy threw open the door. By the light of the candle he carried, she could barely discern two figures on cots across the room.

"Take Gordon to another cell until we're through with the earl," Montgrave ordered the guard accompanying them. "Her Majesty wishes to speak to His Lordship in privacy."

The guard roughly pulled Gordon from his cot and pushed him toward the door.

A curse erupted from the other cot. "Goddammit, be careful, you fool," Robert MacDarren said sharply. "Let him walk by himself. Do you wish to open his wound?"

The guard didn't answer as he pushed Gavin Gordon past Elizabeth. She caught a glimpse of tousled red hair, bloodshot blue eyes, and freckles dusting a parchment-pale face. Why, he was only a boy. She doubted if he had reached his twentieth year. A strange choice to guard the man they called Black Robert.

"On your feet," Percy said to MacDarren as he placed the candle on the table. "Can you not see who is honoring you with her presence?"

The dark figure on the cot didn't move. Arrogance, Elizabeth thought. Well, she had no quarrel with arrogance. She had an abundance of that quality herself, and a touch of it in him would serve her well.

"Leave us, Percy." She moved forward into the cell. "Come back when I call."

"But, Your Majesty," Percy protested. "It's not safe. He will—"

"Throttle me? Ridiculous," she scoffed. "He may be without manners, but he's no madman. Go."

Percy hesitated before stepping back and slamming shut the door.

"Now that he's gone, do you suppose you could bring yourself to display courtesy?" she admonished.

"You do not have to prance and pose to show how brave and uncaring you are."

There was a moment of silence, and then MacDarren chuckled. "Good evening, Your Majesty." He stood up and bowed. "Forgive me. I judged you incorrectly. I assumed you had a fondness for poseurs like Montgrave. Naturally, in my precarious situation I wanted only to please you."

She peered into the shadows but could discern only the white blur of his shirt and the fact that he was big, very big. "I cannot see you. Come closer."

"I fear I'm both disheveled and aromatic. I understand your senses are very delicate, and I would not offend you."

Mockery. She suppressed a flare of anger. One of the reasons she had chosen him was his lack of reverence for authority, and she could not have it both ways. However, it might be wise to remind him that authority had certain advantages. "My feelings are not so sensitive that I could not bear to witness you punished for your insolence. This tower has witnessed the breaking of stronger men than you, my lord. Now, come here and let me see you."

He let a moment pass before strolling forward into the pool of light.

God's blood, he was comely.

She had always had a fondness for dark men. Her own dear Robin had this same Latin coloring. No doubt it was MacDarren's Spanish mother who had given him his gypsy-black hair, the brows that slashed over deep-set dark eyes, and the skin that was more golden than tan. Unusually high cheekbones hollowed his cheeks and made his well-shaped lips appear all the more sensual in contrast. His body was tall and fit, his legs powerful and bulging with muscle in their hose, and he had moved with a sleek, animallike grace that stirred her senses. Comeliness was not necessary for her purpose, but she was pleased that he possessed it.

"But you have no desire to break me," he said softly. "Do you, Your Majesty? You have something else in mind."

She gazed at him with wariness. "You think so? That must have given you comfort, lying here in this dark cell."

He smiled. "It did, actually."

Good white teeth, she noticed, and, though charged with mockery, that smile had a certain bold charm.

"I'm sure that disappoints you," he continued. "Did you picture me lying here trembling in fear of your royal wrath?"

"It would not be unheard-of in your situation."

He shook his head. "If you had wanted me dead, Montgrave could have accomplished that end in Edinburgh. Instead, you brought me to London at some little bother to dear Percy."

"More than some little bother. Two dead men, I understand."

"But you thought it worthwhile to forfeit their lives for your purpose."

"Perhaps I wanted to show my people I will not tolerate piracy."

"Unless you receive a generous tribute from the Spanish treasure chests."

She didn't bother to deny it. "But you gave me no tribute and did not confine yourself to Spanish ships. You attacked one of mine."

"Did I?"

"And led the captain of that ship to believe you were acting on the orders of your Scottish king. James was not pleased when I sent him a protest. Not only had he not received the tribute that might have soothed the sting of my note, but he had most certainly not sent you forth to raid my ships."

His smile didn't waver. "I didn't exactly say I was acting on James's orders."

She snorted. "Quibbling. You were amazingly restrained in that attack. You took booty but no lives. I believe you attacked my ship for only one reason. You wanted me to believe that James was interfering with my fleet."

His lids lowered to veil his eyes. "Why would I do that?"

"That's one of the things I want to know. You have questions to answer."

"I so detest questions."

The mockery was back, and she was suddenly impatient with him. "That boy they took out of here is your kinsman?"

"Gavin?" His smile vanished. "Yes, my cousin."

"And I understand as chief you act as father and protector of your clan. Unless you wish to rescue him from a very unpleasant fate, it would be wise to answer me clearly and fully."

An expression flickered over his face that caused her to take a step back. She was actually afraid of him. The knowledge amazed her and then sent a tiny thrill through her. There had been no reason for her to be afraid for many years, and absolute safety was always a little boring. As queen she was protected and guarded by her very position, but MacDarren cared nothing for her crown. Deadly, Percy had said about him. She had an idea he was more deadly than the man knew.

"Ask your questions," he said coldly.

"Why my ship?"

"You seem to have guessed. I did it to annoy James. The opportunity presented itself, and I took it."

"But why in this way?"

He hesitated, then shrugged. "It was a chance to divide you. James is powerful enough already, and everyone knows you're considering naming him as heir to your throne. It would not be to my advantage to have him king of England as well as Scotland. He has no liking for Highlanders."

"Particularly for you."

He inclined his head. "We have had words on occasion. Is that all you wish to know?"

"For the moment. I know a good deal about you already and have guessed more. If I think of something else, I will let you know."

"But it's not only information you want from me, is it?" he asked softly. "It's action."

It was true, but he could not possibly have guessed her purpose. She was curious to know what conclusions that agile mind had drawn. "And just what action do you think I wish from you?"

"Assassination?"

"What?"

He studied her astonished expression. "No?" He shrugged. "It was a reasonable conclusion."

"Assassinate who?"

"James."

She looked at him, surprised. "You believe I chose you to kill a fellow monarch?"

"There would be certain advantages. I'm a Scot, and everyone knows I have no love for James. That would draw suspicion away from you. You've kept James's mother, Mary, captive for nearly twenty years because you fear her claim to the English throne. Now, rumor has it the Parliament has asked you to end that captivity . . . violently."

"She instigated a plot to take my life," she said quickly.

"But with Mary of Scotland dead and James suddenly removed as well, it would throw Scotland in turmoil. What a perfect opportunity for you to march across the border and restore order." He added, "And gather Scotland up like a goose for the cooking."

He *was* clever. If the circumstances had been the same fifteen years ago, she might have decided to do just as he supposed. "If that was what I wished to do. It is not. Though she has been a constant threat to me,

I have avoided executing Mary for years." She cracked her fist down on the table. "I have *no* wish to see her die. She is a queen, and the lives of royalty should be sacrosanct. All monarchs walk a thin line between life and death. If I take her life, who is to say that tomorrow another king won't deem I should also die? To put her to death is to put myself in danger."

"Then you will disregard the order of execution drawn up by Parliament?"

She did not answer directly. "I do not wish to see her die." She lifted her gaze to his face. "And if I wished to kill James, it would be in battle, not by assassination. So you are wrong on both counts. But you are correct that I do intend to use you for my own purpose."

"And that purpose?"

"I intend to make a bridegroom of you."

He stared at her, stunned, before he threw back his head and laughed uproariously. "Good God, are you proposing to me? The Virgin Queen who has refused half the royalty in Europe?" He swept her a low bow. "I accept. And when shall we wed, Your Majesty?"

"You know I did not mean myself," she said, annoyed. "Your impudence is beyond belief."

He clutched his breast. "Stabbed to the heart. And just when I thought happiness was to be mine."

Another side of him was suddenly before her. For an instant his grimness had vanished, and his face was alight with wicked mischief. She struggled to suppress a smile. "Percy is right ... you are a rogue. Since you're so eager to wed, you will have no objection if I choose the bride."

"I did not say that. Alas, I fear it's you or no one for me."

Her smile vanished. "And I fear, if you do not do as I tell you, that you will be without a henchman."

The coldness returned to his expression at the threat. "I do not wed at England's command."

"Nor at Scotland's, evidently. James has sent you three candidates for your inspection."

"Because he wants a claim on Craighdhu and sees no other way to get it. He finds our trade routes with Ireland appealing." He smiled crookedly. "As I'm sure you do also, Your Majesty."

"I don't care a whit for your Irish trade routes."

He lifted a skeptical brow. "Then why are you trying to furnish me with a bride from your court?"

"She is not from my court. The girl lives in the Midlands. She is Mistress Kathryn Anne Kentyre. The child has reached her sixteenth year and is in good health, has been well schooled, and is not unattractive. She has no title, and, though of gentle birth, is not legitimate. You must take her away at once and never bring her back to England." She went on briskly. "Naturally, there will be no dowry. You're lucky to escape with your head still intact. The wedding will take place at once, and you will—"

"Where in the Midlands?" His gaze was fixed on her face, and she could almost see the wheels of thought turning.

"Sheffield," she said reluctantly.

"One of Shrewsbury's lands." He was silent as he stared at her. She could almost see the moment when he made the connection. He gave a low whistle. "By God, it's true."

"I fear I don't know what you're talking about."

"She *did* have a child."

She gazed at him without speaking.

"I may be a poor ignorant Scot, but even I've heard about Bess Shrewsbury's charges." He sat down on the cot and leaned back against the stone wall. "I assure you, everyone in Scotland found the scandal very interesting."

"I did not give you permission to sit in my presence."

He ignored the sharp injunction, his gaze searching her face for any change of expression. "She's Mary's daughter?"

"Everyone knows that Mary has only one child, and he sits on the throne of Scotland."

"Not according to Bess Shrewsbury. She claims her husband and Mary enjoyed the closeness of Mary's captivity to the utmost. What was her story? That Mary bore him two children while he was holding the queen captive for you on his estate all those years?"

"Bess Shrewsbury is an ambitious, spiteful woman. I reprimanded her for spreading such rumors."

"And neatly silenced her."

"The earl of Shrewsbury gave himself selflessly to the task of keeping Mary comfortably imprisoned. He's a loyal servant of the crown."

"And Mary was a beautiful young woman and known to be selfish and headstrong ... a lonely, passionate woman held captive away from the world. It's only reasonable she would reach out to the only man within her reach. Was there just the daughter and not another issue?"

"I told you, Bess Shrewsbury was a liar."

"So there was only one. . . ." His tone was musing. "But that was more than enough. You couldn't let it be known, could you? There was already too much outcry about you keeping Mary prisoner. Since half of Scotland already looked upon Mary as a harlot, I'm sure you had no trouble convincing her to give up the child. But if the truth had come out, there was always the chance she might have claimed the earl had raped her, and that would have given her supporters in the north of England cause to join with France or Spain to overthrow you."

"This is all supposition."

He leaned forward. "Then let's carry the supposition a little further. Suppose this child *is* Mary's daughter. Suppose she *is* the illegitimate daughter of the queen of Scotland."

"Mary is no longer queen. She abdicated in favor of her son."

"But James has never been popular with the people. There are many nobles who would be pleased to find another Stuart to rally around. That wouldn't please you, would it?"

God's blood, he had a facile mind. She had known he would probably reach this conclusion, but not with such quickness. "Supposition again. You're very good at it. However, the child is only sixteen, hardly a threat."

"You were not a good deal older when you ascended to the throne, and they called you a young lioness."

A rush of fierce satisfaction surged through her. "Yes, by Judas, they had to reckon with me. I sank my teeth into them and made them know a woman could—" She shrugged. "But I was extraordinary. Even if this is Mary's daughter . . ." She trailed off, then added, "And I don't say that she is. Do you think I'd fear a child unschooled in court intrigue?"

"Yet you fear something, or I would not be here."

"I fear nothing." He continued to stare skeptically at her, and finally she said, "*If* the child is who you say she is, she could be used as a pawn. It would be wise to remove her from English soil."

"So you send her to Scotland where James would be eager to dispose of any claimant to the throne and rid you of the task."

"No!" She tried to temper the harshness of her voice. "I send her to Craighdhu. You will wed her and take her to your island and keep her there."

"Oh, I will?"

"There are already too many rumors in the air concerning the child. I've tried to keep her isolated, but if someone should discover— No, she must be taken away as soon as possible."

"And why by me?"

"Because you're the most suitable. Do you think I

chose you blindly? I've searched over three years for a solution to this problem. You're not perfect, but you'll have to do. You hate the Spanish, so you'll not go running to Philip with the girl. You're of noble blood and warrior stock. You have no bonds to anyone but your Highlanders and show no ambition to climb higher than you are in the world."

"Because there is no place higher to climb than to be lord of Craighdhu."

He meant it. The simple words were spoken with absolute sincerity and authority. She had seen rulers of nations who did not exude that air of power.

"Nonsense. But it suits me to have you believe that arrogant folderol. As long as you cling to that notion, you will not use the child to try to seize a crown." She frowned. "But you must stop raiding Philip's ships."

"Indeed? But I may continue to raid yours?"

"I believed you when you said that you did that just to prick at James, but you must not indulge in such mischief again. I won't have you killed on the seas when you should be at Craighdhu protecting the girl. You must keep her safe."

"I could see how my death could be inconvenient to you," he said ironically. "I regret to refuse you, but I have no desire to become embroiled in your plots, and certainly no desire to wed."

"You must wed sometime."

He shrugged. "When I do, it will be with someone who can bring something to Craighdhu besides bloodshed."

"You've not shown any reluctance to shed blood in the past."

"But it's an oddity of mine that I prefer to choose when and where I fight." He met her gaze. "And it won't be in your cause, Your Majesty."

"Nor in James's, evidently. What will you fight for?"

"Craighdhu," he said simply. "Only Craighdhu."

"Good," she said. It was the answer for which she had hoped. "Then if the girl is at Craighdhu, she will be secure."

"Perhaps I'm not making myself clear. I will not wed the girl."

"You *will* wed her." She paused. "Or I will take your henchman out and hang him and then have his body dismembered into so many pieces, there will not be anything left to bury in your precious Craighdhu."

He went still. "I've not heard that Your Majesty is in the habit of killing innocent men to enforce your will."

"The girl is innocent too. I will *not* have her caught in a trap because of her birth. I thought her safe for a few more years at Sheffield, but now I cannot . . ." She stopped. "You must take her away at once. I will have your word on it."

"You expect me to keep a vow forced on me?"

"You will keep it. Percy tells me a Highlander's vow is sacred. You will give me your word to wed her and take her to Craighdhu."

He was silent.

"Do not make me prove I mean what I say. I have no desire to kill your clansman. There is too much death in the air right now," she added wearily.

He still did not speak, his gaze searching her expression for any sign of weakness. She showed him none.

He muttered a curse and then said between his teeth, "You have my vow."

"That's not enough. Give me the words."

He said with icy precision, "I promise to wed the girl and take her to Craighdhu."

Relief flowed through her. It was done. "Very sensible. You will be released at dawn and given back your purse and horses. You will go directly to Sheffield, where the girl resides in a cottage a few miles from the village. She's cared for by the vicar and his good wife.

Sebastian Landfield is a godly man and has devoted the last thirteen years to her well-being. Percy will give you a letter I've written bidding the vicar give you custody of the girl. She will be no trouble. The vicar assures me she is presentable and has been raised to be a loyal Protestant and a meek, virtuous maiden." She moved toward the door. "You've made a wise decision, my lord."

"I didn't make it, you did. I prefer to make my own choices." He rose slowly to his feet. "And when I don't, it makes me . . . annoyed."

He was more than annoyed. He was in a cold rage, and she again felt that intriguing thrill of fear. She had all the weapons in this encounter, and yet she still experienced a moment of uncertainty and regret. There were so few interesting men in the world, and she would probably never see him again. It was a pity she was being forced to sacrifice him to the girl. "Someone must win in every battle."

"You have not won yet, Your Majesty."

"I have your word."

A flicker of indefinable emotion crossed his face. "Yes, you have my word."

"Then I have won." Her lips thinned. "And upon my oath, if I hear of you mistreating her, I'll send an armada of my own to Craighdhu to punish you." She crossed the room and shouted, "Percy! Let me out of here. I'm done with him."

"That's not quite true, Your Majesty," MacDarren said softly. "You're not done with me yet."

"What do you—" She glanced over her shoulder and saw in his expression not only anger but implacable resolution. MacDarren clearly had no intention of permitting her to walk away a complete victor. Perhaps she had been wrong, and she might indeed see him again. It was not a totally unpleasant thought.

She smiled at him. "Good evening, my lord." As the door opened, she swept out of the cell.

• • •

"A bridegroom," Gavin murmured. "What a felicitous thought. You staying close to the hearth while your meek young wife hovers over her loom sewing a fine—"

"I'm glad you find this so amusing," Robert said grimly. "I should have let Her Majesty chop you to pieces."

Gavin winced. "The idea is obscene. I choose not to dwell on it. Besides, it's time you wed. I've grown weary of all this traveling about."

"Then *you* wed and go sit by the fire."

"But no one has arranged such a fine marriage for me." He quickly changed the subject as Robert shot him a lethal glance. "We go direct to Sheffield?"

"The queen was most explicit. It appears she's in a great hurry."

"Why?"

Robert was silent a moment, thinking about it. "Mary. She's going to let it happen."

"You think she's going to sign the order to execute Mary? But she's been avoiding it for weeks."

And Elizabeth had said twice to him that she did not want to execute Mary of Scotland, Robert remembered. Yet he was well aware that desire and necessity did not always go hand in hand. God knows, some of the decisions he was forced to make as chief of his clan were not to his liking. The urgency with which she had insisted that the removal of Mary's daughter from England take place at once did not make sense unless she had decided to take that final, deadly step in her dealings with Mary. He said slowly, "I believe she will either sign the order or find a way to have Mary executed that will shift some of the blame from her own shoulders."

"So she's feeling a twinge of guilt and wants the lass away from the uproar before she kills her mother. What a gentle lady." Gavin shook his head. "You think the girl will bring trouble to Craighdhu?"

"I won't let her."

"Trouble follows royalty like bees do flowers."

"I won't let her," Robert repeated, enunciating each word with precision.

"You're angry."

"Oh, yes."

"But you're going to obey the queen?"

"I gave my word." He paused. "But the way I keep it may not be in the fashion she wishes."

Gavin gave a low whistle. "We may have some interesting times ahead." He moved restlessly on his cot. "It's cold in here."

Robert turned his head. "You were hot before. Do you have the fever again?"

"I don't think so," he said.

Muttering a curse, Robert got up from his cot and threw his own blanket over Gavin. "Don't lie to me. I'm going to have enough trouble hauling a woman over those mountains in wintertime. Do you think I want to carry your corpse all the way back to Craighdhu too?"

"May the saints forbid I cause you such trouble." Gavin settled himself more comfortably under the layers of blanket. "In order to prevent such an inconvenience, I'll reluctantly accept your generosity. I would never want to—"

"Be quiet."

"My, you are testy. But I'll forgive you. It must be bridegroom nerves that—"

"Gavin."

A low chuckle issued from the younger man.

Robert settled down again on his cot and closed his eyes. Gavin's depression regarding his failure as a henchman had entirely vanished, and his usual puckish humor was rapidly rising to the forefront. Ordinarily, Robert would have welcomed the transformation, but his mood was too savage for him to appreciate drollery. He wanted to *break* something, dammit. No, not just something, he wanted to break the neck of that royal red-haired bitch who had so arrogantly involved him in her intrigues. Well, she would not succeed. To wed Mary's daughter would be to put the only thing he held dear in jeopardy. He would not have Craighdhu made into a battleground for the factions that were tearing England and Scotland apart. Let them all destroy themselves fighting over their religions and ambitions for the throne. When they were all gone, Craighdhu would still be there, stronger than ever.

By the Saints, he would see that it was.

He was almost asleep when Gavin spoke again. "Would you like me to play the pipes at the wedding? I know they're generally played only for battle, but there *is* a certain resemblance in this case, isn't there?"

"No pipes."

"Or I could—"

"Gavin, go to *sleep*."

2

"*My husband is not* here," Martha Landfield said, scowling at the two men through the crack in the door. "You will have to come back tomorrow."

"I'll be halfway to Scotland tomorrow," Robert explained. "Give me his direction so that I may seek him out."

"I'm not sure where he is," she told him. "What is your business?"

"My business is with your husband." The woman's rudeness irritated Robert. Everything about this blasted affair irritated him. He and Gavin had traveled at full speed from London in an icy downpour, Gavin looked pale and weak as a newborn kitten, and now to be kept standing on the doorstep in the rain by this surly harridan was an annoyance not to be borne. "And I must see the vicar today. My friend is not well—may I leave him here while I seek your husband?"

The woman started to close the door.

Robert muttered a curse and thrust out a booted foot to prevent it from shutting. With an arm he hurled the door open wide. "Madam, perhaps you did not understand," he said with soft menace. "I *will* see your husband, and my friend *will* stay here until I return."

Gavin grimaced. "I think I'd rather go with you, Robert."

Robert ignored him. "You'll give him a chair by the fire and a hot drink. And if he asks any service, you will give it with a smile."

"A smile?" Gavin gave the woman's flushed, enraged face a skeptical glance. "She'll probably poison me. Yes, I definitely think I'm well enough to go with you."

"Be quiet." Robert shoved him into the foyer as he fixed his eyes on the woman. "You understand?"

"You cannot make me—" She stopped, her expression becoming wary as she met his gaze. Grudgingly, she said, "I suppose he may stay."

"And you have in your care a Mistress Kathryn Kentyre. While I'm gone, have her pack her bags and ready herself for a journey."

"Kathryn?" She repeated the name in bewilderment. "Why should you have ... ?" She paused. "You come from the lady?"

"Lady?"

"The queen. You have come on orders from the queen?"

Robert smiled bitterly. "You might say I'm under orders."

"And you're to take the girl away?"

Robert nodded.

The news appeared to dissolve the woman's rage. "My husband ... he will not like it. But," she rushed on, "he'll have to obey the queen, won't he?"

"It appears we all have to obey Her Majesty," Robert said sardonically. "Prepare the girl."

"She's not here," she said, her brow furrowed in thought. "He went after her."

"What?"

"It was the horse," the woman muttered. "That old plug of a horse. I told him it was a mistake to give it to her."

"Horse?"

She made an impatient gesture. "What difference does it make? The willful girl has been gone two days."

Willful. A meek, virtuous girl, the queen had described her, Robert remembered sourly. Meek and virtuous young women did not leave their homes and venture forth into the world alone. Elizabeth had obviously saddled him with a chit as spoiled and wild as her mother.

"Where is your husband searching for the girl?"

"The forest. He thinks she's hiding in the forest. She tried the road last time she ran away, and he doesn't believe she'll go that way again. Caird is too slow." She smiled in satisfaction. "And he'll find her. Sebastian grew up here and knows every inch of that wood."

"What part of the forest is he searching today?"

She shrugged.

"What does the vicar look like?"

"Thin, white hair ... he was wearing his warm gray cape."

"Pack the girl's garments." He turned away and mounted his horse.

"Tell me where he is," Sebastian coaxed as he roped Kate's wrists together in front of her. "You know I'll find him eventually. Why should you make us both suffer like this? You're shaking with cold, and you must be hungry."

She did not answer. Stupid, she had been so stupid. She should not have stopped to rest. She had known her only chance to escape someone who knew these woods as well as Sebastian was to keep moving. No matter how exhausted she had been, she should have kept on.

"A horse is such a large, cumbersome creature. It's not easy to hide one even in the forest. You know how determined I am. I'll find him, Kate."

"You won't find him. You'll never find him."

"And if I don't, the beasts of the forest will. Caird's old and unable to defend himself. Isn't it better to let me put him to death than have them feed on him?"

The thought sent a shudder through her. She had not considered the woodland predators. How clever of Sebastian to strike at her weakest point. But she had hidden Caird well and had left enough grass to last him for a while. She would have to rely on fortune to protect him until she could get back to him. "He's safe. He's not going to die."

"So stubborn. So strong in your corruption." He mounted his horse and tied the rope to the saddle. "Tell me when you change your mind."

He nudged his horse forward, and the rope tightened as the animal started slowly down the path. She plodded after him, knowing the ropes would bite into her wrists if she did not keep the pace. One foot after the other. The trees were shifting around her, but she would not faint. It was only a little more than three miles to the cottage, and she could surely stay on her feet that long. She knew if she fainted, he would not stop. He would pull her after him through the forest until they reached the cottage.

"You're wrong, you know." Sebastian turned in the saddle to look at her. "So wrong and full of sin." He kicked the horse into a trot. The rope drew more tightly, jerking her forward.

She had to remain on her feet. She must not fall.

She stumbled forward, lurching from side to side as she tried to keep up.

"Tell me where you've hidden the horse."

She dimly heard the words through a haze of pain. Her wrists were starting to bleed.

One foot after the other.

She must not fall.

White hair. Gray cloak. A tight, ascetic expression that was an unpleasant reminder to Robert of the priests in

Don Diego's castle in Santanella. Sebastian Landfield. It had not been as difficult a task as he had feared to locate the vicar.

"Master Landfield?" He spurred ahead toward the man coming down the trail. As he drew closer, he noticed the man was dragging something behind him that looked like a small muddy tree or branch.

Sebastian Landfield tensed as he reined in the horse at Robert's approach. His glance raked over Robert. "Yes, I am Sebastian Landfield. Who are you?"

"Robert MacDarren, earl of Craighdhu. I have a letter to you from Her Majesty."

"You came from the queen?" He darted an uneasy glance at the burden pulled by the horse. "I was not expecting a message."

"I was not expecting to deliver it." As Robert drew even with him on the trail, he reached beneath his cloak for the envelope and then thrust it at Landfield. "And I was certainly not expecting to have to chase you through the—"

The muddy object on the trail behind Landfield stirred. It was not a tree.

"God's blood!" Robert got down from his horse. "What the devil is this?"

"The girl isn't hurt," the vicar said quickly.

"Girl?" He knelt down and turned over the now inert form. She looked little more than a child, slight and frail, her bound wrists chafed and bleeding. He brushed aside the long, wet strands of hair clinging to her cheeks. Aside from a faint bruise on her temple, the portion of her face not covered by the mud of the trail was undamaged. She appeared to be in a faint.

"She was merely being punished for her transgressions," Landfield said calmly, then hesitated before continuing. "However, the queen may not understand. It might be better not to tell her of—"

"I have no intention of telling her anything." Robert drew his dirk and cut the ropes that bound the girl's wrists. "I assume this is the girl under your guardianship? Kathryn Kentyre?"

"It is."

He lifted the girl into his arms and rose to his feet. Even with the heavy mud clinging to the skirts of her gown, she weighed almost nothing. He felt another flare of anger. He was not above violence himself but he hated cruelty to the helpless. No matter what the girl had done, she couldn't have deserved this. "You'll be relieved to know she's no longer in your gentle care."

"What?" The vicar's eyes widened in alarm. "Because of this small incident? All young girls must be punished. Their natures are—"

"Read the letter." Robert strode back to his horse, mounted with some difficulty, and cradled the girl in front of him. "I'll see you back at your cottage."

"Who . . . ?" It was only a breath of sound, but it came from the girl in his arms.

He glanced down at her.

Huge eyes that appeared more gold than brown stared up at him.

"Don't be afraid. I'm taking you home."

"I don't . . . have a home." The words were spoken with stark desolation. Her lids slowly closed again. "Not afraid. You're not—" She was once more in a faint.

Not what? he wondered. Not Sebastian Landfield? It appeared any man, any stranger, was acceptable, as long as it wasn't the man who had brutalized her, he thought savagely.

As he spurred his horse into a gallop, his arms tightened around her with instinctive possession.

"Where can I put her?" Robert demanded as he strode into the cottage.

"Where is my husband?" Martha Landfield asked.

"Following. Where?"

She pointed to the staircase. "Her room is at the top of the stairs."

"Heat water, and then come up to change her garments," he ordered as he started up the steps.

"This is the bride?" Gavin strolled into the hall and stood at the bottom of the stairs looking up at him. "Is she hurt?"

"Landfield assures me she's not," Robert answered, continuing up the steps. "How can being dragged through the forest at the end of a rope hurt a person?"

Gavin followed him. "I take it the good vicar is as pleasant as his charming wife."

Robert didn't answer as he placed the girl on the narrow bed in her room.

"We're staying the night?" Gavin asked.

"It's already late afternoon, and I can hardly take her away from here until she can ride. We'll start early tomorrow morning."

Gavin looked critically at the girl's face. "It may be more than one day. She doesn't look well. Are you sure she doesn't need a physician?"

"She has no broken bones, and she woke for a moment on the trail." Robert took off her muddy slippers and soggy stockings and tossed them on the floor. "Let's hope she's resilient."

Gavin was still staring at Kate's face. "Do you think she looks like Mary Stuart?"

"How do I know? I've never seen Mary."

"I saw a painting once, and we've both heard her described. . . ." His gaze went over the small nose, the mouth with its fuller lower lip, the arched brows. "What color are her eyes?"

Golden-brown eyes staring up at him without fear.

"Brown."

"Well, that's the same, but her features have no regularity. She's certainly not as comely as Mary."

"Maybe she takes after her father. Shrewsbury is no

Adonis." Where the hell was that woman with the hot water? The girl's feet were ice cold.

"Maybe." Gavin's eyes began to twinkle. "I was hoping for something better for you. However, the lass is scarce more than a child. Perhaps she'll improve with age. I'd hate to have you saddled with an ugly wife."

Robert gave him a quelling glance. "Go back downstairs and sit by the fire."

"You'd send me back to that dragon?" He sighed and moved toward the door. "Very well."

"And keep Landfield from coming up here," Robert called.

"It's doubtful he would try to hurt her while you're here," Gavin said as he pulled the door closed.

That wasn't what Robert was worried about. He wasn't certain if he could keep himself from skewering the man if he came within striking distance. He knew the anger he was feeling was all out of proportion. Though the punishment appeared extreme, custom gave guardians the full right to punish their wards in any way they saw fit. The girl was not hurt badly, and she was nothing to him.

No, not nothing. She was going to be his wife. He had thought of her only as the "girl," the albatross Elizabeth was trying to fasten permanently around his neck. Now, suddenly, this scrawny bit of flotsam was a person and soon to be his possession. It did not seem to matter that he intended that possession to be of the most temporary nature.

He reached out and gently brushed a strand of mud-coated hair from the girl's cheek.

And, by God, no one damaged something that belonged to him.

Kate slowly opened her lids to see a man's face only inches from her own. Dark eyes . . . hollow cheeks, well-shaped lips that made her want to reach up and trace their curve. How odd, when she had never wanted to touch any man before . . .

Safety. Well-being. Home.

The overwhelming impression came out of nowhere but was not unfamiliar. Though she could not recall where she had seen this face, she could remember a warm sense of security connected with it. Strange, when he did not appear either secure or tame now that she studied him.

He reminded her of one of the wild Gypsy folk who occasionally traveled through the village, but his clothing was much too fine. The large round pendant hanging from a heavy gold chain shimmered against the black velvet of his doublet, and the short cape he wore was simple but elegant.

"Who . . . ?" Her voice was so thin, she could scarcely hear it herself. She tried again. "Who are you?"

"Robert MacDarren." His deep voice held a hint of a Scots brogue. "How do you feel?"

"Well."

"Liar," he said crisply. "You're covered from head to foot in mud, and you're probably one big bruise."

The lack of gentleness in his tone jolted her to full wakefulness and immediately dispersed that feeling of contentment. She must have been mad to think this man safe when he was clearly hard, distant, and without compassion. Memory swirled back to her. The trail. He had been the man on the trail. "What are you doing here? Are you a physician?"

He shook his head.

No, he didn't have the look of a healer, but Sebastian never let strangers into the house unless there was need. "Are you—"

"I'm the earl of Craighdhu. I come from the queen."

"The lady?" Another messenger. That explained the fine clothes and air of bold confidence.

His dark eyes narrowed on her face. "Why do you call her that?"

She looked at him in confusion. The other messengers had not had to be told. They had phrased their orders with care, making certain that the source of their authority remained anonymous. "Because no one must know, of course."

His lips tightened. "I see. And I suppose no one must know how Landfield treats you? I'm sure that must—"

"You'll have to come down and talk to him, Robert."

Her gaze flew to the man who had spoken and was standing in the doorway. Curly red hair, freckles, not much older than herself. Another stranger, but one far less intimidating than the Gypsy in the chair beside the bed.

"She's awake?" The man came a step into the room, his face alight with interest as he studied her. "Ah, that's better. The eyes are really magnificent. You may not be as bad off as I feared, Robert." He bowed. "I'm Gavin Gordon, and I'm delighted to meet you, Mistress Kentyre."

Robert didn't give her a chance to reply as he asked impatiently, "Why should I come downstairs?"

Gavin's glance shifted to Robert. "Oh, the old man is roaring. He wants to see you."

"Later."

Gavin shrugged. "As you like, but he won't let the woman bring up the hot water to wash the mud off her."

MacDarren made a low exclamation, and the chair scraped against the floor as he stood up. "Damn him, the stuff is beginning to cake on her." He started for the door and then paused to look back at Kate. The harshness was gone from his voice when he said, "Try to go to sleep. Everything's going to be fine."

Gavin followed him out of the room and closed the door.

Everything's going to be fine.

The words had been spoken with such cool authority that for a moment she almost believed him. He came from the lady, and Sebastian was always careful in dealing with those emissaries who came to receive reports and give instructions regarding her upbringing. Perhaps she could appeal to him to save Caird. He appeared to possess a boldness and arrogance that had not been apparent in the other messengers. He might intercede with Sebastian on her behalf.

But then he would go away.

They always went away, and she would be alone again. She was always alone. Sebastian would be free once more to do whatever he wished.

However, the man was here now and distracting Sebastian's attention from her. She must not depend on anyone but herself. She had to seize the opportunity that presented itself.

She threw back the blanket and slowly sat up on the bed.

She gasped as pain shot through her shoulders. MacDarren was right about the bruises. Every muscle in her body cried in protest at the movement.

She was barefoot, she realized. Where were her shoes and stockings? She found them and put them on with stiff, fumbling fingers.

She could not leave by the front door, but that presented no problem. The bedroom window had been her escape many times before. She had only to hang by her arms from the windowsill and let herself drop to the ground.

She shuddered at the thought of putting extra strain on muscles already oversore. She cast a longing glance at the bed. How she wanted to lie back down and draw the covers up around her.

But if she didn't go now, heaven knows when she'd

get another chance to escape, and Caird was alone in the woods.

She took a deep breath and opened the window.

Sebastian Landfield stood in front of the hearth with his hands clasped behind his back, the flames lighting the meagerness of his wiry body.

"You wanted to see me?" Robert asked as he strode into the parlor.

"I most certainly do." Landfield fixed him with a stern glance. "I've been trying to be patient, but I find your interference intolerable, my lord."

"How unfortunate," Robert said dryly. "But if you've read Her Majesty's letter, you'll realize you no longer have any right to object. The girl is mine."

"No!" Landfield took a deep breath and then said with less violence, "I'm sure Her Majesty does not realize what a mistake it would be to take her from my care at this delicate time. She is not ready to be left without supervision."

"As her husband, I'll provide any supervision necessary."

"You'll not be able to provide the guidance she needs. You don't understand her. If she leaves me now, you'll undo all I've worked to accomplish."

"I believe I'm capable of controlling one frail girl." He smiled grimly. "And, if I have difficulties, I can always drag her behind my horse for a mile or two."

"You think me cruel?" Landfield asked harshly. "You know *nothing*. The punishment would scarcely affect her. She has a strength you would find unbelievable."

Robert had a fleeting memory of the pitiful fragility of the girl he had just left. Od's bodkin, the man was crazed. "The matter is closed. Tell your wife to take the water upstairs."

"The matter is not closed." Landfield's pale eyes blazed with fury. "You will listen to me. I will not see her sent out into the world to wreak destruction as her mother has done. The queen must have told you whose child she is when she arranged this marriage. Do you know what evil lies waiting within her? Every day she changes and grows more like that Catholic whore at Fotheringhay. You cannot marry her. She must wed no one. She is a Lilith."

"Who the devil is Lilith?"

"The first wife of Adam in Eden, the temptress, the mother of wickedness. Once she has you in her clutches, she will tempt and lure until you are helpless before her. She will mold you like wet clay."

Robert heard a sound like a smothered snort from Gavin, standing in the doorway behind him. Gavin's re-action mirrored his own. The idea of that mud-soaked urchin upstairs being a Lilith and able to turn strong men weak was totally ludicrous. He had had enough of this nonsense.

"Gavin, go to the kitchen and help Madam take that hot water upstairs." Robert turned back to Landfield as Gavin left the room and said coldly, "I appreciate your concern, but I assure you I'm in no danger from a fledgling lass."

"You think you can master her when I still have not conquered her after all these years?" His lips thinned. "But I *will* conquer her, body and soul. Her Majesty must give me the opportunity. She must not be taken away."

He was tired of talking to this vicious old man. "As I said, the matter is closed. We will leave at dawn if the girl is well enough."

Two bright spots appeared in Landfield's cheeks. "You cannot let her—"

"Robert?"

They both turned to see Gavin in the doorway, an uneasy expression on his face.

"She's gone," he said.

Robert stiffened. "What?"

"She's gone. The window was open. And . . ." He waved a hand. "Gone."

"How could she be gone? Her chamber is on the second floor, and she could barely lift her head—"

"I told you." Landfield smiled triumphantly. "A will of iron. Can't you see what trouble she will bring you? She needs a firm hand to keep her in—"

"Come on, Gavin." Robert cut off the vicar in midsentence as he strode toward the door. "She can't have gone far, and she'll be easy to track in all this mud."

"Shall I get the horses?"

"No time. We'll go on foot."

She was being followed!

Sebastian?

Kate paused a moment on the trail and caught a glimpse of dark hair and the shimmer of the gold necklace about her pursuer's neck. Not Sebastian. Robert MacDarren.

The wild surge of disappointment she felt at the realization was completely unreasonable. He must have come at Sebastian's bidding, which meant her guardian had persuaded him to his way of thinking. Well, what had she expected? He was a stranger, and Sebastian was a respected man of the cloth. There was no reason why he would be different from any of the others. How clever of Sebastian to send someone younger and stronger than himself to search her out, she thought bitterly.

She turned and began to run, her shoes sinking into the mud with every step. She glanced over her shoulder.

He was closer. He was not running, but his long legs covered the ground steadily, effortlessly, as his gaze studied the trail in front of him. He had evidently not seen her yet and was only following her tracks.

She was growing weaker. Her head felt peculiarly

light, and her breath was coming in painful gasps. She couldn't keep running.

And she couldn't surrender.

Which left only one solution to her dilemma. She sprinted several yards ahead and then darted into the underbrush at the side of the trail.

Hurry. She had to hurry. Her gaze frantically searched the underbrush. Ah, there was one.

She pounced on a heavy branch, backtracked several yards and held it, waiting beneath the dripping trees.

She must aim for the head. She had the strength for only one blow, and it must drop him.

Her breathing sounded heavy and terribly loud. She had to breathe more evenly, or he would hear her.

He was almost upon her.

Her hands tightened on the branch.

He went past her, his expression intent as he studied the tracks.

She drew a deep breath, stepped out on the trail behind him, and swung the branch with all her strength!

He grunted in pain and then slowly crumpled to the ground.

She dropped the branch, ran past his body and darted down the trail again.

Something struck the back of her knees. She was falling!

She hit the ground so hard, the breath left her body. Blackness swirled around her.

When the darkness cleared, she realized she was on her back, her arms pinned on either side of her head. Robert MacDarren was astride her body.

She started to struggle.

"Lie still, dammit." His hands tightened on her arms. "I'm not— Ouch!"

She had turned her head and sunk her teeth into

his wrist. She could taste the coppery flavor of blood in her mouth, but his grip didn't loosen.

"Let me go!" How stupidly futile the words were when she knew he had no intention of releasing her.

She tried to butt her head against his chest, but she couldn't reach him.

"Really, Robert, can't you wait until the vows are said before you climb on top of her?" Gavin Gordon said from behind MacDarren.

"It's about time you got here," MacDarren said in a growl. "She's trying to kill me."

"Aye, for someone who couldn't lift her head, she's doing quite well. I saw her strike the blow." Gavin grinned. "But I was too far away to come to your rescue. Did she do any damage?"

"I'm going to have one hell of a headache."

Kate tried to knee him in the groin, but he quickly moved upward on her body.

"Your hand's bleeding," Gavin observed.

"She's taken a piece out of me. I can see why Landfield kept the ropes on her."

The ropes. Despair tore through her as she realized how completely Sebastian had won him to his way of thinking. The man would bind her and take her back to Sebastian. She couldn't fight against both MacDarren and Gavin and would use the last of her precious strength trying to do so. She would have to wait for a better opportunity to present itself. She stopped fighting and lay there staring defiantly at MacDarren.

"Very sensible," he said grimly. "I'm not in a very good temper at the moment. I don't think you want to make it worse."

"Get off me."

"And have you run away again?" MacDarren shook his head. "You've caused me enough trouble for one day. Give me your belt, Gavin."

Gavin took off his wide leather belt and handed it

to MacDarren, who buckled the belt about Kate's wrists and drew it tight.

"I'm not going back to the cottage," she said with a fierceness born of desperation. "I *can't* go back there."

He got off her and rose to his feet. "You'll go where I tell you to go, even if I have to drag—" He stopped in self-disgust as he realized what he had said. "Christ, I sound like that sanctimonious bastard." The anger suddenly left his expression as he looked at her lying there before him. "You're afraid of him?"

Fear was always with her when she thought of Sebastian, but she would not admit it. She sat up and repeated, "I can't go back."

He studied her for a moment. "All right, we won't go back. You'll never have to see him again."

She stared at him in disbelief.

He turned to Gavin. "We'll stay the night at that inn we passed at the edge of the village. Go back to the cottage and get her belongings and then saddle the horses. We'll meet you at the stable."

Gavin nodded and the next moment disappeared into the underbrush.

MacDarren glanced down at Kate. "I trust you don't object to that arrangement?"

She couldn't comprehend his words. "You're taking me away?"

"If you'd waited, instead of jumping out the window, I would have told you that two hours ago. That's why I came."

Then she thought she understood. "You're taking me to the lady?"

He shook his head. "It appears Her Majesty thinks it's time you wed."

Shock upon shock. "Wed?"

"You say that as if you don't know what that means. You must have had instructions on the duties of wifehood."

"I know what it means." Slavery and suffocation

and cruelty. From what she could judge from Sebastian and Martha's marriage, a wife's lot was little better than her own. True he did not beat Martha, but the screams she had heard from their bedroom while they mated had filled her with sick horror. She had thought she would never have to worry about that kind of mistreatment. "But I can never marry."

"Is that what the good vicar told you?" His lips tightened. "Well, it appears the queen disagrees."

Then it might come to pass. Even Sebastian obeyed the queen. The faintest hope began to spring within her. Though marriage was only another form of slavery, perhaps the queen had chosen an easier master than Sebastian for her. "Who am I to marry?"

He smiled sardonically. "I have that honor."

Another shock, and not a pleasant one. Easy was not a term anyone would use to describe this man. She blurted, "And you're not afraid?"

"Afraid of you? Not if I have someone to guard my back."

That wasn't what she meant, but of course, he wouldn't be afraid. She doubted if he feared anything or anyone, and besides, she wasn't what Sebastian said she was. He had said the words so often, she sometimes found herself believing him, and she was so tired now, she wasn't thinking clearly. The strength was seeping out of her with every passing second. "No, you shouldn't be afraid." She swayed. "Not Lilith . . ."

"More like a muddy gopher," he muttered as he reached out and steadied her. "We have to get to the stables. Can you walk, or shall I carry you?"

"I can walk." She dismissed the outlandish thought of marriage from her mind. She would ponder its implications later. There were more important matters to consider now. "But we have to get Caird."

"Caird? Who the devil is Caird?"

"My horse." She turned and started through the

underbrush. "Before we go, I have to fetch him. He's not far. . . ."

She could hear the brush shift and whisper as he followed her. "Your horse is in the forest?"

"I was hiding him from Sebastian. He was going to kill him. He wanted me to tell him where he was. . . ."

"And that was why he was dragging you?"

She ignored the question. "Sebastian said the forest beasts would devour him. He frightened me." She was staggering with exhaustion, but she couldn't give up now. "It's been such a while since I left him. . . ." She rounded a corner of the trail and breathed a sigh of relief when she caught sight of Caird calmly munching grass under the shelter of an oak tree. "No, he's fine."

"You think so?" MacDarren's skeptical gaze raked the piebald stallion from swayback to knobby knees. "I see nothing fine about him. How old is he?"

"Almost twenty." She went over to the horse and began to tenderly stroke his muzzle. "But he's strong and very good-tempered."

"He won't do," MacDarren said. "We'll have to get rid of him. He'd never get through the Highlands. We'll leave him with the innkeeper, and I'll buy you another horse."

"I *won't* get rid of him," she said fiercely. "I couldn't just leave him. How would I know if they had taken good care of him? He goes with us."

"And I say he stays."

The words were spoken with such absolute resolution, they sent a jolt of terror through her. They reminded her of Sebastian's edicts, from which there was no appeal. She moistened her lips. "Then I'll have to stay too."

MacDarren's gaze narrowed on her face. "And what if Landfield catches you again?"

She shrugged and leaned her cheek against Caird's muzzle. "He belongs to me," she said simply.

She could feel his gaze on her back and sense his exasperation. "Oh, for God's sake!" He picked up her saddle from the ground by the tree and threw it on Caird's back, then began to buckle the cinches. "All right, we'll take him."

Joy soared through her. "Truly?"

"I said it, didn't I?" He jerked off the belt binding her wrists, picked her up, and tossed her into the saddle. "We'll use him as a packhorse, and I'll get you another mount to ride. Satisfied?"

Satisfied! "Oh, yes. You won't regret it. But you needn't spend your money on another horse. Caird is really very strong. I'm sure he'll be able to—"

"I'm already regretting it." His tone was distinctly edgy as he began to lead the horse through the forest. "Even carrying a light load, I doubt if he'll get through the Highlands."

It was the second time he had mentioned these forbidding Highlands, but she didn't care where they were going as long as they were taking Caird. "But you'll do it? You won't change your mind?"

For an instant his expression softened as he saw the eagerness in her face. "I won't change my mind."

Gavin was already mounted and waiting when they arrived at the stables a short time later. A grin lit his face as he glanced from Kate to the horse and then back again. "Hers?"

Robert nodded. "And the cause of all this turmoil."

"A fitting pair," Gavin murmured. "She has a chance of cleaning up decently, but the horse . . ." He shook his head. "No hope for it, Robert."

"My thought exactly. But we're keeping him anyway."

Gavin's brows lifted. "Oh, are we? Interesting . . ."

Robert swung onto his horse. "Any trouble with the vicar and his amiable wife?"

Kate's hands tensed on the reins.

"Mistress Landfield appeared overjoyed at giving me the girl's belongings." He nodded at a small bundle tied to his saddle. "And the vicar just glowered at me."

"Perhaps he's given up."

"He won't give up," Kate whispered. "He never gives up."

"Then perhaps we'd better go before we encounter him again," Robert said as he kicked his horse into a trot. "Keep an eye on her, Gavin. She's almost reeling."

Sebastian was waiting for them a short distance from the cottage. He stood blocking the middle of the path.

"Get out of the way," Robert said coldly. "I'm not in the mood for this."

"It's your last chance," Sebastian said. "Give her back to me before it's too late."

"Stand aside, Landfield."

"Kathryn." Sebastian turned to her, and his voice was pleading. "Do not go. You know you can never wed. You know what will happen."

Robert rode forward, and his horse's shoulder forced Sebastian to the side of the trail. He motioned Gavin and Kate to ride ahead. "It's over. She's no longer your responsibility." His voice lowered to soft deadliness. "And if you ever approach her again, I'll make sure I never see you repeat the mistake."

"You'll see me." Landfield's eyes shimmered with tears as his gaze clung to Kate. "I wanted to spare you, Kathryn. I wanted to save you, but God has willed otherwise. You know what has to be done now."

He turned and walked heavily back toward the cottage.

"What did he mean?" Gavin asked as his curious gaze followed Landfield.

She didn't answer as she watched Sebastian stalk away. She realized she was shivering with a sense of impending doom. How foolish. This was what he wanted her to feel; this was his way of chaining her to him.

"Well?" Robert asked.

"Nothing. He just wanted to make me afraid." She straightened her shoulders. "He likes me to be afraid of him."

She could see he didn't believe her, and she thought he would pursue it. Instead, he said quietly, "You don't have to fear him any longer. He no longer holds any power over you." He held her gaze with a mesmerizing power that frightened as well as soothed her. "I'm the only one who can hurt or help you now."

3

The lights of Tabord's inn gleamed warm and welcoming ahead of them.

But not welcoming for her, Kate remembered suddenly, stiffening. Dear heaven, she had been so weary and dazed at the bewildering changes in her life, she had let MacDarren lead her where he would.

She reined in Caird. "No."

Robert looked impatiently over his shoulder. "What the devil is wrong now?"

"I can't stay here."

"The hell you can't. You wouldn't stay at the cottage, and now you won't stay here. We're not camping by the side of the road tonight. I'm tired and almost as dirty as you are from that roll in the mud. I need a bath and a bed, and this is where we'll get both." He turned and kicked his horse into a trot. "Now."

He didn't understand, and she was too numb with weariness to explain further. He would find out soon enough.

Master Tabord threw open the door and came out into the stable yard. The light from the candelabra he carried revealed the broad smile on his face as his gaze instantly appraised the richness of MacDarren's garments. "Ah, my lord, welcome. I am Peter Tabord, the owner of this inn."

Robert inclined his head. "I'm Robert MacDarren, earl of Craighdhu."

"And how may I serve you?"

"Beds, food." Robert got down from his horse and came around to Kate's horse. "And above all, tubs of hot water for baths."

"We have the finest of all three. You took a fall?" Master Tabord shook his head sympathetically as he watched Robert lift Kate from the saddle. "I hope the lady was not—" He broke off, his eyes narrowing. He stepped closer, the candle held high, peering at Kate. She knew by the tightening of his lips the minute he recognized her. "Good evening, Kate." He turned abruptly back to Robert. "I'm sorry, my lord. I can give you no shelter here. I have no room."

"You had rooms before," Robert said slowly.

"Not now." The innkeeper turned back to Kate. "Go home. Have you not caused the vicar enough woe with your wild ways? I will not have you come whoring under my roof. You're not to—"

"Quiet!" Robert stepped forward, and his dirk was suddenly pressed to Tabord's plump stomach. "No more. By thunder, I've had enough. You'll find two rooms in this 'crowded' hovel of yours, and you'll give me what I ask or I'll slit your gullet."

"Please refrain," Gavin said, flinching. "You know how I hate the sight of blood."

Robert ignored him as he pressed the knife harder against Tabord's stomach. "You will find a maidservant to wait on my wife, and you will give her both the respect and service she requires."

Master Tabord's lips set stubbornly. "You cannot intimidate me, my lord. I will do what is right. You cannot— Your wife?" Master Tabord's expression mirrored Kate's shock as he grasped the full meaning of Robert's words. "Kate? She is not your—"

"We are wed." Robert sheathed the dirk and turned to Gavin. "Take the horses to the stable."

"Wed?" Gavin gave a low whistle. "So that's how you're going to do it."

Master Tabord still frowned at them. "It is odd your man does not seem to know of this marriage."

"Have I taken this woman in marriage, Gavin?" Robert asked.

"Aye." Gavin smiled as he gathered Robert's and Kate's horses' reins and turned toward the stable. "You've taken her right and fast."

Robert's hand closed on Kate's wrist, and he pulled her into the inn. "Hot water, a tub, and a maid-servant."

Master Tabord slowly followed them into the hall. "There is only my daughter, Carolyn."

"She will do."

"No," Kate said quickly. "Not Carolyn. I won't have her waiting on me."

For the first time the innkeeper's expression softened. "Carolyn will not mind, Kate. She's never stopped talking about you."

Robert pulled Kate up the steps. "Where is our chamber?"

"The second door," Master Tabord said. He stood in the hallway gazing up at them. "You're truly wed?"

Robert turned and said with precision, "I will not tell you again. She is my wife, and you will treat her as such." He led Kate down the short hall and opened the chamber door.

Kate tore away from his grasp and whirled to face him as the door closed behind them. "You lied to him."

"I don't lie." Robert slammed the door, took off his short cape, and threw it on the chair.

"Don't do that, you'll get mud on those fine embroidered cushions." She picked up the cloak and dropped it on the floor.

"I don't give a whit about Master Tabord's cushions." He looked at her. "And I'm surprised you do, after the way he flayed you."

"It's not his fault. He's a better man than most." Her own damp cloak seemed an unbearable weight on her shoulders. She took it off and threw it down beside his. How strange they looked together, she thought vaguely. Rich velvet and shabby wool, as different from each other as she was from this man who had whirled into her life. "He was very kind to me when I was a child. I used to play with his daughter, Carolyn."

"He didn't seem overkind to you tonight."

"When I grew older, Sebastian decided it wasn't good for me to have the company of the villagers. He forbade me to come to the village, and he told everyone . . ." She stopped at that remembered hurt and then continued, "He told everyone that I was a harlot, and that he must watch me closely to keep me from sinning."

"And they believed his lies?"

"Why not? He's the vicar, a man of God. And he did not think it a lie. He believes I have the soul of a harlot, and they believe him." She met his gaze and suddenly felt a flare of anger. "But I'm not a whore. I will not be anything he says I am. And I will not let you make me into the harlot he thinks me."

"I have no intention of making you my whore."

"I'm not ignorant. Sebastian made sure I know what constitutes carnal sin. We occupy the same chamber; you lie and say we are wed when we are not. Do you have any intention of marrying me?"

"We are wed."

The statement was spoken with such absoluteness that she gazed at him in shock. "Are you mad? We cannot be wed just because you say it is so."

"Oh, but we can." He smiled grimly. "And that is the only way we'll ever wed. Handfast."

She repeated the unfamiliar word. "Handfast?"

"Handfast is an entirely legal marriage in Scotland.

There is no religious ceremony, but the man and the woman announce the bonding before witnesses and then live together for a year. If the match proves to give contentment to both, or a child is born, the marriage is declared permanent. If not . . ." He shrugged. "They are both free to go their own way."

"It sounds most strange," she said suspiciously.

"But entirely legal and binding . . . for a year. I'll take you to Craighdhu and acknowledge you as my wife. In a year we will part." His lips thinned. "In spite of any more permanent plans devised by Her Majesty."

He was angry, but it wasn't with her, she realized. "You don't wish to stay married to me?"

"God, no!" He smiled crookedly. "Forgive my lack of gallantry, but you're the last woman I'd consider marrying. I have enough problems without burdening myself in that fashion."

"Because I'm who I am. Because I'm *her* daughter," she said. It was not a question. Sebastian had always made it clear that she was not worthy of marriage, that no man would ever want her in any but the carnal sense.

"Exactly."

An odd pang of hurt shot through her at the decisive word. It was the answer she had expected, but the hurt was still there. She threw back her shoulders and forced herself to stand up straighter. "Well, I certainly don't care. I don't want you either. I don't want to marry anyone." She wished he would leave her. She had thought she had armored herself against pain, but somehow he managed to get beyond the barriers to make the loneliness worse. It was only because she was so tired, she told herself. Every emotion was distorted when you were on the verge of collapse. "I don't know why the lady—Her Majesty thought it necessary to have me wed."

"You don't?" He studied her before muttering,

"Evidently the good vicar neglected to advise you on the political implications of being Mary's daughter."

"Political?" She looked at him in bewilderment. "I'm nothing to anyone. I have no power. I'm illegitimate, my lord."

"So was William the First. There are—" He stopped when they both heard the sound of voices on the stairs. "They're bringing up the tub. We'll talk later." He started for the door. "And my name is Robert. Since we are wed, I prefer less formality ... Kathryn."

"Kate!" As he turned to look at her with a quizzical expression, she tempered the passion of her tone. "*He* calls me Kathryn."

"And you won't be anything he says you are," he quoted softly. "What did Landfield mean?"

The question confused her. "What?"

"What he said about you knowing what he had to do."

"He always told me I had to be saved or destroyed," she said. "He means to destroy me now."

"You appear to accept that quite calmly. I would think—" A knock sounded on the door, and he opened it.

A tall, dark-haired young woman stood smiling at them. Kate recognized Carolyn and instinctively tensed.

"I'm Carolyn Tabord, my lord." She gestured behind her. "Simon is bringing a tub for the countess. We've placed another in the next room for you and filled it with hot water. Your man is now bathing in the kitchen. I hope that is satisfactory?"

"Quite satisfactory." He glanced back at Kate for an instant and then turned on his heel and left the chamber.

Carolyn swept into the room, her dark eyes twinkling. "And I'm sure the countess finds his lordship very satisfactory as well," she murmured as she came toward Kate. "By the saints, he looks as lusty as that stallion we watched mount Megan that day in the field. Is he?"

Kate was caught off guard. There was no hint of censure or restraint in Carolyn's manner. It was as if they had parted yesterday instead of three years ago. "I'm not sure. I mean— Hello, Carolyn. How are you?"

"Fine. You know I'm always fine." She grinned as she swept up the cloaks from the floor. "I'm to marry also."

"Who?"

"Timothy Kanut, the blacksmith." She opened the door and threw the cloaks out into the hallway. "I'll hang them before the fire in the kitchen to dry and then dust the mud off. Merciful heavens, you're dirty."

Kate vaguely remembered Timothy Kanut. He was some years older than themselves, a tall, strapping man with a sweet smile, enormous muscles, and a wife whose tongue was as sharp as a dagger. "I thought he was already married."

"His wife died last year. Poor dear." She shut the door and turned with a grin. "Just in time to save me from sinning in the hayloft to persuade Timothy to run away with me."

Her eyes widened. "You would have done that?"

She nodded. "I love the man, and it would have been foolish for me to let him stay with a shrew who only made him miserable. That would have been a greater sin than fornication, and you know I've never been a fool."

No, Carolyn had always been shrewd, bold and free-thinking, or she would never have had the courage to become Kate's friend. "Your father would have been brokenhearted."

Carolyn nodded. "Sometimes he doesn't see things clearly." She paused, and for a moment there was a faint awkwardness in her manner. "He shouldn't have believed Sebastian. I tried to tell him . . . I went to the vicarage many times that first year, you know."

"No, I didn't know."

"She wouldn't let me see you. I tried to persuade her, and then I shouted at her. I did everything I could to convince her, but she looked at me with those cold eyes. . . ." She shrugged regretfully. "Finally, I gave up and didn't go back again."

"I wouldn't have given up," Kate said fiercely. "I would have kept on trying to see you, if it had taken a hundred years."

"I did the best I could. I knew you wouldn't understand." She made a face. "I could never be all you wanted me to be. You always demanded too much. You were never able to accept me as I was."

One part of Kate realized that she could not expect those days of freedom and friendship to be as precious to Carolyn, but she still fiercely resented the abandonment. Kate had never told her about her life at the cottage; she had wanted to keep their hours together free from any taint. Still, if Carolyn had truly cared about her, wouldn't she have sensed how alone Kate would be if she permitted Sebastian to separate them? No, Carolyn didn't understand loneliness, she thought wearily, just as Carolyn had never really understood Kate herself. "I suppose it doesn't matter."

"Well, not anymore, at least." Carolyn's smile was back. "Now, you're a fine countess with a husband who can make even my father take a step back. Everything always works out for the best. I heard nothing about your marriage in the village. How long have you been wed?"

"Not long." She still wasn't sure if MacDarren's words about their being married had been true. It all sounded most peculiar. She lifted her hand and rubbed her temple.

Carolyn noticed the gesture and immediately went to the door. "You're tired, and I'm standing here keeping you from your bath. I'll see what's keeping Simon. We can talk while you're in tub."

Everything works out for the best.

How wonderful it would be to believe that were true in this world where her fate seemed left to the whim of a stranger. Yet two good things had already come out of Robert MacDarren's arrival in her life, she realized with a little flare of hope. She had found she had not been completely abandoned by the only friend she had ever had, and she was free of Sebastian. At least for the time being. She could worry about the rest later. She was too tired to think now.

"And where is our bride?" Gavin asked as he watched Robert come down the steps an hour later.

"Presumably in a tub of hot water. I just got out of one myself." He glanced around the common room. "Did you tell the innkeeper to fix food?"

Gavin nodded. "It will be ready shortly." He thrust a cup of ale into Robert's hand. "And he has a fine sturdy mare. He's asking more than she's worth, but I think I can get him down to a reasonable sum." He paused. "You still intend to take the piebald?"

"I said so, didn't I?" Robert drained his cup. The liquid was warm and comforting, but it didn't soothe his bad humor. He didn't even know why he was in such foul temper, only that it had something to do with the way Kate had stood there looking at him, muddy, weary, and yet arrow straight, refusing to surrender to her own weakness. He crossed the room, sat down before the fire, and stretched his legs out before him.

"May I ask why?" Gavin inquired politely as he followed him across the room and leaned one arm on the mantel.

"No, you may not." He was silent a moment before he finally answered, "The girl will give us less trouble if we take the horse."

"Oh, I see. And I thought it was because the poor lass had touched your heart." His eyes twinkled. "Or perhaps your more carnal body parts. I suppose I should have known better."

"Aye, you should." Robert leaned back in the chair. "I have better taste than to wish to couple with a mudlark."

"I'd say she's much too fierce for a mudlark. Besides, you've been without a woman for weeks. Considering your somewhat voracious appetites, even a mudlark should look good to you after that time."

"Not this mudlark. Even if I was tempted, she's the one woman I would not bed."

Gavin's brows lifted. "Surely a strange attitude toward your bride." Then he understood. "Ah, the bairn. If you got her with child, the marriage would become permanent whether you willed it or not."

"Exactly."

"Of course, some risks are worth taking."

"Not that one."

Gavin made a face. "It would be difficult, but you could always take precautions."

"Why? I have no desire to couple with her."

"The poor lass." Gavin grinned. "In the full spring of youth and not to know the joys of the flesh. Have you told her?"

"I've little time to discuss anything in detail." Robert paused. "She has no idea what a danger she might pose."

"To you?"

"To me, to James, to everyone." He was silent a moment and then exploded with unexpected violence. "Christ, she doesn't *know.*"

"It probably suited Her Majesty to make sure she was kept in blissful ignorance."

"Ignorance can lead to mistakes, and mistakes can lead to the block."

"She's scarcely more than a child. You had to realize this was a possibility. Why the sudden concern?"

He had realized, but he hadn't let himself think of

anything beyond what he must do to avoid the trap Elizabeth had laid for him. Which was exactly what he must continue to do. The woman upstairs was nothing to him, and Craighdhu was everything. "I'm not concerned. I just think it foolish of the queen not to have had her warned of the—"

"Please, my lord."

Robert turned to see the innkeeper's daughter standing in the arched doorway.

The girl's eyes were wide with fear. "Please, my lord, come quickly. I cannot wake her."

"What?" Robert jumped to his feet. "What the hell do you mean, you can't wake her?"

"She fell asleep in the tub. That is, I think she is asleep. She may be ill. I shook her, but she only stirred and won't—"

"Christ!" Robert was already out of the common room and taking two steps at a time.

Kate was lying in the hip bath, her head lolled back against the rim, her dark lashes arcs on her thin cheeks.

"Kate!"

She didn't stir. He knelt beside the tub and shook her. "Kate!" Her color seemed good, and he could see the pulse pounding in her throat. Why the hell wouldn't she wake up? He had heard of instances where men wounded in battle had managed to function perfectly until hostilities ceased and then succumbed to their wounds. Perhaps she was even now drifting away from him.

The thought made his grasp tighten on her shoulders. He shook her harder. "Are you deaf? *Talk* to me."

Her lashes fluttered and then slowly opened. "What do you want me to say?" she whispered.

Relief tore through him. His grip loosened. "That's enough. Now, stay awake until I get you out of this tub." He turned to the servant hovering at his side. "Toweling."

The woman scurried across the room and snatched a large piece of linen from the stool in front of the fire.

"She does appear to move from disaster to disaster, doesn't she? I can only hope it's not a sign for the future." From behind him Gavin added politely, "Should I be turning my back?"

"You should be going down and getting her something to eat."

"Right away."

He heard Gavin's steps fade away as he took the towel from the maid and ordered, "Turn down the bed."

He began to dry Kate's long hair. Her eyes were beginning to close again, he noticed with exasperation. "Don't do that," he said sharply.

She didn't open her eyes. "Tired . . ."

"You can sleep later. You have to eat now."

She shook her head.

"Christ!" He stood up and jerked her to her feet. Her lids flew open, but her eyes were still misty with sleep.

After quickly wrapping the toweling around her, he lifted her into his arms, then carried her across the room and set her down on the bed. She gazed dumbly at him. He doubted she even knew he was there.

Carolyn was beside him, nervously nibbling at her lower lip. "Is she well?"

"Well enough."

"It's not like her to be— Shall I go for the physician?"

"No, leave us," he ordered curtly.

"I think—" The girl broke off, hesitated, and then left the room.

He began to dry Kate briskly, starting at her shoulders and going down her torso. She wasn't as thin as he had thought, he noticed absently, and her small breasts were exquisitely shaped.

Her eyes had closed again.

"How long has it been since you slept?"

"Three . . . days. I was afraid . . . Had to keep moving."

"And how long since you ate?"

"Berries . . ."

Exhaustion and starvation and the terror of being stalked as prey, and yet she had borne that punishment with a stoicism that any of his clansmen would envy.

"Food," Gavin announced from the doorway. He carried the tray he was bearing to the table in front of the fireplace and set it down before turning to appraise Kate. "She still looks asleep."

"She's awake. She's in a sort of stupor." He wrapped a blanket around Kate and lifted her in his arms. "And she'll be better once her belly's full."

"If you can manage to get anything down her." Gavin shook his head as he stared at Kate. "Why don't you let her sleep now and eat later?"

"Because she needs strength, and food will give it to her." He carried her to the chair by the fire. God, she felt light in his arms. He sat down and arranged her on his lap with her head on his shoulder. "Once she goes to sleep, I doubt if she'll wake for hours."

"So much for the plan to leave at dawn." Gavin reached down and touched Kate's cheek. "Who was to guess what wonderful skin was lurking under all that mud? Like satin . . ."

Without thinking, Robert quickly shifted Kate in his arms so that Gavin's hand fell away from her.

Gavin's eyes widened in surprise. "I wasn't going to hurt her."

Robert's response had startled himself as much as it had Gavin. He had acted instinctively, mindlessly, when he had seen Gavin's hand on her. "She was slipping."

"Was she? It looked like you were holding her tight

enough to me." He yawned. "Well, unless you need me, I think I'll go and take my own rest."

"I don't need you." He put a bit of meat to Kate's lips. "Open."

Though her eyes remained closed, her lips obediently parted, and he put the pork on her tongue. She automatically began to chew.

At Gavin's chuckle he looked up to see his cousin still standing at the doorway watching him. "You find something humorous?"

"She looks like a bairn, not a bride. And you look like a nursemaid who—"

"Good night, Gavin."

Gavin took one look at Robert's expression, and the smile vanished from his face. He quickly closed the door.

Robert resumed feeding Kate but managed to get her to eat only a few bites before she rebelled.

"No more . . ." she murmured, nestling closer.

He put the fork down. There was no use forcing her. He was surprised he had gotten her to eat as much as she had.

He started to get up from the chair.

"No!" Her eyes remained closed, but her hand clutched wildly at his doublet.

"Bed," he said firmly. He was tired and hungry himself, and had no intention of sitting here all night.

Her head moved in an almost imperceptible shake of negation. "Safe . . . here."

Safe. The words struck him like a blow. She had probably had precious little security in the past, and it was doubtful she would have it in the future, but at this moment she felt safe with him. God only knew why; he had certainly not been overgentle with her. His arms tightened instinctively around her. Dammit, he supposed it would do no harm to stay here by the fire a little while longer. When she fell into a deeper sleep, he would move her to the bed across the room. She was so exhausted that it shouldn't take long. He leaned back in the chair and gazed into the fire.

The scent of burning cedar logs and the wax of the candle on the table drifted to him. And something else—the clean smell of soap.

The girl. He glanced down at her. Her hair was a wild shining brown-gold tangle against the gray blanket, and her skin was clean and glowing as the bairn Gavin had called her.

But she wasn't a bairn. She was old enough to marry. She had a woman's fleece, and her breasts, though small, were crowned with exquisite nipples that could nurse a child.

Or a man.

The thought of his mouth enveloping that breast sent a bolt of heat through him. He was hardening, readying. It shouldn't have surprised him. Gavin was right—his appetites were strong, and it had been too long. But, God's blood, he did not need this tonight.

He was unbearably conscious of the soft, womanly weight of her resting against him as he grew in dimension. He shifted her in his arms, but it did no good. She was *there*, her nakedness covered only by the thin wool of the blanket. With one hand he could brush aside the cover, and she would be open to fondling and more intimate exploration. He could turn her on his lap, free himself, and in one thrust be inside her.

He was throbbing, flexing, heat moving through him with every breath. Why not? She was nothing to him. A wife was for the taking, and no man would fault him for coupling with her. He did not have to spend within her. He could enjoy that tightness and then draw out before he loosed the seed that could be a danger to Craighdhu. He could satisfy his lust and steal something for himself from this devil's bargain with Elizabeth.

He shifted her so that she sat squarely on him. His hands moved down to cup her slim buttocks before they pressed her small body down against him. She was so tiny. A shudder racked him as he wondered how much of him she could take, how tight she would be when she closed around him. He pushed the blanket from her shoulders. Her shining hair flowed over her breasts, half-veiling the pink tips from view. Would she wake when his tongue touched her? Not yet. He wanted to feel the textures of her. He shifted her again, and his hands caressed down her naked back.

She flinched and murmured something.

And he saw the red weals on her back.

He knew those marks well. He had earned many himself during those years in Santanella.

Sebastian again. It appeared the bastard had given her more cause to run away than the threat to kill her horse.

Pity, anger, and frustration exploded through him. Dammit, he didn't want to pity her. He wanted to be inside her. He wanted to plunge in and out and rid himself of—

But he could not do it. In his anger and lust he might have ignored her exhaustion, but those whip marks had reminded him how defenseless he had felt under the lash. He would not inflict that sense of helplessness on anyone but his greatest enemy.

So what should he do? Sit here in torment while she slept peacefully through the night? He was not such a fool.

She stirred against him. "Safe . . ."

Goddammit!

She was being carried.

Kate opened her eyes to see Robert's face above hers and felt a surge of relief. For a moment she had been afraid, but it was all right. Safety . . . home.

"No arguments," he said grimly. "I've been sitting in that damn chair for hours, and I don't intend to spend one more minute in it."

Chair? The fog of sleep surrounded her, and she couldn't grasp what he was talking about. She was only aware that everything was right. Her lids were too heavy to stay open, but it didn't matter. All was still as it should be.

He was gone! She forced her eyes to open again. He was sitting on the bed next to her but no longer touching her. "Please ... don't go."

"Close your eyes," he said between his teeth as he took off his boots. "I'm not going anywhere."

He was displeased about something, but he had promised to stay. It was all right to let go. As long as he was here, nothing bad could happen.

Home ...

He was half turned away from her, and the noon sunlight streamed over his face, illuminating high cheekbones and the beautiful line of his jaw. He lay quite still, strength and power suppressed, but a living force nonetheless. His black hair was tousled, and yet Kate received no impression of careless disarray. Even now she could sense the control, the discipline that surrounded him. How terrible it must be to be this on guard even in sleep, she thought drowsily. She wanted to reach out and touch him, comfort him—

Dear Lord, he was naked!

So was she.

Shock jolted through her as she scrambled upright in the bed and clutched the blanket to her chin, staring at him.

"I was wondering if you were ever going to stir." He turned to face her, his lids opening to reveal eyes fully awake and alert. His lips tightened with displeasure. "You're looking at me as if you'd just found a snake in your bed."

"I'm surprised ... I did not know ... Why are you here?"

"We're man and wife. I belong in your bed. You'd

be wise to become accustomed to it." He sat up and swung his legs to the floor. "Though you may not have an opportunity to get used to such a civilized piece of furniture. It's possible we may not see another bed before we get to Craighdhu. You can travel days in the Highlands without running across an inn." He went to the washstand and splashed water on his face. "How do you feel?"

She stared at him in shock. The back he had half turned to her was crisscrossed with white scars that tiger-striped his dark skin and gave him an air of savagery. She supposed she should have felt sympathy, but she was too aware of his physical presence to respond with anything but helpless fascination.

She couldn't take her eyes off him: the tight buttocks, the bulging muscles of calf and thigh, the triangle of black hair on his golden-brown chest that tapered to a thin line at his waist. He looked completely and overpoweringly male.

He cast her an impatient glance over his shoulder. "Answer me."

For a moment she couldn't remember the question. "Oh, very well."

"You said that after Landfield dragged you through the forest. I want the truth. Are you able to travel?"

"Of course."

He reached for the toweling by the basin and dabbed at his face. "Then get up and get dressed."

She could feel the heat in her cheeks. "I'm waiting until you leave. I'm not so shameless about my lack of clothing as you are."

He smiled mockingly as he threw the toweling aside. "You do not find me pleasing in this state? It would be wise of you to become accustomed to that also."

"I see no reason why I should," she said haltingly.

"I didn't either until last night. The situation has ... changed." He reached up to smooth his rumpled hair, and she watched his abdomen flatten, the muscles of his upper arm ripple. "Why should I be modest? You displayed little of that quality last night."

Her eyes widened in sudden alarm. "Didn't I?"

"You don't remember?"

She thought for a moment and then shook her head. "I remember Carolyn and then sitting in the tub. . . ."

"You also curled naked on my lap before the fire." The mockery deepened. "You were quite shameless. Evidently you found the experience less memorable than I did."

Her heart started to pound with fear. Shameless. He had called her shameless. Let it not be true, she thought fervently. Yet even as she woke, she had wanted to reach out and touch him, she remembered with panic. But she could not have— "Did I . . . mate with you?"

"Your eyes are big as saucers. What difference does it make? It's a wife's duty to give her husband pleasure."

"Answer me! Did I let you—did we fornicate?"

He stood looking at her for a moment and then slowly shook his head. "I assure you that I'd have made sure you remembered if we had." He watched her curiously as her breath expelled in a rush of relief. "What a violent response."

"I thought . . ." She swallowed and began again. "For a moment I thought he might be right."

"Sebastian?"

"He always said I was a lewd creature, unable to control my passions. He said without his guidance I would give myself to any man who crooked his finger." She straightened against the headboard and lifted her chin. "Of course, I knew he was wrong. It was foolish of me to even think I would be so weak."

"Very foolish." He paused. "But passion is not a totally undesirable quality in a wife."

"He said I would never confine myself to one man."

His lips tightened. "Now that I would find highly undesirable. So undesirable, I might respond in a manner better fitting our friend the vicar."

She could sense tension beneath the displeasure in his voice. "Why are we discussing this?" she asked impatiently. "You did not find me pleasing, or you would have taken me last night."

"Would I? Even though you were weak and hurt and unable to defend yourself?"

"Men do not care for such things. They regard women only as animals for their pleasure."

"Ah, more wise words from the vicar? If you don't believe other things he says, why believe all men are steeped in lust?"

For an instant she was uncertain, but then she remembered the cries from Martha in Sebastian's chamber. If Sebastian was driven by lust, then surely it must be so of all men? "Are you saying they are not?"

He opened his lips to speak and then wearily shook his head. "No, for once he spoke the truth. Beware of us. We can be mindless beasts when the need comes on us too strong."

Strong arms holding her, peace, a feeling of supreme contentment.

The memory came out of nowhere, colliding with his words and bringing bewilderment in its wake. "I see nothing to fear in you. In spite of what Sebastian said, I'm no Lilith who bewitches a man. I'm not even as comely as Carolyn. And if I do not please you, you will not bother me."

"No?" He smiled. "Don't be too sure. I can be more lewd than your Sebastian ever dreamed, and I indulge my passions as I see fit." He looked down at his lower body. "And I clearly do find you pleasing."

Her gaze followed his to that part of him at which she had avoided glancing. Her eyes widened as she saw the hard, bold arousal springing from the nest of dark hair.

Scorching heat flew back to her cheeks. Her chest tightened until she could scarcely draw a breath.

"You see?" He strolled over to stand in front of her. "Lustful heathen that I am, it takes little to please me. But I find much about you that draws me." He reached out and touched her hair. "Soft and glossy and of a fine length. Unbound it comes down past your waist." He draped a strand over the blanket that covered the curve of her breast. "When you were naked last night, it veiled you. But veils are meant to be pushed aside."

The soft weight of her hair felt heavy against her breasts, and she realized with astonishment that her nipples were hardening, peaking, pushing against the wool of the blanket.

"And your mouth pleases me." His voice was soft, thick, and she stared up at his face, mesmerized. Plum-rich color now darkened his cheeks, and his nostrils were flaring slightly. "It has a certain look to it. . . ." His index finger traced the full curve of her lower lip. "Open."

She didn't obey him. She felt frozen—no, that was too cold a term for what she was feeling, for the heat moving through her. She was . . . beguiled. She could do nothing but stare up at him, waiting for the next word, the next touch.

His finger slipped between her closed lips to touch her tongue. "Wonderful mouth," he murmured. "It looks as if it were created to accept . . . anything." He gently, rhythmically stroked her cheeks with the thumb and forefinger of his other hand, forming a coaxing circle about her mouth. "Will it?"

His finger was callused, hard, faintly salty against her tongue. His words were bewildering and seemed to come from far away. Aware only of those dark, glittering eyes holding her own and the textures of that intruding finger, she wasn't certain of the moment when her mouth closed around him, holding him captive.

He jerked as if she had struck him, and a shudder went through him. "Aye," he said thickly. "It most certainly will." He looked down at her, his chest rising and falling with his labored breathing. "But at the moment I could have wished you hadn't done it." He slid his finger from her mouth and took a step back. "I'm sure the memory is going to bother me exceedingly while we're on the road today."

Reality returned the instant he was no longer touching her. "Why did you—"

"Because I wanted to," he interrupted. The mocking smile was back. "I always do what I want to do."

That wasn't true, she thought. No one could have such an air of disciplined power and be that recklessly self-indulgent.

"But I'll be damned if I prove your Sebastian right after all those painful hours of knightly restraint I went through. I can wait." He started to dress with movements that were jerky. "Though not long. And, dammit, not at all if you insist on wriggling naked on my lap."

She drew a shaky breath. "I was not myself. And it is not courteous of you to remind me of it."

His mocking smile faded. "You're right. I wasn't fair. God knows, it's bad enough to be accountable for our actions when we're in control of our senses."

His reaction surprised her. She had judged him to be far more self-willed and arrogant than Sebastian, and yet he had admitted to fault, which Sebastian would never have done.

"Why are you looking at me like that?" he asked impatiently.

"Sebastian believes that people are accountable for their sins every moment, whether waking or sleeping."

"That doesn't surprise me." He turned to face her. "Which doesn't make it true."

"But sometimes when someone says something

over and over, it seems like the truth." She moistened her lips. "Everything fades together, and it gets harder to remember which is the truth and which is a lie."

His expression became arrested. "I know."

He did know. She had thought them so different, but there was no doubt in her mind that he knew exactly what she meant. She abruptly remembered the scars on his back. Had there been a Sebastian in his life? she wondered.

He turned away and put on his doublet. "And when that happens, you just fight harder."

She nodded. How odd it was to sit here and watch a man clothe himself. Odd and yet just as strangely familiar.

"I'm no Sebastian Landfield." He didn't look at her as he sat down on the bed and pulled on his left boot. "You will not find me a gentle man, but I will be fair with you. I realize you do not wish to be caught in this coil any more than I do. Submit to my will, cause me no problems, and you will lead a comfortable, untroubled life for the next year."

"And afterward?"

"Afterward you will not be my concern." He pulled on his other boot. "You will be free to do as you wish."

"Free?" she asked, startled.

"I will give you a small allowance until you marry again. I would advise you to leave Scotland. The danger will be less if you're out of James's reach. Perhaps France would be a good choice."

It suddenly dawned on her that he was talking as if she were menaced. But that realization made little impact compared to what he'd said earlier. "I will truly be free to do as I wish?"

"Did I not say it?"

"You'll never send me back to Sebastian?"

He stood up. "Whatever happens, you will never have to see Landfield again."

She doubted if that was true; Sebastian would not

relinquish her easily. But just Robert's avowal that he would never give her up to him was like a heavy stone removed from around her neck.

"You promise?" She waved an impatient hand. "Oh, not about Sebastian. I can deal with him. But you'll set me free? Truly?"

His face softened as he saw the eagerness in her expression. "By the Saints, do I perceive something besides distrust? Be good, obey me, and cause me no worry this next year, and you'll be free to do as you wish."

It seemed too much to believe. Excitement soared through her. If he was willing to give her so much for peace of mind, perhaps she could win something even more precious from this distasteful marriage. "What you wish is not impossible," she said cautiously. "But you do realize I could cause you a great deal of trouble if I chose? Sebastian found me most unsettling."

His gaze narrowed on her face. "What are you trying to say?"

She paused, then said in a rush, "A house. I want a house."

"Indeed?"

"Only a small house, but it must be built of good, strong stone."

"Like Sebastian's cottage?"

"I will see that it bears little resemblance to anything that belongs to him, but it must be of stone." She added, "And it will have to have enough ground for a garden. Every home should have a garden."

"And you refuse to promise your cooperation without this piece of property?" he asked silkily. "I have no liking for greed, Kate."

"It's not greed to demand compensation for services given." She glared at him. "I'm not asking for a palace, only a house. Something of my own."

He studied her expression. "This means a good deal to you. Why?"

"I've not been so sheltered that I haven't found that property is everything in this world," she said evasively.

"But that isn't why you want this house, is it?"

She did not want to answer him. This desire was secret and innately her own. She did not wish to share it. "It's not your concern."

"It is if I'm being forced to give it to you."

He would not let it pass, she realized with frustration. "I want a place of my own," she said baldly. "A special place that's mine alone, a place that no one can take away from me. There, I've said it. Are you satisfied?"

"For the time being."

"And you'll give it to me?"

His thoughtful gaze was still on her face, as if he were waiting for something. He nodded. "I'll give you your house."

"A stone house?"

He nodded again.

Relief and joy streamed through her. She smiled brilliantly. "I . . . thank you."

"You *can* smile. I was wondering." He smiled faintly himself. "I had every intention of providing you with a residence, you know. It would not have been suitable to do anything else."

Her smile vanished. "Then you should have told me so at once."

"But then I would have lost the opportunity to see you with your wall of thorns down. It was most interesting."

"I do not like to be considered interesting." She added sharply, "And I do not like to be probed and prodded. You would not like it, if I did it to you."

"No, I wouldn't, but that's one of the sweet prerogatives of power." He opened the door. "Get dressed and be downstairs in fifteen minutes. At this rate we'll be lucky if we get on the road before dark."

She felt feather light, sun bright, as she tossed the blanket aside when the door closed behind him. Now that he was gone, she could permit her exhilaration to spring free. No one was here to see or take this happiness away. She felt as she had during those magical childhood moments when she and Carolyn had been able to forget everything but the joy of being alive, when every day was a new adventure. Complete freedom was not hers yet, but it beckoned on the horizon, and life with Robert MacDarren could not be as terrible as living with Sebastian Landfield.

True, it appeared he might make demands on her person that the vicar would never have thought about, but she could bear that for a year. She felt that strange heat move through her again as she recalled the instant when his finger had stroked her lip.

It was not lust, she quickly assured herself. She was *not* shameless. She had been caught by surprise, and her response had been— She was not what Sebastian called her. She would not think about it and let it spoil this moment.

It was the earl's right as her husband to couple with her, but the next time he touched her, she was sure she would show the proper restraint when enduring his fondling. He did not appear to be a cruel man, and if time proved her wrong, she could always run away from him as she had from Sebastian.

She experienced a flicker of uneasiness as she remembered how relentless Robert had been when tracking her down. He did not possess Sebastian's fanaticism, but his quiet determination might make him even more difficult to elude.

Well, she would not worry about that now. For the first time in years she felt eager and hopeful and . . . and *young*. She would enjoy it while it lasted.

"*It's about time.*" *Gavin* nibbled at a slice of beef as Robert came into the common room. "You've missed breakfast. Would you care for dinner?"

"No." He glanced at the apple and beef on Gavin's plate before turning to Carolyn, who was serving Gavin. "But take up some of that fruit to my wife."

"At once, my lord." She hesitated. "She is better this morning?"

"Much better."

Carolyn smiled in relief and hurried from the room.

Robert pulled on his leather riding gloves and turned back to Gavin. "What kind of night did you have? Did your wound bother you?"

Gavin shook his head as he finished the beef on his plate. "I slept well." He grinned. "And you certainly gave me plenty of time to rest. I was wondering if you were going to stir before evening."

"So was I. The girl was exhausted."

"And of course you had to pamper the child."

"Why the devil do you keep calling her a child?" As he saw Gavin's smile of satisfaction, Robert tempered the violence in his tone. "And I didn't pamper her. Every commander knows that to push a soldier when he's exhausted is to court trouble."

"Hmm." Gavin popped a slice of apple into his mouth. "And here I was, sitting here imagining you in the toils of Cupid. Oh, I know she was exhausted last night, but you had all morning to consummate the happy nuptials." He snapped his fingers. "But that's right. You have no use for mudlarks. How could I forget?"

"You forget nothing you wish to remember."

"But she did clean up well, didn't she?" He smiled mischievously. "You weren't even tempted to linger awhile?"

Robert had a fleeting memory of Kate staring up at him, her eyes wide, uncertain, that pouty mouth closing around his finger. Dammit, he was hardening again. He turned abruptly toward the door. "Let's go to the stable. I want to take a look at that mare."

Gavin didn't move. "The mare's fine. And you didn't answer me. Weren't you tempted to—"

"I don't want to talk about this, Gavin."

"I think you *were* tempted. Poor Robert. It's very difficult, isn't it?"

"I'm sure you're going to elaborate on that."

"Aye, I feel it's my duty." He took the last slice of apple and chewed it thoughtfully. "You want to bed her, but you can't because she's your wife. It's very amusing."

"I'm glad you find it so. I assure you, if I choose to bed her, I will do so."

"Ah, the wind's shifted." Gavin laughed in delight. "I thought I saw the signs last night. But I still don't think you will. In fact, I'll wager you won't. Two pounds. Taken?"

"Why are you so sure?"

"Because in many ways she's still a child in need, and you've been trained to care for those who need you, not steal from them. Everyone at Craighdhu knows that."

"But she doesn't belong to Craighdhu," Robert reminded him softly.

"But she belongs to you."

"For a year."

"All the more reason not to steal something that will bring pleasure to the next man who takes her in marriage."

The next man who lay in bed with her, who plunged between her thighs and sampled that tightness he had just denied himself. Robert's expression carefully hid the rage that tore through him at the thought. "But I'm so good at stealing."

"Only from the Spanish, not from big-eyed children."

His lips tightened in annoyance. "I told you, she's not a child. I assure you, there's no one more wary or barbed than—" He broke off as he saw Kate coming down the stairs.

She was dressed in the same brown wool cape she had worn previously, but her hair was now in a neat single braid. She moved with a springy step, color bloomed in her cheeks, and her eyes flashed with life. He had never seen a woman more boldly alive, and yet there was still a touch of that fragile eagerness he had seen in her when he had told her he would give her a home of her own.

Gavin gave a low whistle. "Never mind. Let's forget it."

Robert didn't take his eyes from Kate. "Never mind what?"

"The wager. You're staring at her as you did that very first galleon we took from the Spanish." He took a step forward as Kate reached the bottom of the stairs. "Good morning, my lady. Do you remember me?"

"Of course I do."

She was smiling at Gavin with an openness she

had never displayed toward Robert. Her attitude had always reflected wariness or distrust toward him. Why did it annoy him? Everyone always smiled at Gavin.

"How could she forget you?" Robert abruptly turned on his heel and strode toward the door. "It's time we got on the road. Bring her along to the stable."

Kate's smile faded as she watched Robert leave the inn. "What did I do?"

"He's annoyed with me, not you. As usual, my tongue ran away with me." Gavin changed the subject. "Did you have time to eat? You came down so quickly."

"I had a bite or two while I said good-bye to Carolyn. I was too excited to eat."

"Well, it's not every day a lass is wed."

"Wed?" She shook her head. "He's going to give me a house, a place of my own."

He chuckled. "And a house is better than a bridegroom?"

She looked at him uncertainly. "Are we truly wed? It all seems most strange."

"Aye, handfast is as legal as standing before a man of God in Scotland."

"But we're not in Scotland."

"Robert is a Scot. That makes it binding right enough."

She felt a rush of relief. "Then it is all right."

He nodded. "And the only way Robert could best Her Majesty. He was not at all pleased with her."

"Why would he want to best—"

"I'll tell you once we're on the road." Gavin took her elbow and guided her toward the door. "Robert wants us at the stable, and I've caused him enough irritation for one morning. It's always best to dole out impudence in small doses so that he doesn't choke on it." He added ruefully, "Or choke me."

She found herself smiling again. How strange that she was so easy in Gavin's presence. She had no desire to withdraw into herself as was her custom. Perhaps it was that his sunny demeanor reminded her of Carolyn's, and she suspected it masked the same kindness. "You don't appear to be overfearful of him."

"That's because I belong to Craighdhu. A certain amount of liberty is always given to the denizens of Craighdhu."

"No, it's more than that." She had noticed a bonding, an easy familiarity that was not that of lord and minion. "You've known each other a long time?"

He glanced at her appraisingly. "You have sharp eyes and know how to use them." He nodded. "We grew up together."

"Like brothers?"

"At first." He frowned. "But later it changed. . . ."

"Why?"

"He changed." He added wistfully, "*They* changed him."

"Who?"

He shrugged. "Robert doesn't like us to talk about it."

It was clear that subject was closed. "But you're kinsmen? Your names are different."

"Most of the clans have intermarried. My mother was a MacDarren and married a Gordon. When he died, she brought me back to Craighdhu. She never liked the Lowlands. No Highlander does."

"What's wrong with them?"

He made a face. "Too rich and fat."

"And that's bad?"

"Aye, you'll know what I mean when we reach Craighdhu." He guided her around a puddle. "But we'll stop overnight with my uncle, Angus Gordon, once we reach the border. He's not a bad man . . . for a Lowlander."

She was amused at the qualification. "I'll look forward to meeting him. He's not fat and rich then?"

"Oh, he's rich enough, but his reiving keeps him lean and hungry."

"Reiving?"

"Raiding," he explained. "He raids the English on this side of the border."

"You mean he *steals*?" she asked in astonishment.

"Of course. But only from the English," he added quickly. "He wouldn't steal from a Scot."

"And you believe that makes stealing right?"

"Well, perhaps not right." He frowned as if trying to work out the ethics. "But it's custom."

She shook her head dazedly as she thought of how Sebastian would view this calm acceptance of the breaking of holy law. "And do you ... reive, also?"

"Well, not exactly. Not from the English." He opened the barn door and stepped inside to let her precede him. "Of course, there was that one English ship, but Robert only meant to— Robert prefers to raid the Spanish."

"I see." She did not see at all. She felt more bewildered and uneasy with every hesitant step into this new world where it seemed it was perfectly all right to be an outlaw, as long as the crime was aimed at the right party.

"You'll be fine." She turned to see Gavin smiling gently at her. "It only takes getting used to. Don't worry, I'll help you."

"Will you?" Her spirits lifted as warmth flowed through her. Why should she be afraid, when this was exactly what she had wanted? She had fought to free herself from Sebastian and all his restrictions, but if she had escaped him before, she would have been alone. Now she had Gavin Gordon to help her through these first steps. "Thank you." A warm smile lit her face. "Then you're right—I'll be fine."

"What do you think of her?" They both looked to see Robert leading Caird and a chestnut mare toward her. "She appears strong and gentle enough."

Kate stepped forward and patted the mare's nose. "She's lovely," she said. "What's her name?"

"I didn't ask," Gavin admitted.

She frowned reprovingly. "Every creature deserves a name."

"Sorry," he said solemnly.

"I'll call her Rachel." She gave the mare a final pat, and then went around her to Caird and began stroking his muzzle. "How are you, boy?"

The piebald neighed and nudged her.

"He's tired," Robert said bluntly. "And he'll get more tired. You said the innkeeper is a good man. We could leave him here."

She tensed. "He is a good man, but he would have no use for Caird. How would I know who he would sell him to? You said he could come."

"Dammit, you like the mare. Look at them together. She's young and fit, and the piebald is old."

"All the more reason to love and take care of him."

"It's no use, Robert," Gavin said. "I have an idea the horse may be her Craighdhu."

She could feel Robert's gaze on her back as she leaned her forehead against Caird. He muttered something inaudible and then said to Gavin, "Saddle our horses and put a light pack on the piebald." He grabbed Kate's wrist in one hand and the mare's reins in the other and pulled them both out of the barn into the stable yard. "You've made a mistake."

His grasp on her wrist was generating a strange heat up her arm, and she tried to pull away. "Let me go."

He ignored her. "The horse is going to be nothing but trouble. He'll slow us down. We can't afford to be slowed down now."

She couldn't deny that Caird would have that effect, so she merely set her jaw and glared at him.

"And don't look at me like that. It makes me want to *break* you."

"You'd like that, wouldn't you? Another prerogative of power. You'll find I don't break easily."

"You're wrong." His gaze narrowed on her face. "All women are easily broken in one manner."

For an instant she didn't understand, and then his meaning became clear to her. She felt the blood rush to her cheeks, and she suddenly couldn't breathe.

"Aye." His hands closed on her waist and lifted her slowly to the saddle. "We'll not see a bed again until we reach the border, and I'd prefer to take you the first time on clean sheets than the cold ground. But don't tempt me, Kate."

She could feel the warmth of his hands through the layers of clothing, and it brought the same burning sensation as his grip on her wrist, spreading upward to her breasts, making them exquisitely sensitive. The response frightened her, and she snapped, "I'm not tempting you at all. It's your own sinful, carnal nature."

An indefinable expression flickered across his face. "Very sinful and very carnal," he agreed softly. "And very impatient." He turned to Gavin, who was leading Caird and their own horses out of the barn. "Wager taken. Two pounds."

Gavin's troubled gaze went from Robert's reckless smile to Kate's flushed face and then back again. "I don't like this. I think I want to withdraw the wager. It makes me feel responsible."

"No? Too bad. The wager stands. And I intend to like it very much indeed." Robert turned away. "Carnal sinner that I am."

Kate watched him mount his horse and trot out of the stable yard before she turned to Gavin. "Wager?"

"It's nothing." Gavin smiled at her. "Only another example of my runaway tongue." He got on his horse. "But it seems you must have a less than discreet tongue yourself. You should not sting Robert until you learn the way to do it without suffering the consequences. Watch me, and I'll show you."

• • •

Robert set a grueling pace that afternoon. In three hours Kate's every muscle was stiff and sore. By the time they stopped at sundown at a clearing near a small brook, she had to struggle just to stay in the saddle.

"I'll take the horses down to the brook to water them," Gavin said as he lifted Kate to the ground. "Sit down and rest."

She shook her head. "They're mine. I can do it." She took the mare's and Caird's reins and led them down the path through the forest toward the brook. She knelt and splashed her face, vaguely aware of Robert and Gavin talking a few yards down the bank but too tired to comprehend their words.

When she lifted her head a few minutes later, Gavin was no longer there, but Robert stood leaning against a tree, watching her.

She tensed, then deliberately sat back on her heels and straightened her shoulders. "You need not wait for me, my lord. I can make my way back on my own. I was just refreshing myself."

"And trying to keep from fainting," he said roughly. "For God's sake, don't lie to me. I know how weak you must feel. I drove you hard today."

"I'm not used to long hours in the saddle. I'll do better tomorrow." She forced herself to get to her feet and gather the horses' reins. "I'll help Gavin to—"

"Gavin doesn't need help."

"His wound—"

"His wound is mending." Robert stepped forward, tossed her up on the mare again, and gathered both horses' reins. "And he would not appreciate your cosseting him. He's a Highlander."

"And Highlanders do not care for each other?"

"We take care of our own. We don't ask help from outsiders."

Outsiders. The word struck a hollow, hurtful note within her. Yes, that was what she was, what she had always been. From the moment she had been born, she had been the one outside looking in.

"For God's sake, why do you look like that?" Robert's gaze was on her face. "Very well, help him. Drive yourself until you collapse. Why should I care?"

"You should not." She had made him angry again, but she was too weary to let it bother her. "I'm nothing to you. I'm an . . . outsider."

"You're more than that. You're a troublesome woman who—"

"The queen forced you to wed," she suddenly flared. "And you're a lawless pirate who would be hanging dead for the crows to pick if you hadn't been given the opportunity to marry me. So I'll hear no more about how much trouble I am."

He went still. "I see Gavin's been talking again."

"He says they call you Black Robert. It was kind of someone to tell me what I must face during the next year."

"A lawless pirate."

"Isn't that what you are?"

"A pirate, yes, but not lawless. I have my own laws."

"How convenient," she said tartly. "And I suppose you change them daily to suit yourself."

His lips were suddenly twitching. "Not daily. Weekly, perhaps."

She stared at him for a moment. The quicksilver change from grimness to humor caught her off guard. "I do not understand you."

"Must you?"

"Yes, I think so. If I'm to live with you, I must come to terms." She moistened her lips. "You see, this is not what I . . . I'm confused. Because I hate Sebastian does not mean I hate God's laws. They are good. And if they are good, then what you and Gavin do is bad. Is that not true?"

"Quite true."

"And yet I like Gavin and find him . . . good. It is most perplexing."

He smiled sardonically. "I notice you're not having any conflict regarding my humble self."

"There's something about you that makes me uneasy." That was not the right word for the dark tumult he aroused, but to use another would reveal more than she wished to show him. She frowned. "Besides, I don't know you. I don't think you want anyone to know you. Not even Gavin."

"Why not?"

"I don't know." She thought about it. "It may be for the same reason I closed myself off from Sebastian and Martha."

"Because they hurt you? I'm not afraid of Gavin hurting me, and I assure you the scamp is never uneasy around me."

"No, but there's something. . . ." She remembered the touch of wistfulness in Gavin's expression when he had spoken of Robert and their childhood together. "I think you make him . . . sad."

He looked away from her. "You're mistaken." They had reached the clearing where Gavin was kneeling building a fire. "Why don't you ask him?"

"He wouldn't tell me. He's kind, but even to him I'm an outsider."

"You seem to have become overly attached to that word," Robert said testily as he lifted her down from the mare. "Did it occur to you that I have little knowledge of you either?"

"What is there to know?" she asked warily. "I've lived with Sebastian and Martha since I was a small child. Surely you can see how uneventful such a life would be. There were no adventures or sea travels for me."

"Sometimes you don't have to travel afar to find adventure. What was it like, living with Sebastian?"

Loneliness, desolation, fear, everything within her

tightening, drying. She met his gaze. "What do you think it was like?"

His lips tightened. "I can guess, but speculation is never fully satisfying."

She said haltingly, "I rose at dawn and helped Martha with the chores. Master Gywnth came at ten and gave me lessons."

"What kind of lessons?"

"Mathematics, French, geography . . ." She made a vague gesture with a hand. "The lady . . . the queen wished me to have the education of a nobleman. That's why she sent word to Sebastian to buy me a horse."

He cast a glance at Caird. "I'd wager she never saw this specimen."

"Of course not. She left everything to Sebastian."

"Did you study a musical instrument?"

She shook her head. "Sebastian said music encouraged licentiousness."

"Aye, I'm sure it would have made you even more wicked than you are. What did you do after your lessons?"

She frowned in bewilderment. These humdrum details could not be of interest to him. "I studied the Scriptures all afternoon with Sebastian when he wasn't traveling the countryside visiting his parishioners." She had a sudden memory of herself sitting on her stool by the window for many hours, trying desperately to keep upright because she knew the brutality of the punishment that would come if she showed a lack of attention. "When he wasn't home, I was permitted to go for walks or ride Caird."

"Alone?"

She nodded. "I told you that he didn't like me to be with the villagers."

"Yes, you did." She could sense an undercurrent of anger in his words. "How could I forget?" He started to turn away. "Sit down and rest."

"I can help."

"You could," he bit out, "but you won't. We'll be traveling from dawn to dusk tomorrow, and I want you to be able to stand the pace."

"I'm strong. I'll stand the pace." She brushed a strand of hair back from her cheek. "But I don't see why I should be forced to do so. I see no reason for such speed."

"Don't you?" He stared at her with an expression that compounded frustration, anger, and grudging respect before he turned on his heel and strode toward Gavin.

She sat watching him as he helped Gavin set up camp. He moved swiftly, gracefully, swooping down on tasks, doing more than his share but not in an obvious way. He let Gavin do enough that he felt useful but not so much that he strained his dwindling strength, and kept him busy with casual conversation so that he was never aware of the disparity. She suddenly realized he had acted in the same fashion on the trail with Gavin. Though the pace had been hard, he had found ways of easing the wounded man's path.

We take care of our own.

She was aware of an aching pang of envy and wistfulness. She was being foolish. These Highlanders and their codes had nothing to do with her. She could take care of herself and had no need of such camaraderie.

It made no sense. She was so weary she could scarcely lift her head, and yet sleep evaded her. It must be the night sounds that were disturbing her. No, it was not the night sounds. She would not lie to herself. She knew why she could not sleep.

She shifted in her blankets and slowly turned toward the warmth of the blaze.

Robert was watching her from across the fire.

She tensed, waiting for him to speak.

He said nothing. He just lay there, his dark eyes alert and unwavering, fixed on her with the same expression they had held in the bedchamber this morning.

Her breasts were lifting and falling as if she were running, and each time they brushed against the blankets covering her, her nipples became harder, more sensitive. The heat from the fire seemed to engulf her, scorching her flesh.

The silence stretched on. She had to break it. "I . . . can't sleep," she whispered.

"I know."

Of course he knew. She had felt his gaze on her for the last hour.

She closed her eyes.

"It won't do any good, you know. I tried it."

She kept her eyes closed tightly, shutting him out.

"The storm," he said.

She opened her eyes again.

"You asked what the hurry was." He paused. "There's a big storm coming. I want to be across the border before it catches up with us."

He made no sense. The day had been bright and sunny, with not a cloud in the sky. "The rains are past. How could you know there is to be more? There's no storm coming," she said firmly.

"You're wrong." He turned his back to her and pulled his blanket around his shoulders. "It's coming."

Gavin reined in on the rise, turned to Kate and pointed to the north. "That's Angus's land."

Fertile meadows rolled gently before them, and in the distance Kate could see a brick manor house and several outbuildings crowning a small hill. The manor was not splendid, but it appeared both substantial and in good repair.

"It's a fine property," Kate said. "And brick is almost as strong a building material as stone."

"I'm glad you approve," Robert said mockingly as he turned to Gavin. "Did I forget to tell you how adamant my wife is on the subject of stone for her future domicile? May I ask why stone is such a passion with you, Kate?"

She looked at him in surprise. "Because it doesn't burn."

"Well, it's true it's very difficult to burn."

"It's almost impossible to burn. That's why Sebastian had the new cottage built of stone."

"The *new* cottage?"

She nodded. "The old one was built of sod with a thatched roof."

"And it burned down?"

He was looking at her with a faint quizzical smile that contained an element of mockery. She had meant to evade the truth, but he appeared so sure, so confident, that it annoyed her, and she suddenly wanted to jar him. "No, *I* burnt it down."

Gavin's lips fell open, but to her disappointment, Robert's expression didn't change. "How extraordinary. I do hope you don't make it a common practice. Being without walls could get a bit drafty this time of year."

"It was an accident, Kate?" Gavin asked.

"I did it on purpose. One night after he had punished me I lit the curtains with a candle." She added fiercely, "He deserved it."

"I'm sure he did," Robert said. "I'm just wondering how he and his sweet wife escaped the flames."

She scowled. "I had second thoughts. I went back in the cottage and woke them."

"Bad judgment," Gavin murmured.

"I had reached only my tenth year," she said in her defense. "I was angry, and I knew they deserved it, but I couldn't let them die. It would have been a sin, and I would have been like my mother." She added defiantly, "But I'm not sorry I did it. I'd do it again."

Robert smiled. "I believe I'm beginning to realize why Sebastian found you so 'unsettling.' "

"It's easy to condemn me now. You weren't *there.*"

"We're not blaming you, Kate," Gavin soothed gently. "Except for your lack of foresight."

"You're hardly the one to talk," Robert said. "I remember how squeamish you were at your first blooding."

"But I'm sure you weren't squeamish at yours," Kate challenged.

"Death is never pleasant, nor is it to be taken lightly." His lips tightened grimly. "But some people deserve to die. I've been wondering what punishment Sebastian invoked on a child of ten to push you to those lengths."

"I'm sure you wouldn't consider the punishment deserving of such an action on my part."

"No? Why don't you tell me and let me judge?"

"I don't like to be judged any more than you do," she said.

"And you don't like to talk about your 'uneventful' life with Sebastian. What did you do to deserve punishment?"

She tried to shrug carelessly. "He caught me looking in Master Brelam's window one evening."

"Master Brelam?"

"He was the baker. His cottage was on the outskirts of the village."

"And why were you peering into his window?"

"Why do you think? Because I liked to do it." She bit her lower lip before bursting out, "It was a long time ago. None of it matters now. Why are you asking me these questions?"

"I have a curious nature."

Gavin said with a frown, "She's right. It's none of our concern, Robert."

"Perhaps not." Robert smiled sardonically. "But I want to know. If she didn't want to answer questions, she shouldn't have told us about burning down the house. What was so fascinating about this baker's cottage?"

"Nothing." She saw him lift his brows and said, "They were . . . they laughed a lot. It was pleasant to see them. He was a young man, and his wife was scarcely older than I am now. I'd go to the cottage at supper-time and watch them prepare their meal. They had a little boy who crawled around the kitchen, getting in their way. . . ." She shouldn't have mentioned that night. Over the years she had tried to block out the desperate hunger that had driven the child she had been to that window. Yet now the memory came back to her as if it had been yesterday. The cheerfully blazing fire in the hearth, the young man with fine, straight hair and a broad smile, and his wife who looked at him with confidence, not fear. "I'd never seen . . . I didn't know it could be like that. I didn't do any harm. I just wanted to see them."

"And what did Sebastian do when he caught you?"

"He dragged me into the house and made me apologize to them and admit my sin." She swallowed. "I was so ashamed."

"What sin?"

"Avarice. He said I lusted after what they had."

"And did you?"

"Yes," she whispered. She had wanted to drink in the love, the trust, and that wondrous lack of fear. She had wanted to fill herself with it, secrete it away to comfort her in Sebastian's cold, barren house. "I couldn't stop crying. They were very kind. They told Sebastian that it was natural for children to be curious. He wouldn't listen to them. He knew me. He knew why I was there." She drew a deep, shaky breath. "He took me back to his cottage and beat me until I couldn't stand, and all the while he did it, he told me over and over that what I'd seen in that house would never be for me. I'd never have a home or people who would care for me. I wasn't worthy. I must reject all thoughts of such a life and resign myself to the knowledge that my destiny would always be with him."

"Christ," Gavin uttered.

Robert said nothing, staring impassively at her.

The impulse that had led her to confide in him had been a mistake. The memory of that hideous night was terribly hurtful, and she already felt too vulnerable and exposed when she was with him. She looked away from him and said, "We stayed at the inn until Sebastian received a sum from the lady to rebuild the cottage. It was while we were there I got to know Carolyn."

"And then he built in stone," Robert said. "Did he suspect you did it deliberately?"

"I told him I did it."

"Another mistake. I imagine your punishment was even more severe."

"That didn't matter," she whispered. "For the first time I didn't feel helpless. I had *done* something."

"You certainly did," Robert said dryly. His gaze went to the manor house in the distance. "Let's hope Angus doesn't raise your ire."

"You know it's not the same," she said. "I would never do anything like that to any but an enemy."

"Then we're lucky Angus is a stranger. He's very fond of his fine brick house."

"He has a right to be. It's very handsome."

"Fat," Gavin corrected with a grin as he spurred ahead. "But he's a good man, so we forgive him, don't we, Robert? I'll see you at the stables. I want to see what new horseflesh Angus has plucked from the English." He glanced slyly over his shoulder at Kate. "And I promise not to tell Angus the danger encroaching on his horizon."

Kate watched him gallop away, the rosy rays of the setting sun shimmering in his red hair as he bent over his horse's neck, urging him to go faster.

"But will you forgive our Angus his transgressions?" She turned to see Robert smiling crookedly at her. "How distressing. Another outlaw for you to weigh in the balance."

"You're not being fair. I've never judged you. I just want to understand. I'm far from perfect, and I've been judged too often myself to judge others." She frowned. "I think you wish to hurt me."

"Now why should I wish to do that?"

"I don't know." She could never tell what was on his mind, she thought with exasperation. All she knew was that he was always watching her, and for the past three days she had been growing more and more tense. She would turn her head with a smile on her lips from something Gavin had said and find MacDarren's gaze fixed on her face with that deep intensity that made her so uneasy.

"I don't want to hurt you." His gaze went again to the manor house in the distance. "Just don't fight me."

The first time I have you, I'd prefer it be on clean sheets.

His words came to her so quickly, she knew she had been deliberately keeping herself from remembering them.

"Aye." His gaze was back on her face, reading every nuance of her expression. "You knew it was coming. I couldn't have made myself clearer. Angus has no use for women in his life, but he has two able-bodied male servants who keep his house tidy and clean, and he can give us what we need."

Clean sheets. She tried to block out the image of him naked and aroused, eyes shimmering down at her. She drew a shaky breath and with an effort made her tone acid tart. "Speak for yourself. I certainly don't need it."

"You will." He smiled. "I have no liking for reluctant women. I'll take care that you need it as much as I do."

"Gavin says it's important we do not have a child. Would you take such a risk for mere lust's sake?"

"Lust is never 'mere,' and there is a certain precaution I can take."

He had an answer for everything, and since she knew nothing of this blasted magical "precaution" she could not argue with him. She kicked her horse into a trot and rode on ahead.

Gavin came riding back to them when they were within a few hundred yards of the stable. "Robert!" He waved a hand back at the stable yard that was teeming with men and horses. "Angus is about to set out to go reiving. He wants us to go with him. What do you think?"

"I thought you'd had enough of blood and glory," Robert said dryly.

"There won't be that much blood, and it will take only a few hours. They're just going to raid the earl of Cavendish's stable of a few choice mares Angus says will be much happier in Scotland. The English have no appreciation for fine horseflesh." Gavin's eyes twinkled. "Of course, if you don't wish to go, I'm sure Angus will understand. I've explained you've just wed and now have a tendency to curl up by the fire like a tame pussy-cat."

"How kind of you."

Gavin waved his hand. "What's a henchman for, if not to smooth the way for you? Do we go?"

"I'll consider it." He glanced at Kate and gestured to a small, square-shouldered man in the center of the group of riders in the stable yard. "Come along and be introduced to my kinsman."

"You're related to him also?" Her gaze went to the man he had indicated. Angus Gordon had shaggy, graying red hair and rough-hewn features, and he bore no resemblance to Robert. "I thought he was Gavin's kinsman."

"And Gavin is my kinsman." He shrugged. "It is all the same. We are all bound together."

A wistful pang rippled through her at his words.

What must it be like to be bound together in that fashion, to ride into a place and know you belonged there? Well, she would know that feeling someday. She would have her own house, a place to come home to. But there was more here than just a house, she realized suddenly. These people belonged together by right of blood and oath. They were family. She had never thought further than owning a house, but would that house be a home without people who cared about it as much as she did?

"Ah, Robert, lad. I hear you've been keeping busy," Angus Gordon boomed as they approached. "Tell me, is marriage to a puling Englishwoman as much diversion as plucking gold from the Spanish?"

"It has its moments of hazard." Robert gestured to Kate. "My wife, Kate. Since she has a kind heart, she will excuse your lack of courtesy, Angus."

"I'm sure she's already found you less gentle than those weaklings with whom she grew up." He looked with cold appraisal at Kate. "Fine eyes, decent breasts, but her hips are too narrow for good breeding."

Kate felt as if she were a sheep at a town market, and in her present agitated state she was in no mood to be treated as livestock She always hated being made to feel her own helplessness, and she would *not* overlook this particular discourtesy. She rode her horse into the circle of horsemen until she was squarely in front of Angus. She ran her gaze with deliberate disparagement over his short, stocky frame, then said sweetly to Robert, "I can see why he wishes you to accompany him, my lord. A man so small and puny must need all the protection he can procure."

Gavin's snort was quickly muffled.

"Protection!" An expression of outrage appeared on Angus's face. "I need no—" He stopped, then he threw back his head and laughed uproariously. "Good for you, lass." He turned to Robert. "Are you sure she's not a Scot?"

"English," Robert said. "And a tired English at that. Will you give us hospitality for the night?"

"When have I ever turned you away?" Angus asked. "Even when Jamie was less than pleased with you. Have you had any more trouble with his man Malcolm?"

"No, but then I haven't been home in over a year. I'm sure Malcolm will furnish me with sufficient distraction once I'm at Craighdhu. And I have to warn you," Robert added, "James is still exceedingly annoyed with me."

"I'll still find room for you and this English." Angus grinned. "But to soothe my conscience, I'll have to take at least three more mares from Cavendish than I planned. I wouldn't want anyone to think I'd turned into a Sassenach lover." His expression turned grim. "The English have grown too confident when they think they can kill a Scottish monarch and get away with no retribution. You've heard about Mary?"

Robert went still. "Mary?"

"They beheaded her four days ago at Fotheringhay." Angus shrugged. "You know I was never one of her supporters, but I don't like the idea of those damn English killing any Scot."

Shock, followed immediately by a wave of sickness, washed over Kate. Mary, Queen of Scots, was dead. Her mother was dead. "You're sure?" Kate whispered. "How . . . did she die?"

Angus looked at her curiously. "Are you all right, lass? You look a bit pale."

"How did she die?" she repeated.

"I told you, the block."

"No, that's not . . . what I mean." She lifted a hand to her trembling lips. "Did she die . . . well?"

"Better than she lived," Angus said. "Aye, I heard she died bold and brave like a true queen. The messenger said she wore a bright scarlet petticoat and a golden-haired wig, and was as comely as when she was a lass. The wig fell off when the executioner beheaded her." His gaze narrowed on her face. "It seems to have come as a great shock to you. Did your people support Mary's claim to the throne?"

She didn't answer. A bright scarlet petticoat . . .

Robert said quickly, "Kate's parents are dead, and I'm sure her guardian had no kind feelings for Mary Stuart." He turned to Kate. "Isn't that right, Kate?"

She nodded numbly.

"And it's no wonder she appears stunned. Your rough tongue is enough to turn anyone's stomach."

The suspicion in Angus's face was replaced by ruefulness. "I thought she was stronger than most English. I didn't mean to sicken you, lass."

"She'll be fine once she has rested." Robert turned to Gavin. "Take her to the house. I'm to have the same chamber, Angus?"

Angus nodded, his gaze still on Kate.

Gavin dismounted and threw the reins of his horse to a young boy. "We're not going reiving tonight?" he asked Robert, disappointed, as he lifted Kate from the saddle. "It would make a fine tale once we get back to Craighdhu."

"We need an early start tomorrow." Robert got off his horse and turned back to Angus. "Do you have time before you visit Cavendish to show me your new acquisitions?"

Angus's attention instantly left Kate, and a smile broke over his face as he slipped from the saddle. "I'll make time. I want to show you what you're missing by living on that barren island with no access to good horseflesh. Though you could always amuse yourself by snatching a few of Malcolm's prime stock." He laughed in amusement at the thought and clapped Robert on the shoulder. "Come along, and I'll show you one of the prettiest mares you've ever seen."

• • •

Kate watched from the window as Angus Gordon and his men rode out of the stable yard and then turned south and thundered toward the border.

There's a storm coming.

She had not understood when Robert had said those words, but this was what he meant. He had known her mother was going to die. He had known when he had taken her from Sebastian that Queen Elizabeth was going to behead her mother.

"Are you well?"

She turned to see Robert standing in the doorway. "Of course." She unclenched her hands and forced a smile. "I don't know why I was upset. It was very foolish of me. I don't even remember seeing her. She never came to visit me, never wrote me a letter. After she gave me up, it was as if I never existed."

"Hearing anyone has been beheaded is never a pleasant experience. It's not surprising you're upset."

"I'm not so squeamish. I always knew it might happen. Sebastian told me someday Elizabeth would grow tired of my mother's sinfulness."

His lips thinned. "Why the devil did you ask Angus to describe her death?"

"All my life I've heard what a sinful life she led. I had to know that it didn't end that way, that she had some worth. Courage is a virtue too." She folded her arms across her chest to keep them from trembling. "It's growing chill, isn't it?"

"No, but I'll build up the fire." He knelt and threw on another log and stoked the flames. "I've told the servants they could go to their quarters. They're more friends than servants to Angus, and I didn't want them gossiping to him about how upset you are."

"I'm sorry to be so much trouble."

"No trouble. I've asked Gavin to see what he can find in the kitchen and bring your supper up here."

"Thank you. You're very kind."

He rose to his feet and replaced the poker. "Good

God, you must be upset to make that bad a mistake in judgment."

"You can be kind. You're kind to Gavin. Sometimes you remind me of a fierce falcon, spreading your wings over him, keeping him from all harm. It must make him feel very safe." A weary smile touched her lips. "But I forgot, he belongs to Craighdhu. That makes him the exception, doesn't it?"

"Aye." He stood looking at her, frowning. "I don't like this."

She didn't know what he meant and was too numb to care. As she moved toward the hearth, her gaze fell on the bed, and his words on the hill came back to her. She said dully, "Clean sheets."

"By the Saints," he exploded. "I'm not so desperate for a woman I'd take one who is capable of no more feeling than a puppet."

"No?" It did not seem to matter. She sat down in the high-backed chair by the hearth and stared into the dancing flames.

"You're to eat your supper when Gavin brings it. Do you understand?"

She nodded.

"And then you're to go to bed and forget all this."

Forget death and loneliness and the woman who died in her scarlet petticoat four days ago. "I shall be quite all right."

She was vaguely aware he was standing there staring at her. Then he muttered a curse and slammed the door.

She leaned her head back against the chair. The flames shimmered scarlet in the gathering darkness, as bold and brilliant as a scarlet petticoat. . . .

Robert looked down at the untouched food on the tray. "You should have made her eat."

"She wasn't hungry. She said she was going to bed." Gavin crossed the hall and vanished into the kitchen. He came out a moment later carrying a bottle of whiskey. "Look what I found. I'm sure Angus won't mind. We can always tell him we only wanted to toast his success against the English. What was the real reason we didn't go with him?"

"Too dangerous. For the next few months every action against the English is going to be laid to Mary's execution. I have no desire for anyone to link my marriage to any sudden interest in avenging her."

"I wondered why you were so quick to distract Angus." He frowned. "But we can trust him, Robert."

"He's curious and curious men speculate. Speculations are dangerous." His gaze went back to the stairs. "How did she look?"

Gavin shrugged. "You saw her."

"That's no answer," Robert snapped. "Dammit, how does she look? Was she any better?"

"She looked as though she were seeing phantoms." Gavin paused and then added, "But we all have to face our phantoms alone. You can't fight them for her."

"Why the hell should I want to try?" Robert strode to the table in front of the hearth. "Bring that whiskey. I feel in need of warming."

"Or blurring." Gavin set the bottle on the card table and sat down opposite him. "I'm sure this isn't what you planned for tonight. You were so hot for her, I thought you'd give in a dozen times on the journey here."

"So did I." He was still hot for her. He had never been in such a fever for a woman as he was for Kate, and frustration was tearing him apart—frustration and that aching tenderness he had been fighting since the moment he had seen her. Why could he not set that softness aside and take what he wanted?

"She's a brave lass. It's hard to see her suffer, isn't it?"

Robert didn't look at him as he reached for the bottle. "Deal the cards."

• • •

Mermaid!

She couldn't breathe! Her lungs were filling with water. Smothering! "Wait, please, wait . . ."

"What the hell is wrong?" She was being shaken hard, being torn from the blue depths. "Wake up!"

Kate opened her eyes to see Robert's face above her.

Safety. Harbor. Home.

She hurled herself into his arms, her heart beating so hard, it felt as if it were going to leap into her throat and choke her. Her arms closed frantically, desperately around him. "She's gone!"

"Shh . . ." Robert buried his fingers in her hair. "You must have had a bad dream."

What was she doing? Instinct had brought her into this embrace, but Robert was no safe harbor. She tried to break free, but he quelled her struggles "Stop it."

She collapsed back into his arms. She would have to rely on instinct; she was too weak to do battle now.

"She's gone." She was sobbing so hard, she could barely get the words past her lips. "Mermaid. Mermaid . . ."

"Easy." Robert began stroking her hair. "It can't be that bad. It was only a dream."

The tears were pouring down her cheeks. "That's what I tried to tell him. Not a sin—only a dream."

"Told who?"

"Sebastian. He wouldn't listen. Martha got . . . the whip."

He went still. "The whip?'

"Because of the dream. Mermaid . . ."

"What does a mermaid have to do with this?"

"It's her. Don't you see? It's her."

"Mary?"

"My mother." The frantic words tumbled out wildly. "He said to dream about her was wicked. But it never felt wicked. It wasn't wicked."

"Christ."

She was silent a moment, trying to control her trembling. She mustn't be this weak. "You can let me go now."

"Hush." His arms tightened around her. "I'll do what I want to do."

She was thankful he hadn't wanted to do what she asked. She felt as if he were the only stable rock in a stormy sea. But the mermaid ruled the sea. . . .

"You don't mind? It will only be for a little while. When you hold me, I feel—"

"Safe," he supplied dryly. "I know."

"Yes, it's strange, isn't it? When sometimes I'm almost afraid of you . . ."

"I'm surprised that you admit it."

"So am I. I believe I'm not myself. Dear God, I hate to feel this weak. It makes me want to vomit with disgust."

"I pray you restrain yourself. I can bear tears, but the other is completely beyond me."

She closed her eyes and let the waves of strength and security he emitted sink into her. She became aware of the scent of leather and spice and whiskey surrounding him.

"Why mermaid?" Robert asked.

She shouldn't tell him. She had told Sebastian and suffered the consequences. But he was not Sebastian, and she *needed* to tell him. She could not stand the loneliness any longer. "Because of the posters."

"Posters?"

"You know what a mermaid is the symbol for?" she whispered.

"Aye, prostitute. But it's not something you should know about."

"I've known since I was a small child. Sebastian told me. He told me everything about her."

"For instance?"

"After her husband Lord Darnley was murdered,

the townspeople of Edinburgh suspected her of complicity. They thought she murdered her husband so that she could marry her lover Lord Bothwell. They put posters everywhere, on every house and wall in Edinburgh." She paused. "A mermaid with a crown on her head."

"And that's what you dream?"

She nodded jerkily. "But it's not about murder or lust." Her voice softened. "I'm somewhere deep in the sea. The water is blue and silky and beautiful, and I'm happy. I feel free and safe, as if I belong there." She paused. "Then she comes."

"And you're not happy any longer?"

"At first I'm very happy. She's so beautiful. Her hair flows about her like brown-gold seaweed, and she smiles at me."

"And then?"

"She leaves me," she said desolately. "She swims away and leaves me behind. I try to swim after her, but she's too fast and the water grows darker and I can't see around me. I see glimpses of strange creatures with huge teeth, and I know they'll devour me if I don't swim very fast and catch up with her. But I can't. The sea isn't safe anymore, and suddenly I can't breathe under the water. The mermaid looks over her shoulder and smiles at me." The tears were falling again, and she wiped her cheek on his shirt. "You see, it's not a harmful dream."

"Except to you."

"Except to me," she repeated. "I'm getting your shirt wet."

"It will dry."

"She's gone for good this time. She'll never come back."

"No, she'll never come back."

"It seems strange. She was such a big part of my life, and yet I never knew her. When I was little, I used to think someday she would come and take me away. I

thought if I could get to know her, get to learn everything about her, that I could do something to make her
love me. But she never came. Children are very stupid,
aren't they?" She swallowed. "I'm still being foolish.
Gavin said you were going to play cards. Did I disturb
you?"

"No, and stop making polite conversation."

"Was that what I was doing?" She laughed tremulously. "How odd. No one has ever taught me that art.
Do you suppose it's my royal breeding emerging?"

"Perhaps."

Her smile faded. "I was joking. I'm not like her.
No matter what anyone says, I'm not like her."

"How do you know? What do you know of her?"

"Everything."

"Everything Sebastian wanted you to know."

"She was selfish and willful and an adulteress."

"So I've heard." He paused. "I've also heard that
she was gay and charming and brave. Half of Scotland
was willing to fight under her banner."

"But not you."

"I fight only under Craighdhu's banner."

"But you would never choose to fight for her," she
persisted.

He hesitated. "No."

She smiled sadly. "You see?"

"I would not follow her because a leader who acts
on impulse is a leader who will lead you to destruction.
Mary was ever ruled by her emotions, not her mind."

"And I'll never be like her."

"Which is why you jump out of windows to rescue
nags not worth tuppence."

"That was different." She lifted her head to look at
him in sudden horror. "Wasn't it? I'm not like her?"

"It's different," he said quickly. "Of course it's different." He went on slowly, searching for words. "We
can't escape where we come from, but we can choose
where we're going. Take what you want and leave the

rest. Take Mary's bravery and leave her lack of vision. Accept her gift of laughter and reject her lust for power."

"Sebastian would say that's not possible."

"And I say it is. You can always control what you become, what you are."

She was again aware of that air of inflexible resolution that was always with him. "Because you do?"

At first she didn't think he was going to answer. Then he said, "Aye, because I do."

"It's not that easy. I can choose while I'm awake, but when I sleep . . ." She had a sudden thought. "Do you ever dream?"

"Everyone dreams."

"Bad dreams?"

He was silent a moment. "Not anymore."

But at some time his dreams had not been pleasant, or he would not have been willing to lower his guard to give her comfort. She opened her lips to ask what those dreams had been about but shut them without speaking.

He lifted a quizzical brow. "No more questions?"

"If I probed and dug, I would be as bad as Sebastian. You don't want to talk about your dreams."

"No, I don't want to talk about them." He paused. "But I'll tell you how I rid myself of them. I'd wake in the night in a cold sweat, unable to go back to sleep. One night I could stand it no longer. I went to the stable and saddled my horse and left the castle. I rode aimlessly for a while and then went to the barrens."

"The barrrens?"

"The north side of the island is nothing but black rocks and steep cliffs. We call it the barrens."

She had a sudden picture of him, alone and tormented, the night wind lifting his hair as he rode along that desolate shore. "Why did you go there?"

"I don't know. But I sat on the cliff all night and watched the seals and the sea lions on the rocks below.

Every spring hundreds of them come to the barrens to have their young. Life . . ." He was silent, remembering. "After that night, every time I woke from the dream, I'd go to the barrens. By the end of the summer I no longer had the dreams."

"You think it healed you?"

"I don't know. Perhaps."

"You do think so. Seals and sea lions . . ."

"But no mermaids," he said softly. "I never once saw a mermaid."

"Will you take me there?"

"Someday."

She wanted to pursue the matter and get a firmer commitment, but he had already given her more than she could have hoped. He had shared his memories and his pain, and that was not an easy thing for Robert.

And he had done it for her, she realized with joy. He had given her a glimpse of his own past to ease her pain and provide comfort. She did not question why the act meant so much to her; it was enough that it filled her with a happiness and contentment she had never known. "I feel very strange . . . as if I were naked inside. It's most unsettling." Something closed and tight was uncoiling within her, but it was all right to let go. She did not have to hold Robert at bay with all the others.

She relaxed against him. "You're being kind to me."

"Am I?"

She nodded. "And I'm not Gavin."

He smoothed her hair back from her temple. "I agree, you don't resemble him in the slightest."

"No, I mean I don't belong to Craighdhu."

"I very much fear you're wrong. I wish the hell that you didn't, but I'm afraid you do belong to Craighdhu now."

"You mean, for the next year?"

There was only the slightest pause. "Aye, that's what I mean."

"And that means you'll be kind to me, just like you are to Gavin?"

She felt him stiffen against her. "I don't think of you in the same way."

"You could, if you gave up this foolishness of wanting to bed me."

"I'm afraid that foolishness will continue." He paused and then said roughly, "But if it will make you happier, I promise I will not attempt you until you come to me and say you wish it."

"And you will treat me as you do Gavin?"

He hesitated. "If possible."

The falcon enfolding her with warmth, protecting her. What a wondrous thing that would be. "That will be . . . pleasant."

"Not for me."

"Why not?"

"Because it means I lose two pounds to Gavin."

She couldn't see what a wager had to do with this, but she was so emotionally drained, she might not be thinking clearly. "Sebastian says gambling will destroy the soul."

"I don't give a damn about Sebastian or his opinions."

"Neither do I. That was very stupid of me. I guess I just couldn't think of anything else to say."

His hand stroked her hair. "Then don't say anything at all."

The suggestion seemed very good, and she relaxed against him and closed her eyes. She could hear the strong beating of his heart beneath her ear, rhythmic and powerful, like the sea washing against the shore. Strange, always before, after the dream fear had made her avoid all thought of the sea, but she felt safe tonight. There might come dreams of seals and sea lions and Robert's dark presence on the cliff looking down at them, but somehow she knew there would be no desolate loneliness and no mermaids.

5

She woke alone at dawn the next morning. The moment she opened her eyes, she was aware something had changed, something was *different.* Memory rushed back to her. Seals and sea lions and Robert holding her through the long night and that feeling that she was safe at last. Robert had gone, but it made no difference. Joy rippled through her like sunlight. He had made her a promise, and Gavin said he always kept his promises. She jumped out of bed and ran over to the washbasin.

As she started down the steps, Robert was striding across the hall toward the front door. "I was just going to send Gavin to wake you. We should be on our way."

She stopped on the stairs as a wave of panic swept through her. Dear God, he was as cool and remote as if last night had never happened. He was closing her out, walking away from her like all the rest. Sickening disappointment was immediately followed by a flare of anger. By Judas, he couldn't take away what he had given her. She had opened herself to him, and she would not go back. Only loneliness awaited her if she gave up now. She ran down the rest of the stairs and marched up to him. "No! I won't have this. Do you hear me?"

His expression remained impassive as he gazed

into her blazing eyes. "Go to the kitchen and get something to eat. Angus is still asleep, but last night I gave him our thanks for his hospitality and we—"

"Why are you so different? You said—you know what you said."

"And I will keep to it. I will guard you as I do Gavin."

"But that's not enough." She had to make him understand. "I know I behaved in a weak fashion, and I can understand your disgust, but that's no reason for you to— You need not offer me protection. I can care for myself, but there's no reason for you not to be my friend as you are Gavin's. Carolyn says I always demand too much of people, but no more than I'm willing to give. We could talk and . . . and laugh and— It would make our time together more harmonious, and I think—"

"Hush."

"I won't hush. You cannot push me away again. I tell you that—"

Robert covered her lips with his hand. "I know what you're saying. You're saying I don't have to shelter you under my wing, but I must coo like a peaceful dove whenever I'm around you."

"I could not imagine you cooing, but I do not think peace and friendship between us is too much to ask." She blinked rapidly as she moved her head to avoid his hand. "You promised that—"

"I know what I promised, and you have no right to ask more from me. You can't expect to beckon me close and then have me keep my distance," he said harshly. "You can't have it both ways, as you would know if you weren't—" He broke off. "And don't *weep*."

"I'm not weeping."

"By thunder, you are."

"I have something in my eye. "You're not being sensible."

"I'm being more sensible than you know," he said

with exasperation. "Why the devil is this so important to you?"

She wasn't sure herself, but it had something to do with that wondrous feeling of *rightness* she had experienced last night. She had never known it before, and she would not give it up. She tried to put it into words: "I feel as if I've been closed up inside for a long time. Now, I want ... something else. It will do you no harm to be my friend."

"That's not all you want," he said slowly as he studied her desperate expression. "I don't think you know what you want. But I do, and I can't give it to you."

"You could try." She drew a deep breath. "Do you think it's easy for me to ask this of you? It fills me with anger and helplessness, and I *hate* that feeling."

She wasn't reaching him. She had to say something that would convince him. Suddenly, the words came tumbling out, words she had never meant to say, expressing emotions she had never realized she felt. "I thought all I'd need would be a house, but now I know there's something more. I have to have people too. I guess I always knew it, but the house was easier, safer. Can't you see? I want what you and Gavin and Angus have, and I don't know if I can find it alone. Sebastian told me I couldn't have it, but I will. I *will*." Her hands nervously clenched and unclenched at her sides. "I'm all tight inside. I feel scorched ... like a desert. Sebastian made me that way, and I don't know how to stop. I'm not ... at ease with anyone."

He smiled ironically. "I've noticed a certain lack of trust in me, but you seem to have no problem with Gavin."

"I truly like Gavin, but he can't change what I am." She went on eagerly, "But it was different with you last night. I really *talked* to you. You made me feel ..." She stopped. She had sacrificed enough of her pride. If this was not enough, she could give no more.

The only emotion she could identify in the multitude of expressions that flickered across his face was frustration. And there was something else, something darker, more intense. He threw up his hands. "All right, I'll try."

Joy flooded through her. "Truly?"

"My God, you're obstinate."

"It's the only way to keep what one has. If I hadn't fought, you'd have walked away."

"I see." She had the uneasy feeling he saw more than her words had portended. But she must accept this subtle intrusion of apprehension if she was to be fully accepted by him.

"Do I have to make a solemn vow?" he asked with a quizzical lift of his brows.

"Yes, please. Truly?" she persisted.

"Truly." Some of the exasperation left his face. "Satisfied?"

"Yes, that's all I want."

"Is it?" He smiled crookedly. "That's not all I want."

The air between them was suddenly thick and hard to breathe, and Kate could feel the heat burn in her cheeks. She swallowed. "I'm sure you'll get over that once you become accustomed to thinking of me differently."

He didn't answer.

"You'll see." She smiled determinedly and quickly changed the subject. "Where is Gavin?"

"In the kitchen fetching food for the trail."

"I'll go find him and tell him you wish to leave at—"

"In a moment." He moved to stand in front of her, lifted the hood of her cape, and framed her face with a gesture that held a possessive intimacy. He looked down at her, holding her gaze. "This is not a wise thing. I don't know how long I can stand this box you've put me in. All I can promise is that I'll give you warning when I decide to break down the walls."

She stared up at him mesmerized, unable to tear her gaze away.

"Do you understand?"

She forced herself to step back, then turned and moved down the hall toward the kitchen. "You'll change your mind once you realize how it would get in the way," she tossed back over her shoulder with a touch of bravado. "I'll be much better as a friend than just a woman for your bed."

"That premise is open to extensive debate, and one in which you're not qualified to participate." He opened the door. "Tell Gavin to give you something to eat while I go to the stable and get the horses."

He was wrong, she told herself. Everything would be fine once he became accustomed to her. Everything would be just the way it should be. She would dismiss this nagging unease and let herself be as happy as she had been when she awoke this morning.

Gavin looked up when she walked into the kitchen. "Well, you look bright and rested. I'm glad to see it. You nigh scared me to death with your screaming."

She flushed. "I'm sorry. I didn't mean—"

"I know," he interrupted with a gentle smile. "It was clear her death was a cruel blow to you."

"It shouldn't have been. I behaved most inappropriately." She changed the subject. "Where is your kinsman?"

"Asleep. Angus came back in the middle of the night, roaring and crowing with glee, and had to toast his cleverness with the rest of that bottle of whiskey I found."

"His journey was successful?"

"Aye. Five lovely little mares and one stallion." He set bread and cheese before her. "Eat. Robert wants to be gone from here. We're too close to the border."

She picked up the piece of bread and began to nibble at it. "This hurry is all foolishness, you know. Even if anyone realized who I was, it would make no difference."

"That's not what Robert thinks." He sat down opposite her and crossed his legs at the ankle. "And he's no fool. Do you suppose there's a possibility he may even know more than a lass who had been buried in the country all her life?"

She grinned and airily waved a hand. "A slight possibility." Quickly, she finished the bread and cheese and got to her feet. "I'm ready. Let's be on our way."

"Such eagerness." He studied her. "I wouldn't know you were the same lass as yesterday."

"I'm not. I feel different."

"How?"

She wasn't sure herself. It was difficult to separate and identify the elements of this strange, euphoric mood. It wasn't only that she had won the battle with Robert. She felt free . . . . No, that wasn't it. She had not felt a sense of liberty when Robert had turned up the collar of her cape. She had felt cosseted, guarded, and robbed of the responsibility she had felt all her life. It was as if a great burden had been lifted from her, and the lack of that load brought a giddy sense of exhilaration. She would probably not tolerate that cosseting for any length of time, but for now it brought a rare pleasure.

She smiled brilliantly. "It's hard to explain." She turned and moved toward the door. "Let's go. Robert is waiting."

They came within sight of the Grampians four days later. The mountains rose stark and wild in the distance, their crests wreathed in mist, the steep slopes only sparsely covered with vegetation.

"Well?"

She found Robert's gaze fastened on her face.

"They look . . . lonely."

"A curious word. I thought you would be more intimidated. Most people find our Highlands less than hospitable."

"What is that dark brown plant on the slopes? I've never seen it before."

"Because it grows principally in Scotland." Robert smiled. "Heather has the good sense to gift us Scots with most of its beauty and bounty."

"Beauty?" Kate made a face as she looked at the scraggly growth. "It's ugly."

"You think so? I'll wager you change your mind."

She shook her head doubtfully. "And it looks prickly. How does it feel?"

He chuckled as he shook his head. "I'm sure you'll find out for yourself. You must have stopped a dozen times today to look at or touch something. I've never seen anyone as curious as you are."

"I just want to *know* things. I've never traveled before, and everything seems so . . . so new." It was more than that, she thought. She herself felt new. It was as if everything within her was stretching, growing, reaching out to touch and see and be. There were still times when she would feel the old fear, tightness, and anger coming back, but those moments were coming more and more infrequently.

"And I suppose you never displayed this trait before?"

She made a face. "Well, Carolyn did say once that I was overly inquisitive. But that was after— Well, never mind. There's nothing wrong with being interested in everything, is there?"

For an instant she thought his expression held a hint of tenderness. "No, there's nothing wrong with that."

"Then what bounty?"

He frowned in puzzlement.

"You said heather gave most of her bounty to Scots."

"Oh, heather serves a multitude of purposes. It feeds our souls and our senses and even our need for forgetfulness on occasion." He shot a mischievous glance at Gavin. "Isn't that true? I remember the night before we left Craighdhu, you imbibed so much of our heather ale that I doubt you remember anything about that leavetaking."

"You're wrong. I remember playing the pipes and then you throwing me off the bridge into the moat."

"At least I kept everyone else from drowning you. You play the pipes only tolerably when sober; when drunk, you're a disaster."

"I was going into battle. It was entirely suitable to play the pipes," Gavin protested. "And it's not kind of you to reveal my sins to Kate when I've been trying to convince her what a fine guide I'll be on this rocky road of marriage she's treading."

"Just as long as you don't try to lead her after you've had a few cups of ale. I'd hate to be forced to pull both of you out of the moat."

She had never seen him like this, teasing, his expression alight with humor. She instinctively guided Rachel closer, to bask in that warmth. "I'm surprised you don't think even drunkenness laudable if performed by a Scot."

"Excess is never laudable, but it's understandable."

"As long as it's done by the people of Craighdhu."

He laughed. "Aye, now you're beginning to understand."

He was being so open, she decided to venture more. "And by you?"

"I never indulge in heather ale."

"Why not?"

"Good God, will your questions never cease?" He answered her just the same. "Because I always drink too deep."

He was drinking deep now, she realized suddenly. He was breathing in the cold air, tasting the flavors and scents of this place, this time. She suddenly wanted to reach out and touch him, join with all the other sensations that were surrounding him, feeding him. "Only of heather ale?"

She knew at once the words were a mistake. She had desired only to draw closer, to find out more about him, but she had subtly shifted the delicate balance between them. He glanced at her, and something flickered in his face. "No, I have a tendency to embrace all excesses, and therefore must never tempt myself too strongly." He kicked his horse into a gallop. "Let's see if we can make a better time than this snail's pace. God knows once we leave the Lowlands, that piebald will keep us creeping along."

She glanced back at Caird. The derogatory remark was not unjustified, but it was the first Robert had made since they had left Angus's manor. "It's not his fault," she told Gavin, since Robert was now far ahead. "He's doing his best."

"His best may not be good enough. We would have been deep in those mountains by this time if he hadn't been along," Gavin said. "And Robert's right. Once we get higher, the thin air will slow him down even more. The mountains aren't kind to the old or weak."

"Then we must be that much more kind ourselves."

Kindness. Her glance went back to Robert. He had been kind to her during these past days. He had answered her questions, he had been polite and courteous . . . and kind. It was not enough. She would just have to try harder to draw nearer to him, to find out everything about him so that she could make him give her the warmth and joy she had known that night. If she had not been so clumsy, she might have made a great stride today, but instead she had reminded him of that side of his nature she wanted him to forget.

She would just have to try harder.

"Pull your blanket up higher," Robert said, his gaze on the girth he was repairing. "The wind is sharpening."

"I'm fine," Kate said drowsily, her gaze on his hands. Beautiful hands, she thought, the long fingers clever and facile. She lifted her stare to his face. The planes of his cheek were hollowed in the firelight, his eyes narrowed as they focused on the leather.

He put the girth down, pulled the blanket higher around her shoulders, and then picked up his work again. The action was done matter-of-factly, almost absently, but contentment rippled through her. Tucked beneath the falcon's wings, she thought dreamily. It was a caring gesture, like one of a hundred he had made in the last two days. He still did not treat her with the same ease he did Gavin, but there was closeness and nurturing and sometimes even laughter. She was drawing nearer to Robert every day.

"Did you like being a pirate?" she asked.

"It had its interesting moments."

"Then will you do it again?"

"I think not."

"Why not?"

"There's no need. I have enough gold for my purposes now."

"We needed the gold to expand our trade with Ireland, Kate," Gavin said. "We needed warehouses and more ships. . . . Craighdhu is a hard land and will not support us."

"I can't believe it." Kate's eyes twinkled with mischief. "From what you've both told me, I thought it must be paradise."

For a few minutes there was only the sound of the crackling fire. "Who is Malcolm?" she asked suddenly.

Robert looked up in surprise.

"Angus Gordon mentioned him, and you said—"

"I remember the occasion, but I wasn't sure you would. You were a trifle upset at the time." He went back to his mending. "Sir Alec Malcolm of Kilgranne. Some of his lands border mine."

She frowned. "On Craighdhu?"

"No, Craighdhu is an island, but our clan also has land on the mainland."

"Then he's a Highlander?"

"He was *born* a Highlander," Robert explained.

"He's a greedy bastard," Gavin put in from across the fire.

Robert smiled. "Gavin has no liking for my cousin Alec."

"Another relation?"

"I told you, we're almost all bound by family ties."

"He'd like to sever that tie and your jugular with the same cut," Gavin said bluntly. "You're too lenient with him, Robert."

"I'm not lenient. I'm just as greedy as my dear cousin. If I kill Alec, then James will have an excuse to send his troops in to avenge his favorite and grab Craighdhu. If I wait for a more propitious time, I stand a chance to make peace with Alec's son, Duncan. He's not a bad lad."

"And keep Craighdhu safe," Gavin added.

Robert nodded. "And keep Craighdhu safe."

"If Alec lets you." Gavin made a face. "There's no telling what we'll find when we reach home."

"Jock will not have let the island be breached." He shrugged. "And any land Alec's taken, we'll just take back."

They were both so casual when speaking about blood and conquest, Kate thought, then realized with surprise that she was no longer shocked, as she had been at first. Had custom hardened her? "Wouldn't that make James just as angry?"

"Perhaps, but not enough to give him an excuse to

march in and try to get it back for Alec. It's all a balance that has to be struck."

"I don't understand."

"You would if you'd ever met your dear brother."

"I've heard he's not overpopular in Scotland." She smiled, reminiscing. "When I was very little, I used to dream about James riding into the village one day, taking me away from Sebastian and carrying me off to live with him at his castle in Edinburgh."

"I assure you, James would have no family feelings toward you. His ambitions exceed even Malcolm's."

"He wants more power?" She shook her head. "I wonder why, when he has so much already."

"Power can be a heady brew."

She thought about it. "I believe I can understand that."

"What?" Robert's head lifted, and she heard Gavin's indrawn breath.

"It must be pleasant to have power. I think I would like it very much indeed."

"Then think again," Robert said harshly. "Unless you have a desire to follow in your mother's footsteps."

Her casual words had disturbed him, she realized with lazy amusement. Another sign that they were drawing closer. She wondered if she could provoke a further response. "I've always hated being helpless. It was like a bleeding sore when I was with Sebastian. And you like power yourself." She softly quoted his own words, " 'The sweet prerogatives of power.' "

"The prime prerogative of power is to use it in staying alive."

He was growing more intense by the moment over a subject that was blatantly ridiculous. She smiled teasingly. "But I'm not as unwise as my mother. I would never make the mistakes she did."

"Christ."

"She doesn't mean it, Robert," Gavin said. "Can't you see she's joking?"

"I'm not so sure." Robert's gaze drilled her own. "Are you joking, Kate?"

She was suddenly not certain how much was jest and how much was truth. She had never thought about herself in connection with power. She had rejected the concept along with all of Sebastian's other views, but now, in this moment of dreamlike contentment, the idea held a subtle allure. "It's a terrible thing to be made to feel defenseless. I will never go back to that again. Yet I don't believe I would want to be in the position of imposing my will on others. Sometimes my temper is unruly, and that would not be good." She frowned, weighing the matter. "Unless I could learn to control my passions. And power would bring safety, wouldn't it?"

"Not for you. You say you're not unwise, but you're a thousand times more ignorant than Mary," he bit out. "And you're no match for James. Dammit, he could have stopped your mother from being beheaded."

Her eyes widened. "How?"

"All he had to do was threaten to invade England if she was executed. Elizabeth wouldn't have risked war to rid herself of a threat who was already her captive. Instead, when Mary was condemned to death by Parliament, all James did was send a weak protest."

"Perhaps he thought that would be enough."

Robert shook his head. "He wants to be king of England as well as Scotland. His mother stood in the way."

"Matricide?" she whispered.

"In a fashion." He held her gaze. "So don't ever decide to throw yourself on his mercy. You pose almost as much of a threat as she did."

She shook her head doubtfully.

"God's blood, *listen* to me."

"All this talk of power and threats is without point. I have no claim to the throne."

"Elizabeth now rules England, yet the Catholics

said she was illegitimate and had no claim to the throne because Henry broke from Rome for her mother, Anne Boleyn. Ambitious men twist facts to suit themselves and are ever looking for pawns to get what they want."

"I'm not a pawn."

"Not now, and if you wish to remain that way, stay away from James and my dear cousin Alec Malcolm and the pope and half the nobles in Scotland. Oh, and Philip of Spain." He shook his head. "Shall I go on? I could, you know."

"Well, I have nothing to worry about at the moment." She glanced away from him. "And I do think you're wrong. If I do not choose to be a pawn, then no one can make me one."

"Don't be too sure."

"I am sure." But she was becoming uneasy with all this talk of pawns and conquests. He was becoming impatient, and she could now sense something violent and angry leashed beneath the surface. She wanted to go back to that moment when she had felt so safe and happy as he had tucked the blanket around her. She settled down and leaned her cheek on her arm. "I refuse to worry about something that will not come to pass."

"I hope to God it won't come to pass," he said. "But you won't prevent it from happening by hiding your eyes from the truth." He stared at her and then muttered savagely, "But I forgot, you make a habit of not seeing what you don't want to see."

She inhaled sharply, her eyes wide with shock. The explosion had caught her completely off guard, as if a tiger had leapt out of the shadows.

"I believe it's time, we all went to sleep," Gavin interjected. "We should reach the foothills tomorrow, and the going will be much rougher. Have you not finished that girth, Robert?"

Robert didn't answer.

Gavin took one look at his face and then shrugged. "Well I, for one, am too weary to hold my eyes open for another moment." He glanced meaningfully at Kate as he settled down in his blankets. "I'm sure you feel the same, Kate. Good night."

"Good night." Robert's gaze shifted back to the girth in his hands.

Kate watched him. The tiger had returned to the shadows, but she was painfully aware he was drawing away from her, from both of them. Everything was suddenly different. It was as if he had withdrawn to a place she could not go, and she wanted to reach out and jerk him back. "I'm right, you know. All this talk of—"

"Good night, Kate," Robert said without looking at her.

The note of finality in his voice was almost as painful as his withdrawal and frightened her more. It wasn't final, she assured herself. She would just ignore this little contretemps, and tomorrow would be the same as the days that had gone before.

The slopes of the distant mountains were not yet shimmering with snow, but they loomed stark and forbidding in the moonlight, and this afternoon Robert had noticed that the sky had turned the nasty pewter color that heralded a storm.

That's all we needed, Robert thought in exasperation. Snow and ice would make the rough trail through the mountains even more treacherous.

"It may not be so bad," Gavin said quietly as he came to stand beside Robert on the rise. "We're only in the foothills. The snow may be over before we reach the slopes."

"But not the ice."

"It will just take us a little longer."

Dammit, he didn't need any more delays. He needed to get to Craighdhu before he splintered into a thousand pieces. "Aye."

Gavin shot him a sideways glance. "You're worried about the piebald?"

"He's laboring."

"We can't push any harder. It would break her heart if anything happened to him."

"Do you think I don't know that?" Robert said savagely. "We should never have brought him."

"But he's here."

"And so it's my fault, my responsibility."

"I didn't say that."

"You didn't have to say it." It was always his responsibility. Craighdhu and his people and now Kate and this Goddamn horse. He whirled and started back down the hill toward the campfire.

Gavin fell into step with him. "What are you going to do?"

"What am I supposed to do? Carry the nag over the mountains?"

"You don't have to bite at me." He paused. "Or Kate."

"What is that supposed to mean?"

"It means you're making her miserable. She was so happy a few days ago. It was as if she were . . ." He stopped to find the right word. "Blooming. She doesn't understand why you're different now."

He knew she didn't understand. He had seen her unhappiness and bewilderment, and it flicked at him like a raw wound, the kind of dangerous pinprick a man can die of without knowing he'd received it. Yet what else could he do? He should have drawn back before this. He had already yielded too much to her. "She doesn't want to understand."

"Maybe it would be better if you did bed her, if it would rid you of this bad temper. You're hurting the lass."

"I'm glad I have your permission."

"I know you don't like me to speak to you of this." Gavin's jaw was set. "But I like her, and there's no need for her to be hurt more by your coldness."

Coldness wasn't the problem, he thought grimly.

He had never been more hot and aching. The frustration was growing every second of the day, and she still expected him to give her the impossible. "You're right, I don't want you to talk of this."

"Well, you're to be kind to her tonight," Gavin said flatly. "I've spent the past hour trying to raise her spirits, and it won't hurt you to smile at her."

But if he smiled at her, she would smile back. She would smile with an eagerness and trust that tied him in knots and kept him from breaking free of her.

They were approaching the fire now and Kate, who sat cross-legged on a blanket in front of it. Gavin said quickly, "And praise her. Tell her how—"

Robert no longer heard Gavin's words as he stared in horror at Kate.

Firelight glittered on metal as three knives whirled in a circle above Kate's head!

"What the hell is she—"

"Shh . . ." Gavin grabbed his arm, his gaze never leaving the knives Kate was juggling. "Don't startle her. Is it not wondrous?"

"It will be wondrous if she doesn't kill herself." Any second one of those dirks could fall blade first into Kate's hand, cutting it to the bone. He knew how sharp those edges were. "Why the hell did you let her do it?"

"I thought it would distract her," Gavin said. "She said she had a trick she could show me. I don't think you need to worry. She seems to know what she's doing."

Robert felt as if he were going to throw up. "Not worry? When she—" He broke off as Kate sent one dirk spinning into the dirt a few yards away and then deftly caught the other two by their shafts.

Thank the Saints, it was over.

She laughed with delight as she noticed them standing there. "They're fine knives, Gavin. It's not often that you find such well-balanced—" She broke off as she saw Robert's expression and drew herself up warily. "You don't need to look at me like that. I didn't hurt them."

"I've never seen such foolishness. You could have sliced your hand off."

"Nonsense. A knife is no different from any other object, if balanced correctly."

"And you know how to balance—"

"Of course she does," Gavin interrupted with a warning glance at Robert. "Such a pretty trick, Kate. Where did you learn to do it?"

Kate kept her cautious stare on Robert. "A troop of strolling players passed through our village every year. Carolyn and I would hide in the woods and watch them practice." She smiled. "Acrobats and rope walkers, and there was a juggler who was truly wonderful. His name was Jonathan the Great, and he could keep five bright-colored balls in the air at one time. After they were gone, Carolyn and I practiced to learn the way of it. She soon grew bored, but I kept on with it for years. I had no balls, but I used apples and potatoes."

"And may I ask why you were so determined?" Robert asked sarcastically. "Or was it just your damnable curiosity?"

"No, of course not. I thought when I ran away from Sebastian, I might join a troop of strolling players."

"As a juggler?"

She raised her chin defiantly. "Why not? It's not such a foolish idea. I knew I'd have to earn my way in some fashion if I was to hide from Sebastian. I'm not so bad now, and with more time to practice I would have gotten better. It was not—"

"God's blood." She didn't even realize the dangers of the life of strolling players, who were nearly always surrounded by whores and thieves and charlatans. Dammit, she didn't know anything. She just stared at him with those huge, luminous eyes filled with eagerness and dreams and expected him to—

He turned on his heel and stalked off into the darkness.

She jumped to her feet and ran after him. "Why are you so angry? I did nothing wrong. One of the blades is a trifle dirty, but I can—"

"Stay away from me."

"But I did nothing wrong, and it's not fair for you to—"

"Be silent."

"I won't be quiet. I want to know why you're—"

He whirled and grasped her shoulders and shook her. "You did nothing wrong! You could have—" He stopped as he saw the expression on her face.

She had gone still. "You were worried about me?" she asked. Then a brilliant smile lit her face. "That is very . . . pleasant."

"Is it?"

She nodded. "I don't remember anyone ever being concerned about me before. Carolyn, perhaps, but that was a long time ago." She took a step closer, her gaze eagerly searching his face. "I told you we would become friends, didn't I?"

"That's what you told me."

"And it's true. Have we not talked and become companionable? Oh, you've been most peculiar for the past few days, but now I understand. You were probably concerned about me then also."

He could feel the warmth of her body reaching out to him through her woolen cloak and the gown beneath it. He should release her, drop his hands from her shoulders. "Was I?"

"Of course. And now you worry about me as a true friend would, as you would for Gavin."

"Why do you keep making comparisons? You're not Gavin."

Her smile dimmed a bit. "I believe you're still angry at me for frightening you. I was quite safe, but I will promise not to use Gavin's knives again if I can find something else. The problem was that I had no balls or apples or potatoes."

Something seemed to explode inside him. "No balls or apples or potatoes," he said through his teeth. "What a pity." He jerked her to him. "Perhaps I should give you something else to amuse you." His hands grasped her hips, and he pulled her against him, letting her feel the hard, jutting strength of his arousal. He rubbed yearningly, sensuously, against her softness, feeling himself swell and grow in dimension. He wanted to loose himself and drag her down to the ground and enter and plunge and rut like an animal. "Shall I furnish you with another toy to keep you occupied?"

He felt her stiffen against him. "Why are you doing this?"

His hands moved around to cup her buttocks, keeping her immobile. She felt so good against him. A shudder racked through him. "Because I'm not your mother or your father or your friend. You told me once if you learned everything about your mother, you'd find a way to make her care for you. Do you think I don't know that's what you've been trying to do to me? Well, you can't do it. You're not coming any closer. If you need a friend, go to Gavin, not to me." He was growing painfully heavier with every word. He couldn't keep on for much longer. "I tried to tell you that, and you wouldn't listen. Do I have your attention now?"

She was too close for him to see her face. He didn't want to see her face. He didn't want to see the disappointment come and the eagerness leave. "Yes," she whispered.

"Good. Then hear me now. If you don't wish to occupy my bed, then stay away from me. I will have no more of this." He released her and strode away from her, careful not to look back.

He knew how she would look—lonely, desolate, as she had when he had comforted her the night after the mermaid dream. He could not help it if she was disappointed. How could she expect him to be what she wanted him to be? He was a man, with a man's needs. It was time she knew there was no place for her in his life other than the temporary carnal one he had first chosen for her.

She would not cry. She'd been foolish, and foolish women deserved to be hurt. Kate drew her cloak closer around her as she gazed blindly into the shadows where Robert had disappeared.

It had all been a dream wrought by her own eagerness and longing. She could see that now. She had deliberately blinded herself, and that must never happen again.

She turned heavily away and started back toward the fire. He had never wanted anything from her but that carnal closeness that men always wanted from women. He had always made that clear, and she had been too stubborn to accept it. She would go to sleep and let slumber heal the hurt. She would come to terms with this pain and be fine by morning.

It was not as if she lost anything that had really been hers.

Robert woke in the middle of the night to see Kate kneeling beside him.

"Shh . . . Don't wake Gavin." She swallowed and then said haltingly, "This won't take long. I have . . . to speak to you."

"Couldn't it wait until morning?"

"No, I cannot sleep. I wish to apologize for being so stupid. I realize now how troublesome I've been to you. You see . . . I had been alone too long." She paused, then continued. "It was because you were strong, I think. Sebastian was strong, but his strength was always used against me. Then you came . . . and you were strong and yet you were so kind to Gavin. It seemed . . . wonderful to me. I wanted it, so I tried to take it. I didn't care what you wanted." She added with sudden fierceness, "But you didn't care what I wanted either."

He had cared. He had been aware of her desperate hunger to be close to someone after those years of loneliness and repression. He had just been unable to give her what she needed.

"You were right, I tried to mold you into what I wanted you to be." She smiled without mirth. "But you wouldn't fit into the mold."

He wanted to reach out and touch her. He did not. "I believe you should go back to your blankets."

"Soon. I have to finish this before I can go on. I lived a life of lies with Sebastian, and I will never do that again. He tried to mold me as I did you. I'm ashamed to have acted as he did." She shrugged. "In truth, I should probably thank you. Sebastian built a shell around me, and you broke through it."

"I had nothing to do with it." It had not been so much a shell as a cocoon from which an exquisite and wonderful butterfly had emerged and tried her tentative wings. "You broke through it yourself."

She lifted her chin. "You're right, I did it. I can have anything, be anything, I want to be. I never really needed your strength. I'm not a child. I don't need anything from you."

He stared at her without speaking.

"That's all. I just wished you to know my foolishness is over and that I won't bother you again. When we reach Craighdhu, we must try to work out an arrangement to see as little of each other as possible." She rose brusquely to her feet. "Good night."

He gazed after her as she went to her blankets. He could almost see the walls of pride and hurt rise around her, shutting him out. The eager, open child of these past days was gone. He should be pleased, dammit. She would no longer trail after him, talking and gesturing, asking him questions, trying to make him into something he could never be. She would distance herself and no longer be a constant temptation to him. It was not likely, but he might even be able to reach Craighdhu without bedding her.

He should be pleased.

Edinburgh

"It is absurd," James said impatiently to Sebastian Landfield. "You cannot expect me to believe such a tale."

"I realized it would be difficult to comprehend, so I took the liberty of bringing a few of the letters Her Majesty sent me through the years regarding the girl's upbringing." Sebastian withdrew the documents from beneath his cloak and presented them to the king. "I'm sure you've received personal letters from Her Majesty and can compare the script."

James did not bother to unfold the letters. "And even if it's true, the girl can be no threat to me."

"She is a threat to all who believe in John Knox."

"She is a Catholic?" James asked swiftly.

"Not at the moment. I've trained her to be a good Protestant, but she is weak and sinful like her mother. It would take little to sway her into the devil's camp. I need not tell you what chaos she could bring down upon both our lands if she tries to lure your Catholic barons under her spell." Sebastian lowered his voice. "And she could lure them, Your Majesty. Imagine your mother, young and winsome but with a fire that Mary never possessed, and you have Kathryn."

James bit his lower lip with annoyance. It was not fair, he thought peevishly. He had just rid himself of one rival, and now there was this new problem on the horizon. A young, winsome, fiery Mary. He, too, was young, but the image in his mirror reflected neither winsomeness nor fire, and his countrymen were easily influenced by both.

And Elizabeth had compounded the danger by marrying the wench to MacDarren. The earl had been a constant source of irritation to him for the last few years and would not hesitate to cause more.

"You will take action, Your Majesty?" the vicar asked.

"I will think about it."

"You must act immediately, while she is still young and uncertain of her powers."

"I said I would think about it," James snapped. "You said MacDarren is taking her to Craighdhu?"

"He mentioned only Scotland, Your Majesty."

"For him Craighdhu is Scotland." James stood up and moved toward the window. "And I might as well be his subject for all he cares for my consequence."

"Then being wed to a man such as he will make her an even greater danger."

"I know, I know," he said impatiently. "How can I even be sure this tale is true?"

"The letters should—"

"The letters are not proof enough. Has the child been with you since birth?"

Sebastian shook his head. "Kathryn was given to me at the age of three. Before that, she was cared for by a wet nurse, a woman named Clara Merkert."

"In your village?"

"No, she lived in Bourse."

"Does she still?"

Sebastian frowned. "I have no idea."

"I'll send a troop to bring her here."

"The woman may not even be alive," he protested.

"I must have proof there's true danger before I move against MacDarren. The nurse is the key."

"Then it must be done quietly. Her Majesty will

not be pleased to have one of her servants taken by you."

"Do you think I don't know that? I need no advice from an Englishman. I will look into the matter."

Sebastian bowed. "I will await news. I'm lodging at an inn near the palace. You will have the goodness to keep me informed?"

James nodded curtly. "But I cannot promise any degree of speed."

"I will wait." Sebastian bowed again and backed from the room.

James grimaced as he turned away from the window. How he detested these religious zealots with their burning eyes and equally burning determination. But this particular fanatic might have done him a service. He certainly could not have royal bastards roaming about the countryside at this delicate time. His countrymen were not at all pleased at his lack of action to prevent his mother's execution, and the whole country could be fanned into flames with a mere breath. Well, what had they expected? Was he to let his mother grab the English throne from beneath his nose? It was all her fault. If she had not involved herself in a conspiracy against Elizabeth, he would not have been put in this awkward position.

And now he had his dear mother's bastard with whom to contend, and he must not be connected with the inevitable demise of that particular threat. The matter must be handled by someone utterly trustworthy and devoted to him.

He turned and walked quickly to the desk across the chamber, sat down, and dipped his quill into the inkwell. It was fortunate he had such a loyal servant as Alec Malcolm sitting on MacDarren's doorstep. He felt a tiny thrill of excitement at the thought of seeing Alec again. He had been most upset when Alec had deserted the court and gone back to his estates in that Highland wilderness and had been thinking of inventing an excuse to call Alec back to his side anyway. He had always been attracted to strong, dominant men, and Alec's driving ambition was an added charm in his eyes. Yes, he would send for Alec and, as soon as he arrived, put the troublesome matter of the girl into his capable hands. He began to write.

> *My dearest Alec,*
>   *It seems an eternity since you left me and how desperately I have missed you. But it seems fate has seen fit to bring you back to me. . . .*

6

"*He'll get over it*," Gavin said in a low voice as he lifted Kate onto her horse the next morning. "You scared him last night. It's natural for a man to strike out when he's afraid."

She tried to smile at him as she gathered the reins. "Thank you for your concern, but you need not worry."

"Oh, no." Gavin smiled ruefully. "You're pale and pinched as a corpse, and Robert has buried himself so deep, I can't even talk to him. Nothing is at all wrong."

She carefully avoided glancing at Robert as he mounted his horse. Even if she looked at him, she would see nothing for her. All during the morning meal he had been as cool and remote as those mountains they were going to climb today.

"You don't understand," Gavin said urgently. "He didn't mean to— He's not a cruel man."

No, it was not cruel to reject what you did not want. It was Gavin who did not understand. It had been her own fault, her own stupidity and blindness, but she did not have to continue being stupid. "How far is it to Craighdhu?"

He nodded at the mountains. "On the other side we'll see the sea. We travel a day along the coast, and we'll be on MacDarren land, another day and we'll be at the crossing."

Relief poured through her. "Then we're almost there. How long will it take us to get over the mountain?"

"The trail is good. Robert and I have made it before in two days."

She would soon be quit of this terrible intimacy she had once thought so wonderful. At Craighdhu she could surely find a way to avoid Robert until a year had passed. "A week then?"

Gavin glanced at Caird and then to the gray sky to the north before shrugging uneasily. "If all goes well."

It couldn't go worse, Kate thought. Sebastian in all those years had not managed to inflict a wound as deep as the one she had suffered last night. She kicked Rachel into a trot. "Then let's get on with it."

The piebald fell to his knees, his sides heaving as he struggled to get thin air into his lungs.

Kate stopped with a low cry, slipped from Rachel's saddle, and ran back down the trail. It was what she had feared for the past four miles. She could hear Robert's exclamation but paid no heed as she fell to her knees beside Caird. "No, boy. Not now," she murmured frantically, stroking the stallion's nose. "You can't rest now. Soon, but not now."

Caird neighed and pushed his nose against her hand.

She could feel tears burn her eyes as she wrapped her arms around the horse's neck.

"He can't make it, Kate," Gavin said gently from behind her. She felt his comforting hand settle on her shoulder. "You can see that for yourself."

"I don't see it," she said fiercely, her grip tightening around the horse's neck. "He just needs to rest. He'll be fine once he—"

"We can't rest," Gavin said. "You don't know these mountains. The storm will hit within a few hours, and before dawn the trail could be impassable. We could freeze to death if we're caught here without shelter." She heard a metal hissing. "Stand aside, Kate."

She looked over her shoulder and saw to her horror that he had drawn his sword. He was going to kill Caird. Gavin, who had always been so kind, was going to do this terrible thing. "No! I won't let you."

"Do you think I want to do it? We have no choice," he said unhappily. "Better to kill him now than leave him here to freeze to death."

She glanced beyond him at Robert, but there was no help there. He sat his horse, silent, impassive, closing her away from him.

"He's *not* going to freeze to death. I'll find shelter where he can rest, and he'll be fine." She jumped to her feet and grabbed the lead rope. "Come on, Caird. Get up. You have to get up."

The horse made a valiant try, then faltered and fell again.

"You see?" Gavin asked. "It's no use."

"I won't give him up." She tugged at the rope. "Both of you go on. I'll take care of him."

"We can't do that. If you stay, you'll die. Isn't that right, Robert?"

He did not answer. He just sat there gazing at her with no expression.

His very impassiveness jabbed thorn sharp at her already lacerated emotions. She whirled to face him and spat, "But then, that would solve all your problems. No wife to endanger your Craighdhu, and it would be no fault of yours. Isn't that true?"

"Quite true," he said quietly.

"Then leave me." She turned back to Caird and again began tugging on the rope.

"Robert?" Gavin asked.

He was asking Robert if he should kill Caird, she

realized in panic. All Robert had to do was nod his head and Gavin would—

"Get behind him, Gavin." Robert was suddenly standing beside her, grabbing the lead rope. "Push, while I pull." He snapped at Kate, "Talk to him."

Hope flared within her. He was going to help her. She scrambled out of the way. "Come on, Caird. Come on, boy," she pleaded. "Just try."

It took another ten minutes before Caird got shakily to his feet. Robert tossed her the lead rope and remounted his horse. "Keep him on his feet. We've wasted too much time already."

She quickly mounted Rachel. "I'll keep him going."

Gavin frowned. "Robert, you know—"

"Of course I know," Robert interrupted. "That's why we're going to try to find shelter before the storm hits."

"What if we can't?" Kate asked.

He met her gaze. "Then I'll cut that horse's throat myself."

He meant it. Her teeth sank into her lower lip. "I won't let you."

"You won't be able to stop me." He kicked his horse, and the stallion moved up the winding trail.

Fear rippled through her as she watched the unyielding line of his spine. She felt helpless as she hadn't at the threat Gavin posed. Robert was a much more powerful antagonist, and she knew no plea would move him once he was set on a course. Well, she would face that threat if they failed to find shelter. At least he held out a thread of hope.

They found the cave an hour later. It was hardly more than an indentation in the side of the mountain, perhaps thirty feet deep with a mouth a scant six feet across. To Kate, it looked like paradise.

"Don't just sit there. Get the horses inside," Robert told her as he got down from his horse. The wind whipped the horse's mane back against his face as he grabbed an ax from his saddlebag.

Kate cast an anxious glance at the roiling, stormy sky to the north. It was much colder now, and the wind had a moist, bitter bite. She slipped from the saddle and grabbed Rachel's reins and Caird's lead rope. "What are you going to do?"

"We'll need wood for the fire and brush to form a barrier to cover the mouth of the cave." His gaze scanned the vegetation on the steep slope on the side of the trail. "And there's precious little of either."

Gavin got down from his horse and pointed to a fallen pine in a stand of trees about a hundred yards down the slope. "That should do for firewood, and those scrawny little trees bordering the trail will do for the barricade. If you'll take the slope, I'll cut down those trees along the—"

"No," Robert said curtly. "Take sufficient food from Caird's packs to get you down the mountain and be on your way."

Gavin's eyes widened in shock. "You want me to go?"

"You heard me," Robert said. "Without the piebald to hold you back, you'll be able to move fast enough to reach the foothills before the trail gets impassable."

"Dammit, I can't do that," Gavin said, then tempered his vehemence with a light "You know how I hate to travel alone. And what kind of henchman would I be to leave you in danger and go to safety?"

Robert smiled faintly. "We've already discussed what an abysmal henchman you are."

"But I'm not a coward."

Robert's smile vanished. "I never thought you were."

"So I'll stay."

Robert shook his head. "If we're stranded here for any length of time, our food will run out. You'll be much more useful where you can gather supplies and help to rescue us if it becomes necessary."

Gavin was uncertain. "You think—"

"I don't have time to argue anymore. Move!" He set out, slipping and sliding on the steep slope as he made his way toward the stand of pines.

Gavin watched him. "I can't go. He needs me."

"He's right, there's no sense in all of us being stranded here." She cast a glance at the sky, which seemed to be darkening even more by the second. "It's coming fast...." She snatched a blanket from Caird's pack and said, "If you want to be helpful, take the horses into the cave and unsaddle them before you leave. I'll help Robert."

She didn't wait for him to answer as she slid down the slope toward Robert.

He barely glanced at her, didn't even stop chopping at the trunk of a fallen tree. "Has he gone?"

"Not yet." She spread the blanket on the ground. "Pile the wood on this, and I'll tie the corners and drag it up to the trail."

He didn't argue, but began rapidly tossing logs and branches on the blanket.

"Is it true we may be stranded here for some time?"

"Aye, it's true."

"Then I want you to go too," she said haltingly. "Caird is my horse and my responsibility. I must stay, but I wish to put no one else in danger. I will be quite safe by myself."

He resumed chopping at the log.

"Did you not hear me?"

"I have no more time to argue with you than I did with Gavin." He swung the ax again, and the blade bit into the wood. "I won't leave you."

"Why?"

He didn't look at her, but his answer echoed her

own words about Caird. "Because you're my wife and my responsibility."

A responsibility he had never wished to bear, she thought in an agony of guilt. "It's not the same."

"No, that nag of yours sensibly accepts help and doesn't plague me with conversation."

He would not be persuaded, she realized in despair. She could only try to add her own strength to help keep them both alive.

In an amazingly short time the blanket was overflowing with wood. He tied the corners and said, "Go."

She started up the slope, struggling with the heavy burden she was dragging behind her.

"Kate."

She turned to see Robert looking at her, the hatchet balanced in his hands.

"Make sure Gavin is on his way."

Gavin, too, was his responsibility, and he was not willing to risk Gavin's life as he was his own. She nodded and continued up the slope. She stopped at the top, her breasts rising and falling with the harshness of breathing.

Gavin came out of the cave and reached for the blanket. "I'll take it. The horses are in the cave, and I've unsaddled them and unpacked the—"

"You're not supposed to be here. Leave." Robert had given her a task, and she would see that it was carried out. "Now."

He looked taken aback at the fierce determination in her voice. "I've been thinking about it, and I don't—"

"Now!" She dragged the blanket toward the cave. "Robert said you have to go."

He hesitated and then slowly moved toward his horse. "I'll give you two days. If the two of you aren't down by that time, I'm coming back."

She didn't answer as she dumped the wood on the

floor of the cave and set off with the blanket down the slope again. When she glanced back at the trail, it was to see Gavin moving at a fast pace up the trail.

She lost count of the trips she made up and down the slope in the next two hours. Robert was working at a furious pace, the hatchet slicing into the wood, the branches flying onto the blanket.

"Enough!" Robert shouted over the wind as she started up the slope. "I have to start cutting down those trees alongside the trail to use as barriers. Stay in the cave out of this wind this time. The trees will be too heavy for you to move."

She didn't have the breath to answer as she struggled up the slope, fighting the burden from behind and the buffeting wind from the front. Inside the cave she leaned against the rock wall, fighting the exhaustion clawing at her. Sweet Lord, she wanted to rest. But Robert wasn't resting. He was fighting the cold and the wind, exerting his strength and his will to keep them alive. She pushed away from the wall and staggered out on the trail again.

Robert was coming up the slope carrying the last load of wood. "I told you to stay in the cave."

"When you do."

He threw the load into the cave, then strode to the edge of the trail and began cutting down one of the small, scrawny trees.

The snow had started falling, hard ice-filled pellets that stung more than the wind striking her cheeks.

He shouted, "Dammit, you *can't* help with this! Go inside."

She shook her head as she grabbed the tree he had just chopped down and tugged it toward the cave. Though small, it weighed more than she did, and the branches were sharp and thorny. It took her an excruciatingly long time to drag it the short distance to the mouth of the cave. Then she went back and started on the second tree Robert had thrown up onto the trail.

The sharp branches shredded her woolen gloves, and she impatiently took them off and tossed them aside.

By the time she had dragged the fifth tree in front of the cave, it was snowing so hard, she could scarcely see and feel her hands. She was working too slowly, she thought desperately. She couldn't keep up with him. He had already tossed two more trees on the trail. She had to hurry. Just two more trips and she would—

"Inside!" Robert was beside her. He picked her up, deposited her inside the cave, and then turned to leave.

She took an unsteady step toward him.

"Can't you understand? It's almost finished. If you must do something, build a fire. I'm almost frozen."

He grabbed a wooden bucket and disappeared beyond the swirling veil of snow outside the cave.

She hesitated, trying to think through the weariness dragging at her. What had he wanted her to do? A fire. He was cold and would need a fire. Strange, she was not at all cold anymore. Her fingers had been icy, but now they felt as if they didn't belong to her as she knelt and began to lay the wood.

It took a long time, and she was vaguely conscious of the tree barrier building at the mouth of the cave as Robert tossed the trees one on top of each other at the entrance.

The wood finally caught fire, and she fanned it furiously. Mustn't let it go out. Robert was cold and would need—

"Good, you've got it lit." Robert stood just inside the cave, snow glistening on his cloak and dark hair. His arms were filled to overflowing with the ugly brown-black shrub he had called heather. He dumped the load on the floor of the cave and pulled the last barrier in place behind him. "Now, help me fill in the holes between the branches."

"With that?"

"I told you this had a multitude of purposes." He began stuffing the heather into the openings. "The snow should freeze it into place and keep the wind out."

She came forward and tried to help, but she could not seem to make her fingers work.

"No, not up there," he said, as she reached high with a handful of plants. "We need a small opening to release the smoke and let in the fresh air." He picked up the blanket she had used to haul the wood and fastened it to one side of the barrier to form a narrow entrance. He frowned as he stepped back to survey his handiwork. "It will have to do."

"Are we finished?"

"I hope you're speaking of our preparations and not our extremely mortal selves," he said. He turned away and moved toward the fire. "It's a hearty blaze. You did well." He glanced over his shoulder and said soberly, "And not only in the building of fires. I could not have asked for a better helpmate."

Through the haze of cold and weariness enfolding her, she felt a tiny flicker of pride. "Neither could I."

"But I'm not a woman."

"I believe that to be an unfair remark. I will have to think on it." She could not seem to think at all at the moment. She moved toward the fire and held out her hands. "This must not be good wood. There's hardly any heat."

"There's plenty of heat." He glanced down at her hands and went still. "They're bloody. Where the devil are your gloves?"

"They were woolen, and the branches tore them to pieces, so I threw them away." She shrugged. "It doesn't matter."

"The hell it doesn't matter." He touched a deep scratch on her palm. "Do you feel this?"

She shook her head.

"God's blood!" He pushed her down on the ground before the fire and dropped to his knees beside her. He jerked off his heavy leather gloves, took her left hand between both of his, and began to chafe it.

"What are you doing?" She tried to draw away.

"Stay still," he said between his teeth. "You have frostbite. You'll be lucky if your hands aren't frozen. I can't believe you—why didn't you go back to the cave when I told you to?"

"You needed me. How was I to know this could happen so quickly? We do not have such weather in the Midlands. Do you have to be so rough? It's beginning to hurt."

"Good," he said, continuing the chafing.

Her skin was tingling, the scratches stinging so painfully it brought tears to her eyes. "Is it not enough?"

He dropped her hand, ordered her to hold it out to the fire, and reached for the other one. "Can you feel the heat?"

"Yes."

"When you start feeling pain in this hand, tell me."

She was already beginning to feel the first tingling sensation, but it was another few minutes before the pain began in earnest. "Now."

"In all the fingers?"

Tears began to run down her cheeks. "The thumb is still a little numb."

He shifted his hold and began to concentrate on her thumb and index finger, bringing them to life.

He dropped her hand and lifted his gaze to her tear-streaked face. "I realize it hurts," he said hoarsely. "But I couldn't leave them like that."

"I know." She wiped her eyes on the back of her hands. "I don't know what's wrong with me. I'm not usually so stupid as to weep due to a little discomfort."

"More than a little. I've had frostbite." He grabbed a clean blanket from the supplies Gavin had piled against the wall and spread it before the fire. "Lie down and rest."

"I have to see to Caird and Rachel."

"I'll do it."

"You're as tired as I am."

He ignored the protest and walked toward the horses tethered in the back of the cave.

Perhaps he wasn't as tired, she thought hazily. He moved with the same indomitable strength and power he had exhibited when he had first gone down the slope more than two hours ago.

Well, she was not so impervious to weariness. She sat down on the blanket and watched as he probed gently at Caird's ankles.

I'll cut his throat myself.

But he hadn't killed Caird. He had struggled and fought to save both the horse and herself at the risk of his own life. Her gaze shifted to the hole at the top of the barrier and she saw the snow falling faster, denser, turning late afternoon into night. They were safe for the time being, but Gavin's anxiety had made abundantly clear that the danger was not over. Her gaze went back to Robert. It would have been terrible to be alone here in this isolated place, but it was even more terrible to be responsible for danger to another human being.

"No swelling. You'll be glad to know the cause of all this trouble is fine," Robert said as he stood up and patted Caird's neck. "I mean, as fine as this bag of bones ever is," he added wryly.

She was too weary to defend the insult to Caird. She curled up on the blanket watching Robert as he took a cloth and began to wipe down the piebald.

Soon she would get up and help, but it would do no harm to rest for a moment. . . .

• • •

Robert sat across the fire, staring into the flames when she opened her eyes.

He looked as he always did: powerful, remote, controlled. Even when he thought himself unobserved, there was no lowering of that wariness that was always with him.

He glanced up as he felt her gaze on him. "I was hoping you'd sleep through the night."

The sky beyond the opening appeared darker, the shadows on the wall of the cave more pronounced. "How long did I sleep?"

"Not long. A few hours."

She sat up and brushed her hair back from her face. "I didn't mean to sleep at all."

"Why not? There's nothing else to do." He poured liquid from the pot hanging over the flames into a cup. "But since you're awake, drink this."

She looked at the milky-looking liquid in the cup he handed her. "What is it?"

"Hot water brewed with the bones of the hare we killed yesterday."

She made a face. "I don't think I—"

"Drink it. It's not much, but it may have some strengthening power. We ate a meal this morning before we set out, so we'll wait until tomorrow to roast the hare. From now on we'll eat only once a day ... and lightly."

"You believe that the storm may last for days as Gavin said?"

He shrugged. "I have no idea. You can never tell this time of year. It could last a day or a week. If it only lasts a day or two, once it stops, we should be able to make it down to the foothills."

"And if it lasts longer?"

"The trail will be impassable, and it may take a month before the drifts melt enough for us to get down."

"A month!"

"If fortune is with us." He met her gaze. "Two years ago one of my clan was stranded in a cave like this for two months."

"What happened to him?"

"He froze to death."

She inhaled sharply. "How terrible."

"Aye, he was on his way from Edinburgh. He told no one he was coming home, or we would have searched for him. By the time we received word, it was too late." He glanced at the cup in her hand. "Drink."

She took a sip and found it as unpleasant as it looked. "Are you sure Gavin will be safe?"

"I can't be sure of anything, but he has a better chance than we do."

"I did not realize that—"

"I know you didn't realize the hazards." He smiled crookedly. "But even if you had, would you have acted differently?"

Her gaze went to Caird. How could she have acted differently toward her old friend and companion? She glanced at Robert. "I couldn't have deserted Caird, but, yes, I would have acted differently. If I'd known the danger was this great, I wouldn't have listened to you. I would have made you go with Gavin. It was not right for me to let you risk your life."

His brows lifted. "And how would you have done that? Hit me on the head as you did in the forest?"

"If necessary."

He chuckled. "I believe you would. What touching gratitude after all my efforts on your behalf."

"I am grateful," she said haltingly. "You have no idea how grateful I am—no one has ever risked their life for me before—but there is guilt also. I should not have let you do it."

"As I remember, I gave you no choice." He made an impatient gesture. "There's no use discussing it now. It's done."

"Yes, it's done." She looked at the pile of wood,

which appeared pitifully small after Robert's chilling
story. It was warm here now, even cozy, but if the trail
became impassable, so would the slope that led to their
only source of fuel. "Should we put out the fire to save
wood?"

"We'll burn it only at night when it's coldest. The
barriers should be tight enough to keep us from freezing during the day."

She involuntarily shuddered at his words.

"I'm not trying to frighten you. I'm trying to be
honest. You deserve better than lies." He met her gaze.
"Believe me, I have no intention of dying."

"Perhaps your clansman didn't either."

"He stayed and waited for the thaw that didn't
come. I'll not make that mistake."

"What will you do?"

"Find a way. There's always a way to be found, if
you search hard enough."

For the first time since she had opened her eyes,
she felt a surge of hope. Robert would never give up.
She should not either. "So what should we do now?"

"Sleep. We'll need it. After we put out the fire tomorrow morning, we'll have to keep moving to keep
warm." He finished his drink and put his cup aside. "By
sunset tomorrow I guarantee you'll be wearier than if
you'd ridden through these mountains all day." He
stretched out and closed his lids.

He suddenly looked younger, more vulnerable,
now that she could no longer see those dark, glittering
eyes. Why, he *was* young, she thought. He seemed
much older and more seasoned than Gavin, but in
years he and his henchman were a scant five apart. He
had a full life yet to live.

And that life could be quenched like the flame of
a candle.

And the blame would be hers.

He had known her only chance to live was for him
to stay and make preparations that would mean sur-

vival, and he had done it. She had made him promise to treat her as he did Gavin, and he had done that also. He had extended his protection as if she belonged to Craighdhu as Gavin did. But Gavin had known the danger and would never have endangered Robert as she had done.

If Robert died, she didn't know how she could live with the burden of guilt. He had saved her life, and she owed him a great debt, a debt that seemed more smothering and intolerable with each passing moment.

Dear God, she did not wish to owe Robert MacDarren anything. Debt was a bond, and she could not bear to be bound to him any longer. She had discovered in these past weeks how hurtful it was to live only on the fringes of his life, and she would do it no longer. She had thought when they reached Craighdhu she would find a way to cut their ties, but she could not do it if she was laden with this overwhelming obligation.

She lay down, cradling her head on her arm, staring at him as he slept.

Now that she was closer to him, he no longer appeared either young or vulnerable. His lips had a wicked sensual curve, and the hollowed plane of his cheeks gave him a look of exotic hunger.

Her heart was beating so hard, it was almost painful, as she sank to her knees beside him. She desperately wanted to scurry around to her former place by the fire. She must not be so cowardly. She had made up her mind, and now she must just do it.

She drew a deep breath, then reached out and touched his cheek.

She flinched back as his lids immediately flicked open. "What is it?"

She drew her blanket closer around her. "I must talk to you."

"I thought it had all been said."

She glanced away from him. "Not everything. I've thought about it and ... It is hard to put it into words. But if you wish it ..."

He stiffened. "Are you saying what I think you're saying?"

"How should I know what you think I'm saying? My tongue is so clumsy, I wonder you can understand me at all." She drew a shaky breath and started again. "You appear to set store by this carnal coupling. After all, we are wed. I suppose I would not mind if you ..." She stopped again and then said in a rush, "Why don't you say something? I told you this was difficult for me."

His gaze narrowed on her face. "I'm trying to decide why you've suddenly chosen to gift me in this fashion. Guilt?"

"Yes," she said bluntly. "And I owe a great debt. In spite of what you say, I believe there's a possibility I may never be able to repay you as I would like." Her hands clenched nervously. "And if I don't repay you, I would feel ... I would never be free of you. This seems the only ... I don't see why you think this act is important, but I would not deny you." She had gotten it all out, she thought with relief. "If you still want it, I believe I can bear it."

"Want it?"

She inhaled sharply as she saw his expression change from wariness to sensuality.

"Oh, yes, I still want it," he said in a thick voice. "I've wanted nothing else since that night at the inn. At times I thought I'd go mad with wanting it." He smiled recklessly. "And I don't give a whit how I get it. I'll accept gratitude as long as I get the rest."

It was going to happen. She had thought her heart was pounding hard before, but now it was trying to leap from her breast. "You'll have to tell me how to do this. Sebastian told me I had the instincts of Lilith, but he must be wrong or I would never be this uncertain." She let the blanket fall to the ground, and the heat of the fire touched her body. "However, I'm not so ignorant I don't know it starts like this. Isn't that so?"

His muscles locked, became rigid, as his gaze fastened on the pink tips of her breasts. "Nakedness is usually not required in the middle of a snowstorm."

"I thought it would be over quicker if I got the disrobing out of the way. I'm not cold." An understatement, she thought. A trail of scorching heat followed his gaze as it moved from her nipples down her body to the soft hair that encircled her womanhood.

"Neither am I," he said hoarsely.

"Should I lie down and close my eyes?"

"So that you won't see the horrible fate that's about to overtake you? Not yet." He reached out and touched her belly. "I want to test your tolerance." His fingers trailed down to the curls that had so absorbed his attention. "I want to see just how much you can bear."

A shock went through her, and her muscles clenched beneath his touch.

"What a violent response," he murmured as he began to stroke and pet her. "And I'm sure I'm not hurting you."

No, not pain, something else. "I feel as I did when I fell out of an oak tree when I was a little girl of six. It was—" She closed her eyes as his hand reached down to cup her. "Why . . . are you doing that?"

His fingers were patting, probing, delicately exploring. "Don't you like it?"

A hot shiver went through her. "All this fondling seems a great waste of time."

"Oh, I forgot, you wished it quickly over. You even undressed for greater efficiency. But I'm afraid you'll have to be patient. There's something I want to do here." His fingers were searching. "I'll try to hurry."

She arched back with a low cry as he found the nub that had been his quest. Shock. Heat. Hunger.

"You like that?" She was in such a haze of pleasure,

she was only barely aware of his gaze narrowed on her face as his thumb pressed and then began moving in a slow, erotic circle. "Ah, I see that you do. How much?"

Too much. She bit her lower lip to keep from moaning as sensation after sensation tore through her, spreading through her body. Her flesh was hot, flushed, her breasts ripening more with every passing moment.

"But I interrupted you." He began plucking at the nub, every pull sending a jolting bolt of need throughout her womanhood. "You were telling me how you fell out of a tree when you were six."

Was she? She couldn't remember anything before the moment when his fingers had started that rhythmic motion.

"You fell out of a tree," he prompted.

"I ... knocked the breath out of myself."

"And that's how you feel now?"

"I believe ... so."

"Don't you know?"

"I cannot think. . . ."

"Good." He removed his fingers. "An excellent sign. Now you can lie down and catch your breath." He distanced himself a few feet and began to pull off his left boot.

She collapsed on the blanket. It was just as well he had told her to lie down, for she was trembling so much, she was not sure she could have remained upright. "You're undressing?"

"It seems appropriate for your first time." He took off the other boot. "I cannot provide you with clean sheets, but I'll not mark you with all this leather." He tossed his leather jerkin aside. "Open your legs for me, Kate. I want to look at you."

"Is that necessary?"

"No, but it will give me pleasure. Isn't that the purpose of all this?"

She felt a flush envelop her entire body as she obeyed him. She could feel his gaze on that juncture where they would join as if it were stroking her as his fingers had done before. She felt totally helpless, totally submissive.

"Beautiful . . . Just a little wider. That's right." He undid his points. "Do you know how many times I've thought about you lying like this, waiting for me to come into you?"

His dark eyes were intent, almost glazed with need. The need was for her, and the knowledge caused that strange melting heat to increase. She was acutely conscious of the womanliness of her body, the swelling of her breasts, the softness of her skin, the vulnerability of her position.

He was completely nude now, as sinewy and beautiful as he had been in the chamber at the inn and even more aroused. She moved her gaze quickly from his lower body to his face, but that was somehow worse. She closed her eyes so that she would no longer see his expression of naked hunger.

"Open your eyes. I want you to look at me. I want you to watch me." His voice was guttural. "I want you to know every minute who is doing this to you. Who is going to be inside you." She opened her eyes to see him kneeling between her outspread legs, unclothed.

"Is it going to happen now?" she whispered.

"Aye." He moved closer. "But not quite yet." Two fingers slid slowly into her.

She arched upward at the incredible invasion of body and senses. His fingers moved in and out slowly, then more rapidly, and then with a jerky, primitive rhythm that drove her to bite her lips to keep from screaming with the erotic sensations that were cascading through her with his every motion.

"Tight . . . God, you're tight," he muttered. "I can't—wait any longer. I have to get *in*."

He entered carefully, fighting the tightness. When he reached the barrier, he stopped, his chest lifting and falling with each labored breath. "Brace yourself, lass."

He plunged to the hilt.

She gasped as pain shot through her. He became still, buried deep, joined, pulsing within her.

She still felt a dull ache, but another sensation was beginning to submerge the discomfort. Fullness ... but still hunger, a hunger she suddenly knew she could not bear not to assuage.

She instinctively clenched around him.

He gasped, and a shudder went through him. He lifted his head to look down at her. "Are you trying to kill me?"

But he had liked it. She had caught that expression of unutterable pleasure on his face. "It felt ... right. It was right, wasn't it?"

He nodded. "You just surprised me."

It had been no surprise to her. Now that he was within her, everything seemed to have its own rhythm, its own primitive inevitability. "But there's more." Her hands reached out blindly to clutch at his shoulders. "There has to be more."

"Aye, there's more." He began to move in and out, with short and long thrusts that came like fiery blows, striking at the heart of her.

Bonding, wild pleasure, hunger, all growing more intense with each driving thrust.

He was not giving her enough, she thought feverishly. She had to take more of him. She began to thrust upward, meeting him with a need so fierce, it made her nearly mindless as she tried to clench around him to keep him within her.

"Easy," he muttered. "It's too good. I can't hold on."

He was speaking foolishly. There could be no ease in this act. It was madness, fire and pleasure, and she could not bear it to either slow or stop.

She thrust upward, her nails digging into his shoulders. "*Help* me."

He froze. "God." He began to move with animal

ferocity, his hands cupping her buttocks in his palms as he drove to the quick. "This?" His voice hoarsened. "Is this what you want? Take it!"

This must be like birth or death, she thought hazily. Whatever it was, it had to go on forever. No, it had to be *done*. She couldn't go on like this with the pleasure building, satisfaction beckoning, climbing, yet just out of reach.

Robert's face above her was flushed, his lips heavy with sensuality, his cheeks hollowed and drawn with a terrible strain. "Now," he said, through clenched teeth. He lifted her higher, closer. "Give it to me. Now!"

Her body convulsed, splintering into hot arcs of pleasure.

He groaned, his spine arching, the tendons of his throat distending as he threw back his head.

He collapsed on top of her, his entire body shuddering, shaking as if with a fever.

She was shaking, too, she realized dimly, as her fingers ran down his back. Roughness against the smoothness of his skin. Scars, she remembered, he had scars on his back. They had hurt him. She felt a wild burst of possessive anger, and her arms tightened around him. Never again. He must never be hurt again.

"Kate."

His voice was deep and caressing as he said her name. How beautiful . . . her name had never sounded so beautiful.

"I'm too heavy on you. Let me go, lass."

He wasn't too heavy, and she didn't want to let him go. She never wanted to let him go again.

Robert lifted his head and brushed her forehead with his lips. "I'd gladly stay here, but I'm already stirring, and I think you've have had enough for the first time." He made a face. "Probably too much. I wasn't as gentle with you as I would have liked."

He *was* stirring, she realized incredulously. He

wanted her again. It could go on, the pleasure could go on. . . .

"No!" he said as he felt her tighten around him. He quickly drew out and moved to one side. "Not now, Kate. Rest now. I can't believe I'm saying that." He chuckled as he kissed her nose. "But you must admit you bore this hideous trial quite well."

Her breath was coming in gasps, and it was as if she were seeing everything through a haze. Only what had gone before was real. "Is it . . . always like this?"

"More or less." His tongue delicately licked her shoulder, and a hot shiver ran through her. "But this is definitely more. You appear to have been created for this kind of sport. I admit I didn't expect such an enthusiastic response from a virgin."

"I did not expect to give it." Panic jarred her into full awareness as she realized what had just happened to her. She had been shameless, uncontrolled, the slut Sebastian had always claimed her to be. With a jerky motion she sat up and wrapped the blanket around her. "It was a . . . surprise. I'm sure I wouldn't have responded with such abandonment if I'd known—"

"Known what?" He smiled teasingly. "That you were born with the kind of passion Aphrodite was said to have?"

Heat flew to her cheeks. "You are making jest of me."

"Am I?"

She nodded. "I'm not the stuff of legends, and you know it. Besides, I would not conduct myself in that foolish fashion. All those goddesses seemed to think only of lust and vanity and deserved all their tribulations."

He chuckled. "Very well, you're no goddess." His hand reached up to cup her breast. "But I believe I'll have to try you again to determine the extent of your earthiness."

Sweet Jesus, it was happening again, she realized in

despair. Her nipple was peaking, readying beneath his touch. "No!" She scooted backward, out of reach. "It was a mistake."

He lifted a brow. "How fleeting is gratitude. . . ."

"I will find another way."

"I like this one."

"And I don't." He was still too close. She stood up and moved around the fire and sat down.

"You like it very much." His gaze narrowed on her face. "And will like it even more once you've learned the way of it."

"I will not," she said fiercely. "I will not be the whore Sebastian called me."

"Ah, there's the problem." His lips tightened. "By Judas, that bastard manages to spit his poison even when he's not in the same country. You're no whore, Kate."

"Pure woman do not enjoy—"

"What of your friend Carolyn? Did you not tell me she was eagerly looking forward to marrying?"

She frowned in confusion. He was right. Carolyn had always had a lustful turn. "It's different for me."

"Because Sebastian told you it was wicked so many times that the truth became blurred. You told me that yourself."

She shook her head helplessly. "You don't understand. If he is right about this, he may be right about other things. I cannot let it happen again."

"But you will." His expression hardened. "You didn't have to give yourself. I would have kept my promise. It was your choice."

"And I've changed my mind."

"It's too late." His eyes glittered in the firelight. "If you think I'll stay in this cave with you, knowing what we could have and letting Sebastian take it from—" He broke off and repeated, "It's too late."

"You would take me against my will?" she asked shakily.

He shook his head. "But we've already discussed how delightfully weak your will is in this particular matter. I'll simply lay assault until it crumbles."

Fear surged through her, and with it a dark, forbidden heat. She knew how determined he could be, and now she also knew the pleasure he could give her. Her lustful body would not wish to fight him, would instead battle to surrender. She searched wildly for an argument that would get through to him. "You said once a child would be a danger to Craighdhu, and that you could prevent— But I don't think you protected that from happening, did you?"

An indecipherable expression flickered across his face. "No."

She did not think he had. She was not sure what action would have been necessary to prevent a child, but their coming together had been so savage, calculating behavior of any sort had seemed impossible. "Then you clearly should not let it happen again."

"You're wrong, I've already made the mistake. You may even now be with child. There's no reason I shouldn't enjoy your body until I find out if it's true."

"There is a reason," she said in exasperation. "I say no."

He suddenly smiled. "And that's reason enough for now. There is probably soreness from your first joust, and I'll not trouble you again tonight." He lay down and pulled the blanket over him. "Tomorrow night will do as well. When darkness falls, and we light the fire, I'll show you how a man can be mounted. You'll find it much more pleasurable than any ride Caird has given you." He met her gaze across the fire. "In the meantime think of how you felt when I came into you. Do you not want that pleasure again?"

She did want it, she realized in despair. Just the memory of that joining was starting an aching heat between her thighs.

His gaze moved down to the fullness of her breasts

outlined beneath the blanket. "I have few fond memories of my time in Spain, but I learned many things there that will bring you pleasure. I'll show you a few tomorrow evening."

"No," she whispered.

"Aye, pleasure is no sin between man and wife. Personally, I'm delighted Mary has gifted you with such a lustful nature. It will be my joy to develop it to our mutual advantage during our stay here."

"I'm *not* lustful."

"But you are, with a clean, beautiful lust such as I've never known before. If you will be honest with yourself, you'll admit that you came to me as much from lust as from gratitude."

Her eyes widened in shock. "It's not true. I knew nothing about this. How could I know I would find this—" She stopped in dismay.

He smiled knowingly, and she realized he had guessed what she had almost blurted out. "You couldn't know, but you were curious, weren't you? You're always curious. You want to know how everything smells and tastes and feels. Curiosity, too, is a form of lust, Kate." He closed his eyes. "Now go to sleep. You'll need your rest tomorrow."

Could he be right? Had she lied to herself about her motives tonight? she wondered, stricken. It was true at one time she had passionately wanted to pierce that wall surrounding Robert and learn everything about him. The desire had been like a terrible thirst, and when she'd been denied the means to soothe that thirst in the way of her choice, it was possible she had tried to quench it in the only way left open to her.

She settled down, her gaze on his face. He was so sure, so confident of victory, the falcon swooping down on its prey. But she was no helpless victim. She could fight him, best him. She had only to ignore what had happened tonight and—

But she could neither ignore nor forget what had

happened. Because, God help her, it was still happening. He had only had to look at her and her body had changed, ripened. Even now, her breasts were still aching and swollen beneath the blanket. She did not know that woman who had moaned and moved and arched at his command. What would be her response if he touched her again? Would she change into the panting, lustful animal she had been only a few moments before? The thought filled her with sickening fear, and another emotion even more terrifying.

A dark, dangerous anticipation.

"Wake up, Kate."

She opened her eyes to see Robert already dressed and pulling on his boots. He smiled. "Get dressed. It's time to put out the fire."

The fire was already burning low, and even beneath the blankets she could feel the chill. When it went out entirely, it would be frigid in the cave. Memories of last night abruptly flooded back to her, and she became acutely conscious of her own nakedness and Robert watching her across the fire. She hurriedly reached for her clothing, dragged it to her, and started to struggle into the garments beneath the blanket.

"For God's sake, what are you doing?" Robert asked impatiently. "You look like a pig rolling in the mud."

"I'm getting dressed."

"Modesty? Did it not occur to you I've already seen what you're trying to conceal?" He smiled sardonically. "Or are you just obeying Sebastian's commands and trying not to arouse my wicked carnal lusts?"

"Modesty is not unknown to me," she said, stung. "And I do not need either Sebastian or you to lesson me in it."

"I have no desire to teach you any such foolishness. I infinitely prefer you as you were last night."

"I do not," she said crisply. "And I wish you would not speak of it. It makes me uncomfortable."

"I passed a few uncomfortable hours myself last night," he murmured. "Would you like for me to tell you in what fashion?"

"No," she said in exasperation. She was sure she had her blasted gown on backward, and how was she to put on her stockings without disarranging the blanket? "I want you to be silent and let me get on with this."

His lips were suddenly twitching. "At the speed you're going, we'll use our entire supply of wood before you manage to clothe yourself."

He was right, she thought crossly. Why should she be forced to this foolishness when it only amused him and discomforted herself? She sat up and tossed aside the blanket. She did not have the gown on backward, but the bodice was buttoned wrong. She quickly corrected the matter. "I meant what I said last night, you know."

"I'm sure you did." He paused. "So did I."

"Then you must change your mind." She started to tug on her woolen stockings. "For I shall not change mine."

"You seem to be having a great deal of difficulty with those stockings. May I help?"

"No! I have no need—" He was already kneeling in front of her, his hands brushing aside her hands. A jolt of heat went through her when his fingers touched her bare calf as he slowly drew the gray wool up her leg.

"You have fine limbs," he said softly. "You gave me no opportunity to study you last night."

She had a sudden memory of herself lying open and defenseless before him. "That's not true." The words sounded breathless, and she deliberately steadied her voice. "You must know every inch by now."

"Not every inch." He pulled her stocking past her

knee. "I was preoccupied with only one portion of your enchanting person. Lust has a habit of making one single-minded." He reached for the leather garter on the blanket beside her. "I'm sure you understand that now." He tied the leather garter, and then his hand moved up to caress her inner thigh. "There's nothing more sensual or pleasing than the sight of a woman's limbs bound by stockings and garters and then to find this lovely surprise of soft flesh."

She stared helplessly at his tan hand against her pale limb. His touch was caressing, its very lightness beguiling, chaining her. She must move away from him.

He touched the leather garter. "This is good leather, butter soft. I enjoy the feel of leather." His cheeks were flushed, and the mocking note had vanished from his hoarse voice. "I'll show you later what a pleasure leather can be." He tore his hand away and reached for the other stocking. "I have a great fondness for most textures, but I have no liking for this rough wool. I'll find you silk stockings when we get to Craighdhu." He pulled the stocking up past her knee and tied the garter. "Silk has a pleasing texture too." His fingers trailed up, and then still farther. "But there are a few textures even more pleasing."

The muscles of her thigh clenched beneath his touch, sending a chain reaction upward to the place he had stroked last night. Why could she not move? It was as if she were frozen in place by his touch.

"I'll try to take more time tonight," he said thickly. "I know I was too quick with you. There are many ways of pleasure, and not all of them so rough."

He had not been rough. There had been wildness but not brutality. If anything, she had been the one who was brutal. She remembered how her nails had dug deep into his shoulders as she lunged upward. She had been an animal, no better than a whore. The thought broke the spell he was weaving about her, and she drew away from him. "I will not learn these ways."

He sat back on his heels and pulled down her skirt. "You'll have no choice."

"I've learned enough about you to know you won't force me."

"I won't have to. You don't have a temperate nature." He met her gaze. "We both know I could have taken you just now, if I'd wished."

She started to deny it and then remembered that moment of mindless fascination when he had held her in thrall. She would do better to search out his weaknesses than deny her own. "Then why didn't you?"

"I can wait." He stood up and drew on his cloak. "You're a little confused, but you're generally a sensible woman. You'll come to see the truth."

"That it's right to be a whore?" she asked scornfully.

"No, that it's right to be a woman," he said. "Entirely a woman, with a woman's right to give and take pleasure. You could never be a whore, no matter what Sebastian told you. You're too strong. A whore is used, and you would not let yourself be used. You're far more likely to use me than I you." He added as he reached out and pulled her to her feet, "And it will be my pleasure to let you use me in any manner you find agreeable."

She stared at him, startled. He was presenting an entirely different picture of her role in the passionate play of last night.

"Power," he said softly. "Is it not a seductive thought? All your life you've had no power, you've been crushed by circumstances and your kind Sebastian into submission. I'm offering you a battleground where you have greater power than any man alive."

It was seductive, she thought, and he was diabolically clever to have presented her with the one argument that would appeal to her mind and emotions as well as her body. "I have no desire to be the Lilith Sebastian called me. I will not walk that path."

"I'm saying you have the strength to be anything you wish, but do you really think I'd let you lure and use me against my will? Your soul is safe with me." He smiled. "I only want your body."

She stared at him incredulously and then found herself laughing. "What a great comfort."

"It would not prove so to most women, but I knew the thought would appeal to you." He took a step forward, draped her cloak about her, and buttoned it at the throat. "You have all day to think about it." He suddenly frowned as he glanced at her hands. "I forgot about your gloves." He took off his own leather gauntlets. "Take these. As soon as I put out the fire, it's going to be icy in here."

She shook her head. "You're no more impervious to cold than I am. You told me you had frostbite once."

He frowned. "Do as I—" He stopped as he saw her expression. "We'll share them. You wear them for the first hour." He met her gaze. "You see how you can impose your will on me? Enough but not too much. It's all in striking a balance. Give me your hand."

She held it out, and he slipped the big glove on her hand. The outside of the glove was hard, rough, but the interior hugged her palms in a soft, pliable caress. She could feel the warmth from his body, and the leather's embrace felt as intimate as his hand on her thigh. He put the other glove on her. "There. It's not too bad sharing with me, is it?" He smiled down at her. "I promise I'll make it very easy for you."

He was not talking about the gloves. She couldn't seem to tear her gaze from his face. She whispered, "You have not . . . convinced me."

"I had no intention of doing so. You're too intelligent a woman to let Sebastian rob you again. I intend to let you convince yourself." He turned and put out the fire. "While we try to keep from freezing to death until it's time to light another fire."

*H*e *kept her on* her feet all day, walking, moving her arms, exercising the horses, allowing her no more than ten minutes in every hour's span to rest. He left the cave only once, with a bucket to gather snow to be melted for drinking water for themselves and the horses. Other than that, he kept to the same regimen he set for her. He was silent, speaking only when necessary. It would have been easier if he had talked to her. It would have allowed her less time to think of his words.

I intend to let you convince yourself.

You have power.

She had not felt powerful when she had been caught in the throes of their joining. She had been a mad, driven creature, caught in her own search for pleasure.

But Robert had been caught in the same quest. He had led but not tried to conquer. He had been as helpless before that overwhelming carnal tide as she had been.

You're too intelligent a woman to let Sebastian rob you again.

Sebastian had always tried to rob her of all the joys of life. How he would rejoice to know that he could put her back in the cage she had just escaped.

No, she would never let that happen. She would fight it to the last breath and—

"Rest is over. On your feet." Robert was standing before her, holding out his hand. "You have to get moving again."

She let him pull her to her feet.

He released her hand immediately and turned and went to the horses. She watched him as he took Caird's lead and began to walk him in a circle around the cave.

Dear God, he was beautiful. Sinuous and graceful, totally male, with that stormy secret intensity she had found fascinating since the first moment she had met him. She had submerged herself, drowned herself in that intensity last night.

She felt a stirring between her thighs. Lust. Sebastian would have said she was completely lost to carnal sin, but Robert said lust could be clean and beautiful. Whom should she believe?

Not Sebastian. Never Sebastian.

"Why are you just standing there?" Robert asked over his shoulder. "You need to walk. It's still—" He stopped as he saw her expression. "Yes?" he asked softly.

She couldn't speak. She could only stare at him and nod.

He became still, and the air between them seemed charged, heavy, hard to breathe. "Then don't look at me like that—we still have at least two hours to go before dark."

She was suddenly no longer cold. She wanted to touch him. Surely it would be all right just to go to him and touch his cheek?

"No," he said harshly, as if he had read her mind. "I'm holding on by a thread. Go get Rachel's lead and exercise her."

"Very well." She went to Rachel and began petting her muzzle. "It's only because what you said has merit. Sebastian would be robbing me if I denied myself this enjoyment." She took Rachel's lead and began to follow him. "And I found you very ... agreeable."

"I know."

"I think you must be very skillful at the act."

"You don't have the experience to judge."

"That's true, but you seem to know ..." She felt her muscles tense as she remembered how he had made her body respond to his every touch. "Everything."

"I had excellent tutors."

"In Spain, you said?"

"Aye."

"Where?"

"At the castillo of Don Diego Santanella."

"It seems an unusual subject to teach someone."

"He was an unusual man."

"In what manner?"

"Will your questions never cease?" he asked between his teeth.

"This is all new to me, and I'm unsure. It makes me feel less nervous to talk about it." With effort she kept her tone even. "I regret if I upset you."

"It doesn't upset me."

"I believe it does. Why else would you be so short with me?"

He whirled to face her, his eyes blazing. "Because I'm hard as a rock and trying to keep from pulling you down on that blanket and coming into you."

The crude words should have shocked her. They did not. Excitement rippled through her. "I do not think that would be such an unwise idea," she said breathlessly. "I'll only get more nervous as I wait, and it would—"

"Christ!" He covered the space between them in two steps and grabbed her shoulders. He jerked her down to the blanket.

He was shaking, the pulse leaping in the hollow of

his throat. He buried his face in the hair at her temple. "Tell me no."

"Why should I tell you that when I just said—" His lips stopped her words, his tongue entering her mouth to toy frantically with her own. She had not known men kissed that way. He had barely touched her lips last night. She found the action darkly intimate and almost as exciting as that more carnal invasion. He did not give her a chance to savor it. He pushed her back, his hands fumbling at the buttons of her bodice. "Don't move—I have to—"

His lips were cold on her breast, but his tongue was moist and warm as he started to suck strongly, frantically. She arched upward, her fingers tangling in his hair. "Robert!"

"Sorry," he muttered. "I didn't want this— No time." His hands were under her skirt, reaching, searching, frantically adjusting his own clothing.

He was inside her, big, warm, club hard, plunging, rutting. His warm breath plumed the frosty air as his chest lifted and fell with his labored breathing.

Cold. Heat. Desire.

She held desperately to his shoulders as she met him, took him, merged with him.

It was over in only a few wild minutes.

She became gradually conscious of the hardness of the ground beneath her, of Robert lying next to her, gasping, his hand still covering her bare breast.

"Did I hurt you?" he asked quietly.

"No."

"It's a wonder," he said bitterly. "I . . . lost control."

The words brought an odd, bittersweet pleasure. Robert, who rarely lost control, had been stirred enough to abandon it for her. No, not for her, for her body. Well, that was still part of her. The pain that qualification brought was not reasonable.

His hand on her breast tightened. "Jesus, look at you. It's freezing cold, and I have you nearly naked."

"I . . . liked it."

"I promised you I'd go slow."

She was tired of him chastising himself. "You're being very foolish. I thought it went very well. How do you know I would even care for this . . . this slowness?"

He chuckled. "Oh, you'll like it. I'll demonstrate just how pleasurable slowness can be later, when we light the fire and get some warmth in here." He rolled over and began buttoning her bodice. "So, fie on Sebastian?"

She smiled. "Well put. Fie on Sebastian."

Kate gazed languidly into the fire. "If you learned all this from the Spanish, then they must be a very decadent people."

He drew her back against him, fitting her into the hollow of his hips. "At times."

How well they fit together, she thought contentedly. During the last hours she had been more aware of that almost magical togetherness than anything else. It was as if they had been two parts of a whole that had been separated and were now coming together. "But I believe I like this kind of decadence, so I've decided they must not be as bad as everyone says."

"Does that mean you're contemplating asking Philip's protection? Forget it." He added lightly, "You mustn't judge all Spaniards by my example."

"But you're not Spanish, you're Scot."

"Yes, I'm Scot." He was silent a moment. "But my mother is Spanish."

She raised herself on one elbow to look at him. "Truly?"

"Truly." His lips twisted. "Doña Marguerita Maria Santanella."

"Will I meet her when we reach Craighdhu?"

"No."

"Why not?"

"Curiosity again? I thought Sebastian's example had taught you to avoid asking personal questions."

"This is different. Dreams are private. But why should you not tell me something everyone at Craighdhu probably already knows? You know everything about me."

"Not everything." His index finger traced the aureole around her nipple. "I'm discovering new and splendid facets at every turn. Did you know that only one woman in a thousand has the ability to grasp a man with the power that you do? I thought I would go mad when you clenched around me and then squeezed until I—"

"Hush!" Heat flooded her cheeks, and she slapped away his toying hand. "Decadence is well enough, but you do not have to put it into words." Then the full meaning of his sentence hit her. "Thousand? Have you truly had a thousand—you are jesting with me."

"Am I?" He blandly met her gaze, and suddenly his lips were twitching. "Perhaps a slight exaggeration."

"A vast exaggeration. You would have time to do nothing else." She frowned. "And I think you said it only to distract me because you didn't want to answer my question. You're not being fair."

His smile faded. "Why is it important to you that I answer you?"

"It would make me feel ... safer." It was not the entire truth. He had possessed her, owned her in a manner that frightened as well as elated her, but she also desperately wanted to *know* him. That desire had obsessed her since the moment she had met him, and she doubted if he would ever be more open to her than he was at this moment. "Why will I not meet your mother?"

"My mother is residing in a convent in Santanella, where she prays for my soul." He smiled without mirth. "Though she is sure that her prayers are of no avail."

"A convent?"

"She considered it her only recourse when I escaped from her brother, Don Diego, and returned to Craighdhu. She had failed, you see. They had tried to mold me into a true Spaniard and had only succeeded in exaggerating my deplorable Scottish savagery." His lips twisted. "What a pity."

"I don't understand."

"You wish to hear it all? I don't know why, it's all in the past."

"I want to hear it."

He shrugged. "When he was a very young man, my father traveled to a shipyard in Spain seeking to purchase a caravel for our trade with the Irish. Don Diego Santanella, a nobleman who owned the shipyard and practically everything else along the coast, invited him to stay at the castillo until the ship was ready. It was there that he met my mother. She was only seventeen then, and very different from the women he had met before. You may have noticed we Scots have a tendency to be deplorably earthy in nature."

"It's come to my attention."

"She seemed shy and pure and very devout. She was also very, very beautiful. My father went mad for her. He had to have her. It didn't matter to him that she was Spanish and a Catholic or that she wanted to go into a convent and forgo marriage. He went to Don Diego and asked for her hand. To his surprise, his suit was looked on with favor. Diego refused to give a dowry, but he acceded to the marriage. They sailed back to Craighdhu as man and wife." His expression became shuttered. "She hated Craighdhu, she found my father detestable, and when I was born, she found me an annoyance. She spent most of her nights avoiding his bed and her days on her knees praying for deliverance. She had no time for a child. When I was nine, my father suddenly died of a stomach disorder. I've wondered since if it was not caused by a drop or two of poison in his food."

Her eyes widened in shock. "You believe she killed him?"

He shook his head. "But her attendants were all appointed by Don Diego, and he appeared on the scene just two weeks after my father's death. He arrived one night, and the next morning at dawn my mother and I were on a ship bound for Spain."

"Why would he want to kill your father?"

"Craighdhu and our trade routes to Ireland are very valuable. Don Diego made it very clear once I was under his wing that was why he'd given my mother in marriage. He was an ambitious man, and the trade routes are a very rich plum. A plum he couldn't pluck while my father was alive, but if he could mold and control the heir to Craighdhu, then he could control the trade routes. I spent the next four years at his castillo at Santanella being 'tutored' by the good priests and Don Diego."

"Tutored in what?"

"I was a Protestant, so I had to be taught to abandon such heresy." He added with irony, "Every day I received my gentle lessons from the priests Diego sent to school me."

She remembered the scars on his back. "With the whip?" she whispered.

"Of course, how else? Protestant or Catholic, it is all the same. They all believe they're right and must prove it at all costs." His lips thinned with bitterness. "First, you're given holy words, and next, the whip to enforce it. You should know that truth. Sebastian used his whip on you."

"But he was afraid of the lady, and I was not left scarred."

"Yes, you were." He touched her forehead with a curiously gentle caress. "But not irreparably. You're strong. In time the scars will fade, and you won't even remember where you got them."

But he remembered where *he* had gotten his scars;

he had permanent reminders. She wondered how many of his dreams concerned those afternoons at the castillo. "Didn't your mother try to stop it?"

"Oh, no, she had been raised by the priests and properly shaped in the way she should go. She even forced herself to sit in the same room while they tried to rid me of my devils. She would plead with me to give in and not to make them do this to me."

"She watched them whip you?"

"The priests would bring the whip to her before they started and she would pray over it, asking God to instill it with His holy power. Then she would kiss it and hand it back to Father Dominic."

She felt sick at the picture he painted vividly before her. She had thought her time with Sebastian a horror, but it had not been a systematic daily regimen of torture overseen by the one person who should have been his most ardent defender. The vision was too hurtful to contemplate. She changed the subject. "I don't understand. You said you learned"—she waved a hand to encompass their extremely intimate situation— "this at Santanella. I'm sure the priests did not teach you."

He smiled without mirth. "Don Diego was not nearly as devout as my mother. He believed there were many pleasurable uses for sin. Many evenings he would send for whores from the town and then summon me to his chamber to demonstrate the pleasures that awaited me if I rid myself of my foolish wish to cling to my homeland."

"But you were only a child."

"I didn't stay that way long. Unfortunately, I was too stubborn and lost in sin to accommodate either my mother or Don Diego, so it went on for four years. Punishment in the afternoon, a deliciously corrupt reward in the evening. When I reached my thirteenth year, I managed to run away from Santanella and made my way back to Craighdhu."

"How?"

"Very laboriously. It's a journey I prefer not to relive."

A boy alone, without means, hiding, afraid, traveling over land and sea. It was incredible he had been able to reach Craighdhu safely. "But if you had to get across the—"

"Enough questions. It's over and done." He suddenly rolled her on her back. "You have an enchanting mouth, but there are uses I would rather put it to than talking." His index finger traced her full bottom lip. "A divine mouth ... Open ..."

For the first time she felt a quaver of uneasiness. She had thought she could embrace this pleasure as Robert did, but was this sense of deep, irreversible bonding entirely customary in these situations? If so, why did it not vanish when the mating was finished? She felt closer to him now than when they had been in the throes of passion.

He pressed on her lower lip. "Open ... I want to come in."

She wanted him to come in. She was being foolish to question this pleasure that was deeper than any she had ever received before. Her arms closed around him as she opened her lips.

Darkness lay beyond the opening in the barrier, but Kate could see no sign of snow drifting through that blackness.

"Why aren't you asleep?" Robert nibbled at her earlobe. "If I wasn't vigorous enough to tire you, perhaps I should try again."

He was teasing her. He could not possibly wish to join with her again after these last hours of erotic play. "I think the snow has stopped."

"Aye, earlier this evening. You were a trifle ... occupied or you would have noticed yourself."

"That's a good sign, isn't it?" she asked eagerly.

"If it doesn't start again."

"But the storm could have moved on. We could be able to leave."

"Don't think about it. The weather is treacherous this time of year. We could be disappointed a dozen times before we manage to get out of here."

But it was difficult to suppress hope. She had never felt so strong, so alive. She did not want to die. "That's a foolish thing to say. How can I think of anything else?"

"You managed earlier." He went on quickly as she started to speak. "Tell me of this fine home you're going to have someday."

"You don't want to know. You're just trying to distract me."

"If I didn't want to know, I wouldn't have asked you. Don't you think I ought to be informed, since it's my gold that's to pay for it?"

It did seem just, but she would rather take advantage of his efforts to distract her in another manner. "Craighdhu. I want to know about Craighdhu."

"You'll see it for yourself soon."

Would she? She shivered as she glanced out into the darkness again. "Tell me anyway."

"It's not a large island. Mountains, steep hills, rocky country. I told you about the barrens."

"Tell me about the castle."

"It's old, very old. It was built by the Norsemen when they first came to conquer and then to settle the land."

"Who was there to conquer?"

"A savage sun-worshiping tribe called the Picts and later the Scots, the first Gaels who came from Ireland." He blew a tendril of hair at her temple. "They all made us what we are."

"The great and fierce Highlanders," she said teasingly. "What does the castle look like?"

"Like any castle. Turrets, stone, a moat. There's

nothing unusual about the castle or my island." He shrugged. "Many find it a forbidding place."

"But not you."

He looked into the fire. "Spain is warm and dry, and white jasmine bloomed in the gardens at Santanella. It was everything that poets call beautiful. On the day I stepped on shore at Craighdhu, I was barefoot and my feet were bleeding and the rocks were cold and rough beneath my feet. Night had fallen and torches were burning bright against the gray walls and mists veiled the mountains. It was chill, harsh, and spare."

"And beautiful," she whispered, her gaze on his face.

"I didn't say that."

He did not have to say it. It was there in his expression. Even if Craighdhu was not beautiful to the rest of the world, it was to him. "Home."

"Aye." He smiled. "Home." He glanced away from her. "I'm sure the home you choose will be much more hospitable."

"I don't know what it's going to be like. Whenever I think of it, it's very hazy. But I'll know it when I see it."

"You're so sure?"

She nodded. "I always know when something is going to belong to me, to truly be mine. The first time I saw Carolyn, I knew she was going to be my friend, and the same with Caird."

He chuckled. "If Caird is an example, then I assume beauty has nothing to do with it."

"No, it's like the pieces of a puzzle coming together. I may have to search for it, but when I see it, I'll know."

"And what if we don't find it? Will you settle for something less than your dream?"

"No, that would not be——" She became suddenly aware he had used the word we. "But you need not worry. Once the year is over, I'll hold you to your promise to furnish me with funds, but I will find my own way."

He stiffened. "I suppose I'm just to let you go wandering over the face of the earth," he said sarcastically. "Perhaps you could even join a troop of strolling players."

His roughness stung her after the gentleness that had gone before. "Perhaps I could," she said defiantly.

His arms tightened possessively about her. "It would be just like your idiocy to— I will not have it."

"You'll have no say in the matter. I will be free of you." Her own words were starting a pain somewhere deep within her. She sat up and moved away from his touch. "You won't even have to set eyes on me again. Your Craighdhu will be safe."

"Come back here."

"I do not wish it." She turned to face him. "And I've decided once we're down from this mountain, we should not fornicate again. It is too disturbing."

"You *like* that disturbance."

"My body likes it, but it is not wise."

His lips tightened. "Sebastian again? I thought we were done with that nonsense."

"Not Sebastian," she said haltingly. "Me. I cannot be like you. I cannot just accept this pleasure. It . . . affects me. I'm beginning to feel . . . something."

"Something?"

"I don't know. It confuses me. It's as if . . ." She tried to put into words the hazy fear that had been looming in the back of her mind. "It's as if whenever we come together, a bell begins striking louder and louder, and suddenly my ears are ringing and everything I am is vibrating with the sound of it. I know I'm part of the ringing, and each time it strikes, I become more a part of it." She nervously ran her fingers through her hair. "It must stop."

"I don't agree."

"But what happens when the bell stops ringing?"

she whispered. "You've seen how determined I can be when I try to hold on to what I want. What if I decided I wanted to make it keep on?" She shook her head. "I know you do not feel as I do and that this is all play to you, but can't you see that I—"

"We'll talk about it later," he interrupted, then reached out and drew her back down into his arms again.

"That may be too late."

"Go to sleep," he said roughly. "I'm tired of hearing about bells and strolling players and—I said we'd talk about it later."

Kate's breathing steadied and then slowly deepened. He was aware of the exact moment when she drifted away from him and fell asleep. His body and mind were so exquisitely attuned to her that he seemed to know her every reaction, every thought.

"You do not feel as I do."

He did not want to know how he felt. All he wanted to do was to keep on as they were now, to feel her tightness around him, to be able to reach out and touch her. She enjoyed what he did to her, and he would pay no heed to her words. There was no reason why he should not continue to have her until he knew she was not with child.

A child.

The fierce possessive joy that surged through him was startling in intensity. It meant nothing, he told himself, it was only primitive instinct. His mind told him a child would be a disaster for Craighdhu, and he must listen to his mind. After he was sure she had not conceived, he must never bed her again. He already knew he had no control when he was within her and would never be able to withdraw before he gave her his seed.

But he did not have to think about that now. Not yet. His hand moved down to caress her belly.

A child . . .

• • •

A band of light was striking her across the face. Too bright, she thought sleepily as she opened her eyes, much too—

Sunlight! Brilliant, beautiful sunlight streaming through the small opening in the barrier. She sat upright, pulling the blankets around her as the chill struck her naked body. "Robert, it's the—"

Robert wasn't there. He must already be outside.

She scrambled to her feet and hurriedly began to dress. She was thrusting her arms into her cloak when Robert pushed aside the blanket at the entrance and entered the cave.

"The sun ... Will it ... ?" She stopped, holding her breath, her gaze fixed anxiously on his face.

A slow smile lit his face, and he nodded in answer to her unspoken question.

Relief made her almost weak. "Thank God."

"You'd best save your thanks until we get down the trail. It's going to be no easy journey."

"When do we leave?"

"Now. The drifts are fairly deep but not impassable, and it's better to travel before the sun melts the snow and leaves us with the ice underneath to contend with." He strode over to Caird. "Put out the fire. I'll saddle the horses." He spoke rapidly as he threw the blanket over Caird's back. "You'll ride Rachel and lead my horse. I'll follow on foot with Caird on a tight rein."

"I should do that. He's my—"

"Responsibility," he finished for her. "I know all about your sense of 'responsibility.' For God's sake, don't plague me with it now. We have to get down the mountain before dark, before the melting snow refreezes. Believe me, you'll have enough to do just keeping the other two horses moving."

When they started out a few minutes later, she understood what he meant.

The pace was agonizingly slow, the horses laboring, struggling to force their way through the deep drifts. It was worse for Robert than for her. Caird's legs gave way three times in the first four hours, and it was a Herculean task to get him moving again. Robert tugged, cursed, and pleaded, and through sheer force of will managed to keep the horse going.

The third time she reined in to wait for him, he turned on her in exasperation. "Why the devil are you stopping? Your sitting there biting your lip is not going to help me. Keep on going, and don't look back."

"I can't do that. Anything could happen." She suddenly burst out, "Caird's not overly bright. What if he suddenly shied while you were pulling him and knocked you off the trail?"

"He's not going to shy. He's barely able to struggle through these drifts." He studied her distraught expression and then smiled with surprising gentleness. "And we can do anything we want to do. It's just a question of in what order we decide to do things. We're going to get off this mountain, Kate."

Strength and purpose showed in every line and muscle of his body as he got Caird back on his feet. He was covered from head to toe with snow, his dark hair was rumpled, and his temper was not at its best, but all of that didn't matter. He was magnificent, spreading his wings over Caird, over her, and she suddenly felt again that wonderful golden sense of security.

She loved him.

The knowledge came out of nowhere, stunning her. She should have known before. All the signs were there for her to see. From that first moment she had wanted to come closer, learn all his secrets, be part of him.

But she could never really be part of him. There could be no life for her with Robert. He had made that clear. The pain that surged through her at the thought was almost too intense to bear. It wasn't fair. She had never had anyone to care about. She *deserved* someone to love.

But who said life was fair? she thought dully. Their situation had not changed because she had experienced this revelation that had shaken her to the core. If she loved him, she would just have to get over it. She had been more wise than she knew to tell him she would distance herself. She had survived Sebastian, and she could survive this too.

She turned in the saddle and resumed her own struggle to get down the mountain.

She almost ran into Gavin as she rounded a curve in the trail.

A smile of joy lit his face. "Kate! I was afraid—" He stopped, his anxious gaze going beyond her to Robert's horse with its empty saddle. "Where's Robert?"

"Behind me. Just around the turn." Robert had said Gavin would probably be safe, but she had not realized until this minute the nagging anxiety that had plagued her about him. She smiled. "You had no trouble making it down?"

"Aye, but I ran out of the storm within an hour after it hit. It's dry as a bone in the foothills."

"If we ever get there," Robert muttered as he rounded the curve. "Which we'll never do if you continue to stand there chatting."

"I'm not only chatting," Gavin protested. Mischief suddenly glinted in his eyes. "I'm storing up the sight of you. What an amusing vision you are, covered in snow, playing nursemaid to that nag. It's going to make a fine tale when we get to Craighdhu."

"And I'm sure you'll make the most of it." He gazed searchingly at Gavin. "You're well?"

The unspoken bond of affection shimmered between them, its strength almost visible to Kate in that moment.

"Aye," Gavin said quietly. Then he smiled again.

"Without the burden of protecting you weighing me down, I fairly flew down the mountain."

"Then turn around and fly back down again," Robert said as he turned and began tugging on Caird's lead rope. "And take Kate with you. Make camp as soon as you reach the foothills. I expect a warm fire and hot food when I finally get this equine misery out of this snow."

"You'll have it." Gavin took Robert's horse lead from Kate. "Come on, Kate. I know it's very entertaining to watch the man flounder, but we must take pity on his humiliation and let him suffer alone."

"Thank you," Robert said. "Your kindness is overwhelming."

She didn't want to leave him. Even though Gavin and Robert seemed to think the danger was over, it was still very real to her.

"Go," said Robert, his gaze on her face. "You can't help, and I'll move faster if I don't have you to worry about."

She wanted him to move fast, she wanted him off this hellish mountain. She tore her gaze from him and nudged Rachel forward, trying not to let him see her fear. "Very well, but see that you don't dally. I want you down before dark, or we'll eat without you."

She heard his surprised chuckle behind her. "Caird and I will most certainly endeavor not to 'dally.' "

Darkness had wreathed the foothills for more than two hours, and Kate was almost ill with worry when she and Gavin caught sight of Robert stumbling down the trail toward the campfire. She could not tell who was staggering more, Caird or Robert.

She jumped to her feet and ran toward him. She was barely aware of Gavin taking Caird's lead as she pulled Robert toward the fire. "You're late." Her voice was shaking, and she was forced to steady it. "Your food is cold, but I might be persuaded to heat it for you."

"Never mind. Too tired to eat . . ." He sank down before the fire and held out his hands. "That feels good." He closed his eyes, his expression blissfully sensual. "I didn't think I'd ever feel warm again."

Alarm tore through her. "You're not frostbitten?"

He shook his head. "Just cold. Come here."

She fell to her knees beside him. He lay down on the blanket and drew her into his arms. "Warm . . ."

She nestled closer, sharing that warmth, her arms closing protectively around him. "You should eat."

He was already asleep.

He was wet, hard, and cold, as uncomfortable as granite ice against her. He would probably not even know if she moved to her own blankets across the fire.

She did not want to move. For the first time he had reached out to her not in passion but in need. Her arms tightened possessively about him. It would do no harm to meet that need.

After all, it was almost over.

She awoke in the night to feel him aroused, boldly hard against her, his hands fumbling with the buttons of her gown. Pleasure, she thought drowsily, pleasure coming . . . She instinctively moved to help him and then stopped in midmotion. "No," she whispered.

"Why not?"

Because comfort was safe, but pleasure was dangerous. She shook her head to clear it of sleep. Dear heavens, she did not want this confrontation now. "You're tired. . . ."

"But I'm not dead." His hand cupped her breast. "And I'm beginning to think I'd have to be a corpse not to want this from you."

Her breast was swelling in his grasp. She cast a desperate glance at Gavin slumbering across the fire. "Gavin."

"He's asleep," he muttered. His mouth closed on her nipple.

She clenched when a bolt of heat tingled between her thighs as he began to suck. "He'll wake up."

"We'd never know." His hand moved down to cup between her legs, rubbing, pressing, exploring. "He'll pretend he's still asleep."

"I'd know," she gasped. He was ignoring her protests, and in a moment she would be swept away. "No!" She rolled away and sat up. She began buttoning her gown with shaky fingers. "Not anymore."

"Why the hell not?" His gaze narrowed on her face. "This isn't about Gavin."

She swallowed. "I told you, it's not wise."

He muttered a curse. "I *want* this. I will hear no more about bells and such nonsense."

Sweet Lord, she wanted it too. "I will not speak it. It just won't happen." She hurriedly moved to the other side of the fire before she could change her mind.

"The devil it won't." He lay there, glaring at her, aroused, angry, his eyes glittering in the firelight. "Very well. I'll accede to this idiocy until we get to Craighdhu. It would distress Gavin to see you struggle." He added silkily, "And shame you to have him see how easily you can be persuaded. But only until we reach Craighdhu, Kate."

She shook her head without speaking.

"You will have me," he said between his teeth. "By God, you *will*."

She closed her eyes so that she would not see his expression. It did little good. She still felt the force of his will touching her, stroking her like a silken whip. She was acutely aware of the aching emptiness between her thighs. She wanted to go back into his arms and unbutton her dress and—

Gavin cleared his throat. "I think I should inform you that I'm awake."

"Then go back to sleep," Robert said curtly.

"It's difficult to do when the conversation is so interesting. And, incidentally, you were wrong. I felt obligated to warn you that you had a listener in case Kate might suffer some later embarrassment."

Kate kept her eyes shut and made no answer. Her emotions were in too much tumult for her to feel shame that Gavin had been witness to their intimacy.

She heard Robert's annoyed exclamation and then the sound of motion. She realized to her relief that he must be turning his back to her. If she opened her eyes now, she would not see that compelling stare holding her own, drawing her toward him.

It was the right thing to do, she told herself desperately. No matter how much her body denied the fact, her rejection was the right thing to do.

Now, it was truly over.

"Should I have kept my mouth shut and pretended not to hear last night?" Gavin asked, his gaze on Robert, who was riding ahead along the shore. "I thought it for the best. At times my humor is a trifle twisted, but I would not purposely cause you pain."

"You didn't cause me pain."

His lips tightened. "But Robert did." He was silent a moment before asking awkwardly, "In the cave . . . did he force you?"

"No."

Relief lightened his expression. "I didn't think he would, but I wasn't sure. I've never seen him as he is with you." He paused. "At first, I thought it might be better if you did couple with him, but you're right to refuse him. He will only hurt you."

He had already hurt her, she thought dully. Just being near him hurt her.

Gavin went on haltingly, "It is Craighdhu, you see. He's a fair man, and he would not mean to cause you unhappiness, but Craighdhu is everything."

"Do you think I don't know that?"

"Perhaps not everything. Did he tell you of his time in Spain?"

"Yes."

"Not much, I'll wager. He doesn't talk of that time."

"He told me how he got the scars on his back." Her lips tightened. "Perhaps I'm fortunate not to have known my mother."

"Mothers can be amazing and wonderful creatures. Mine was." He wrinkled his nose. "Doña Marguerita was amazing but never wonderful. I was only a lad of four years when she took Robert away, but my memories of her were not pleasant."

"Robert said she was beautiful."

"Quite perfect, but so hard and stern, she reminded me of the barrens. If she was warm, it was only to her God. Robert wasn't at all like her. He was wild and full of mischief, and he laughed—except when he was with her. He was different when he came back."

"He was older."

Gavin shook his head. "They changed him. Not the way they wanted to, but he wasn't the same. For a while he was like a wild animal, not trusting any of us, watching the horizon for anyone who might come to take him away." He turned to look at her. "Most of his wariness is gone now, but I believe his vigilance will last forever. No one will ever again be allowed to take him from Craighdhu or Craighdhu from him."

"Why are you telling me this?"

"Because I love him," he said simply. "And I like you. I want you to understand why you must never come too close to him. I would not have you hurt."

"You need not worry. What was between us is over."

He shook his head. "It did not seem so last night."

"It is over," she said determinedly. "And will stay so. I cannot—"

"By all that's holy!" Gavin's exclamation brought

her gaze flying to his face, but he was no longer looking at her.

Her gaze followed his, and her eyes widened in surprise.

A troop of horsemen were riding toward them along the shore. There were ten or twelve in the party, and they were coming fast.

"You know them?"

"My dear cousin Alec," Robert said grimly as he rode back toward them. "Be ready, Gavin." He turned to Kate and said rapidly, "If there's trouble, *any* trouble, run. Don't stop for that damn horse, don't stop for anything. You'll come to a MacDarren croft a day's ride north from here. Tell them who you are, and they'll give you protection." He turned his horse and galloped forward to meet the oncoming band of men.

Alec. Sir Alec Malcolm of Kilgranne. As she and Gavin moved more slowly after Robert, Kate tried to remember what she had heard about the man who was causing this sudden bristling tension. Something about greed and danger . . .

The man who reined up before Robert was tall, well muscled, with a fine figure, and looked to be in his early forties. His hair might once have been blond, but was now a pale brown streaked liberally with gray. She could not tell the color of his eyes from this distance, but they were pale beneath well-shaped brows. His features could not have been described as comely, but they were very strong, and his cheeks were ruddy.

He smiled. "Good day, Robert. I heard rumors you'd been taken by the English."

"You were devastated, I'm sure." Robert smiled with equal politeness. "Were you coming to rescue me? This troop is a trifle small to take on Her Majesty."

Alec laughed. "Very funny." He genuinely seemed to think the idea amusing. "I believe your Jock may be planning to do that very thing. I thought such action a bit absurd when we didn't even know whether your capture was truth or rumor. You know what a peace-loving man I am."

"Of course I do. And I know how fond you are of me."

"Are we not kin? And see, I was right, the story that you'd been taken to the Tower was pure fabrication."

"So you traveled all this way to welcome, not to rescue me? I'm truly touched."

"I would have been delighted to welcome you, but this is purely an accidental meeting. I'm on my way to Edinburgh. James has sent for me on some trifling matter or other."

"I know how he values your opinion."

He made a face. "Too much at times. I do not look forward to this trip through the mountains in winter." His gaze went beyond Robert to Gavin and Kate. "Good day, Gavin. It's been a long time."

Gavin nodded. "How is Duncan?"

"Well."

Gavin hesitated, then asked, "And Jean?"

"As bonnie as ever. I took her to Edinburgh last year, and she was very well received. I've had a dozen offers for her." His glance wandered to Kate. "And here's another bonnie lady. Yours, Gavin?"

"Mine," Robert said. "My wife, Kate."

Alec Malcolm's gaze immediately shifted back to Kate with new interest. "And you weren't going to introduce me? How rude, Robert. You must tell me all about the match. Where did you find this treasure?"

"England."

"So you were in England. You see how these rumors start?" He chuckled as he snapped his fingers. "Bridal bower. Tower. They sound alike, but one signifies a beginning and the other an end." He rode forward and stopped before Kate. "Permit me to introduce myself, since Robert has forgotten his manners. I'm Sir Alec Malcolm." He took Kate's hand and lifted it to his lips. "We're neighbors, and I'm sure we will be very close friends." He met her gaze. "Extremely close."

Kate was vaguely aware of Gavin moving protectively nearer but was too occupied in absorbing impressions of Alec Malcolm to grasp the significance. His eyes were a cool blue, she saw now, his manner forceful but not unpleasant. He exuded vigor, dominance, and a cheerful charm. "I've heard Robert speak of you," she said noncommittally.

He laughed. "I'm sure you have. I've always endeavored to be interesting enough to be the subject of conversation."

He was still holding her hand, and she withdrew it. "I assure you I found it very interesting."

"But I know nothing about you. When I return, I will pay Craighdhu a visit, and you must prove equally informative. I have an uncommon thirst for knowledge." He glanced over his shoulder. "Robert will tell you."

"You have an uncommon thirst for many things," Robert said without expression. "And we're keeping you from one of them. I know how impatient James will be to see you. We'll bid you good day."

Alec nodded cheerfully. "You're right, I mustn't tarry even in such engaging company." He bowed to Kate. "I can't tell you of my delight that Robert has taken a wife. I'll look forward to seeing more of you."

"How kind of you," she said quietly.

Alec nodded at Robert and Gavin, then raised his gloved hand and motioned his men forward. A few minutes later they were a quarter of a mile down the trail.

Gavin expelled his breath in explosive relief.

"He's not what I expected." Kate's gaze followed them. "He was actually quite pleasant."

"Oh, he can be very pleasant," Robert said. "His smile is sweetest when he's cutting a throat or raping a child."

She turned to look at him. "He's that evil?"

"He doesn't think it's evil. He has no concept of right or wrong. If he wants to do it, he does it. That makes it right."

"And James likes him?"

Robert shrugged. "James is not without vices of his own, and Alec panders to them. He's clever enough to mask his more heinous villainies before the court. I understand he's thought to be very charming." Robert looked at her. "But I'd advise you not to become better acquainted with my cousin."

She shivered. "I have no intention of doing so. Will he truly come to Craighdhu?"

"If it suits his mood." He turned his horse. "But you have nothing to worry about. You'll be safe. No one can breach Craighdhu's defenses." He gave her a level glance over his shoulder. "You may not even see him. I intend to keep you too busy in the bedchamber to entertain guests in the hall."

Anger flared through her. It was an unnecessarily intimate remark in front of Gavin. However, when she shot Gavin a glance, she found him gazing with a frown after Alec Malcolm.

"No," Robert said firmly, turning to Gavin. "Don't even think about it, Gavin."

Kate suddenly realized that Robert's intimate remark had been spoken absentmindedly, and his impatience and intensity were directed entirely toward Gavin at this moment.

Gavin didn't look at him. "I know your views on the subject."

"But I notice you don't promise to adhere to them."

"I . . . can't, Robert," Gavin said, troubled.

"You'll get yourself gutted," Robert said with more violence than she had ever heard from him. "And, by God, you'll deserve it."

Gavin shook his head as he watched Malcolm disappear from view. Then he turned his horse and kicked him into a headlong gallop.

"What's wrong?" Kate asked as she watched him fly ahead of them down the trail.

"*Damn* him."

"Tell me why he's upset."

"Ask him yourself. I can't even talk about his madness without blaspheming." He put spurs to his horse and rode after Gavin. "The damn lunatic."

8

She had no opportunity to ask Gavin anything for the
rest of the day. Instead of staying by her side as he usually did when on the trail, he led the pace. It was not
until they were making camp that evening that she was
able to speak to him.

She knelt beside him as he was laying wood for the
fire. "May I help?"

"To lay the fire? Or," he added ruefully as he
glanced at Robert, who was watering the horses several
yards away, "to save me from Robert's wrath?"

"Either." She began to encircle the wood with the
stones he had gathered. In the past weeks she had become closer to Gavin than anyone in her life except
Robert, and yet it was still difficult for her to intrude
on his privacy in an intimate manner. It was an indica-
tion of how much she had changed that she could do
it at all. She kept her gaze on her work as she said awkwardly, "I've never had any friends but Carolyn, but I
have a true fondness for you, Gavin. It makes me . . . I
do not like to see you unhappy."

"I don't like being unhappy. It's not my nature. It
shouldn't be anyone's nature," he said wistfully.
"Wouldn't it be a wonderful world if we just let every-

one find their own happiness, without interference or censure?"

"A fine world," she agreed gently.

"But it doesn't happen that way." He struck flint to the kindling. "So we must attempt to find our way around the obstacles."

"What obstacles?" She added quickly, "If you wish to tell me. This isn't curiosity, Gavin. I truly wish to help."

"I know." The kindling caught, and he fanned it to life. "It's Jean, Alec's daughter. I'm going to wed her."

She tried to remember Malcolm's reference to his daughter. "And Malcolm does not know this?"

He made a face. "Alec would string me on the rack in his dungeon and break every bone in my body if he even suspected I was going to take Jeanie. He has plans for her that don't include a landless henchman who serves his enemy."

She was beginning to understand Robert's frustration and concern. If Malcolm was as ruthless as she had been told, this involvement could be deadly for Gavin. "You've been away. You could not have seen her for a long time," she said gently. "Perhaps your feelings have changed."

"Some things don't change. I knew the first time I saw her at the gathering at Kilfirth. I was only a lad of fifteen and she was four years younger, but it made no difference. We belonged." He added more wood to the fire. "We still belong."

"What are you going to do?"

"Take her from Malcolm. Wed her. Love her." He smiled. "It's very simple, really."

"If you aren't killed while doing it."

"Oh, yes, there's always that problem. That was one of the reasons I went to sea with Robert. I'm not a great warrior, you see. I thought there were things I should learn to protect my Jeanie." He added, "And I'll need my share of the booty when I have to leave Craighdhu."

She looked at him in bewilderment. She knew he loved Craighdhu almost as much as Robert did. "Why would you leave Craighdhu?"

"Jeanie. I couldn't expect Robert to harbor her when Alec comes after her. It would give Malcolm the excuse he's been seeking to try to take Craighdhu."

And Craighdhu must always come first with Robert, she thought sadly. "Have you talked to Robert?"

He nodded. "He says I'm a madman to give up everything for a woman." He straightened his shoulders as if shrugging off a burden. "But maybe madmen are more content than sane ones. What do you think, Kate?"

She thought she was frightened and sad and a little angry at this woman who would cause Gavin to risk so much. "I think you should ponder this decision very carefully."

"I have no intention of running straight to Jeanie the minute Alec's back is turned." His face lit with an impish smile. "I'll wait, at least until he's in Edinburgh and harder to reach by messenger." His smile faded as he reached out and gently touched her cheek. "Stop frowning. All will be well."

"When you have to leave the home you love?"

He shrugged and got to his feet. "It's a choice I had to make. I can do nothing else."

Craighdhu.

The island lay fifteen miles from shore, looming ghostlike in the gray-green sea, its mountains wreathed with swirling mists and clouds. The castle on the north side of Craighdhu looked as wild and dark as the mountains themselves, as if it had been hammered by the winds and sea until it seemed to have been wrought not by man but by Nature.

"Merciful God, no!" murmured Kate, stricken.

"I told you it wasn't pretty." Robert's tone was sharp as he saw her expression. "But I didn't expect you to hate it this much."

"No, it's not pretty," she said dully.

"Well, you'll have to put up with it for only a year." He got down from his horse and moved to the large raft tied to the pier. "Help her dismount, Gavin."

She was barely aware of Gavin lifting her to the ground.

Some things are meant to be, Gavin had said, but surely this cruel jest was not fashioned by the hand of God. She had accepted that she was not to have Robert because of his idiotic misconception of her importance, but this new loss was too much to bear.

Craighdhu. Her own special place. Home.

"Jock's not going to be pleased with either of us," Gavin said as he dipped his pole into the water. "What do you say we go back to Edinburgh, Robert?"

Robert grinned and shook his head. "Better to face him now than give him a chance to brood about it."

Jock. Kate vaguely remembered Gavin talking about a Jock Candaron, who seemed to occupy a position of some authority on Craighdhu, but surely his consequence was minimal in comparison to Robert's. This sudden concern from both the laird of Craighdhu and his henchman was puzzling.

"Why should you have to worry about his displeasure?"

Robert and Gavin exchanged glances, and they both grimaced.

"Jock makes sure he's the subject of concern of everyone around him," Robert said. His gaze shifted to the shore. "I think I see him on the dock."

"We can still turn around," Gavin suggested gloomily.

Kate could see three ships anchored at the dock, one galley and two large caravels, but the figures on the dock were indistinguishable to her from this distance. "How did he know we were coming?" she asked.

"Edinburgh can be very pleasant this time of year," Gavin said.

Robert answered Kate. "There's always a watch on the harbor. The word would have gone to the castle the moment we stepped on the raft."

"I believe Angus urgently needs my company. Would you not like to go reiving, Robert?" Gavin asked wistfully.

Robert turned and said, "I'll send you wherever you like, if you promise to stay away from Malcolm."

Gavin shook his head. "You know I cannot do that." He smiled with effort. "And you're right, we mustn't let Jock brood."

Jock Candaron was standing on the dock waiting for them when the raft reached the island.

He was close to his fortieth year, but the only signs of age were the faint creases at the corners of his eyes. He was a giant of a man with a deep chest, arms corded with muscle, and legs as thick as tree trunks. His hair, tied back in a queue that hung halfway down his back, shone white-gold in the pale winter sunlight. His cloak was thrown open as if he did not feel the chill wind that was causing the men behind him to stamp their feet and blow on their hands. He reminded Kate of one of those wild, strong Viking raiders her tutor had told her stories about.

"It's about time you came home," he said. Then he motioned to two men standing behind him and ordered, "Take the horses. We'll walk back through the town. They'll want to see him." He turned back to Robert. "You could have sent word, dammit. Your ship arrived two months ago with news you'd decided to stop over in Edinburgh, and then we received word from MacGrath you'd been taken by the English."

"It was true."

Jock scowled. "You must have been careless. Have I taught you no better?"

Robert laughed and clapped him on the shoulder. "I stand chastised."

"It was my fault," Gavin said. "I took a sword thrust."

Jock turned to him. "Not serious?"

Gavin shook his head.

"You're entirely well?"

Gavin nodded.

"Good." Jock's huge fist lashed out and connected with Gavin's stomach.

Gavin fell to his knees, gasping for air.

"You failed your duty," Jock said without expression. "You should have kept him safe."

Gavin clutched his stomach. "Dammit, Jock, you didn't have to hit so hard."

"A weak blow would not be remembered." Jock reached out and pulled him to his feet. "You deserved it."

"I know," Gavin wheezed. "But I think you broke my rib."

Jock smiled faintly. "You would be certain if I had. I was careful."

"No more, Jock," Robert said. "He served me well."

"So I heard from your crew. That's why I didn't break all his ribs." He shrugged. "It had to be done. Now it's over."

"Thank God," Gavin breathed. A warm smile lit his face. "How have you been, Jock?"

"Doing my duty to Craighdhu, as you should have been."

Kate gazed at them in bewilderment. It was clear a strong bond of affection existed between Jock Candaron and Gavin, and yet it seemed impossible her friend would accept that punishment without even a hint of bad feeling.

Robert turned and helped Kate onto the dock. "This is my wife, Kate, Jock."

Jock did not change his expression, but she could sense an almost imperceptible stiffening. He bowed formally. "Welcome to Craighdhu, my lady," he said without taking his gaze from her face. His eyes were Nordic blue and cool as the sea lapping against the dock. "A surprise, Robert. Where did you find her?"

"England."

Jock shrugged his massive shoulders. "A foreigner. I suppose England is better than Spain. I would have preferred you to choose one of our lasses, but when did you ever listen to me?"

"When you gave me a blow as you just did Gavin." Robert laughed. "She's a brave honest lass. She'll give us no trouble, and I expect you to protect her as you would me." He kissed Kate's palm lightly before turning away and starting down the dock. "Bring her along, Gavin. I'll go ahead with Jock so he can tell me all the news."

"If I can still walk," Gavin muttered as he took Kate's elbow and escorted her after Jock and Robert.

"The news isn't good," Jock said.

"I didn't expect it to be," Robert assured him. "Alec was much too self-satisfied when we ran into him two days ago on his way to Edinburgh."

"He has a right to be," Jock said. "I wasn't sorry to hear James had sent for him. We need time to mend bridges."

"While he may be preparing to tear down others." Robert frowned. "Send a messenger to Bobby MacGrath in Edinburgh right away. I want to know what Alec's movements are while he's there and why James sent for him."

Jock nodded. "It never hurts to keep an eye on the devil. However, your concern should be centered here, not in Edinburgh. You're not going to like Alec's latest . . ."

Jock's words became inaudible to Kate as he and Robert drew farther ahead. She turned to Gavin. "Did he hurt you?"

"Aye, but it could have been worse. If Robert had been wounded, instead of me, I wouldn't have been able to get out of bed for a week."

She shivered. "He's brutal."

Gavin shook his head. "Just. I failed my duty, and that's not permitted."

"Who is he? Another cousin?"

He shook his head. "He came to Craighdhu when Robert and I were children. Robert's father took him in, and he became one of us."

"An outsider?"

"He earned his place. Even as a young boy he had the makings of a superb warrior, and he became Robert's father's henchman. When Robert's father died and his mother took him to Spain, the clan appointed Jock acting head of the clan until Robert returned."

"And he didn't mind giving up his power when Robert returned?"

He shrugged. "He didn't seem to, but who can tell what Jock is thinking? He's not easy to read."

She believed him. She had not been able to detect anything beneath that impassive exterior and those icy blue eyes.

"Anyway, he immediately stepped down and began to train Robert in what he should know." He made a face. "He wasn't always an easy taskmaster, but Robert learned."

"And did you?"

"I had no talent for weapons, but he taught me to defend myself."

"Does he still live at the castle?" she asked, her eyes on that stronghold in the distance.

"No, both he and I have our own lodgings here in town. Jock prefers to stay in his unless Robert is gone for an extended period."

Relief surged through her. She could not imagine living harmoniously with Jock Candaron. "Who is this Bobby MacGrath in Edinburgh Robert was talking about?"

"When Robert and James had words three years ago, Robert sent one of our lads to Edinburgh to live so that he would have a man in the enemy camp and know what James was about." His gaze shifted to the pair walking ahead of them, and he gave a low whistle. "Evidently, Jock wasn't exaggerating the trouble Malcolm's been concocting."

She looked at Robert and saw that he was frowning. He was obviously displeased at something Jock was telling him. "The town appears very peaceful. What trouble could there be?"

"Plenty. There's always trouble with Malcolm about. It's just a question of where and on what scale."

She didn't want to think of Malcolm or this brutal Jock or anything but Craighdhu itself. She wanted to see it, smell it, touch it. She hungrily absorbed it all as if she had been starved all her life for the sight of it.

Warehouses, taverns, and small shops had formed a neat crescent around the harbor, but once they turned the corner, all sense of orderliness vanished. The town was built on three low hills, and thatched sod houses and shops clung precariously to the steep slopes. Yet, even though the impression was of an erratic, rambling landscape, she did not find it displeasing. The shop- and stall-bordered cobblestone street on which they were walking appeared to be the main thoroughfare and led to the castle.

"It's very clean." She sniffed. Not even the foul stench that usually pervaded a village. It was as if the blustery sea winds had scoured and buffed Craighdhu to pristine cleanliness. "It even smells pleasant."

"Jock has a sensitive nose and a profound dislike for disorder. When he was acting in Robert's stead, he passed a law that no chamber pots were to be emptied in the street. Twice a week a wagon is sent around to collect foul matter, and there are penalties for anyone who doesn't keep his property immaculate."

She wondered why no one had thought to do the same in Sheffield. Heaven knows, it smelled far sweeter here than the village where she had lived all her life.

The street was crowded with men, women, and children, all of whom were laughing, talking. Jock had said the people would want to see Robert, but they wanted more. They reached out and touched him in affection and greeting. It was not the return of a feudal lord, but the homecoming of a family head.

Kate felt alone, the outsider, as she watched. "They love him."

"Aye, as much as he'll let them."

She turned to look at him.

"He gives them everything, food, riches, safety. . . ."

"But not himself?"

He nodded. "Sometimes I think he's lonely, that he wishes he were different, but he cannot be. They changed him."

She would *not* feel sorry for Robert. He had everything she wanted, and if he was foolish enough not to be satisfied, then he deserved this loneliness. She changed the subject. "Why do some of the men wear those short skirts?"

Gavin looked outraged. "Not skirts, kilts. And they're short because we Highlanders are not afraid of a little weather or rough country, as Sassenachs are."

"Angus didn't wear them."

"He's a Lowlander and has been corrupted by the easiness of the life."

She had evidently struck a sensitive subject, and his defensiveness amused her. "Neither do you and Robert." She smiled teasingly. "Have you also been corrupted?"

"Robert says it's better to blend into the crowd when you're in enemy territory."

She took another look at the short green, purple, and dark blue plaid kilts that a good portion of the men wore. "Well, you certainly would not go unnoticed in that garment." Seeing him start to frown, she gestured to the small, beautiful church they were passing. It was like a finely polished gem set in the busy square. "Robert said his mother was very devout. Was that her church?"

"No, she had her own chapel at the castle. She would have nothing to do with our religion or the dominie."

"When will I meet this dominie?"

He caught the wary note in her voice and understood immediately. "All men of the cloth are not like your vicar, Kate. This dominie is a kind, gentle man who does much good in the parish. You'll seldom find him in that fine church. He travels from place to place both here and on the mainland comforting the sick, performing marriages, and baptizing the children of the clan."

A few minutes later they were starting across the castle moat when Kate suddenly chuckled. "Was this where Robert threw you into the water because you played the bagpipes?" she asked, remembering Robert and Gavin's badinage.

"He was most unfair. I wasn't that bad. Well, maybe I was, but it was the ale that made me so."

They shared so many memories, she thought wistfully, experiences that wove their lives together in a common tapestry. Even wild, brutal Jock Candaron had his own place in Robert's life.

They had entered the courtyard of the castle, which was as clean and neat as the village. The flagstones were damp and gleaming and looked as if they had been scrubbed only minutes before.

"Jock Candaron again?" she asked.

Gavin shook his head. "This is Deirdre's domain. Jock wouldn't interfere."

She couldn't imagine Candaron not interfering with anyone or anything that suited him. "Deirdre?"

"Robert's housekeeper." He opened the tall brass-studded front door. "Deirdre O'Connell. Jock brought her to Craighdhu six years ago from Ireland after he killed her husband."

"What?" she asked, shocked.

"Oh, it's all right. She didn't mind."

"How fortunate," she said dryly. "I thought it was only acceptable to kill English or Spanish."

"Well, Deirdre's husband was an exception." He closed the door, and his shout echoed off the high-arched ceilings of the hall. "Deirdre!"

"I'm coming. You don't have to bellow like a bull." Kate looked at the direction the voice had come from and saw, at the curve of the stairwell, a tall, strongly built woman in a gray gown. "I have enough to do without running when you raise your voice, Gavin Gordon."

"Sorry," Gavin said meekly as he took Kate's arm and pulled her forward. "I just wanted to introduce you to Robert's bride."

"I'm not so lacking in courtesy I wasn't coming to greet her," Deirdre O'Connell said as she marched down the steps. She was not a woman in her first youth, but she exuded a vitality that was almost overwhelming. A few threads of gray already streaked the shiny black hair drawn back in a bun, but she had firm, glowing skin and sparkling hazel eyes.

She reached the bottom of the stairs and sketched a quick courtesy to Kate. "Welcome to Craighdhu, my lady. We weren't expecting you."

"I wasn't expecting to be here," Kate said.

"Robert and Jock are in the library with Tim MacDougal. I'll show you to your chamber." She turned to Gavin and commanded, "Come with us."

"I had every intention of doing so." Gavin followed them up the stairs. "You take a bit of getting used to, and I didn't want Kate running through the town screaming for help."

"I'm not as bad as you would have her believe," Deirdre said as she led them down a long hall. "I have no use for fools, but I don't devour children like her without cause."

"But she might give you cause. Kate has teeth, and she's not above using them."

Deirdre glanced over her shoulder and gave Kate an appraising glance. "I would not have guessed it." She opened the door. "This is your chamber. Robert's is next door."

Kate stood still in the doorway. This chamber was to be hers. It did not seem possible. It was the finest chamber she had ever seen, much finer even than the rooms at Tabord's inn. A fine ivory, rose, and green carpet covered the stone floor, and real velvet curtains of the same dark green enclosed the four-poster bed. The huge fireplace on the south wall was crafted of gleaming gray limestone that contrasted with the muted rose, green, and brown colors of the ancient tapestry that was mounted on the wall above it. The tapestry depicted lions and unicorns and a bare-chested man in a MacDarren kilt slaying a man in full armor.

"If someone had been kind enough to let me know, you would not find me so unprepared." Deirdre swept across the room to the windows and threw them wide open. "I had no chance to air it, but there's a fine breeze today, and it will smell fresh in an hour or so."

Gavin shivered as a gust blew into the chamber. "If she doesn't freeze to death first."

"Which won't happen if you'd stop complaining and build her a fire." Deirdre turned to Kate. "There's a fine view from here."

Kate slowly walked to the deeply recessed windows. The panes, made of stained glass which she'd never seen except in a church, were exquisite. Depicted on one window was a kilted warrior kneeling before a unicorn; on the other was a woman in a red gown weaving at a loom. The sun sparkling on the multihued glass made the figures seem to shimmer with life.

"Well?" Deirdre demanded.

Kate hurriedly glanced at the view Deirdre had summoned her to see.

Far below she could see a swath of green that stretched alongside the castle. To the north was the rocky coastline she had seen from the mainland. Rough waves crashed against dark rocks that looked as stark and dangerous as the waves themselves.

"It's beautiful," she whispered.

"You find it so?" Deirdre asked curiously. "I was wondering if you'd like it. It's not a sight to everyone's taste."

"Not everyone has a fondness for all that tame greenery you Irish call home," Gavin said as he struggled to light the fire in the hearth. "Some us have a liking for more interesting scenery."

Deirdre snorted. "Rocks are all the same, and Craighdhu is but one rock after the other." Another blast of wind shook the curtains around the bed. "Perhaps it is a little chill." She took Kate's arm and led her toward a cushioned chair by the hearth. "Sit here and rest, and I'll bring you up a cup of hot cider." She pushed her down onto the chair and then frowned as she tucked Kate's brown wool cloak more closely about her. "Where did you get this garment? It's so poorly made and the wool so porous, I wonder it keeps out the cold at all." She didn't give Kate a chance to answer. "Gavin, go fetch that coverlet on the bed."

"Fetch and carry, fetch and carry," Gavin grumbled as he rose from the hearth, crossed the room, and brought back a cream-colored wool coverlet that had been tossed on the bottom of the bed. "Anything else?"

"I'll tell you if there is." Deirdre tucked the cover around Kate's shoulders.

The soft coverlet was so finely woven, it instantly

blocked the sharp breeze blowing through the room. Kate's fingers caressed the cloud-soft texture. "It's wonderful. I've never seen anything so fine."

For an instant Deirdre's expression turned mild, and a flush of pleasure colored her cheeks. "No?" Then she straightened, turned away, and moved toward the door. "Of course you haven't. I made it myself."

She was gone before Kate could reply.

"She's not as hard as she seems," Gavin said. "Well, that's not true. She's every bit as hard as she seems, but she's still a good woman. You're fortunate to have her."

"Am I?" Kate asked faintly.

Gavin nodded. "She keeps all the servants jumping, you won't see a speck of dust in any chamber of the castle, and the meals are excellent."

"She's very"—she hesitated, trying to describe that sense of explosive energy that Deirdre exuded— "vigorous."

Gavin nodded ruefully. "She has so much energy, she has to be busy every minute and keeps everyone busy with her."

"Even Robert?"

"At times." Gavin grinned. "For the first year he was ready to slash Jock's gullet for bringing her here, but after that they became more comfortable with each other."

"Does she have children?"

Gavin shook his head. "She's free to devote all her attention to the castle."

Kate wasn't sure she liked the idea of Deirdre's devoted attention. She had hoped to absorb Craighdhu at her own pace, but it appeared Deirdre was a major force here, and her pace was anything but slow.

"You'll become accustomed to her," Gavin assured her. "She's a bit rough, but she means no disrespect. Here in the Highlands servants consider themselves part of the family."

It was not disrespect about which Kate was concerned. Her gaze went back to the windows; Deirdre had not given her time enough to study them. "I've never seen stained-glass windows with anything but religious figures."

"There are windows like that all over the castle. The stained glass was added by Robert's grandfather when he wed. His bride complained how depressing the castle was, and so he brought artists and glassmakers from France to replace the windows. This castle was built to resist siege, and there was little he could do to make it less grim, but he thought the glass would help." Gavin made a face. "Robert's mother found them just as heathen as she did the rest of us."

"Then she's a fool. Nothing that beautiful could be sinful."

"I've always thought that too." Gavin's gaze followed her own to the window. "When I was a boy, I used to stare at those windows until I was well-nigh dazzled by them. I'd pretend I was that warrior with his mighty muscles and his grand sword. . . ." He shook his head. "That might be one of the reasons why I wanted to follow Robert when he went to raid the Spanish. I still saw myself as that warrior. I found out soon enough I didn't have the stomach for it."

"You should not regret finding that out. You're fine the way you are."

He nodded. "I think, when Robert has no more need for me as a henchman, I might become a bard."

"A bard?"

"Aye. A laird usually has a storyteller to tell the tales of the past and present of the clan."

"Aren't such tales usually written down?"

Gavin flinched. "You have no soul. There's no comparison between hearing a great storyteller weave his tales and reading dry parchment."

"I'm sorry," she said solemnly, trying to hide a smile. "I have no experience with bards."

"That's very clear. I'll forgive your ignorance since

you're a stranger here." He smiled eagerly. "I'll even entertain you. Robert is sure to be busy with Jock for a while anyway."

"You're going to tell me a tale?"

"Oh, no, you should be welcomed to Craighdhu in a more splendid fashion." He started to turn away. "I'll go fetch my pipes."

"I've never heard the bagpipes played before," she said cautiously. "Will I enjoy it?"

"Oh, it's a fine, winsome instrument," he answered, beaming. "You'll like it. Trust me."

"Cease." She covered her hands with her ears. "I can bear no more."

Gavin didn't hear her. It was not surprising with that beastly caterwauling erupting from the bags of the instrument he was blowing with such blissful enthusiasm.

She strode forward and jerked the mouthpiece from between his lips. "No, Gavin."

He looked hurt. "But you've not given it a chance, Kate."

"I've listened for over an hour. It's all the chance that instrument of torture will get from me."

He lowered the bagpipes to the chair beside him. "I guess a woman is too gentle-natured to be stirred by the pipes. But I admit to being sorely disappointed in you."

She felt a flicker of remorse. "Perhaps you're right. I'm sure you played very well."

"He played abominably." Robert stood in the doorway. "We never let Gavin pipe when we're going into battle. The troops would exhaust themselves trying to kill him instead of the enemy."

"You malign me," Gavin protested, then changed the subject. "What news from Jock?"

"We leave for Ireland at nightfall."

Gavin pursed his lips in a low whistle. "We just got here. That bad?"

"Worse," he said grimly. "Nine months ago Malcolm appeared at the port near Kilgranne with a ship built especially for cargo. For the past six months he and his men have been going from town to town on the coast trying to frighten the merchants and craftsmen into dealing with him instead of Craighdhu."

"Why didn't Jock take care of it?"

"He would have done so, but he thought reassurance should come from the head of the clan. Me." His lips twisted. "He had no idea Elizabeth would take it into her head to delay my arrival."

"So you must visit the merchants and council members and assure them they needn't fear Malcolm if they continue to deal with us?"

"With all due speed. Malcolm's agent and a troop of men are in Ireland right now. See who you wish to greet and then meet me at the ship in two hours."

Gavin shook his head.

Robert stiffened. "No?"

"I've been away too long. I don't wish to go on another voyage."

"We'll be gone no more than four weeks."

"Take Jock. You know you should have taken him last time."

"I want you."

"Take Jock," Gavin repeated. "Kate needs me here to protect her and tell her the things she must know about Craighdhu." He added lightly, "Perhaps, given time, I can even teach her appreciation for my bagpipes."

"Perhaps I should be the one to go to Ireland," Kate murmured dryly.

Robert met Gavin's gaze. "I could order you to come."

"Don't do that, Robert," Gavin said gently. "It would grieve me to disobey you."

Robert stood looking at him for a moment. "Damn you. You'd better be here when I get back." He turned on his heel. "Come with me to the courtyard, Kate."

She followed him from the chamber and down the winding stone steps. "Four weeks?"

"Do you wish it were more?" he asked caustically. "Ireland is no great distance from Craighdhu, and with good winds I'll be back in your eager arms in no time." He jerked open the heavy brass-studded front door. "So be prepared to give me a warm welcome to your bed."

She shook her head. "I will be glad to see you return safely, but that part of our lives is over."

"Oh, is it?" He turned on her, the suppressed frustration and anger suddenly unleashed. "It's not over until I say it's over. I've given up too much not to reap some benefits from this damn alliance."

"You've given up nothing," she said fiercely. "You have your life and your Craighdhu, and this danger you claim I bring is not even real. Go to Ireland, but don't expect me to give you anything but a smile when you return. Perhaps not even that if you continue to be such an arrogant, stupid coxcomb of a—" She whirled and slammed the door. She marched across the foyer and up the stairs, fighting back the tears that stung her eyes. She should be relieved he was leaving and she'd be spared the battle she had dreaded. By the time he returned, she should know whether or not she was with child and might have even a stronger argument to hold him at bay.

Dear God, she did not want to hold him at bay. She did not want him to go to Ireland, where danger might be lying in wait. She wanted to welcome him to her bed and her heart. She wanted to live in Craighdhu and have his children. She wanted the life she was denied.

"Kate?" Gavin was coming down the stairs toward her.

She quickly wiped her eyes on the back of her hand. "He's gone."

"Jock will take care of him," he said.

"Yes." She swallowed. She was foolish to cry over something she could not have. She must just enjoy what she was given. She smiled tremulously. "I must go to the stable to see that Caird and Rachel are properly cared for, but then will you keep your promise?"

His eyes glinted with mischief. "To teach you to love the bagpipes?"

She flinched. "Heaven forbid. No, to teach me what I should know of Craighdhu."

"What do you wish to learn?"

"Everything." Her smile had a touch of feverish recklessness. "I want to know how to be mistress of this great heap of stone. I want to meet the people. I want to walk the streets and talk to the craftsmen. I want to be *part* of all this."

"You'll expend a great deal of effort for a short return. Wouldn't it be better simply to try to live on the surface for the next year?"

She knew the suggestion was wise, but there was no question of her taking it. These months might be all she would have. "I can't do that," she whispered.

He nodded sadly. "I can see that." He turned to leave. "Give me a short time to refresh myself, and I'll meet you in the courtyard."

"Where are you going?" Deirdre asked as she suddenly appeared around the corner of the stairwell.

Gavin grinned. "I'm going to show Kate a bit of the village before dark. As is natural, she has a curiosity regarding her new home."

"Very natural," Deirdre said. "But you're going about it wrong. You must see and learn everything regarding the castle before going to the village." She frowned. "Gavin really knows nothing of the running of this castle. I shall have to be the one to teach you. By the time Robert returns, you shall be well on the way to being a proper mistress of Craighdhu." She turned to Gavin. "Run along now. I must introduce her to Tim MacDougal, Robert's agent, and then we will tour the castle." She didn't wait for Gavin to obey as she beckoned imperiously to Kate. "If we set about immediately, we shall accomplish much before supper. Afterward you will inspect the servants' quarters and meet with the . . ." Her words became inaudible as she turned a corner.

"I didn't want her to show me the castle," Kate whispered to Gavin. "I wanted you to—"

"No one knows it better," Gavin said uneasily. "Perhaps she's right. It's best you start out on the right foot."

"But not at a dead run. I'd like to go to the village and meet—"

"Ah, there you are." Deirdre had returned and was standing at the end of the hall. "We will never accomplish anything if we dally like this."

Kate instinctively responded to the sternness in the housekeeper's tone and started down the hall. After all, she did want to see every inch of the castle, she told herself. Her journey to the village could wait for a little while.

"I'll come to take you to the village tomorrow morning, Kate," Gavin called after her.

"We shall be much too busy tomorrow," Deirdre answered for Kate as she started down the hall again. "Perhaps in a week."

"A week?" Kate shook her head. "Tomorrow, Gavin."

Gavin gave Deirdre's retreating back a nervous look. "We can try."

God's Blood, he didn't want to leave.

Robert's hands closed tightly on the wooden rail, his gaze on the stone battlements of the castle as the ship drew away from the shore. Since that moment in the cell when he had confronted Elizabeth, events seemed to conspire to leave him with this feeling of helplessness and frustration. Even as a boy in Santanella, he had never been thrown into such emotional turmoil.

"I could have gone alone," Jock said quietly.

Robert unclenched his hands from the rail and turned to look at him. "No, you're right. It's best I go."

"I'm glad you agree," he said. "If you hadn't, I'd have been tempted to knock some sense into you. She has a fine, lovely look about her, but Craighdhu is more important than fornication."

"You don't have to tell me that."

"She seemed a quiet enough lass when I met her at the dock." Jock's lips quirked with amusement. "However, I understand she was less than docile when she bade you good-bye."

Robert should have known Jock would learn about Kate's outburst. Everyone at the castle still gave Jock unlimited loyalty, and nothing happened on Craighdhu without his hearing about it. "Quiet is not how I would describe Kate."

"Good. We had too much silence when your mother was here." Jock glanced back at the castle. "Why did you wed her? Did she have something Craighdhu needed?"

How well Jock knew him. "No."

"Then why?"

"I'll tell you at some later time." He smiled ruefully. "At the moment I have no intention of giving you cause to tell me what a fool I am."

Jock's eyes widened in surprise. "You care about the girl?"

"I did not say that," Robert said quickly.

"You do not have to." Jock's words came as blunt and sharp as hammer blows. "You stare at her as if you would like to devour her, but I thought it only lust. It seems I was—"

"It is lust," Robert interrupted.

"Then your problem is easily solved. You can slake it with one of those comely lasses you found so willing the last time you visited Ireland."

He did not want to bed one of Jock's Irish lasses, comely or not. He wanted Kate, dammit.

Jock shook his head, his eyes narrowed on Robert's face, reading every change of expression. "No? Then it may be worse than I thought. I remember the day your father brought your mother to Craighdhu. He had the same besotted, puppy-dog look you do now."

"I'm not besotted. Leave it, Jock." He turned away. "I'll talk no more of this. Tell me which merchants we will have the most trouble convincing."

"Very well, we'll not talk of it." Jock paused and then said softly, "But I should give you warning. I'll not fail again."

"Fail?" Robert smiled. "You never fail at anything, Jock."

"I failed once. When I let them take you to Spain. After your father died, my duty was to you. I should have kept you here."

The words came as a shock. Jock had never spoken of that night since he had returned to Craighdhu. "I've never blamed you. She was my mother and Don Diego my uncle. There was nothing you could do."

"I could have stopped her." Jock shifted to meet his glance with glacier coldness. "As I would stop her now. With a dagger in her heart."

"A woman?"

"A woman or a man, it makes no difference." Jock smiled mockingly. "No, a woman is worse. You think they are no threat with their beauty and softness and let them curl close to your breast, under your armor." He shrugged. "You have no defense when they sting you."

"Kate has no intention of stinging me."

"That is good. For I'll not let another woman hurt either Craighdhu or you again." Before Robert could reply, Jock changed the subject and answered Robert's question regarding the situation in Ireland. "Shaughnessy is the most frightened. He sent word that he would no longer supply us with goods. Reardon is uneasy, but more prone to fight Malcolm than surrender. Kenneth O'Toole is wavering in our direction, but he'll need . . ."

9

"*Come quick, we must* leave at once." Kate grabbed
Gavin's arm. "Deirdre's in the scullery inspecting the
pots and pans. If we hurry, we can—"

"I thought perhaps you'd locked her in the stable.
You seemed a trifle annoyed when she wouldn't let you
leave yesterday morning."

"It's been three days, and I've seen nothing but
stone walls and stables and sculleries and—" She cast
an anxious glance over her shoulder. "Come on!"

Gavin started to chuckle as he allowed himself to
be propelled toward the door. "What if she catches us?
Will we be set to scouring the pots?"

"Worse. She'll find something else it's my duty to
do. I spent the entire afternoon yesterday going over
last month's accounts. She had poor Timothy
MacDougal explain every sum he spent down to the
last pence."

"It all sounds very laudable."

"Oh, yes, very laudable," Kate said with exasperation. "Everything she does is laudable. She's firm but
kind to the servants. She's canny and works harder than
anyone I've ever seen. She clearly wishes only the best
for Robert and Craighdhu and labors from dawn to
dark to see that all is well." She threw open the door

with barely contained violence. "She's about to drive me *mad*."

"Robert had a similar response when she first came here."

"It could not be as bad. She's like a river that sweeps everything in its path to the sea. She keeps me moving from task to task until I'm too weary to think."

"You're not so meek you could not refuse. Why have you let her rule you in this?"

She scowled. "I don't know. It's something about her that— She's always so sure she's right that she makes me believe I'm foolish to— Stop laughing."

He tried to keep a straight face. "You said you wanted to know everything about Craighdhu. It's sometimes dangerous to be granted your wishes. I know exactly what you mean about Deirdre. It's a terrible bane to be around a person who is always right. Why do you think I have lodgings in the village?"

"I'll not be so cowardly, but I—"

"Where are you going?"

Gavin and Kate turned to see Deirdre striding toward them across the hall.

"You know where we're going," Gavin said lightly. "The same place we've been trying to go for the last three days. I thought I'd take her to the village to see—"

"We have no time for that," Deirdre said. "Today we must go to the stable and—"

"I've already seen the stable," Kate interrupted. She did not care if it was cowardly or not, she had to escape. She took Gavin's hand and ran down the steps. "Come on, Gavin."

They hurried across the courtyard like two children fleeing punishment.

Kate cast a glance over her shoulder and saw Deirdre on the top step, a frown wrinkling her smooth forehead. "Do you think she'll come after us?" she whispered

Gavin shook his head. "She doesn't get along with the village women. They find her too ..."

He hesitated, and Kate supplied him with a word. "Annoying."

"Well, she did try to tell them how to best run their concerns. Of course, in most cases she was right, but that didn't make her observations more welcome. They bristle every time they see her coming toward them."

"It doesn't surprise me." Her pace quickened as she started over the drawbridge. "I grew very weary of her telling me what I must and must not do. I wish to learn everything, but not all at once. I'd like to go more slowly and savor. And there must be more ways of doing a task than Deirdre's way."

"It's a very good way, judging by the result."

"But it's not *my* way." She shifted her shoulders as if shrugging off a burden. "I don't wish to think about her anymore." They had crossed the moat and were approaching the village, and her pace eagerly quickened.

It was early, and the village only beginning to come alive, and yet there was already much to see. Young apprentices were busily taking down shutters, opening the shops, setting up small stalls, readying wares.

A young woman carrying a huge basket moved through the crowds crying, "Cherry ripe, apples fine!"

As they passed through the streets, Kate was assaulted by other merchants calling their wares. "Fine cobweb lawn, pins, points, and garters!"

"Do you not need a fine cabinet, my lady?"

"Will you not buy Spanish gloves? The finest leather!"

"Hot oat cakes!"

As they passed a bookseller's shop with the unlikely sign naming it the Brazen Sheep, Kate paused at a trestle stall to look at a heap of volumes. "I've never seen so many books," she said with wonder.

"Didn't you have a bookseller in your village?" Gavin asked.

She shook her head. "Sebastian thought reading

anything but Scriptures was corrupt and condemned it from the pulpit."

"Well, if Sebastian didn't like it, we must certainly buy you one." He scanned the titles and chose a thick red leather volume. "Ah, here's one that's quite satisfactorily corrupt and yet suitable for a lady." He paid the shopkeeper and handed the book to Kate with a bow. "With every sentence you read, think of Sebastian. It will give you added pleasure."

She chuckled as she accepted the book. "Thank you. I will certainly do that." She lovingly cradled the book as they walked on. "Everyone looks so busy and prosperous."

"Aye, there's no hunger on Craighdhu. Robert wouldn't permit it. He takes care of his own."

"You said Craighdhu was too land poor to support its people. How does the clan make its living?"

"We trade with the Irish."

"I know, but is that all?"

"It's more than enough. All the world wants fine woolen goods. We buy from the Irish and sell to the English and half the countries in Europe. Since Robert's great-grandfather's time it's given us a very generous living."

She stopped by a shop window where the MacDarren plaid was displayed. "That's fine cloth. I've never seen such fine weaving or truer colors."

"Irish. All the cloth you'll see in the shops on Craighdhu will be Irish."

That answer seemed odd to her. "No cloth is made here?"

"Sometimes the women do a little weaving for their families' use, but there's really no need for it. Robert makes sure there's plenty of cloth available for their needs at cheap prices, and they can't produce anything like this. The Irish weavers are magnificent, and the quality of the work is superb."

"I see that," she said, remembering the beauty of

the quilt Deirdre had tucked around her that first day. "And the wool is from Irish sheep, no doubt."

"Aye, Craighdhu is too rocky to provide much pastureland for sheep."

"So we reap the benefit of both fertile Irish land and skillful labor."

Gavin nodded. "All the world wants fine wool, and we provide it."

"It's the Irish who seem to provide. We merely buy and sell."

Gavin raised his brows. "That seems to upset you."

"I don't know why it should." She made a face. "I suppose I want Craighdhu to be all things."

"That's not practical. You must realize—" He broke off as he caught sight of a man coming up the street toward them. "There's Ian Mactavish. Come, I'll introduce you." He led her toward a young man coming down the street. "He's Jock's lieutenant, and if you need anything, he's the one to ask."

"Deirdre would give you argument there," she said dryly. "She seems to think she's the only one with answers." The dark-haired man approaching appeared only a little older than Gavin, but his air was far from youthful. He moved with a heavy, purposeful stride, and his earnest expression was just as weighty. She had a vague memory of seeing Ian Mactavish among the men who had met them at the dock. "I thought you'd be in charge when Robert wasn't on the island."

He shook his head. "I've no talent for giving orders. I have a tendency to wander off when I should be applying myself to serious things."

"And Ian Mactavish does not?"

"Never, he's a very serious lad. Of course, trailing in Jock's shadow would tend to make a man sober." He halted before Mactavish. "Ian, I have the honor to present you to the countess."

Ian Mactavish bowed. "My lady, an honor indeed. Naturally, I was going to pay a visit to the castle to express my willingness to serve. If there's aught I can do for you, you've only to send for me."

"Thank you." She smiled. "You're very kind, but I'm sure I won't need your help. Craighdhu seems a very safe and pleasant place."

"It's when all seems safe that the danger is greatest." He bowed gravely again and started up the hill.

"Good heavens, you're right," Kate whispered. "I can see why Jock Candaron chose him. He's terribly sober."

"And depressing. That's what comes of being weighed down by responsibility." Gavin grinned. "While I'm light as a feather." He half skipped as he pulled her toward a stall a few yards away. "Taffy. Kenneth Cameron makes the best candy in all of Scotland. Come, I'll get you a piece."

By the time they returned to the castle, it was almost dark, and Kate was so weary, she could hardly walk. Perhaps it wasn't weariness but happiness, she thought. She was giddy, drunk with sights and scents and sounds. She felt as if she had met every woman, man, and child in the village and strolled down every twisting street.

"Careful, you'll fall into the moat," Gavin said as he watched her weave across the drawbridge. "And you don't have the excuse I did. You've had no heather ale."

"I feel as if I had. Or, perhaps not—I've never had too much liquor before. I've never had too much of anything." She whirled in a circle. "Does it feel as if your head is filled with air and the colors are brighter and—"

"Yes, all of that." He grabbed her as she wandered too close to the side of the bridge and pulled her back. "And it makes you venture a little too close to danger. Which is why I got thrown into the moat."

"Then I am drunk. Drunk on Craighdhu." She ran forward across the courtyard, almost colliding with a stable boy who was exercising a gray mare. What was his name? Colin. "Good evening, Colin. Isn't it a splendid night?"

"Aye." He grinned indulgently as he saw her glowing face. "But you'd best get inside now, my lady. Deirdre has been out here twice looking for you."

A little of her exhilaration faded as she thought of the housekeeper. She had successfully dismissed Deirdre from her thoughts all day, and she wouldn't let her destroy her mood now. "Presently. How are Caird and Rachel?"

"In fine fettle," Colin said. "I'll exercise them tomorrow, but I thought they could use a bit of rest. The piebald looked a wee bit tired."

"More than a bit," Gavin said as he joined them. "He could use a month's rest, perhaps a year."

"You can be sure I'll take good care of him." Colin nodded politely and turned away. The horse's hooves echoed on the flagstones as he led the gray across the courtyard toward the stable.

Kate watched him. "Perhaps I should go see Caird."

Gavin smiled knowingly. "You can't avoid facing Deirdre much longer unless you'd care to sleep in the stable."

"It would do no good. She'd come and get me, brush me off and scour me like she does everything in the castle." She turned and started toward the steps leading to the front door. "I'll guess it's time I went in to face her."

"And it's time I bid you good evening," Gavin said.

"Coward."

He looked hurt. "I merely remembered having pressing business with Ian."

"And you're also a liar." She opened the door. "I expect you here tomorrow morning to rescue me."

"Two mornings in a row?" he asked dubiously. "She won't be pleased."

"And I won't be pleased if you desert me. I haven't

visited the docks yet." She gave him a stern glance. "Be here."

She didn't wait for an answer but swung the heavy door shut.

"Oh, you've come back." Deirdre came brusquely forward. "You're a bit tousled. Run up to your chamber and put yourself in order while I tell them you're ready to be served supper."

Kate's hand instinctively went to tidy her hair.

"No, that won't do. Go up to your chamber. I'll send a maid to help you." She started to turn away.

"No," Kate said suddenly.

Deirdre turned back to look at her. "My lady?"

Kate had not known the rejection was coming until she had spoken. Yet now she knew she could not retreat from the confrontation. "I said no. I don't wish to go tidy myself. I'm going to bathe and go to bed. You may send up a tub and water."

"After your supper."

"I don't wish to have any supper. I'm not hungry." She started up the stairs. "I ate while I was in the village."

"Sausage, fruit tarts, and candy, I'd wager," Deirdre said with a frown. "You'll probably be ill. You'd have done better to have waited to eat properly."

Kate realized she was already feeling a bit queasy. Merciful heavens, why must the woman always be right? She continued up the stairs. "I enjoyed it. I intend to have exactly the same food tomorrow when I go back."

"Not tomorrow. Tomorrow is our day for making candles. You must be there to learn how to supervise the—"

Kate stopped and turned around. "No."

"The candles are needed. We use a good many here," Deirdre persisted. "It's necessary we—"

"I don't care." She drew a deep breath and said with clear precision, "I'm going back to the village tomorrow with Gavin. You will not tell me what I will or will not do. I will make the decisions. Do you understand?"

Deirdre gazed at her impassively. "I'm not stupid. Of course I understand." She turned and walked away.

Kate stared after her in a muddle of frustration, exasperation, and guilt. She wished the woman had stayed, so she could have argued, vindicated herself. It was maddening to fight against a woman who was doing only what was best for her and Craighdhu.

She turned and ran up the steps. She had been right. She had done the only thing possible to establish her independence and position in the castle. If she had not acted to prevent it, she might be as much a prisoner here as she had been with Sebastian.

Yet, if that was true, why did she keep remembering that moment of softness on Deirdre's face that first day as she had tucked the coverlet around her? It must be that Deirdre was not an enemy as Sebastian had been, and Kate was not accustomed to challenging opponents who were not enemies.

No, that was not true. Robert was not an enemy, and there had been conflict between them from their first meeting.

She must not think of Robert. She had done very well. She had been aware of thinking of him only a few times today, and tomorrow would be better.

She was lying to herself. She had not been aware of thinking about him because he had been there before her all day. Everything she had seen had been Robert's world, and every step, every word, every person she had met, had led her deeper into the intimate byways of his life. He had been as much a living presence as if he had led her through those streets instead of Gavin.

Fierce rejection surged through her. She didn't want to remember that this was Robert's Craighdhu. For this short time she wanted it to be hers alone. She wanted to *make* it hers.

She frowned at the sheer selfishness of the thought. Was it this meanness of spirit that had driven her to be so resentful and impatient with Deirdre? It was possible, and she did not like the petty vision of herself it reflected.

She knocked firmly on the door of Deirdre's chamber.

No answer.

Surely she must be in her chamber at this hour. Everyone in the castle had retired for the night, and even Deirdre did not work this late. Kate didn't think she could have the wrong room. The housekeeper's room had been omitted from the inspection of the servants' quarters, but Deirdre had carelessly indicated it in passing.

She knocked again. "Deirdre, may I come in? I need to speak to you."

"Come."

Kate opened the door and was immediately struck by a brilliant blast of light. Besides the fire burning in the stone fireplace across the chamber, dozens of candles in tall candlesticks gave the room an almost daylight brightness.

"Is something wrong?"

Kate's gaze shifted to the opposite side of the room. Deirdre sat at a bench before the largest loom Kate had ever seen, enclosed in the structure of beams and thread like a spider caught in a web. The massive structure made her appear smaller, more vulnerable, in comparison. Her dark hair hung loose on her shoulders, and she was clothed in a white linen nightshift and dark blue wool robe, the informal attire lending her a less formidable air.

"No, nothing is wrong," Kate said as she came into the room. "Why didn't you answer me?"

"I didn't hear you. This pattern is difficult, and I have to give it my full attention." Deirdre gave her a quick glance over her shoulder, her appraisal taking in

Kate's nightgown and robe. "Have you changed your mind about supper? Are you hungry?"

"No, I couldn't sleep. I wish to speak to you."

"Shut the door. I'll be with you in a moment." Her gaze flew back to the shuttle of the loom. "You might as well sit down."

Kate moved to the stool beside the fire, sat down and wrapped her arms around her knees, all the time watching the quick, facile movements of Deirdre's skilled fingers. She had never seen anyone so adept at the art of weaving. The cloth on the loom was large and white and must be a blanket. The design was a beautiful barbed purple flower of some kind, and it was growing, coming alive beneath Kate's gaze.

She looked curiously around the chamber. The furniture was sparse, without embellishment, but there were touches of beauty in the purple coverlet lying on the bed, the sparkling white linen curtains at the window.

"What do you wish of me?"

Kate's glance moved back to Deirdre. The housekeeper's fingers were still moving on the loom as she stared levelly at Kate.

"I felt we should talk."

Deirdre smiled grimly. "You felt guilty for speaking sharply to me. The soft ones always do."

"I didn't feel ... Well, perhaps I did, but I shouldn't have."

"But the soft ones always do. They bite and then try to lick it better."

Kate suddenly chuckled. "That sounds disgusting."

"I believe in truth, not sweetness." She looked down at the pattern. "You didn't have to come here. I'm used to being snapped at."

"Perhaps it wouldn't happen if you wouldn't provoke it. People don't like to be constantly told what to do."

"It's my nature," Deirdre said. "I've always done

things better than others, and I cannot bear to see them struggle when they'd improve so much if they'd only do as I tell them."

"It could be they want to do it their own way even though it's not as good."

"Do you think that thought has not occurred to me? But it makes no sense, so I ignore it." She looked back at the work on the loom and asked in a low voice, "Do you wish me to leave Craighdhu?"

Kate was silent a moment, hesitating. Her life might be easier if Deirdre weren't here, but she was not sure she wanted life easier if it meant robbing this woman of her place at Craighdhu. "Why should I send you away? It's unreasonable to dismiss someone because they're too clever and work too hard."

"Are you having trouble finding excuses? I'm annoying. Everyone knows that to be true." The shuttle flew faster. "And I'm very disrespectful."

"I've not been a countess long enough to be offended by disrespect." Kate said. "But I can't argue that I find you annoying," she added bluntly. "Just listen to you. You're even telling me the proper manner to dismiss you. Do you wish to go away?"

"Why should I wish to leave? I'm very comfortable here."

"Then I see no reason why we cannot work together," Kate replied. "I do wish to learn from you, but in my own way and time. If you can accept that, we can try again."

"I cannot promise to stop guiding you in the direction you should go," Deirdre said crisply.

"And I will not promise I won't tell you to go about your tasks and leave me alone."

"Fair enough." Deirdre looked up and met her gaze. "Is that all?"

It was all Kate had come to say, but she had a curious reluctance to leave Deirdre yet. "Do you mind if I stay and watch you?"

A flicker of surprise crossed her face. "If you like. But don't expect me to converse with you. As I said, this pattern demands attention."

"And light." Kate's gaze went to the dozens of candles that had startled her when she had first entered the room. "You said we use a good many candles."

Deirdre stiffened. "I have Robert's permission to use as many as I wish. I have no time for weaving during the day, and I make many fine things to bring comfort to this great barn of a castle."

"I don't doubt it. I've seen many of them. I was not accusing you of waste."

Deirdre relaxed and turned back to her loom.

"But I would think you'd be too weary to weave so late at night."

"I need only a few hours sleep a night to rest me. I've always had a great deal of energy."

That was a huge understatement, Kate thought ruefully. "That's a beautiful design. I've never seen a barbed flower like that before."

"It's not a flower, it's a snowflake."

"Oh." She had clearly made a big mistake. She was silent a moment before cautiously venturing, "A purple snowflake?"

Deirdre did not answer.

Kate tried again. "It's a lovely shade of purple anyway. What plant did you get the dye from?"

"The root of the bell heather."

Heather again. "Robert told me there was no end to heather's uses."

"He's right. Depending upon its age, it also gives me yellow, orange, and gray-green dyes."

"Where did you learn to weave so well?"

"From my mother, and she learned it from her mother," Deirdre said. "By the time I could scarce walk, they started to teach me the way of it."

"I was taught spinning and weaving, too, as a

child, but I never dreamed of creating anything this fine."

"Because you did it for necessity. I did it for the trade."

"And that makes a difference?"

She nodded. "The trade was everything in my village. If the work was fine enough, then a house was paid a shilling bonus for every bolt of material. Naturally, every household strove to earn that bit of extra."

"And I'm sure you always made that extra shilling."

"Of course. I was the best weaver in the village," she said matter-of-factly.

"How many families in your village worked in the trade?"

"Nearly all of them. The women wove the fabric, and the men raised sheep."

"And they all sold to Craighdhu?"

She nodded. "The MacDarrens have always been fair to us. We trust them."

"Even Jock Candaron?"

She glanced at Kate. "They told you he killed my husband?"

"It surprised me that you came to Craighdhu."

"I bore him no ill will. My husband was a bully and a drunkard. He was always brawling. One day he picked on the wrong man." She shrugged. "I had just lost a child and was too ill to work. Jock Candaron brought me here and had me nursed until I was well again. After that, he offered to send me back to Ireland, but I chose to stay here."

"Why? You don't appear to have a fondness for it."

"One place is much like another."

"I don't agree."

She smiled faintly. "No, you're like the rest here. You think there's no place on earth as fair as this storm-tossed rock."

"Why did you choose to stay on this storm-tossed rock?"

Deirdre ignored the question and said sternly, "I told you I could not talk to you, and yet you plague me with questions. If you stay, you must be silent and not bother me."

Deirdre had not considered it a bother until the questions had become more personal in nature, Kate noted as her gaze went to the snowflake pattern on the quilt. Deirdre was a little like that snowflake, serene and yet barbed, substance one moment and melting out of reach the next.

Kate rose to her feet. "I'll leave you to your work. May I come again tomorrow night and watch you?"

Deirdre met her gaze. "Why would you want to?"

She was not sure herself, but there was something vaguely pleasant sitting here by the fire with the scent of burning wood and candles drifting to her while she unraveled the guarded puzzle of Deirdre O'Connell. It could be that she had never had a woman friend except Carolyn and was lonely for that companionship. Good God, she could not have chosen a woman less likely to assuage that need. "Sometimes I cannot sleep. It would be pleasant to have company. May I come?"

Deirdre looked away from her. "You're mistress here. You may do anything you wish."

"May I come?" she asked again.

Deirdre started moving the shuttle. "Very well, come. It makes no difference to me."

"Did you like being a weaver?" Kate asked.

"A woman always likes doing something she can do better than anyone else."

"But if you did nothing but weave all day . . ."

"It was only monotonous when I had to repeat the pattern over and over. I grew very bored with the MacDarren tartan." She added quickly, "Though no one turned out a finer plaid than I."

"I'm sure of that."

"And even when I was a child, I liked the waulking."

"Waulking?"

"After the wool is dyed and woven, it has to be stretched, and all the children would gather to do it, and there would be singing and joking. . . ." Her smile faded. "But that changed when I grew older and they saw what an excellent weaver I'd become. I was allowed to do nothing else. My father wanted both the shillings and the honor of turning out the finest goods in the village. He was no different from the other men. The trade was everything, and the men of the family ruled the trade." She shrugged. "I was never a handsome lass, but all the lads in the village were after my hand. They knew what a fine provider I'd be."

"Did your father arrange your marriage?"

She snorted. "Why should he marry me off when I had such value for him? No, I chose Sean myself. He was a big, handsome man, with a pleasing way about him. I paid no heed to the stories about his drunkenness." She suddenly bent over the loom. "Be silent now until I finish this bit."

Kate knew very well by now that Deirdre could master any difficulty in the pattern with her eyes closed, and this was only a signal she wished to drop a subject. Kate had learned much about the woman in the hours she'd spent in this candlelit room during the last week, and she was sure Deirdre had learned an equal amount about her. She was still sometimes tentative in the housekeeper's company, but those times were becoming less frequent. "You never told me why you chose to stay here at Craighdhu."

"It's as good as any other place. I could be busy here."

"You were the finest weaver in your village. Surely you were busy there also."

"Yes, but I know the loom so well, it takes no

thought." She looked down at the coverlet. "If your mind is empty, the memories come. It's a foolish woman who lets the past come knocking, if she doesn't want to let it in."

"The child?" Kate asked softly.

For a moment Kate didn't think she would answer, but then Deirdre nodded jerkily. "I wanted a babe. I was barren for fourteen years. When I found myself with child, I thought it was a miracle." The shuttle moved faster. "Sean was happy about the babe. A man is always proud when he can get a woman with child. Then he got drunk one night, and his pride didn't matter as much as his lack of money. I was ill most of the time while carrying the babe and wasn't producing as much as I had before. He beat me, and I lost the child." Her hands halted in their movement, and she gazed unseeingly down at the shuttle. "I've been clumsy. I'll have to start this section again."

Kate got to her feet. "I'm distracting you. Perhaps I'd better leave you and go to bed."

"You're being kind," Deirdre said. "You needn't go because you think I may weep. I don't weep anymore. I work." The shuttle moved again. "There's great satisfaction in work. It gives you purpose."

For the first time Kate was beginning to understand that almost frantic energy that drove Deirdre.

"And fulfillment," Deirdre continued. "A woman needs nothing else, if she knows her own worth."

Deirdre was clinging to work as Kate had clung to her dream of a home. But Deirdre had closed herself off from the truth Kate had discovered.

"You're wrong," Kate said quietly. "I once thought as you did, but there are other needs as important. We can't hide away and live alone. It's hollow without others to share it."

"A husband?" Deirdre smiled bitterly. "I rejoiced when I was released from that bondage. Do you think that was the first time he beat me? I was a woman, and so could be used and punished when I did not fulfill expectations. No one in my village thought of punishing him because he killed my child. Just because you have a fine man is no reason to believe it is—" She stopped as she saw Kate's closed expression. "I know you fought with Robert before he left, but you must not let that poison you. He's a good man. I've watched him these many years and have never found him cruel or greedy. Believe me, I have no liking for most men, so my words have value." She grimaced. "Of course, he's impatient on occasion, but I tend to arouse that response."

Kate stood up and started for the door. "I think it's time I retired. I'll see you in the morning, Deirdre."

Deirdre gave her a dry smile. "By all means, you must not get overweary. Good night, Kate."

A few minutes later Kate stood at her chamber window looking out over the sea. She had not fooled Deirdre; the housekeeper had known Kate had left to avoid discussing Robert. She must rid herself of this impulse to run away every time Robert was mentioned. She had no right to lesson Deirdre on hiding when she was doing the same thing herself. In truth, she had no real quarrel with the meat of Deirdre's solution. Work did bring forgetfulness, and God knows, she desperately wished to forget both Robert and their time together.

But she had no wish to close out the people of Craighdhu. With every passing day she was drawing closer to the clan. They were beginning to accept her, to draw her into their circle. She wished Deirdre could have the benefit of that warmth. In these last days Kate had learned to admire and like Deirdre. The woman would not admit it, but at times she must feel terribly alone. If only the villagers could ignore her arrogant self-assurance and accept her for her virtues. No one was more clever or fair or hardworking than Deirdre. She had so much to give them, and they her. It was a pity that—

Kate inhaled sharply, her hands tightening on the oak windowsill as a sudden thought occurred to her.

Was it possible?

"Can we do it?" Kate eagerly asked Gavin.

"I believe you've already made up your mind on that subject," Gavin said. "Affirmation on my part is hardly necessary."

She grinned. "But it would be pleasant to have your support."

"You know you'll have it." Gavin smiled. "But I'll need Ian's help to deal with the carpenters. I suppose you've already chosen the women?"

"Meg Kildare, Sarah and Mary Cameron, Catherine Mactavish, Elspeth MacDonald. I've already spoken to them and they're agreeable," she added, "but I want you to go visit their husbands and explain what a fine thing this will be for them."

Gavin sighed. "I'll see what I can do."

"You'll do very well." Kate moved toward the door. "You can be very persuasive when you try."

"No more than you. When do you speak to Deirdre?"

"Tonight." She would need more than persuasiveness to convince Deirdre, and the woman seemed to be most approachable during those hours they spent together in her chamber.

"Don't you think you should have spoken to her first?"

Kate shook her head. "I wanted to get everything in place."

Gavin nodded. "I can see why. She's going to be the most difficult obstacle you'll overcome. I don't envy you."

"You're very quiet tonight," Deirdre said as she sent her shuttle flying. "Did Gavin bring you disturbing news?"

"No." Kate's hands, which were clasping her knees,

nervously clenched as again the reed thwacked on the loom, forcing the thread in place. Ordinarily, she found the heavy, rhythmic sound soothing. Tonight it only increased her edginess as she tried to find a way to broach the subject. "I suppose you could say I brought disturbing news to him."

Deirdre smiled and said nothing.

"You're not going to ask what news?"

"You'll tell me when it suits you. You're not one to keep your silence when something is bothering you. Everything has to come blurting out."

"It's really not bothering me. It's just something I— Yes, it is." She drew a deep breath. "I wish you to teach the women of Craighdhu your skill in weaving."

Deirdre did not change expression. "Indeed."

"I thought we would start with five women, and when you feel they're competent, then you could teach five more."

"This is nonsense. I have no time for it."

"It's true you'd need to spend at least four hours a day with the women, and you'd have to work harder than you ever did in your life," Kate agreed. "But I don't believe you'd mind the work. Perhaps we could get more help from the village, and I'll do all I can. I have learned a great deal about managing things here at the castle."

At last the shuttle stopped, and Deirdre turned to look at her. "Why? What is your purpose in doing this?"

"I see no reason why you Irish should reap all the profits. Surely, Scottish women are not so stupid they cannot learn to do as well."

"So I'm supposed to take the shillings away from my own people?"

"They're not your people anymore. You belong here with us. In spite of what you say, you know that as well as I do. Besides, there will be plenty of work for everyone. Gavin says the wool trade is like a thirsty giant. The whole world wants woolen goods."

"That is true."

"Then you will do it?"

"No."

Kate frowned as hope plummeted. "Why not?"

"No village woman would listen to me. They don't like me."

"I thought of that possibility."

"It's more than a possibility," Deirdre insisted.

"They don't have to like you. They only have to respect you and not be antagonized by your manner. I chose women who seemed confident enough to speak their own minds to you. I believe that may help. If I'm wrong, we'll choose five other women." She added, "And I'll be there at first to smooth any feathers you might ruffle. You're a fine woman. They need only to know you as I do."

Deirdre was silent for a time, thinking. "It won't work," she finally said flatly.

"It will work. I want this for Craighdhu."

"And so it must come to pass." She shook her head. "It would drive me mad to teach those fumble-fingered fools."

"They won't be fumble-fingered forever. You'll demand that they get better, and they'll do it."

"They'll walk out after the first lesson."

"If they do, they'll come back."

"Why should they?"

"For the same reason you would. It's a chance to be of value, to be respected for their own talents, to be sought for their skills. It's not often a woman is given the opportunity to earn, instead of being given, her place in the world."

"Not every woman wants that."

"Then we'll teach them to want it."

"So that their men can take it away from them?"

"That won't happen on Craighdhu."

"Man's nature is the same the world over."

"Do you think Robert would permit their husbands to treat them as your husband treated you?"

Deirdre was silent again. "Perhaps not."

"Then will you do it?"

"What about the looms?"

Hope flared bright. "Ian Mactavish is talking to the carpenters tomorrow."

Deirdre snorted. "What does he know about building looms? I'll have to go and choose the wood and tell them how to do it properly."

Oh dear, Deirdre was starting already, but Kate had won so much, she didn't wish to jeopardize success by arguing. "I'm sure he'll appreciate your help."

"He won't, but he'll have it anyway. I can't have those helpless ninnies working on bad looms." She turned back to her loom. "And four hours a day will not be enough. They'll have to work at least six. Even so, it will take at least three years to make them even adequate, five for them to compete with the trade."

Kate would not be here in four years. She would not see this seed she was planting grow, she realized with a pang. Well, Craighdhu would be here, and wherever she was, she would know she had enriched it. "I want to have them ready in four. Is it possible?"

Deirdre turned back to her, and a faint smile lit her face. "Oh, yes, give me real women and not ninnies, and it's entirely possible."

Edinburgh Castle

"Of course, it could all be a ruse. This Sebastian Landfield seems none too stable." James frowned. "But I could not let the matter go unquestioned."

"No, you were right to send for me." Alec Malcolm

lifted his goblet to his lips. "And at least some of what Landfield said is true. I encountered MacDarren on my way here and met this Kathryn."

"You did?" James's frown deepened. "Is she as winning as Landfield said?"

Malcolm thought back to that meeting. Comeliness in a man or woman meant nothing to him, but he had realized as a child that others found a pleasant exterior important. He had always found it odd, but had soon learned to mold their weakness to his advantage. When he had met Kathryn MacDarren, he had assessed her as he did everyone else, weighing her for threat or pliability. He had been more aware of the intelligence and directness of her regard than her beauty. "I suppose she's comely enough. And I would say she is no fool."

James swore beneath his breath. "That's not good news."

"It's neither bad nor good until we find out the truth. You've brought this wet nurse, Clara Merkert, here?"

James nodded. "The troop I sent to fetch her arrived two days ago. She's in the dungeon."

"Has she been questioned?"

"She claims she knows nothing of any child born to my mother. She says the girl is the offspring of a minor nobleman and a strumpet of the town. However, it seems suspicious that the woman comes from a village near where my mother was permitted to go to take the waters."

Malcolm chuckled. "And where she was persuaded to take Shrewsbury as well."

"As you say, we do not know if that is true," James said. "Everything was going so well. I detest all this trouble."

"That's why you sent for me." Malcolm's tone was light. "To take all your troubles away."

James's frown vanished. "I truly missed you, Alec,"

he said softly. "I was very angry at you when you left me."

"I couldn't stay in Edinburgh forever. I have my borders to guard." He met James's gaze. "If you would remove MacDarren as a threat to me, I'd feel safe to visit you more frequently here at court."

"You know I can't move against a nobleman as powerful as MacDarren without just cause. You must settle your own disputes."

Alec had known that would be James's reply. James enjoyed the dominance Alec wielded over him, but he never let it interfere with his own ambitions or well-being. "Then you must do without my company."

"Are your petty little forays more important to you than me?" James asked peevishly.

Malcolm felt a flare of impatience. He knew the answer James expected, and if necessary he would give it to him. It wasn't necessary, he decided. He could please himself and give James a glimpse of the dominance he craved. He replied, "Yes, of course, they're more important. I will fit you into my life when it is convenient to do so."

James's cheeks flushed with anger. "You go too far, Alec."

"That is precisely why you enjoy me. I will have no more of this whining." He changed the subject. "Have you put this woman to the torture?"

"Not yet. I was waiting for you." James's tone was still offended. "You have a great talent for causing hurt."

He'd like to slap the sulky brat's face, but it was time to soothe instead of punish. "Only for your ultimate benefit." He smiled warmly. "You know I care for you."

The boy snatched the bone thrown to him like a starving dog with a leg of lamb. "Truly?"

"Did I not travel over the mountains and come to you in the dead of winter?"

"It's just that you're so harsh with me at times. It's not at all kind when I have such great burdens."

"Well, I'll lift one burden from your shoulders now." He finished his wine in one swallow and set down his goblet. "How old is this Merkert woman?"

"Near her fiftieth year."

"That's not too old for the rack. I've found when subjects near their sixtieth year, their bones tend to crack more easily and the whips are more efficient."

James made a face. "I don't want to hear about it. Just do it."

"I'll want only my own people in the dungeon, and no interference."

"Whatever you like."

"Those are the words I want to hear." He rose to his feet. "See that you remember them . . . later."

James's face lit with eagerness. "You will come to me tonight?"

"How could I resist you?" He immediately balanced the sensual softness with a hard edge. "But I must attend to more important things first." He moved toward the door. "I'll attend to your personal needs when I have the time."

As he walked down the corridor, he analyzed his meeting with James. On the whole he thought it had gone very well. He had reasserted his dominance over the boy and would reinforce it on a physical level later. Now, he must determine whether bringing this Merkert woman here was only a ploy to get him back to Edinburgh, or if there was a valid threat to James. The entire tale sounded preposterous, but if there was a particle of truth in it, the situation had definite possibilities.

It was only a question of how he would bring those possibilities to fruition.

"I want at least six sheep." Kate's brow wrinkled in thought as she finished the mutton on her trencher.

Gavin's lips quirked. "By the Saints, you must be hungry tonight."

She waved the comment aside. "I'm serious. I think we should purchase six fine sheep from the Irish and start our own herd."

"May I remind you that the island can't support these herds of sheep?"

"But if they get rid of their cattle, the crofts on the mainland can. I'm sure the reason they haven't run sheep before is that all of Craighdhu is accustomed to thinking of sheep in connection with the trade."

Gavin chuckled. "It's not enough that you've turned the village upside down with your weavers, you must turn us all into shepherds."

"Not at all," she corrected. "We'll start out slowly, but by the time my weavers are ready, I'd like to be able to supply them with our own wool."

"Tell me, aren't the weavers enough to keep you busy?"

"Deirdre has them well in hand now. I only have to be there in case of disputes." In truth, the weaving lessons had gone better than she had dreamed possible. The women of the clan had shown an astonishing determination and patience, and Deirdre's enthusiasm had begun to sweep them along in her wake. Six hours of lessons had become eight, and the housekeeper often stayed late at the weaving cottage with one or the other of the women. Kate had great hopes the enforced intimacy would reap benefits for Deirdre as well as Craighdhu. "It's time I turned my attention to something else. There's no reason why we can't convince the members of the clans on the mainland that they don't have to go to Ireland to enrich themselves."

Gavin threw back his head and laughed. "No reason at all."

He was laughing, but she had only stated her firm belief. She could not understand this male way of thinking that it was necessary to search the world for what could be found at home with a little effort. She supposed it was men's nature to seize and women's to nurture and build. But, by God, given the chance, *she* could build. She could show them all what could be done with Craighdhu.

Craighdhu had taught her much in these last weeks. She had learned to subdue her temper, to listen, to think before she spoke. She found the people of Craighdhu to be honest and blunt, with a dry wit and a belief that no one on earth was better than a Highlander. At first they had treated her only with the respect they would give the wife of a brother, and she'd been forced to earn all else given to her. She found that challenge as exciting as Craighdhu itself, but to continue to meet that challenge she must work harder, learn more, do more. That hunger was growing more intense with every passing day, and her time here was growing shorter. "Then will you get me my sheep?"

"You'll have to wait a bit or else ask Ian." Gavin looked down into the depths of the wine in his goblet. "I'm going away tonight."

"What? Where are you—" She stopped as she realized his purpose. She had been so involved in her own new life, she had almost forgotten Gavin's determination regarding Malcolm's daughter. "No, Gavin, please."

"Jeanie needs me." He looked up and smiled. "And I need her."

"It's clear Robert thinks it's too hazardous."

"Less so now that Alec is in Edinburgh. I'll never have a better chance." He lifted his glass in a mock toast. "Wish me good fortune, Kate."

He was not going to be dissuaded, she realized. "How will you do it?"

"I've been paying retainers in Malcolm's house for years to arrange meetings and to send word of Jeanie. Stop looking so frightened," he said soothingly. "I'm just going reiving. It won't even be as dangerous as stealing one of Cavendish's horses."

"What about her brother, Duncan?"

"Duncan likes me, and he has no fondness for his father. I'd wager he won't come thundering after us."

"I hope you're right," she whispered. "Where do you intend to take her?"

"I think Ireland. I know people there who will hide us." He paused. "But first I'll bring her here for a day or two and make my peace with Robert. That's one of the reasons I've waited this long. Robert should be back within a few days, and I'll be able to see him before we have to leave for Ireland."

Relief surged through her. She had feared for a moment she would never see him again. She had not realized until this moment how very dear he had become to her. "You believe he'll be terribly angry."

Gavin nodded. "He'll be afraid for Craighdhu, you see. That's why I waited until he was gone. I feared he would try to stop me . . . or help me. I'm putting Robert into a dreadful coil. I'm endangering Craighdhu, but I still belong to him. I'm one of his own." He grimaced as he rose to his feet. "But I can't worry about him when I have troubles of my own."

"When can I expect you back?"

"In no more than four days. All I ask is that you have a chamber and a warm welcome prepared for my Jeanie."

"I'll have the chamber in readiness, but I can't promise to take this woman to my heart." Kate's lips compressed. "She must be very selfish to endanger you in this fashion."

He shook his head. "You'll change your mind when you meet her." He took her hand and squeezed it gently. "Pray for me?"

"Of course," she said gruffly. "Though anyone who is so foolish doesn't deserve it."

"But it's the foolish who need prayers most." He turned and walked out of the hall.

• • •

Edinburgh

He must be careful not to reveal the excitement surging through him, Alec thought as he approached the door of James's chamber. The king must see no sign that would arouse his suspicions. He must be the dominant taskmaster and then the gentle soother of body and spirit James required. Jesus, it was going to be difficult. Who would have guessed he would have been given this chance? Of course, it was too bad the woman had died—a live witness was always better in these cases—but still he had the confession. It would be enough. He would *make* it enough.

He was permitted to pass unchallenged by the two guards at the door of James's apartment. A good sign.

James sat at his desk, writing. He wore a purple-and-gold velvet dressing gown that made his face look sickly pale in contrast. The boy was overfond of purple, Alec thought contemptuously. James thought the brilliant color reinforced his kingly air and made him appear more authoritative. Alec could have told him that such trappings made no difference. It was what a man had inside that gave him the power to rule those about him.

James glanced at him and then looked down at the parchment again. "I'm very angry with you. It's been two days."

So angry he had given the guards orders to let him come to him at any time. "The woman was strong. I needed to concentrate on my service to you."

"It is done?"

"It's done."

"And the result?"

He smiled. "The vicar is as mad as you suspected."

"Then the woman was telling the truth?"

"Not entirely." He had decided that his lie should be more creative than the one the woman had told

James previously. "The girl is the offspring of the marquis of Frandal. He impregnated the daughter of a Catholic tradesman in the village. Our chaste Elizabeth was furious with the young libertine, but she had a fondness for the lad and wished to protect him from the calumny of associating with papists, so she involved herself in the disposition of the child."

"You're sure of this?"

"When have I ever failed you? At the last the woman was raving with agony. She could not wait to confess the truth."

James sighed. "It's a great relief to me."

"I thought it would be. Shall I tell you of the interrogation?"

"No."

"Perhaps later." He took off his short cape and threw it on the chair beside the door. "I have had my fill of dungeons and such. Sometime I will make you come with me to one of these little sessions."

"No, please, I would not like it."

He meant what he said. James had no stomach for torture itself, but the thought of Alec performing it gave him a secret excitement he would not admit even to himself. Alec had whipped a servant once in front of James, and when it was done, the king had taken his hand and looked at it, testing it for power, stroking it. "We will talk of it later." Alec sat down in the chair and stretched his legs before him. "That color becomes you. I have never seen you look so well."

"Indeed?" James flushed with pleasure. He reached up to stroke the velvet of the robe's lapel. "I'm glad it pleases you. I will wear it more often."

"See that you do." Alec leaned back in the chair. "It's good to have that pesky business out of the way. Of course, I will have to remove the vicar. We mustn't let his ravings disturb the nobles at court at this delicate time."

"What of the Merkert woman?"

"Dead. I thought that would be your wish in case Elizabeth took umbrage at your treatment of one of her subjects."

"You've thought of everything."

"Isn't that why you sent for me? My affection is such that all you need to do is call and I'm here to do your bidding." He paused. "But now you must do my bidding. Remove my boots."

As usual, James hesitated, but Alec could see the flicker of excitement in his expression. The king rose slowly to his feet and came toward him. He tried to sound offhand. "I suppose you deserve a reward." He turned his back and tugged at Alec's boot. "How long will you stay with me?"

He wanted to leave this minute, tomorrow at the latest. The excitement and anticipation within him was growing with every passing second. It was the opportunity he had waited for all these years and now he was forced to pamper the desires of this weakling.

"Alec?" James drew off the boot and started on the other one.

But he must not let his impatience cause him to make any false steps. Every move now must be planned and executed with utmost cleverness and surety. James must be petted and made to feel secure.

It should not be too onerous a task with a throne beckoning as a reward.

"I will stay a week." With a faint, cruel smile, he added, "If you're very, very good and obey my every wish."

10

The knock was loud. "Kate! Open the door."

Gavin, she recognized sleepily, and he sounded— *Gavin!*

She bolted upright, jumped out of bed, and flew across the bedchamber.

She threw open the door. "Gavin, are you safe? It's been only two days. What happened?"

"Of course I'm safe." He was smiling jubilantly, his freckled face alight with eagerness in the halo of light cast by the candle in his hand. "I'm sorry to wake you in the middle of the night, but we've just arrived." He turned and held out his hand to someone behind him. "This is my Jeanie."

Kate stiffened as her gaze followed Gavin's.

Jean Malcolm drifted gracefully out of the shadows until she stood at Gavin's side. "You are very kind to have me," she whispered with a tentative smile. "I pray I'll be no bother to you."

Looking at her, Kate experienced a sinking sensation in the pit of her stomach. She had hoped after Gavin had seen his Jeanie again that he would realize no woman was worth the danger he was taking, but she could now see why Gavin had been willing to risk so much. The woman was exquisite. Under a matching cloak she wore a velvet gown with wide panniers as fashionable as those of the ladies Kate had sometimes seen passing through the village on their way to London. The deep blue of the velvet offered a lovely complement to her violet eyes and shining flaxen hair. She was of medium height but so fine-boned and tiny-waisted, she appeared smaller, almost childlike, an impression enhanced by her gentle, timid air.

"Welcome to Craighdhu," Kate said formally.

"There, you see, I told you there would be no trouble." Gavin smiled down at Jean. "How could anyone resist you, love?"

How indeed? Kate wondered in despair. Jean Malcolm was a figure from a troubadour's tale, the helpless princess every man wished to rescue. "Have you eaten?"

Gavin shook his head. "I wanted to make sure she was safe first. I have no time to eat. I must leave at once and go back to the mainland to fetch the dominie for the wedding." He waved a hand excitedly. "You should have seen me, Kate. I slipped into the castle like a ghost, seized Jeanie and was out of there in a—"

"He was magnificent," Jean Malcolm interrupted with a glowing smile. "A true knight." She gave Gavin a pleading look. "But I believe I'm more weary than I thought. I feel quite weak. Could I rest here while you fetch some fruit or cheese?"

"I'll wake up Deirdre and tell her to—"

"No." She swayed. "Please. Could you go to the scullery yourself? I don't want to face any more strangers right now. Could you . . . ?" She trailed off and smiled sweetly at him.

Kate could see Gavin melt like the last ice of winter before that smile.

"Care for her, Kate." Gavin lifted Jean's small hand to his lips. "I'll be right back." He turned and moved swiftly down the hall.

"Would you care to come in?" Kate asked, standing to one side. "May I get you a cup of water or wine?"

"No, thank you." The girl floated into the chamber and sat down in the chair by the door, watching as Kate lit a candle in the silver holder. "We don't have much time. Gavin will be back soon, and we must reach an understanding before he comes." She slipped back the hood of her cloak, met Kate's gaze with bold directness, and said crisply, "You need not worry about him. I'll keep him safe."

The words were as shocking as the girl's change in demeanor. It was as if the woman had taken off a glittering, bejeweled mask. "*You'll* keep *him* safe?"

Jean Malcolm made an impatient gesture. "Of course, we both know Gavin needs someone to look after him. You were bristling like a porcupine when you first saw me and thought I might be a danger to him." She frowned. "He talked a good deal about you on the way here. It troubled me at first. I thought you might have a passion for Gavin yourself, but I believe you are only friends."

Intrigued, Kate asked, "And what if you had decided I had such a leaning?"

"Oh, I would cure you of it." Jean smiled. "Or perish in the attempt."

The words were spoken with utmost gentleness, but there was an underlying resolution in her tone that held a chilling threat.

Jean added, "I could not have my Gavin constantly tempted by another woman, you see. It would make life most uncomfortable for us."

"But you won't be here. Gavin says you're going to Ireland."

"But we will not stay forever. Gavin's heart is here." Her lips tightened with determination. "I will not have him made unhappy by this marriage to me."

At least the woman seemed to have a genuine affection for Gavin. "Have you spoken of your decision to him?"

"Not yet. He must be accustomed to me before I let him see what a harridan I can be." She grinned, and her delicate features were suddenly transformed by impishness. "It's easier to let him see the sweet, gentle maiden the world perceives me to be."

Kate said deliberately, "You're speaking of deceit. You lie to him."

The girl stiffened. "I do not lie. I merely—" She fell silent and then said quietly, "Aye, I lie. Gavin and I have been able to snatch only a scant few times together. I love him. I want him to love me. Men seem to find it easy to love meek, docile women, and I found a long time ago, there are ways of using the weakness they embrace to my own advantage."

Kate shook her head uncomprehendingly.

"I'm not like you," Jean said. "Gavin told me how fierce you can be. He admires you for it, but I regard ferocity as stupidity when there are other means to get your own way." She made a face. "Though I fear deceit becomes a practice difficult to break. I have been what my father wants to see for so long, it has become natural to me."

Kate felt a wave of sympathy. Who was she to judge the methods the woman had used to survive a father like Alec Malcolm? "You cannot go through life fooling Gavin."

"I don't want to lie to him forever. It's just best that I have control over him right now." She shook her head. "We walk a dangerous road. My father is a monster. I watched him crush my mother until he finally killed her with his cruelty. I must not let him hurt Gavin." She met Kate's gaze. "We are surely in agreement in that, if nothing else. Do you believe me?"

"Yes." She was not sure she understood Jean Malcolm, but she did believe she loved Gavin. "But I'm not certain how you can prevent it."

"Neither do I. I will think on it."

A sudden suspicion occurred to Kate. "It seems very strange that Gavin had such little trouble plucking you from Kilgranne."

"He had sent word he was coming," Jean said. "I bribed the stable boy and drugged the guard on watch." She frowned. "Naturally, you will not tell Gavin. It would spoil his pleasure."

Kate's lip twitched. "No, we wouldn't wish to spoil Gavin's pleasure."

Jean rose brusquely to her feet. "Now I will leave you to your rest. We must start planning the wedding tomorrow. Gavin wishes to wait until Robert is back from Ireland to wed, but I will give him only two more days. We cannot expect my father to linger long in Edinburgh with Robert back at Craighdhu, and we must be long gone from here."

"Wedding? You'll not wed handfast?"

Jean shook her head adamantly. "We'll wed before God and man for all time. I'll have none of these temporary—" She stopped as she saw Kate's expression. "Ah, so it's that way with you? No wonder you gave only friendship to my Gavin. I do not know Robert well, but I believe he is a hard man. It's not a simple path you've chosen."

She was angry with herself for revealing that moment of hurt to this stranger. "I've not chosen any path at all. It's been chosen for me."

"Then you have no one to blame but yourself," Jean said bluntly. "A man always tries to choose a woman's path, but there are ways of avoiding taking it. You must find the one right for you. It's clear you've let them muddle your thinking. I will not—" As she heard Gavin's footsteps in the hall, she said quickly, "We will talk later."

Gavin came into the room bearing a wooden tray containing cheese, bread and an apple. "Is this enough?" He frowned anxiously down at the tray.

"Would you like wine? Why didn't you give her something to drink, Kate?"

"Kate was all that was gracious." Jean smiled lovingly at Gavin. "I feel much better. If you will show me where I am to sleep, I'll eat a little of this wonderful repast and go to bed."

"I'll take you." Kate picked up the candleholder. "It's the third chamber down the hall."

"Go back to bed, Kate." Gavin didn't take his eyes off Jean. "I didn't mean to disturb your rest. I only wanted you to meet Jeanie. Is she not everything I told you?"

"Gavin, please . . ." Jean gave Kate an enchanting shy smile.

"No," Kate murmured as she passed them and moved down the hall. "Your Jeanie, is much, much more than you told me."

The *Irish Princess* was sighted near noon of the second day after Gavin brought Jean Malcolm to Craighdhu. The village was instantly thrown into a whirlpool of excitement, and word reached Kate while she was at the weavers' cottage. She was glad the turmoil that erupted all around her hid her own sudden tension and unrest. What if Robert was back? Nothing could come of his presence. She would return to the castle and wait with dignity until he came to her. Why should she run to him like a puppy starved for affection?

He was home.

She found herself walking slowly through the winding streets that led to the dock, jostled by the crowds running to meet the ship, drawn helplessly as if to a lodestone.

He had come back to her.

No, not to her but to Craighdhu. She wasn't important to him in anything but a physical sense. Someone whose body brought pleasure and ease to his loins.

The thought should have quenched the jubilation soaring through her.

It did not. She didn't care. She would see him.

He was here.

She was here.

He had not expected her to be at the dock. She had been so angry with him when he had left that his last memory of her had been of blazing eyes and hotter words. Yet there she was at the back of the crowd, the wind whipping her brown cape away from her slight body.

"Evidently, your gentle wife has gotten over her displeasure with you," Jock remarked. "I could have hoped otherwise."

Robert ignored him as he strode down the gangplank. Christ, he felt the same excitement he had experienced when he had come back to Craighdhu those many years ago. No, not quite the same. The sight of Craighdhu had never made him ready like a stallion before a mare in heat.

He pushed through the crowd to stop before her. "You look in good health."

She nodded without speaking.

"How is Gavin?"

"Good. Very good." She was silent again, her gaze clinging to his, before asking haltingly, "Was your journey pleasant?"

Not as pleasant as knowing she was glad he was back. "Profitable. We accomplished what we set out to do." He wondered what she would do if he carried her into the warehouse across the street, slammed the door, and tore off her clothes. "I brought you a gift."

"A gift?"

How he loved her mouth. He loved the way she smelled of lavender and woman. He loved the courage, boldness, and defiance she showed him that was more tempting than another woman's compliance. By God, he had missed her. "It's in the cargo hold. I'll have it brought to—"

"Haven't you forgotten something, Robert?" Jock stood beside them. "Good day, my lady. I hate to interrupt this sweet greeting, but it's necessary that I consult Robert on the disposition of an item of cargo." He shifted his great bulk to one side to reveal a tall brown-haired young woman with sparkling blue eyes and plump breasts brimming over the low-cut bodice of her gown. "What do I do with this charming creature?"

The woman chuckled and laid a caressing hand on Jock's arm. Her words had a pleasant lilt as she said, "Why, the same as you did on the journey over. I have no complaints. Don't change a thing."

Kate looked from the woman back to Robert in bewilderment. Robert silently and venomously heaped every curse in his memory on Jock. He had no doubt the bastard was deliberately trying to cause trouble.

"Aren't you going to introduce our visitor from afar?" Jock asked.

"Mistress Norah Kerry," Robert muttered. He took Kate's elbow and began propelling her down the dock.

"I'll fetch Norah to the castle at nightfall," Jock called after him. "There's no use bringing her here and not using her services."

Damn that interfering son of a bitch. Robert could feel the tension charging Kate's body, the bewilderment and uneasiness now veiling that tentative happiness he had sensed in her.

"What services?" Kate asked.

"Never mind. Has Gavin shown you the island?"

"Only the town. I've been busy." She glanced back over her shoulder at Jock and Norah. "What services?"

There was no use trying to avoid the truth. Kate's curiosity and obstinacy were very much in evidence. "She's a strumpet."

Under his hand he felt shock harden the muscles of her forearm. "I see. Then I'm sure your journey was even more pleasant than you said." She jerked her arm away and began to walk faster. "But you should not have left her so rudely just because you thought I might have been offended. It was very foolish of you. I know how similar we are in your eyes."

"You don't know anything of the sort," he said roughly.

"Of course I do. We're both in your life only until you cast us out, good for pleasing you in bed and nothing more. I actually feel a certain kinship with her."

"She's not my—"

"You needn't deny it to save my feelings. Considering your carnal nature, it would be mad of me to expect you to abstain when so tempting a woman appears." Her words were coming fast, tumbling like rocks loosened by a landslide. "She seems very good-tempered. I'm sure she proved most accommodating."

"Yes, she did, but not to me. It was Jock who bedded her."

"And now it's your turn?"

"If I'd wanted to bed her, I would have done so. Jock and I have shared women before." Another mistake. He could see she didn't like the picture that brought to mind either. "Jock is bringing her to the castle for—"

"I have no interest in your strumpets." She kept her face turned away, but he could see the color burning in her cheeks. "It's just as well you did bring her for your pleasure, for I'm not with child. You would not want to endanger Craighdhu by touching me."

The words struck him with such force, he knew he had been avoiding thinking of the possibility. He had thought only of Kate, the things he would do with her, the ways he would take her, bind her to him. "You're certain?"

"I've had my flux, and even if I had not, I would not let you come to my bed. So you can feel free to go to your Norah and—"

"Dammit!" Blind frustration and rage exploded within him, and he knew it was caused not by her words but the barrier that now existed between them. He overtook her in two steps, grabbed her arm, and jerked her into the alcove of the butcher's shop they were passing. "I don't need your permission to take a whore or to take my own wife. I will do either, if I see fit."

"Let me go!"

"When you stop talking and listen to me." He put his hands against the wall on either side of her, holding her captive. He could feel the warmth of her body and wanted to rub up and down like a cat against her. "I did not bring the woman for myself. I brought her for Gavin."

"Gavin!" Her eyes widened in shock. "Why?"

"Jock says she's a cheerful and diverting lass, and God knows Gavin needs diverting." He scowled. "Before he gets himself drawn and quartered."

"Oh!" Her teeth sank into her lower lip. "I don't think it's Gavin who is in danger at the moment. You'd best keep the woman away from the castle."

"You don't understand these matters." He tried to be patient, though he wanted to reach out and shake her. No, take her, plunge into her, make her accept every bit of him. But he couldn't do that. Craighdhu was now safe, and he had to quench the fever. Gavin. He would think of Gavin. He couldn't do anything to rid himself of his own obsession, but he could try to save Gavin. "There will be no shame. I promise the woman will not intrude. You'll scarce see her, but Gavin needs—"

"Gavin has all he needs at the moment," she interrupted. "And if you wish this woman to live to give pleasure to any other man, you'll not let Jean know she's on the island."

He stiffened. "Jean?"

"She's here." She added simply, "Gavin went reiving."

He closed his eyes. Christ, this was all he needed. "How long have they been here?"

"Two days. They're to wed at sundown this evening."

"The hell they will."

"You cannot stop them unless you wish to kill Gavin. He will not be swayed. They leave tomorrow for Ireland." She smiled bitterly. "So you need not worry they will endanger your Craighdhu."

"Malcolm will follow them."

"Gavin says he knows people who will hide them."

He shook his head. "It's madness. Malcolm will slice Gavin's throat and make Jean a widow before the month's out." He turned to her. "And then shall I tell you what he'll do to that sweet, shy child? It will make Sebastian's treatment of you seem gentle in comparison."

"She's willing to take the risk, and she's stronger than you think. If you wish to prove it, just send that strumpet to Gavin and see what happens."

His arms dropped, and he slowly stepped back. "I have to talk with him."

"He thought that would be your wish. That's why they waited, instead of leaving at once." She left the alcove and started walking toward the castle. "I believe he wants your blessing."

"He won't get it."

"Then you must give him your good wishes," she said. "I won't have him going into danger with bad feelings lingering. He doesn't deserve such treatment."

"He deserves a knock on the head to clear his brain."

"Because he had the temerity to endanger your precious Craighdhu? Well, I'm glad he did. He should have something better than stone and earth to cling to in this world. I don't fully understand Jean Malcolm, but she's a brave woman and I think you're a fool not to realize Gavin has—" She broke off and stalked ahead of him down the street. "What are you going to do? You can't send her back."

"You won't permit me?"

"Gavin won't permit you." She lifted her chin. "And no, I won't either. They're going to be no bother to you. There's no reason for you to spoil their happiness."

"No reason, but to save their lives."

"It's not your concern. Gavin is no child. He has chosen his way."

"Just as you've chosen yours."

"*I've* chosen?" She started across the drawbridge. "I had nothing to do with this. Elizabeth gave me to you, and you took me and brought me here."

"If I remember, I agreed to pay highly for your acquiescence."

"A home? It's proved to be an empty promise. You cannot give me—" She stopped and drew a deep breath. "We were talking of Gavin and Jean."

"Is it not better to talk *to* them?" Gavin asked.

They looked up to see Gavin and Jean strolling toward them across the drawbridge from the castle. Gavin's hand was clasped tightly around Jean's, his face a trifle pale but his expression resolute. He stopped before Robert and braced himself. "I'm glad you're home, Robert. You're just in time for the wedding."

Robert stared at him. "You realize the consequences?"

"I welcome the consequences." Gavin drew Jean closer. "Some things are meant to be."

"Then heaven help you." Robert strode past them across the bridge and into the courtyard.

"At least he didn't throw me into the moat this time. I consider that an excellent sign." Gavin smiled down at Jean. "First battle over, love."

"And you fought it well." She smiled back at him

before her gaze wandered after Robert. "But perhaps I will also speak to him, later, when his temper cools."

Kate did not see Robert for the rest of the day. After speaking to Tim MacDougal, he had returned to town to seek Jock. She deliberately kept herself too busy with preparations for the wedding feast to spare a thought for him.

However, she made sure she was in the courtyard when Jock Candaron rode through the gates a few hours before dusk. He reined in his horse and shook his head at the stable boy, who ran toward him to take the horse. "I won't be staying." He gestured to the pack-horse behind him. "Take the trunk to my lady's chamber. It's a gift from her devoted husband."

Kate barely glanced at the huge leather trunk. She was concerned only that the woman Norah Kerry was not with him.

He smiled coolly when he saw her relieved expression. "I left the lady at the inn in town. I saw Robert down at the docks, and he said her services were not required. Pity."

"Gavin doesn't agree with you."

"But he was always one who thought with his heart, not his head." He paused deliberately. "Not at all like Robert."

"No?"

"Robert is much like me. He usually confines his passions to objects that cannot hurt him."

"Such as Norah Kerry?"

He shook his head. "Robert chose her for Gavin. His own tastes run to more spirited females. For instance, you've quite captivated him." Bluntly, he continued, "Are you with child?"

Shock ran through her at the rudeness of the question. "No."

"That's good. Then we all may be safe. Robert is

no fool to endanger Craighdhu twice, no matter how much he wishes to bed you."

"He told you who my mother ... who I am?"

"Did you think he would not share such knowledge of a danger to Craighdhu with the man who defends her? I told him what an idiot he was." He paused, then added deliberately, "But he assured me it was only lust, and Robert and I both know how fleeting that emotion can be."

He was trying to hurt her and succeeding admirably. She tried not to let him see how deep that thrust had gone home. "Then you've nothing to worry about, have you?"

"I didn't think so, until Robert and I talked to Deirdre and some of the townspeople this afternoon. You've been busy while we've been gone. Actually, you've done very well. You have a brain in your head and a gift for leadership."

"I've only tried to help," she said.

He shook his head. "You've been making a nest for yourself."

She met his gaze and knew she could not deny it to him as she had to herself. She had followed the instinct blindly, working, weaving a life in this place she most wanted to be. "Since there's no child in the nest, there's no threat to you."

"Not yet." He smiled. "But I thought I should point out that I would be most displeased if you decided to lure Robert into that particular danger."

She felt a chill run through her. The threat was clear, and Jock Candaron a very dangerous man. "And what would you do if I chose to disobey your advice?"

"Whatever my duty bids," he said softly. "I always do my duty, Kate. It is a passion with me." He turned his horse. "Now you must excuse me. Robert is waiting for me at my lodgings to discuss matters of business."

For the first time he had called her by her first name, foregoing the formal title of respect. She knew it was deliberate. He wished to show her he had no more deference for her than he had for Norah Kerry.

"You may *not* call me Kate," she said through her teeth. "I prefer you to call me Kathryn, as my other enemies do."

He smiled. "I look forward to seeing you at the wedding, Kathryn. Such a joyous occasion . . ."

She shivered as she watched him ride away. Duty for Jock could be anything from political machinations to a knife thrust. He would not allow her to—

Good Heavens, what was she thinking? Jock had no right to forbid her anything. He might be the guardian of Craighdhu, but he could not enforce his will on her.

The sudden rage flaming through her was white hot in intensity. It was not fair! Robert and now Jock mouthing these foolish fears. Couldn't they see how unimportant she was to anyone in the outside world? Craighdhu was a universe in itself. She could live here in peace with Robert, their children around her. She could have everything she wanted, everything that had been denied her. It wasn't right for her to be cheated this way.

She stomped into her chamber to find Jean on her knees by the open leather chest, her arms overflowing with a rainbow of velvet and silks. "What wonderful gowns. Perhaps I won't be as hard on Robert as I planned," she murmured. "He's certainly not stingy with the shilling. Powerful men usually hold their purse strings much closer than—" She stopped as she saw Kate's flushed cheeks and blazing eyes. "They don't please you?"

Kate scarcely glanced at the finery in the trunk. "Such garments do not suit me. Take what you wish."

Jean shook her head. "I brought clothing aplenty with me. There was no sense in spending Gavin's gold when I had all those gowns my father was forced to buy when he presented me at court." She sat back on her heels. "And these gowns would suit you much better than those drab feathers you clothe yourself in."

"Feathers!" Kate slammed down the lid of the trunk. "I'm no weak, fluttering bird, and if I'm trying to make a nest for myself, it's only because I wish to be happy. Is that too much to ask?"

"Not of me." Jean rose to her feet. "But men are more foolish than women. Sometimes when they cannot see, we must lead them until everything becomes clear to them."

The idea of Kate putting Robert on a lead was ludicrous. At the moment she would much rather put a noose around his neck. "He's not so tame."

"Only when he wants to be." Jean nodded at the chest. "And he's already given you the weapons to use against him."

"I don't want to fight him. I just wish to be left alone to make a life for myself."

Jean studied her thoughtfully. "I think that's the last thing you wish. Why are you lying to yourself?"

Because she was afraid she would be hurt again if she reached out and took what she wanted. The truth came to Kate out of nowhere, unbidden and unwelcome.

Jean nodded. "I'll have a tub brought up for your bath."

Kate shook her head. "Not now. I still have too much work to do. I have to supervise the setting up of the tables on the green, and the cooks tell me they need more mutton than they thought, and we need flowers for the—"

"I'll send for Deirdre. She'll enjoy ordering everyone about." A slight edge sharpened Jean's words. The one time Jean and Deirdre had met had not been a cordial occasion. Deirdre had no use for helpless females, and Jean's charm had reaped only a bounty of tactless criticism.

"Deirdre has her own work. I can't—"

"I'll send for Deirdre," Jean repeated firmly. She gave Kate a commanding glance over her shoulder as she moved toward the door. "Give me a little time, and I'll make you into the woman you should be."

"I'm the woman I should be now. All of this finery will not make me more so."

"Weapons," Jean said again.

Kate frowned. "Why should you wish to do this?"

"Many reasons. Because it's always a good thing to let men know our power. Because your contentment may have an effect on Gavin's and my happiness." She smiled, and it was not the enchanting smile she used to beguile the world. "And perhaps because I'm beginning to have a true fondness for you."

The door closed behind her.

A ripple of warmth tempered the rage and hurt Kate was feeling. She and Jean were different in nature and thinking, but she was beginning to have a fondness for Jean as well. She turned and slowly lifted the lid of the trunk.

I have a fondness for most textures.

She remembered Robert's words as she reached out with a tentative finger and stroked the nap of the yellow velvet gown on top.

Jean meant for her to make herself into a woman Robert would not be able to resist, to lure him back into her bed in spite of his objections. She could have told her that was not possible. She had tried to make Robert belong to her before and only been hurt.

But at that time she had been a child, chasing after a dream. She had changed. She was a woman now, with a woman's strengths and a woman's goals.

Even if the path Jean suggested was possible, such blandishments were not Kate's way.

Still, the lady of Craighdhu should at least be presentable.

Textures . . .

*A*s *Kate came down* the steps, Gavin blinked, and
then a slow smile lit his face. "You look beautiful, Kate.
Is all this splendor in my and Jeanie's honor?"

"Of course." She quickly glanced away from him as
she touched the crimson velvet of her skirt. "Jean said
I must dress as befitted her wedding, and would not be
satisfied with anything but this gaudy color. She says it
suits me."

"Ah, Jeanie is the clever one. I should have known.
She's right, as usual. It's a fine bold hue for a fine bold
lass."

"You look very fine yourself." He looked more
than fine, Kate thought affectionately. An amethyst-
bejeweled silver thistle embellished the wide MacDarren
sash that crossed his chest and half hid the sparkling
white of his linen shirt. His jauntily plumed hat sat
slightly askew on his red hair, giving him an air of rak-
ish insouciance that was at odds with the eagerness he
was trying to hide. Dear God, he was scarcely more
than a boy, not even able to see through the mask worn
by the woman he loved. How was he to evade the evil
that would follow him when he left here? Trying to hide
her fear with a mock frown, she let her gaze wander to

his bare knees exposed by his green, purple, and dark blue kilt. "But will you not get cold in that skirt?"

He flinched. "Kilt. Women wear skirts, men wear kilts. How many times must I tell you that—" He stopped as he saw her smile. "Och, you were teasing me."

"A wee bit."

"Well, I could wear nothing else on such an occasion. It would not be fitting."

"It will be less fitting to freeze your nether parts on your wedding night," she said teasingly.

"You need not worry, my blood is running too hot to even feel the chill tonight." He looked beyond her up the stairs. "Where's Jeanie?"

"Getting dressed." She grabbed his arm as he started up the steps. "And you'll see her at the church and not before."

"I couldn't run up and show her how grand I look?" he coaxed.

"No, but you can come to the cellar and choose the wine to serve at your wedding feast. We've set up tables on the glen in back of the castle with food fit for a king, but I've had little experience in selecting wine. You must help me."

"Oh, very well." He moved grudgingly away from the stairs and followed her down the hall, through the scullery to the door leading to the storage cellar. "But not wine. Ale. Heather ale."

"Wine." She lit the candle on the table beside the door before preceding him down the winding steps. "This is a very special occasion."

"Which is why we should have the ale." He went past several rows of wine and paused before a large box filled with pottery jars. "Ah, here we have it. These bottles of ale were prepared last year. The spirits should be more heady than the strongest wine."

"But I don't think—" She gave in when she saw

his pleading expression. "Oh, very well. It's your wedding."

A brilliant smile lit his face. "Aye, that it is."

She felt a surge of affection mixed with apprehension as she looked at him. He was bursting, exploding with happiness, giddy and daft as a baby bird just out of the nest. She wanted to reach out, protect him, plead with him to take the safest route.

He lifted his brows. "You're looking at me as if I were a corpse, not a bridegroom. What's wrong, Kate?"

"Nothing." She forced a smile. "I just want everything to go well for you."

"It will go well." He stooped to pick up a few bottles of ale. "How could it not? I have Jeanie."

The woman whose depths he had not even fathomed yet. "I ... believe Jean loves you very much, but she is ..." She trailed off as she realized she could not betray the girl. He was so besotted, he probably would not believe her anyway. She asked brusquely, "Are you going to carry this box upstairs, or should I call a servant?"

He continued to study the bottles. "Do you know, heather ale isn't what it seems. On the surface it's smooth as silk, but underneath there's strength and a bite." He lifted his gaze to her face. "I love the one as much as the other."

She stiffened as she searched his expression. He was not speaking of ale, and he was not the naive boy she had believed him to be.

"I'm not a fool, Kate," he said gently. "Do you think I could love a woman as much as I do Jeanie and not know her true nature? She's had a hard life, but someday she will trust in me enough to let me have all of her." He stooped and picked up two jars of the ale. "I'll take these with me. Robert is at Jock's lodgings, and maybe if I can get him drunk enough, I can persuade him to show up at the church for the wedding."

"Do you think there's a possibility he won't?"

He shrugged. "He was angry. Robert doesn't forgive lightly. We'll have to see." He moved his shoulders as if shrugging off a burden and turned and moved toward the steps. "Come along. We'll send a servant for the rest of these bottles. It's almost sundown." His soberness had vanished, and he almost bounced up the steps. "Did I tell you about the bagpipes?"

"Bagpipes?" She hurried after him, alarmed. "No bagpipes, Gavin."

"Jeanie told me you'd made no arrangements, so I took care of it myself. I know it's not customary at weddings, but this isn't your usual wedding. They have a fine stirring skirl, and I want to hear it when I see my Jeanie coming toward me."

"What about the lute?" she asked frantically. "The lute has a lovely romantic sound to it. Just right for a wedding."

Gavin shook his head. "The bagpipes." He frowned. "I just wish I could pipe her to the church myself. But I'm so excited, I fear I could not do her justice, so I've asked Tim MacDougal to do the honors."

She had not even known Robert's agent could play the bagpipes. She had a sudden picture of the small gray-haired man with his pursed, tight mouth and the permanent crease between his eyes, the furthest anyone could envision from a musician. She had worked so hard to make this wedding beautiful, and now it was going to be a disaster. "Will you not reconsider?"

"You'll see, it will be splendid." Gavin beamed. "Tim is almost as good a piper as I am."

Robert turned with a frown as Jock opened the door of his lodgings. "Ian was just here. Did you know that there was a message from Bobby MacGrath from Edinburgh while we were gone?"

Jock shook his head and threw off his cloak. "What did he have to say?"

"Not enough. Alec is still at court. When he first arrived, he spent two days in the royal dungeons."

"Occupied with his favorite sport, no doubt. Do we know who was the subject of his attention this time?"

Robert shook his head. "James is being very secretive. The guards were sent away, and Bobby hasn't been able to find out who the woman was. He says he'll continue to try."

"Woman?"

"That's all Bobby knows. It was a woman whose body was taken from the prison after two days of torture."

"Pleasant."

"Bobby said he'll keep an eye on him while he's in Edinburgh, but Alec appears to be doing nothing at present but acting as James's dear companion."

"I can't see any connection in this to our affairs."

"Neither can I." Robert shrugged. "But Alec has surprised us before." He threw himself in a chair and reached for the goblet of wine he had poured before Jock had entered. "I want you to go back to Ireland tomorrow."

Jock nodded. "I thought you might. Gavin?"

"Find a haven for him." He leaned back wearily. "If there is such a place."

"I'll do my best. It may not be enough."

"I know." He sipped his wine. "What a fool he is."

"He's not alone," Jock said. "I'm not at all sure I should leave you and go off to Ireland."

Robert said coldly, "I don't want to hear it, Jock."

"But it would not be my duty to leave it unsaid," he said mockingly. "I should stay and protect you from the harm looming on the horizon. By the way, I just returned from visiting your enchanting countess."

He stiffened. "Why?"

"You see how protectively you bristle? Very dangerous."

"Why?"

"I only delivered the gift you brought her from Ireland," he said innocently. "What else would I be doing? And we both know she doesn't need your protection. As we saw this afternoon, your lady-wife has managed to inveigle her way into the hearts of everyone on Craighdhu while we've been gone."

"There's nothing wrong with that."

"I'm sure that's what some people said of her mother's winsome ways."

"Kate's not like her mother."

"No, she burns much brighter."

A faint smile tugged at Robert's lips as he remembered how Kate had burned down Sebastian's cottage. "More than you know." He looked down into the depths of his wine. "She's hungry. All of her life she's been starved, and now she wants to taste everything around her. How can you blame her?"

"I can blame her." Jock paused. "If she gobbles up Craighdhu."

"I won't let her do that."

"Or you."

Robert was silent. It was not Kate's fault, but he felt as if he were being devoured by his emotional obsession.

"I notice you're not answering," Jock said. "Could it be because it's—"

"Robert!" It was Gavin, and he was pounding on the door. "Jock! Open the door. I have two bottles of the best ale in all of Scotland."

The wail of the bagpipes sang wild and sweet, triumphant yet melancholy, as it soared over the courtyard.

Kate stood on the stone steps staring in amazement while Tim MacDougal slowly circled the courtyard wringing such melodies as Kate had never imagined possible from the dreaded instrument. The last rays of the setting sun bathed the scene in shadow and light, rose and darkness.

She swallowed to ease the tightness from her throat and watched Jean take her place beneath the canopy of MacDarren's plaid carried by four kilted clansmen. She looked more like a fairy-tale princess than ever in her gown of ivory-colored brocade. Her long silver-blonde hair flowed free to her waist as was the custom, her only hair ornament a wreath of spring flowers. Thirty clansmen in traditional kilts and carrying burning torches formed a guard on either side of the canopy.

"Kate, come on," Jean called impatiently, an eager smile illuminating her delicate features. "Would you have me late for my wedding?"

"No, of course not." Kate hurried down to take her place behind the canopy as the procession began to file from the courtyard over the drawbridge. Ahead of her the streets were lined with townspeople, and in the distance the bell of the church began to sound, blending with the wild, splendid fanfare of the pipes.

She could see the mist-shrouded mountains in the distance, their reflection mirrored in scarlet in the sea.

Beauty. Craighdhu. Home.

It was all too much. She was overflowing with exultation, never having known a moment like this. She was no longer even concerned that Robert might not be at the church. He had to be there. God was not always fair, but He had created both Eden and Craighdhu and would not let a time of this perfection be marred.

As they approached the church, Gavin hurried down the church steps, his face alight with a radiance equal to Jean's. In their way they were as beautiful as Craighdhu.

Her Craighdhu.

She saw Robert on the top step of the church, dressed in leather vest and MacDarren kilt, his black hair shining in the dwindling sunlight.

He was hers too, she thought fiercely. There was no one in this world who could love him as much or give him more. What had she been thinking to meekly give in when they told her she could not have the two things she most wanted in the world?

She would not surrender either of them.

"My God," Robert murmured.

Kate was dressed in a crimson velvet gown with elegant wide skirts and long, full sleeves that were fashionably cut to reveal the gold chemise beneath it. A pleated gold-embroidered half-ruff framed her face but left her throat and upper breasts bare. The triangular crimson cap on her head was trimmed in glittering gold and vaguely reminded Robert of a coronet. The rosy light played on her, caressing the silky textures of her loose brown-gold hair, the smoothness of her breasts. Her color was high, her step proud and bold. Robert had never seen her look more beautiful . . . or more compelling.

"Christ, she looks . . ." Robert trailed off.

"Like a call to arms," Jock said dryly, his gaze on Kate. "And as reckless as her mother was reputed to be. I suspected as much."

She was staring challengingly at Robert. He was hardening, the blood rushing to that part of him that always responded to her nearness. If that was all in him that responded, he would be much safer.

Gavin and Jean entered the church where the dominie waited.

Kate started up the steps, her gaze holding Robert's.

She was as regal as a queen, as alluring as Circe, as defiant as a warrior going into battle. Yet he could see in her the hint of childlike uncertainty that had always moved him.

She stopped before him and slowly held out her hand.

She was asking for more than an escort into the church.

"Robert," Jock murmured warningly.

He needed no cautioning. He had been aware this moment of decision would come since she had told him she was not with child. He knew the consequences better than Jock and Kate. If he let her come near again, it would be with full knowledge of the pitfalls, the only question being whether the obsession that possessed him was worth the risk of losing all he held dear.

He looked down at the hand she was extending to him, so small yet strong and capable.

It was trembling.

He stepped forward and closed his hand possessively over Kate's. "My lady."

He led her into the church.

Torches flared brightly over the green, glittering on the four swords laid on the grass, and the dancers moving with stylish grace to the strains of the bagpipes.

Kate watched them in fascination as she stood beside Deirdre, handing out cups of ale at the long trestle table. Dancing and music and laughter: All the things that Sebastian had said would never be hers were here on this green tonight.

"Why do you not try it yourself?" Deirdre asked. "I can see you're yearning to. They'll be starting a reel as soon as the sword dance is through."

"I don't know how to dance."

"You'll learn soon enough. It's simple enough."

Kate was tempted as she glanced at the long tables laden with all manner of festive food. Leg of mutton with gallandine sauce, boiled capon, salmon, shrimp, sausages, quince pie, tart of almonds, and huge slices of gingerbread dripping with almond butter were fast disappearing as the evening progressed, and Deirdre and the other servants could certainly preside over their distribution.

No, this feast was her responsibility, her first social duty as the countess of Craighdhu, and she wouldn't shirk it to run and play. "I'll stay. There will be other feasts."

"Perhaps not such a fine one as this," Deirdre said. "You did well."

Kate flushed at the praise that always came sparingly from Deirdre. "I thank you for your help."

"I would have given it sooner if you'd—"

"It's time for us to go." Gavin was suddenly beside her. "The lads are getting a bit rowdy. Will you go get Jeanie for me?" He indicated his bride, who was at the center of a group of women at the far side of the glen. "They might embarrass her with their rude remarks if I'm the one to take her away."

She doubted if Jean would be as discomposed as Gavin thought, but it was sweet of him to be so sensitive to his bride's feelings. She nodded as she set the bottle of ale she was holding on the table. "Of course. I'll help her slip away and send her to you at the castle."

He shook his head. "We must first go beneath the swords ... I hope." He hesitated and then asked, "I have another boon to ask. Will you ask Robert to do the honor of the sword? I ... Tell him I'll understand if he chooses otherwise."

She looked at him in puzzlement. "He was at the church. Why is this different?"

"Because his presence there only indicated the laird's approval of the match. The walk beneath the swords is much more."

"In what way?"

"Acceptance of Jeanie into the clan, a promise of protection for her should I not be around to give my own. That and many other things. Will you ask him?"

She did not want to ask Robert anything that would disturb the bond between them that had been forged when he had taken her hand and led her into the church. Though they had parted when they had reached the green for the wedding feast, the excitement and anticipation lingered, charging every action, every moment of the evening. "Why don't you ask him yourself?"

"Please, Kate. I need this."

She would not be able to grant him many favors in the future. Gavin and Jeanie were going away tomorrow into exile, and Heaven knows what dangers they would face. She sighed. "I'll ask him."

She went first to Jeanie and whispered Gavin's summons in her ear, then strolled slowly across the green toward the place where Robert, Jock, and several more men were playing ball. She stood on the sidelines with the spectators while the men dodged and grappled for the big ball. Robert, like the others, was naked to the waist, his chest and arms gleaming with sweat in the torchlight. As she watched, he fell to his knees, diving for the ball, his kilt flying up to reveal hard, muscular buttocks. His head lifted, and he was laughing, dark eyes glittering, black hair tousled. He was completely sensual, absolutely male.

Robert glanced up and saw her, his laughter fading as he read her expression. He stood up, tossed the ball to the young man next to him, and started toward her.

She knew the same mixture of triumph and joy she had felt when he had taken her hand and led her into the church. She did possess power over him. She could draw him to her side with only a look. She could move him, stir him, even if it was only to desire.

He smelled of salt, leather, and ale, and when he drew closer, the warmth of his body was like a blast of heat from a campfire. Her breath was coming quicker, and her palms tingled with the urge to touch the springy triangle of dark hair on his chest.

"Yes?" he asked quietly.

"Gavin . . . They're ready to go." She met his gaze. "He sent me to ask you to do the honor of the swords."

He stiffened, and his expression became shuttered. "Oh did he, indeed?"

"It's not for himself. He wants Jean protected. He wants her to have a home if something happens to him."

"Sanctuary," he said grimly.

"They're leaving tomorrow for Ireland. He has no intention of endangering Craighdhu. It's not asking much to give him peace of mind."

"It's asking a great deal. They're wed before God, and that tie means forever. If Jean is taken into the clan, she's one of mine."

"Then you won't do it?"

He met her pleading gaze, and then a reckless smile lit his face. "Oh, what the hell. It would probably come to the same thing anyway. I doubt I could refuse her if she came to me in need." He turned and called to Jock across the green. "The swords!"

An uproar greeted the words. The ball game was forgotten as men ran to the sidelines to don shirts and scabbards.

Robert turned and picked up his own shirt from the ground. "Make ready to leave."

"Leave? But Gavin says the celebration goes on until dawn."

"It does." He shrugged into the shirt. "And we will. But not here. I have another celebration in mind."

She felt her chest constrict, and she suddenly found it difficult to breathe.

His lips twisted. "Why do you think Gavin sent you to plead his case? He knew there was a chance lust would cloud my judgment. Every man in Craighdhu can tell just by looking at me that I can hardly wait to bed my wife." He met her gaze. "And so can you. This is what you wanted, isn't it?"

She felt the same triumphant exhilaration she had before. "Yes, that's exactly what I wanted."

He picked up his scabbard. "Then make ready to leave. I'll tell Tim MacDougal to start the skirl."

The men of the clan stood facing each other in a double row that stretched across the glen, with Robert and Jock forming the first duo. The wail of the bagpipes rang out as Gavin and Jean stepped forward.

"Robert, I know you don't wish to do this," Gavin said in a low voice. "I would not ask it if it wasn't—"

"Present swords," Robert called out, interrupting him.

Scabbards hissed and swords gleamed beneath the torches as the arch was formed.

"Thank you, Robert." Gavin grabbed Jean's hand. "Come on, love."

Kate watched them walk down the arch of swords. Jean was now one of them. Embraced, held tight within the arms of the clan.

"Kate."

She turned to see Robert holding out his hand to her.

She stared at him in shock.

"By God, no!" Jock said as he lowered his sword.

"Kate," Robert said again.

She moved slowly to stand beside him. The protection of the clan, a victory she had not even sought. She was now Robert's responsibility in every sense, officially part of the world that was so precious to him. She belonged, even though it might only be for the next year.

Unless there was a child.

She gripped his hand with eager strength.

"Are you mad?" Jock muttered.

"It's a night for madness," Robert said recklessly. He pulled Kate under the arch of the swords and began to run down the gauntlet. He was laughing, and she found herself laughing too.

She could hear the bagpipes playing, and their song was for her.

The wind touched her cheeks. It was blowing for her, bringing her the scents of mist and earth that were Craighdhu.

She could see the clansmen laughing approvingly. The approval was for her; she had worked and won it in these last weeks and would hold it forever.

She was part of Craighdhu, part of all of them.

And, most of all, part of Black Robert of Craighdhu.

Robert slammed shut the door of her chamber and unbuckled his sword. "Undress."

Her hands went around to unbutton the back of her gown and then stopped. No, she could not do it. If she used her wiles to lure Robert in the way she wished him to go, she would be the harlot Sebastian had called her. "There's something I should tell you first."

"Not now." He tossed his scabbard on the chair by the door.

"Now." She squared her shoulders and then gestured to the gown she wore. "I'm seducing you."

"Good."

"No, I deliberately set out to do it. I gowned myself and made myself smell sweet. . . . I wanted you to want me."

"Then you'll be glad to know you succeeded."

"I am glad, but I can't—I'm not like Jean. It's not easy for me to lie to you, even in a good cause." She added fiercely, "And it is in a good cause."

"*Your* cause?"

"Yes, but it will do no one harm to give me my way in this."

He shrugged out of his shirt. "My dear Kate, I'm fully prepared to let you have your way with me, but I'll not lie to myself. It may do great harm."

"Then why do you do it?"

"As Gavin said, some things are meant to be." He added simply, "I have to have you."

The raw need in his voice stunned her. "For how long?"

"Until the madness passes."

"But I don't intend for it to pass." She paused and then said baldly, "I mean to get with child."

"I know." He came toward her wearing only the kilt. "I knew the instant I saw you at the church. If that happens, there is a remedy, but I hope to God I don't have to take it."

"Remedy? What remedy?"

"For God's sake, will you take off your clothes!" His every muscle was tensed, his eyes glittering, nostrils flaring. She could almost feel the waves of desire he was emitting.

Why was she standing here arguing with him? This was what she wanted. He was *hers.* She quickly slipped out of the velvet gown and gold chemise, but there were still the corset and panniers and— It was too much. She turned her back to him. "I'll never get out of all this. Jean took hours fastening me into it. Help me."

"Gladly," he muttered.

She heard the snapping of the cords and looked over her shoulder at him. He stood there with a dirk in his hand, and as she watched he slashed through the last of the corset strings. Seconds later the rest of the undergarments fell in strips around her.

"I don't remember you wearing all this in the cave. Why the hell bother now?"

"I told you, to seduce you." She bit her lower lip as he threw away the dirk, and his hands slid around to cover her breasts. They instantly swelled, the nipples hardening in response. So long. It seemed a lifetime since he had touched her. "I thought only of what you said about textures, but . . ." His warm tongue plunged into her, and a hot shudder went through her. "Jean said I needed this too."

"I don't remember saying anything about textures. But that's not surprising. I wonder I can think at all."

His hands left her breasts, and he made a quick adjustment before he brought her back against him. A shock ran though her as she realized he had pushed up the kilt, and she could feel his arousal against her bare buttocks. His hands moved around to stroke her abdomen as he slowly rotated his hips, rubbing against her in that most sensual of caresses.

"You said you . . . liked . . . the feel—" She paused as his fingers brushed against the tight curls and then went exploring farther down. "Of leather . . . and silk . . . and—" Her neck arched back against his shoulder as he found the nub for which he had been searching.

"This is the only texture I have any interest in at the moment." His thumb pressed and released, pressed and released, as he continued the circular rhythm against her buttocks. "This softness . . ." His breath came harsh and quick in her ear. "I thought of this all the time I was in Ireland. How you felt . . . those frantic little sounds you make when I come into you."

She was already making those sounds deep in her throat as sensation after sensation tore through her.

"Yes, that's it, give it to me." He pulled her down to her knees on the floor. She tried to turn around, but he gently pushed her forward on her hands and knees. "No, this way."

He came into her with one deep plunge. Substance, hardness, fullness. She cried out and sank forward, her breasts resting on the carpet.

He began moving in and out of her, deeply, frantically. His hands were on her buttocks, kneading, caressing. Her breasts lightly grazed the carpet with every stroke, and she found her nipples becoming harder and more sensitive with every touch. The stroking within her and the outer abrasion were both incredibly erotic, and the heat was growing until she could scarcely bear it. She bucked back against him, trying to take more of him. Yet it still was not enough. There was something missing. "Robert, I need . . ."

"Shh ..." He drove to the quick. "Only a little more. I have to ..."

"No ... your face ... I want to see your face."

He muttered something beneath his breath, and then she was on her back looking up at him.

His face was contorted with terrible need, his cheeks hollowed. "Satisfied?" he asked hoarsely.

Her hand reached up and touched the plane of his cheek. She could never be satisfied, but it was enough for now. She could see how much he wanted her.

He didn't wait for an answer but drove into her again and began to take ... and give.

It was fever, madness, and need.

She arched upward, her nails digging into his shoulders as the fever rose to an unbearable pitch, and then she cried out when the climax burst over them in a fiery torrent of sensation.

She lay there on the floor, her arms holding him tightly, feeling the shudder that racked him as he turned from strength to helplessness. "I'm too heavy for you," he gasped.

He was heavy, but she didn't want to let him go. "No."

He moved off her anyway and drew her close. It was minutes before his breath steadied enough for him to speak again. His lips brushed her ear as his hand moved to possessively cup her breast. "I suppose we should move to the bed."

"Soon," she murmured. "I like lying here on the floor. It reminds me of the cave. ..." She didn't want to move ever again. She wanted to lie here with Robert in this firelit room forever. Nothing could be more perfect than this moment. Yet she vaguely came to realize she wanted something else. ...

She made a motion to get up, and Robert's hand instinctively tightened on her breast. "No."

"I'll be right back." She stood up and brushed back her hair. She was still wearing the little velvet cap, she realized with amazement. It seemed impossible after the storm she had just gone through. She quickly moved over to the deep embrasure of the window.

"Where the devil are you going?"

"I wonder if I can hear . . ." She threw open the window, and wild music drifted up to her from the glen below. "Yes, I can. Do you?"

"The bagpipes?" He nodded. "Have you suddenly developed a liking for them?"

She nodded dreamily as her gaze traveled over the men, women, and children still moving about in the torchlit glen. "When Gavin isn't playing them. They're part of Craighdhu." She looked at him over her shoulder.

And Robert was all of Craighdhu. He was the silences and the mysteries, the passions that excited her and the cozy fires that warmed her. She felt a surge of love for him so strong, it almost took her breath away. "Can't you see that this is how it should be?"

He didn't answer, and she turned to face him, a touch of defiance in her stance. "I tell you, I was right to do this."

He smiled slowly and held out his hand. "Then come and do it again."

He would not admit this passion he had for her was not a mistake. Well, she mustn't ask for too much. She had only begun and had already won a great deal tonight.

She smiled as she started toward him, unconsciously keeping pace to the faint martial strains of the bagpipes drifting from the glen. "I intended nothing else."

At noon the next day Jock, Jean, and Gavin boarded the fishing boat that was to carry them to the coast of Ireland. Robert and Kate were at the dock to bid them good-bye.

"May fortune bless you," Kate said as she gave Gavin a hug. "Be careful."

"I will." He turned to Robert. "I won't tell you where we're going. I want you to be able to tell Malcolm in all honesty that you've no knowledge of us."

"I would have no problem lying to Alec," Robert said, then thrust out his hand and added gruffly, "Be careful, damn you. Don't trust anyone."

"We won't," Jean said as she drew closer to Gavin. "Gavin has a trusting nature, but I've learned how men can become corrupted by fear. You'll not hear from us for a long time, but I hope you won't forget us. We do not wish this separation to last forever."

"Jeanie, no!" Gavin said. "You know we cannot come back to Craighdhu."

"We can," Jean said as she met Robert's gaze. "If he will let us."

Robert gazed at her a moment, then smiled faintly. "Perhaps. We will see what time brings." He turned and took Kate's elbow. "Good journey."

They stood watching on the dock as the ship sailed out of the harbor and put out to sea.

"They look so happy," Kate said wistfully. "I've never seen anyone as full of joy. Surely, God will protect them."

"Well, I'd bank more on Jock than any deity," Robert said. "God sometimes forgets to keep an eye out for men like Alec Malcolm, but Jock never does."

"But Ireland should be safe?"

"It would have been safer a year ago, before Alec had men in every town along the coast." He saw the anxiety in her expression and said, "I won't lie to you. Jock will find him the safest haven possible, but they will be in danger as long as Alec lives." He frowned. "Stop looking like that. I didn't mean to frighten you."

"You didn't frighten me. It just doesn't seem fair that things are going so well for me and not for Gavin.

This morning when I woke up, I felt so full of—" *Love.* No, it was too soon to tell him that. She substituted the word he would accept. "Hope."

He smiled. "Spring is the time for hope."

She shivered beneath the weight of her cloak. Last night on the green it had seemed much warmer, but it was always cold here at the dock. "It doesn't feel like spring."

"Perhaps not to a puny Sassenach like yourself, but the sun is shining and the ground is warming. We may even have an early blooming of the heather."

She looked at him skeptically.

"You don't believe me?" He lifted her onto Rachel's back. "Come, I'll prove it to you."

Her spirits lifted higher when she saw the mischievous smile he gave her over his shoulder as he mounted his horse. "Where are we going?"

"The barrens."

"But I have to go to the weavers and tell them—"

"You've told them quite enough. I found out yesterday that I have a minor insurrection on my hands."

She glanced at him warily, but he was still smiling. "Well, you deserved it. Within four years our own people will be making the finest woolens in all of Scotland *and* Ireland."

"If you have your way."

"Why should I not have my way when the way is right ... and profitable?"

"A good question."

"And you won't have to worry about a thing," she said quickly. "Leave it all to me. I'll take care of everything."

"That's what I'm afraid of. You obviously have a taste for running things. Who's to say you won't decide I'm dispensable to Craighdhu?"

She gazed at him uncertainly. "You're joking?"

He chuckled. "Aye, I'm not afraid of being ousted

by the clan. I believe I still have some small value in
their eyes."

"They love you. I could never replace you." She
suddenly grinned. "But in a year you will not be able to
replace me either. You're right, I *like* running things."

"Well, you can forgo it for one day." He turned his
horse and nudged him into a gallop. "I want to show
you something."

A short time later they had left the town behind
them, but it was over an hour's ride before they
reached the northern tip of the island.

He dismounted, helped her down, and then led
her up the steep, sloping hill leading to the edge of the
cliff. He pointed downward. "Spring."

Seals. Hundreds, perhaps thousands, of seals moving on the black rocks below. Sparkling blue water
washed against the dark rocks burnishing them to an
onyx shimmer. Scarcely an inch of rock remained unoc-
cupied by sleek brown-black bodies. Males and females,
babies with big gentle eyes and sleek, soft coats, plunging into the water or basking lazily in the sunlight.

Kate laughed in delight. "I wouldn't think they
would come back this early."

"They usually come a little later, but they're good,
hearty Scottish seals. Not at all like—"

"Puny Sassenachs," she finished. "They come here
to give birth?"

Robert nodded. "And to breed. The females birth
and then mate only a few days later."

"And don't give birth until the following year?
That must mean they're with child almost all the time."

"They don't seem to mind."

"The babies are so sweet." She watched two baby
seals flopping after their mother, their grunts of protest
sounding almost human when they couldn't keep up
with her. "Can we go down to them?"

"Not unless you want considerable damage done
to your enchanting person. The mothers are very pro-

tective." His smile faded. "You know, when I come back from Spain, I wasn't sure there was a God."

She looked at him, shocked. Even at the worst of times, she had never doubted the existence of a Supreme Being.

"In this world where Protestants and Catholics are tearing each other apart, vying to find who can be crueler, it seemed unreasonable, if there was a God, that he would let that happen in His name." He gestured to the scene of sea and earth and life below. "But that's God, Kate. That's the God that makes sense."

"Yes, that's God." She felt as if she were bursting with love for Robert at this moment. She loved the man of thought, the bold warrior, Gavin's friend, her lover, every facet, every movement, every breath he took.

He kept his eyes on the seals as he asked, "Do you ever dream anymore?"

"Not since I came to Craighdhu." She breathed in the salty air. "There's magic here."

He turned to look at her.

"Home," she said simply. "I knew it the first moment I saw it."

"My God." He was silent a moment. "Then I suppose I shouldn't be surprised at your determination to stay here."

"I *will* stay here."

He shook his head. "It cannot be. I'm warning you, Kate, what ever happens between us, you cannot have Craighdhu."

"I'll persuade you otherwise. You're not usually so blockheaded. There's no reason why we can't live in harmony here."

"There's every reason. Why the devil will you not—" He broke off as he saw the stubborn set of her chin. "Why am I wasting my breath?" He took her hand and turned her away from the cliff. "Let's go back to the castle."

"Why? I like it here."

"We'll come back another time." He smiled crookedly. "It may be spring, but it's too cold to take you on the ground, and I feel the need to have you demonstrate just how harmonious we can be together. I trust you have no objection?"

She looked down at the baby seals on the rocks below. If all went well, God might grant her a babe herself by the time the seals came back next year. "No objection at all."

"You fool!" Alec snarled as his hand cracked against his son's cheek. "Can I trust you for nothing?"

Duncan fell to the stones of the courtyard, and before he could rise, Alec kicked him in the ribs. "I leave Kilgranne for only a short time, and you let this happen. How long has she been gone?"

"Two weeks." Duncan scrambled away from another kick and rose to his feet. "I couldn't help it. Gavin snatched her away before we knew he was here."

Alec doubted the truth of his words. Duncan was soft as a woman where his sister was concerned. He would never have dared defy Alec if he'd been here at Kilgranne, but he was capable of working behind his back. "Where did he take her?"

"How should I know?" Duncan asked evasively.

"You should know because you should have pursued them," Alec thundered. "But since you did not, I'm sure you've gathered rumors from the families in the glen. Did he take her to Craighdhu?"

Duncan hesitated.

"Duncan, I need an heir, so I cannot kill you, but I will make sure you do not rise from your bed for a month if you fail to answer me."

"They're not at Craighdhu," Duncan said reluctantly. "They were there only to wed before they moved on." He added hastily, "Or so I hear."

"And what else do you hear?"

"That they sailed from Craighdhu on a fishing boat the day after they wed."

"To what destination?"

"I don't know."

Alec believed him this time. Gavin was no fool and would not bandy about such news. But there were always ways to find out information. The MacDarren clan were closely linked to families here on the mainland as well as on the island itself. Someone would know.

Someone would be persuaded to speak.

And what then? It went without saying, the boy must be punished for his actions and his daughter learn the penalty of defiance. Dammit, if Gavin and Jean were still at Craighdhu, he might have had the opportunity to seize the prize fate had offered him, the prize that was now in Robert MacDarren's possession. Since Robert had sent the newlyweds away, he had no excuse to call on James for help to invade Craighdhu, and the island was impregnable without the assault only the king could provide. Yet there must be some way he could use this temporary defeat to his advantage.

He had only to seek it out.

12

A glory of purple heather covered the slope leading to the edge of the cliff overlooking the barrens.

Kate stared in wonder at the stunted growth that had been transformed from brown ugliness to a symphony of graceful lavender stalks.

"Beauty to feed the soul," she murmured. "I didn't believe it when you told me." She slipped down from Caird and ran up the slope. "It's ... wonderful." She stood on the edge of the cliff and exultantly held out her arms and let the sun stream down on her, the scent of heather and sea surround her. "Dear God, I love this place."

"Well, don't love it so much you fall off the cliff. You look like you're going to take off and fly."

"I might. It's a day bright enough for miracles." She glanced back over her shoulder to find him still at the bottom of the hill quietly watching her. "Someday I might see if I can."

"It wouldn't surprise me if you could, if you willed it so."

"But isn't it wonderful, Robert?"

"Wonderful." He smiled indulgently as he took a blanket from his pack and then followed her up the slope. "But then you find everything about Craighdhu wonderful."

"It is. And if you don't see it, then you've become entirely too jaded and critical. It's fortunate I've come to show you Craighdhu's true worth."

"I'm humbly grateful for your condescension in doing so." He spread out the blanket, then sat down beside her and looped his arms around his bare knees.

He looked a barbaric, primitive figure, she thought contentedly, all gleaming bronze skin and tousled black hair. She loved him best like this, with no trace of the wary, cynical man she had first known. He had taken to wearing the kilt almost constantly during the two months since Gavin's wedding and had shed his shirt during the ride to the barrens. She felt a sudden urge to touch him, to reach out and stroke the tight, corded muscles of his abdomen, but she restrained the impulse. Not yet. That would only lead to passion, and she wanted to savor this special moment. "And you're never humble. I never saw a man with less doubt of his own self-worth."

"Your acquaintance with men has been very limited to date. I hardly think you'd say your Sebastian was lacking in self-esteem."

"True. But you Scots are far more arrogant. I've decided that it's the primary trait of your nationality."

"Then, as the daughter of the queen of all the Scots, you should have more than your share."

Two months ago the mention of her mother would have sent a faint uneasiness through her, but nothing could disturb the euphoric state she was in today. "Oh, I do have my share of arrogance. But we women have need of that quality when men are constantly trying to subdue us. It's our only way to survive."

"Your mother didn't survive."

His tone was still casual, but she could detect the slightest hint of grimness and quickly directed their badinage in a more cheerful direction. "But Elizabeth has survived for over thirty years, and you say she's the most arrogant woman on the face of the earth."

"Or in heaven or hell," he said grimly.

"Yet she tried to be kind to me."

"Not kind enough to make sure the guardian she chose was adequate for the task."

"You resent her still? I think you condemn her too harshly. She was only doing what she thought best for me."

"Elizabeth seldom considers the good of any individual when her own good or the good of her country is in the balance."

"Then you should approve of her. You said you would not follow my mother because she was a woman of impulse."

He scowled. "I do *not* approve of that red-haired bitch."

She had never seen him like this, she thought in amusement. He was like a sulky little boy. "Because she bested you and made you do her will." She grinned. "But would you follow her in battle?"

"I told you I fight only under Craighdhu's banner."

"But if you had a common purpose? Would you?" she persisted.

"Aye," he growled.

She clapped her hands in delight. "And you would not follow James, and he is a man. You see, arrogant women do have a place in the world."

"It's not her arrogance, it's her mind and will that have value."

"But how else could she prevail? Meekness does not serve a ruler well."

"I'm tired of this talk of Elizabeth."

Her lips twitched. "Because it reminds you of how she bested you?"

He was suddenly straddling her, looking down into her face. "You're right," he murmured silkily. "The thought of being bested arouses my temper and makes me want to dominate everything and everyone around me. Would you care to be dominated, Kate?"

She frowned. "I've never liked it before."

"But I'd do it quite differently from your Sebastian. Let me try."

"Oh, very well. If you think I'll enjoy it." He had never done anything she did not enjoy. It was all pleasure and joy. Her hands slipped under his kilt to cup his hard buttocks in her palms. "I've decided I like this garment. It's very convenient."

"I noticed you've found it so. I admit I've worn it more in the last month than ever in my life." His lids half closed as he smiled wickedly down at her. "But then I could scarcely do anything else. I wouldn't want your immodesty to go unmatched."

He meant the habit she had taken to of wearing a minimum of underclothing herself, as she wanted to make herself available to him at all times. She chuckled. "Well, you would not give me a kilt of my own."

"Because I didn't want to let my clansmen know what an eager wife I have. It would only have made them unsatisfied with their own lot." He leisurely unbuttoned her gown to the waist and then parted it to bare her breasts. "Aye, very eager."

Her breasts were beginning to tauten beneath his gaze. "Then do something about it," she demanded.

He shook his head. "I like to look at you."

From his position on top of her she was aware that he would like to do more than stare, but he sat there, unmoving, intent, watching her body ripen.

"Oh, I like that," he said softly. "What a woman you are. It takes only a look and you respond."

He swung off her and began to undress her, taking his time. She tried to help him, but he stopped her. "No, let me. I told you I was in the mood to dominate."

"How can you dominate, if you wait on me?" she scoffed.

"By controlling the speed of the play." He now had her naked except for her silk stockings and the leather garters that held them in place above the knee. He untied the garter on her right limb and began slowly to roll the stocking down her leg, his fingers trailing a feather-light path along the flesh of her thigh.

A shudder went through her, and muscles clenched beneath his touch.

"I'm glad you got rid of those woolen stockings," he murmured. "These are much more pleasant." He rubbed the sensitive spot behind her knee.

She arched upward off the blanket as the touch generated a flash of heat that seemed to strike directly into her womb.

"What a fascinating sensitivity you have there. I can't tell you how happy I am that I discovered it." He drew the stocking off and gently touched the sole of her foot. "And here."

The muscle of her calf spasmed as her foot arched. She drew a deep breath. It was all very well for him to play his games, but this was taking entirely too long. "That is not the sensitive place to which I wish you to apply yourself."

"Presently." He untied the other garter and put it aside. "Perhaps."

"Perhaps! If you think—" She stopped as she saw his mischievous grin. He looked wicked, reckless, and infinitely sensual. She had never seen him quite like this, and the sudden change intrigued her. His mood might be devilish, but she knew he would not be able to keep himself from giving her satisfaction or taking his own. But if she could restrain herself, perhaps he would grow impatient, and that end might come sooner. She met his gaze and then deliberately lay back on the blanket. "It's possible that I may grow bored with all this folderol."

"Ah, a challenge." He sat back on his heels and looked at her lying naked before him. "Now what can

I do to meet it?' He reached down and picked up the two leather garters. "Shall I show you one of the things I learned in Spain?"

"You've already shown me any number of things."

"But this has to do with textures. You displayed an interest in them at one time, and I've always had a certain preoccupation with them." He took one of the garters and bent over her. "No, lie quite still. You know I wouldn't hurt you."

"What are you doing?" She watched as he encircled her left breast with the strip of leather and then slowly tightened the spiral until both the tip and an area about one inch in diameter were thrown upward in relief.

"How does it feel?"

"Strange. There's . . . pressure."

"But it doesn't hurt?"

"No." The butter-soft leather was smooth and warm against her flesh and the pressure slight. "I can barely feel it."

"You will." He was binding her right breast with the other garter. "Even this little stricture will cause the blood to rise to your nipples and make them very sensitive." He finished tying the leather and sat back and looked at her. "It's already starting," he said thickly. "Do you feel it?"

She was beginning to experience a faint tingling, and when she glanced down at the leather bonds against her flesh, the tingling deepened.

"Yes?" Robert asked.

She looked at him and realized at once that the act had excited him as much as it did her. Surely, he could not continue very much longer. "Perhaps a little." She feigned a yawn. "Though I think I'm growing sleepy."

"Then we must certainly wake you up." He sat down beside her and leisurely spread her legs and looked at her. "But I think this part of you needs little stirring." He reached behind her. "However, we will do it anyway."

Coolness against her hotness, a faint earthy roughness against the heart of her.

"What are you—"

He held it up to show her. He had plucked a stalk of heather and had been rubbing it against her. The stalk was fully twelve inches long, with a thick purple stem, close-leaved green shoots, and feathery spikes of bell-shaped flowers.

"I told you there were any number of uses for heather." He brushed the flower across her belly and watched the muscles contract. "Textures, Kate. Wonderful, wonderful textures."

His blasted textures were driving her mad. The spike of petals trailing over her body was leaving paths of fire in its wake, bringing the blood to the surface until she felt as if her entire body were hot, touched, possessed.

"Still sleepy, lass?"

She couldn't answer.

The heather was brushing lightly against her distended nipples, and she bit her lip to stifle a groan. They were now as exquisitely sensitive as he had said they would be. Her breasts began to rise and fall with every breath.

"Somehow I don't think so." He stayed at her breasts a long time, circling the rosy globe the slight pressure had brought to the surface, then applying the plant to the nipples. His gaze was narrowed on her face. "If you ask me sweetly enough, I might be persuaded to put an end to this." He blew on one engorged nipple. "Tell me what you want."

She wanted his tongue on her; she wanted him to draw her into his mouth and relieve this fever of need he had ignited. But he had used the word "might," and she would not give the teasing devil the satisfaction of surrender unless she was sure it was over. Dear heavens, surely he could not continue this for much longer.

He trailed the heather over her rib cage and then down her abdomen. He toyed with the indentation of her belly button, watching as the muscles tensed. He moved the stalk farther, ruffling the curls surrounding her womanhood. "Now this is one of my favorite textures in all the world. Texture against texture. Don't you find the blend interesting?"

"No." Her voice sounded strangled even to herself.

"Ah, then perhaps I'd better do something to capture your attention." He parted her thighs even wider and began to run the heather up and down the most intimate part of her.

She wanted to scream. Her nails dug deep as her hands clenched on the blanket.

"Oh, you do find that interesting?" He used the stem to rotate the nub. "And this?"

She couldn't stand it any longer. "Yes," she said between set teeth.

"You're beautiful down here," he whispered. "Even more beautiful than the heather. You're opening and quivering like a flower at dawn."

He reversed the heather and moved it farther down. "It's a fine thick stalk," he said softly. He probed gently with the feathery spiky tip. "Would you like to feel it in you?"

The silken words flowed over her, inciting a forbidden excitement. She was panting, her head thrashing back and forth on the blanket. It had to stop. She needed— "Yes!"

"Not bloody likely." He threw the heather aside and was in her with one bold plunge. "I'm a jealous man, and I'll be damned if you know anyone or anything but me."

He suddenly was giving her everything he had denied her. While his hips moved strongly, frantically, he lifted her over his arm and began sucking strongly at her breast.

It was too much. She could feel the tears running down her cheeks as both her limbs curled around his hips, desperately holding him to her. The pleasure was so intense, she was mindless, moving to every command, taking until she could take no more.

The explosion that came a few minutes later left her limp and weak.

She was barely conscious when he roused himself, untied the leather garters from her breasts and threw them aside. He chuckled. "I believe you enjoyed being dominated. Perhaps you'll allow me to do it more often."

"I don't . . . think I could stand it," she gasped. She rolled over into his arms. "And, besides, it's only fair I have my turn with you. I know just the place I want that leather garter to be."

"What a bawdy wench you are."

She held him close. The pagans who had first come to Craighdhu must have felt as she did now. She could hear the soft grunt of the seals and the rush of the sea crashing on the rocks below. The sun was hot on her naked flesh, and the smell of earth, heather, and Robert was all around her. Every time with him grew sweeter, more passionate, more complete, and yet always different: bright jewels for her to polish and put away in her treasure chest. Surely it could not be that way for her and not for him. He had never said the words, but she could feel the bond strengthening between them with every day that passed. "My turn," she repeated. "And soon."

"Perhaps we'll forget about domination from now on," he said warily, then kissed her. "Besides, you didn't respond appropriately. Submission was required, not eagerness. You're clearly not suited for this particular kind of play. Or perhaps it was all that talk of Elizabeth and her queenly ways that influenced you to display more spirit than called for."

"Perhaps." She suddenly raised herself on her elbow and looked down at him. "But I shall also be a queen, you know. The best queen in all the world."

He stiffened as she had known he would, and his eyes narrowed. "Indeed?"

She laughed and threw herself back into his arms. "The queen of Craighdhu."

He relaxed. "Are you trying to depose me again?"

"Only in favor of your son or daughter."

His arms tightened around her. "No, Kate."

"Yes." She cuddled closer, her lips brushing the hollow of his throat. "Craighdhu's the only kingdom I'll ever want. *Give* it to me."

"I've told you that's not possible."

Ordinarily, she would have dropped the subject, but she was too full of happiness and confidence not to make the attempt. "And I've told you that your reasons are foolish."

"Listen, Kate, you're the one who is blind." His hand gently stroked her hair. "So blind. Can't you understand— No, Sebastian did his work too well."

"What do you mean?"

"I used to wonder why you couldn't see the danger Elizabeth and I and the rest of the world could see for you. I thought at first you just didn't want to know, but then I realized it was Sebastian again. He told you what a danger you were, and you rejected that truth along with all the lies. Believe me, you are a danger, Kate. To yourself and to Craighdhu."

"And to you?" she teased.

He was silent a moment. "And to me."

He was so sober that for an instant a flicker of fear dimmed her happiness. "This is all nonsense. I would never hurt you. I only want to make you happy. Is it so bad to wish to give you a babe?"

"You're not with child?" he asked swiftly.

"You know I had my flux last month. It's not yet time." His apprehension hurt her even though she knew its source. "So you need not be concerned." She tried to smile. "Besides, you once said you had the remedy to the problem if I ever got with child."

"I do."

"And what is that?"

"We would go away from Craighdhu," he said simply. "Forever."

Her eyes widened in shock. "Exile?" she whispered. "You don't mean it. You love Craighdhu."

"Aye, I love Craighdhu."

"It would kill you to leave it."

"It would kill me to destroy it."

He meant it. She started to tremble uncontrollably as she saw the implacable resolution in his face. "You'd hate me."

He shook his head. "Why should I hate you? I had to have you. I knew the penalty. I made the choice."

She buried her head in his shoulder.

"Stop shaking," he said gently. His hands moved up and down her back, comforting her as if she were a small child. "It hasn't happened yet. We still have time."

And she must use that time to prove to him that he was wrong, that a child would not be the end of Craighdhu for him. "Can't you see what a mistake you'd be making?"

"Shh ... Let's speak of something else."

"I would never hurt you." Her voice was unsteady. "Never. Not for Craighdhu. Not for anything. Do you believe me."

"I believe you."

But he also believed that she was destined to take him away from Craighdhu, and that would hurt him worse than the stab of an assassin's dagger.

Her arms tightened passionately around him.

Why else would God have brought them together if He hadn't meant them to be together here on

Craighdhu? There was no order or reason in the world if He would let them be torn apart because of an accident of birth. Robert had to be wrong, and God had to give her the power to show him his error before it was too late.

Two evenings later Jock Candaron strode into the hall where Robert and Kate sat playing chess before the fire. "How blissfully serene you both look," he said tartly. "I regret to disturb you, Robert, but Malcolm is at the dock requesting an audience. What shall I tell him?"

Robert muttered a curse as he pushed his chair back and rose to his feet. "I thought he was being too quiet."

"What shall I tell him?" Jock repeated.

"Bring him here. I'll have to see him, of course."

"I wasn't sure." Jock's gaze went to Kate sitting by the fire. "Of late, you seem to have let other things distract you from your responsibilities." He turned on his heel and left the room.

"Why do you suppose he's here?" Kate whispered.

"I have no idea. It could mean anything with Alec."

"I didn't even know he had returned from Edinburgh."

"Six weeks ago."

Her eyes widened. "You didn't tell me."

"Why should I? There was no use worrying you until he made a move."

Her hands clenched on the arms of her chair. "He said he would pay a social visit. Could it be a peaceful—"

"Hardly," Robert cut through her sentence. "Not after we've aided the elopement of his daughter."

She had known her suggestion was foolish, but she had been clutching at straws. Malcolm's arrival cast a shadow blocking the sun, and she could not bear this happy time to come to an end. "No, I suppose not. He must be very angry."

Alec Malcolm did not appear angry when Jock ushered him into the room a few minutes later. His cheeks were flushed with high color, and he was smiling.

He smiles most sweetly when he's raping a child or cutting a throat.

Robert's words came back to her as Alec Malcolm crossed the room and bowed before her. "Ah, more enchanting than ever. How I regret not being able to come to you before this. I trust you're in good health?"

"Very good health."

"And how could you help being well in spirit as well as body with such joyous festivities going on? I hear there was a wedding at Craighdhu."

She looked him in the eyes. "A splendid wedding."

"But how unkind of you not to invite me when my Jean was one of the participants. She must have made a bonnie bride."

"Lovely." Robert moved across the room to stand beside Kate's chair. "Is that why you're here? I'm afraid you'll be disappointed. Gavin and Jean are no longer on the island."

"Oh, I'm aware of that fact. Of course, it didn't surprise me that you sent them away. Craighdhu has always been the only thing that mattered to you. You'd never jeopardize it even to accommodate me." He grimaced. "Such a pity. I would have much preferred accomplishing my goal by killing you and taking Craighdhu than wasting my time chasing all over Ireland."

Jock straightened. "Ireland?"

"Oh, you hid them very well, Jock. It took great effort for me to find the happy couple." He smiled. "However, now I fear they are no longer quite so happy."

Kate stared at him in horror. The very casualness of his tone sent a shiver through her.

"Am I distressing you?" He turned back to Kate. "I see you've grown quite pale. Did you develop a fondness for that young scalawag?"

Her lips felt numb as she said, "Have you hurt him?"

"Not much . . . as yet." He glanced at Robert. "You look quite lethal. I don't have to tell you that I wouldn't be here if I wasn't in a bargaining position of some strength."

"If you already have Gavin and Jean, I have no bargaining position at all," Robert said coldly. "And when a desperate situation of that nature comes to pass, only violence remains."

"But you have an excellent bargaining position, and violence would do you no good now. Your kinsman and Jean are safely back at Kilgranne, and my captain of the guard has orders to cut Gavin Gordon's throat if I don't return by dawn."

"No!" Kate cried.

"Ah, you do have a fondness for the lad. Women are such sweet, gentle creatures. I'm sure you'd do anything to keep him from more harm."

"What are your terms?" Robert said curtly.

"Nothing outrageous. I'd not be such a fool to ask for Craighdhu or even retribution for the trade you inveigled away from me from those Irish merchants."

"The terms," Robert said between his teeth.

He gestured to Kate. "Only a woman."

Kate heard Jock inhale sharply, and she was too stunned to speak.

"Impossible," Robert said impassively. "The woman is my wife."

"But handfast marriages are so easy to dissolve."

"It was not handfast. We were wed in the church."

Malcolm shook his head. "Handfast. Oh, your

clansman would not tell me, but my sweet Jean was quite informative."

Kate shook her head. "She wouldn't have told you anything."

"I admit she was under considerable stress." He turned back to Robert. "You were foolish not to wed this lovely lady in the eyes of the church. It would have made her acquisition by anyone else more difficult."

"A man usually doesn't have to do battle to keep his wife."

Alec smiled. "A man doesn't usually wed the daughter of a queen."

Robert's expression remained unrevealing. "I have no idea what you mean."

"You're beginning to make me a trifle impatient. We both know this enchanting lady is a rare prize for an ambitious man."

"And who do you believe she is?"

"Her guardian, Sebastian Landfield, proved quite upsetting to James. Fortunately, I was able to pacify his concern with a few well-chosen untruths."

"And I suppose you had a reason for that?"

"The best reason in the world. Why should I bother with Craighdhu if I can have a throne?"

"I'm not . . . I will have no throne," Kate said.

"Ah, but you will. It needs only the right man to pave the way to it." He turned and walked toward the door. "I'll return to Kilgranne and leave you to think about the matter, Robert. But don't ponder too long. I'm very angry with your kinsman, and I believe you'll be able to guess what task will be occupying me while I wait for your answer."

"I don't trade in human beings," Robert said.

"Let me clarify my position. If you don't give me the woman, Gavin will die, I'll return to Edinburgh and tell James the truth, and the woman will also die. It would not be my choice, but it would serve to increase my influence with him." He turned to Kate and said coaxingly, "Tell him to release you. Don't be frightened. Let me guide you, care for you. You're young and comely, and those are the only qualities I'll demand of you. I'll do the rest. You don't know what power awaits you. I'll make you ruler of both England and Scotland. You could be the most powerful queen the world has ever known. Why would you want to stay here with such a future on the horizon?"

Kate stared at the door as it closed behind him, too stunned to move.

Robert whirled on Jock. "Dammit, I told you to keep Gavin safe."

"I did what I could," Jock said. "We both knew there was a chance it wouldn't be enough. It's hard to hide a man like Gavin. He's rarely discreet."

No, discreet was not a word to describe Gavin, Kate thought dimly. Others suited him far better: rueful, funny, gentle, and loveable. . . .

"Alec will teach him discretion," Robert said. "You heard him, the bastard will be—" He broke off and drew a long breath. "Talk will do no good. We have to get Gavin away from Kilgranne."

"Alec will be expecting a move. He'll have a full complement of men at the castle."

"Then we'll have to send a large enough force to overcome them. Send out a call to every man on the island. I'll go to the mainland and see Robbie MacBrennon and Jamie Grant and try to persuade them to call their clans to ride with us. Meet me at sundown at Kilfirth Glen tomorrow with our own people, and we'll lay plans."

Plans for war, Kate thought, battle and blood and death. Her fault. All her fault.

Jock nodded and strode out of the room.

Robert turned back to Kate. "I'll leave a guard on the island in case this is one of Malcolm's tricks. Don't worry, you'll be safe here."

Safe. She would be safe, but Gavin and Robert and

how many others might die? "No!" She jumped to her feet. "It will be too late. He'll kill Gavin. Let me go along. Maybe I can—"

"God's blood!" He whirled on her savagely. "Can't you see that's what he wants? He'd like nothing better than to lure you away from Craighdhu so that he can pluck you like a ripe plum."

"Then let him do it," she answered just as fiercely. "Gavin wouldn't be a prisoner except for me."

"No, he'd be dead. Alec would have no reason not to make Jean a widow unless he wanted something."

"It doesn't change the fact that Malcolm will—"

"Shut up!" His eyes were blazing down at her. "Didn't you hear what I told that bastard? I won't trade you for Gavin or anyone else."

He strode out of the room, and she followed him. "Listen to me, I couldn't bear to—"

The front door slammed behind him.

Fear and sickness made her dizzy, and she reached out a hand to steady herself against the wall. Robert had told her this might happen. Why had she not believed him when he told her she could destroy Craighdhu? She knew the answer. She had not wanted to believe it because it would rob her of both Robert and Craighdhu.

Her fault. All of it her fault. Perhaps Robert was right that Gavin's actions had been partially to blame this time, but what of next time? Even if they laid siege to Kilgranne and rescued Gavin, Malcolm would still crave the power she represented. It would go on forever. Craighdhu could be taken, men would die.

Robert might die.

Panic soared through her at the thought. Just like her mother. Everything Sebastian had called her had come true. She was a destroyer, just like her mother.

No! She would not be a destroyer. She would not be made into a mirror of her mother.

She would fight.

• • •

When Jock Candaron opened the door to his lodgings, he could not hide the flicker of surprise that crossed his usually impassive face. "You have need of me, my lady? I fear I have little time at the moment." He gestured to the two men standing behind him at the table on which a map was spread. "As you can see, I'm making—"

"I, too, have little time." She stepped around him into the room and pushed back the hood of her cloak. She nodded politely at the two men. The younger clansman she recognized as Jock's lieutenant, Ian Mactavish, but the other was unknown to her. "Gentlemen, if you'll excuse us?"

Jock's lips tightened with annoyance as he turned to his men. "Wait for me in the other room. I'm sure my lady will only be a moment."

A far from gentle hint that he would like to be rid of her as quickly as possible. She crossed to the window and looked down at the street below as Jock conversed with the men in a low voice. Then she heard the door close.

"You should not be here, you know," Jock said. "It's hardly proper for the laird's lady to—"

"Do you think I care!" She whirled to face him. "I wish you to take me to Kilgranne and trade me for Gavin."

He went still. "Indeed? I don't believe Robert will approve of such action."

"But you would," she said bitterly. "It would please you, wouldn't it? You and Craighdhu would be done with me."

"Not if Robert decided to ride after you." His eyes were glacier cool as he added, "We both know he's quite mad about you."

"Yes," she whispered. Mad enough to take the chance of losing Craighdhu. She had fostered and reinforced that sensual madness with every wile at her command. Of late, she had begun to think his hunger for her was not only of the flesh, that he was beginning to love her as she did him. Well, that was all gone. She would never know now. "We'll face that problem when we get Gavin safely away from Kilgranne. If Robert does decide to lay siege to Kilgranne to free me, at least Malcolm won't be holding a hostage he'd be willing to kill. How long will it take us to get there?"

"After we reach the mainland, it's a half day's ride to Kilgranne."

"That means, if we leave at once, we could be there by dawn?"

"Aye, but I'll not be the one to take you. Like Robert, I don't trade in human beings."

"Would you rather see Gavin tortured to death? Malcolm will not harm me—he wants only to use me. If you exchange me for Gavin, he will live, and so will I."

"As long as Alec deems you have value to him," he conceded. "But if he decides otherwise, he'll derive great pleasure in depriving Robert of you in the most painful way possible."

She motioned impatiently. "We're wasting time. If you don't take me, I'll go by myself. You're so fond of performing your precious duty. Do it now. In one stroke you can save Gavin and buy time for an attack on Kilgranne that will be of your choice, not Malcolm's. You know my plan is sound."

He studied her. "Aye, the plan has merit."

She whirled and strode toward the door. "Then let's go. Rachel is tied outside, and I've packed my satchel in readiness."

"You were so sure I'd take you?"

"I knew you'd welcome any chance to rid Craighdhu of my presence." She opened the door. "I'm aware you've always disliked me."

"I've never disliked you," he said quietly.

She looked at him in surprise.

"In truth, you have a boldness and honesty that I

find pleasing. It's the threat you present I dislike." He turned and picked up his cloak. "Give me a moment to give instructions to Ian, and I'll join you downstairs."

Kate breathed a sigh of relief when she saw Jock ride out of the gates of Kilgranne and gallop up the hill where she waited.

"Gavin?"

"Malcolm assures me he's still alive, but the bastard won't let me see him."

"He agreed to the exchange?"

He nodded. "He wants you to come for Gavin yourself."

"Is that wise? If he's as treacherous as you say—"

"It isn't and he is."

"Then what other course is left open to us?"

"We could make a stand and wait and see if he's bluffing."

"No." She nibbled on her lower lip. Jock was supposed to meet Robert at sundown, and she did not want Robert here at Kilgranne. "I'll go." She nudged Rachel into a trot. "There's no use for you to go back. Stay here and wait for word."

Jock was immediately beside her, his horse's pace matching her own.

"I told you to stay here."

He didn't answer.

"Your duty is to Robert, not to me."

"True," he said calmly. "But Gavin is one of ours; therefore, if you commit this folly for his sake, it's my duty to support you in it."

"You define your duty on a very broad scale."

"It's only right to let a man interpret the light that guides his life as he sees fit." He did not look at her. "Alec is a clever man. I've seen him twist men's minds as well as their bodies. It's possible he wants to test your mettle for weaknesses."

"To see how easily the pawn can be fashioned for his purpose?"

"Perhaps." He smiled faintly. "He has seen little of you. He may think you're only what you seem."

Through the open gates she could see Alec Malcolm waiting in the courtyard and involuntarily tensed. "And what is that?" she asked.

"Robert's lady, good only for bed and childbearing."

A little of her tension ebbed as a smile tugged at her lips. "I hope Robert would vouch for the first, and I've been valiantly striving for the second." But that was over, she realized bleakly, even the brief amusement fading. No babe, no Robert, no Craighdhu lay in her future, only this task that must be performed to right the wrong she had done. "I won't let Malcolm twist my mind. The question is, how can I twist his?"

"I don't know." He shrugged. "A man who cares only for his own well-being has few weaknesses. Your one method of defense is not to let him see yours."

She didn't want to defend but to attack. "That's not enough."

"No?" He smiled curiously. "It would be, for most women."

They were riding through the gate, and she braced herself. No weakness.

"Ah, I can't say how delighted I was when my friend Jock told me you were joining me." Alec Malcolm stepped forward and lifted her from the saddle. "I could see at once that you were an intelligent woman, but now I see you have a great heart. How kind to sacrifice yourself for that sweet lad Gavin."

"Where is he?"

"Right this way." He cast a glance at Jock. "You, too, my friend; I know that you can't wait to see your clansman." He led them across the courtyard toward the tower. "Jock tells me that Robert is not aware of your decision. How fortunate for Gavin that your heart is not as hard as your husband's." He nodded at the guard standing before the heavy door, and the man unlocked and opened it. "I regret making you go to him, but he's not able to come to you."

She felt a sudden sickness at his words and was glad that he was in front of her, negotiating the steep, curving stone steps leading down into the dungeon. No weakness.

She heard Jock following behind her.

Alec opened a door at the foot of the stairs and threw it wide. "My lady." He stepped aside to let her go first.

The foul smell of mold, decay, and feces assaulted her from the darkness.

"Be careful," Jock murmured in her ear.

He meant that whatever she saw, she was not to show that it affected her. She knew that, she thought impatiently. She had spent most of her life hiding pain from the enemy. She kept her face expressionless, but could not stifle a gasp of horror.

Gavin was hanging by his wrists four feet from the floor of the dungeon, his head slumped on his chest, his eyes closed in a faint. His ragged clothing hung in strips from his strained body, his legs looked limp and oddly crooked, and his face ... Dear God, there was not an inch that was not bruised or bleeding.

"Was this necessary?" she asked unsteadily.

"Aye, I told him to speak," Alec said, "but he wouldn't obey. Obedience is very important to me."

This was why he had brought her here, she realized. It was to lesson her in her role in the future. She was to be intimidated and cowed at the result of disobedience to him.

"Cut him down." The whisper came from the darkness in the corner. "Please cut him down. . . . Pain . . ."

It was Jean, but a Jean Kate had never seen. She was huddled against the wall, her clothing as ragged as her husband's, her eyes haunted as she gazed at Gavin's hanging body.

"You'll have to forgive my daughter's dishevelment," Alec said. "Nothing would do her but that she stay with her beloved husband."

"Cut him down," Jean whispered.

"Yes, cut him down," Kate said briskly. "And send one of the guards for a wagon. You should have told us he would be unable to travel. This is most inconvenient."

She could see that her coolness had surprised him, but not to the extent of discomposure. "Not yet." He smiled. "I haven't decided what to do with him yet."

"Jock is going to take him to Craighdhu," she said firmly. "It's far the best move." She turned to Jock. "Cut him down, Jock."

Jock drew his sword and stepped toward Gavin.

"You forget where you are," Malcolm said softly. "I command here."

"He does not look well," Kate said coldly. "If you kill him, that will enrage Robert, and he will attack Kilgranne. That's not what we want now."

"No?" He looked intrigued. "And what do *we* want?"

"What you promised me. The crown. Why else do you think I'm here?" She met his gaze. She was acting purely on instinct. Was she striking the right note? "I don't deny I found the boy likable, but not enough to risk what I had at Craighdhu. You offered me something I wanted more, but don't mistake me. I'm no tender blossom to be nurtured and guided unless I so choose."

"You were contented enough at Craighdhu until I came."

"I wanted the island, but Robert will never give it to me. He even refused to marry me in any way but handfast." Her lips tightened scornfully. "He found me pleasant enough to bed but was afraid for his precious Craighdhu."

"You're very blunt."

"It's as well we understand each other at once. You wish to use me, and I wish to be used. You will find me a strong ally. Isn't that better than a weak puppet?"

"Landfield said you could be dangerous," he murmured.

"Not if we're striving for the same goal." She paused. "And we will not win the crown by dissipating our strength in battles over trifles." She nodded at Jock. "Take your man and get him out of here."

She held her breath, but this time Malcolm made no objection.

Jock fetched a stool from across the dungeon, stood on it, and holding Gavin around the middle with one arm, he cut the ropes binding his wrists.

"Be careful." Jean struggled to her feet and ran forward out of the darkness. "His legs are broken."

Jean's face was as bruised as Gavin's, and pity and rage brought bile to Kate's stomach. Jock placed Gavin carefully on the ground and knelt beside him, his hands running exploringly over the younger man's body.

"The wagon," Kate prompted Malcolm.

His musing gaze had never left Kate's face. "You may just be right in this."

"I am right. I've thought the matter over very carefully." She saw him hesitate and said fiercely, "We mustn't make blunders now. All my life I've been without importance to anyone. Now, I have a chance to be a queen. I won't let you spoil my prospects."

He threw back his head and laughed. "You may be a more exceptional queen than I anticipated." He turned and sauntered toward the door. "Very well, Your Imperial Majesty, I'll tell the guard to fetch the wagon."

As soon as the door shut behind him, she flew to Gavin and fell to her knees. "How bad?" she asked Jock.

"Not good. Both arms out of the sockets, right leg

broken in two places, left in three, his back is lashed to ribbons." He glanced down. "Three fingers broken on the right hand."

"Will he live?"

He nodded. "I think so. He may even come out of this without being a cripple, if I can set those bones right away."

"Can you do that yourself?"

"It's a battlefield skill I would have been foolish not to have learned." He frowned. "I only hope there's no damage that I can't see on the surface."

"That's all," Jean said dully. "The whip and then the rack." She looked at Kate. "He made me watch. I told him about the handfast. I would have told him anything to make him stop."

"By the saints, do you think I don't understand? I would have done the same." She looked down at Gavin's poor bruised face and felt tears rise to her eyes. "It will be all right. Once you leave here, you'll be able to care for him and get him well."

"If my father lets me go with him," Jean said.

Another problem, Kate thought wearily. Now she had to think of a plausible reason why Malcolm should send Jean along with Gavin.

"What a tender picture," Alec said from the doorway. "You look quite the ministering angel, my lady."

The hint of suspicion threading his voice must be instantly banished. "I hear my mother was splendid in that same role while she nursed her husband Lord Darnley." She met his gaze. "Before she went off one night to a party, and gunpowder blew his house to shambles. Naturally, she claimed she knew nothing about it."

The suspicion in Alec's face disappeared in a roar of laughter. "I had forgotten that story."

"I have not. I've studied every strength and every weakness she possessed." She stood up and brushed the dirt from the skirt of her gown. "Jock will need a board or stretcher and another guard to help carry Gavin."

"I'm surprised you don't wish me to do it," he said mockingly.

"You've done enough for the moment." She moved toward the door, then turned as if a thought had just occurred to her. "Oh, the girl is to go with him."

"No!" Malcolm said sharply.

"If we don't kill Gavin Gordon, then we have no use for her. They were married in the church, and you can no longer negotiate an advantageous marriage for her. She was formally accepted by the clan, so there's even a possibility of them trying to take her back if you don't release her."

"Then perhaps I should rethink killing the lad," he said softly.

"Why? You don't need her now, and you can do it without cost to us after we have the throne."

"Very reasonable." His gaze narrowed on her face. "Perhaps you're a little too reasonable."

She had gone as far as she could. If she ventured more aggressively, it might destroy everything she had accomplished. She shrugged casually. "Do what you like. It's nothing to me. I only thought to save us trouble." Perhaps it would be wise to show a bit of womanly weakness. She opened the door. "Now I must get out of here before I faint from this stench. I'll wait for you in the courtyard."

When she reached the courtyard, she drew a deep breath of cool morning air. Had she overplayed her hand? She did not think so, but she didn't really know Malcolm. She could only wait and see. She began to pace to release the stored-up tension of the last minutes. Why did they not come?

The dungeon door was thrown open, and Jock and one of Malcolm's guards carried a stretcher bearing Gavin into the courtyard.

Jean?

Jean walked into the courtyard a moment later, and Kate breathed a sigh of relief. As Malcolm came out of the dungeon, she turned away so that he wouldn't see her expression. "I'll be with you in a moment. I must give Jock a message for Robert."

She walked across the courtyard, watching as Gavin was carefully slid onto the bed of the wagon. Jock covered him with his cloak and then moved around to the front of the wagon.

Gavin gave a low groan and opened his eyes, startlingly blue in his swollen, livid face.

She stepped closer, glancing eagerly down at him. "How do you feel?" she whispered.

"Terrible . . ." He shook his head. "Sorry . . . Didn't mean . . ."

"Shh . . . Just get well."

"Broken . . ."

"Jock says he knows about setting bones. I'm sure your legs will be fine."

"Not my legs." He attempted to smile but could only flinch with pain. "Fingers . . . Tell him to fix my fingers."

She didn't understand. "I'm certain he'll set everything that needs fixing."

"Important . . . How else . . . will I play the . . . bagpipes?"

She blinked back the tears. Those blasted bagpipes. "I'm not sure anyone in the clan would thank him for that."

He shook his head. "Important . . ." He fainted again.

Jean crawled into the wagon and cradled Gavin's head on her lap. In the strong light of day she appeared even more haggard than she had in the dungeon. It was as if every artifice she had cultivated had been burned away, leaving only a pale husk of the enchanting woman who had come to Craighdhu. Her expression was hard as she looked at her father, standing across the courtyard watching them. Her lips barely moved as she said softly to Kate, "I want him dead, Kate."

Kate looked down at Gavin and felt the same rage she knew Jean was feeling. "He will be." She turned and walked to the wagon seat where Jock was now sitting. "Try to delay Robert from coming here as long as you can."

"Why?"

"Just do as I say." She moistened her lips and smiled recklessly. "And give him a message for me. Tell him he wouldn't give me Craighdhu, so I decided to take Scotland instead."

"And I'm supposed to make him believe it?"

"Why not? He knows I'm not without ambition. Turn him against me. It's the opportunity you've been wanting since I came to Craighdhu. Isn't that true?"

"Aye, it's true enough," he said slowly.

"Then seize the opportunity."

"What opportunity?" Alec Malcolm was approaching the wagon.

"The opportunity to save his life by leaving me and getting this wagon out of here. You must have heard how loyal he is to my husband. He doesn't wish to relinquish what he perceives to belong to Craighdhu." She stepped back and motioned for Jock to go.

He gazed at her with his usual impassiveness and then snapped the reins to start the wagon rolling.

"Ah, he may be loyal, but it appears he's not a fool, my lady," Alec said.

Kate watched the wagon roll away from her and for an instant felt very much alone. She might never see any of them again and would certainly never see Craighdhu. Then she squared her shoulders and turned to Malcolm. "My lady? But why are you so formal?" She gave him a brilliant smile. "I wish you to call me Kathryn."

· · ·

A single tent occupied Kilfirth Glen when there should have been at least twenty.

Robbie MacBrennan reined in beside Robert on the hill overlooking the glen. "What is this? You told me your lads would be gathered here."

"They're supposed to be. I told Jock I wanted him here by sunset," Robert said grimly. That was Jock's horse grazing nearby, but there were also two work-horses and a wagon drawn close to the tent. "I don't like this. Wait here until I signal you to come ahead." He spurred ahead down the hill toward the tent.

Jock Candaron came out of the tent. Both his linen shirt and his fair hair were darkened by sweat. He wiped beads of perspiration from his forehead on his sleeve as his gaze went beyond Robert to the men on the hill. "You must have been very persuasive. How many?"

"Three hundred strong. Jamie Grant and his men will join us in an hour or so." Robert jumped down from his horse. "Where the hell are our own forces?"

"I told Ian I'd send for them if they were needed."

"What the devil are you talking about? We do need them. Now."

"Perhaps not. You may even decide to send Grant and MacBrennan back home." He nodded at the tent. "I have Gavin."

"What!" His gaze went to the tent. "How is he?"

"In a faint. A state for which I'm sure he's fervently grateful. All day I've been setting broken bones and repairing the damage Alec inflicted. That little fluff of a wife he chose has more backbone than I thought," he added. "She was a great deal of help to me, and it wasn't easy for her to see him in agony."

"Jean is here too?"

"Aye, don't you think that's a brilliant coup?"

"How the hell did you do it?"

"I traded Kate."

The words tore like a sword thrust through Robert. For a moment he couldn't even speak, and then shock was followed by rage. "You son of a bitch. I'm going to cut your heart out."

"I thought that would be your response." He shrugged. "That was the chance I took. Your lady-wife gave me little choice. She said I would either make sure the trade took place or she would see to it herself. I thought if it was to be done, it should be done right."

"And you could get rid of a threat to Craighdhu."

"Aye, I admit that part appealed to me." He paused. "She gave me a message for you. She said to tell you not to come after her. She said since you wouldn't give her Craighdhu, she would take Scotland instead."

Robert rejected the words immediately. Kate had a fine mind and a taste for power, but cold calculation would never be her way. "And I suppose you believe her."

Jock hesitated and then said quietly, "I believe Alec was right in one thing. She would make an exceptional queen." He shrugged. "But I think she lied. If she gets the throne, it won't be through Alec Malcolm. She has a softness toward you and Gavin and wishes to save you both."

"By sacrificing herself?" Robert asked thickly.

"I doubt if she has that in mind." Jock's smile had a curious element of pride. "She was no pale, trembling martyr at Kilgranne. She intends to best Alec Malcolm."

"And she has as little chance of that as Gavin of besting you in battle. Alec has years of experience on his side."

"You did not see her as I did." He paused. "But if you have doubts, perhaps you'd better help her."

"Indeed?" Robert's eyes narrowed suspiciously. "May I ask why this change of heart?"

"You will obviously not be content until you rescue her from Alec's clutches." He smiled. "And I'm not sure that it wouldn't be safer for Craighdhu to have her safely under our eye at the island than on the throne of Scotland. At least we'd have a measure of control over her there."

"You didn't exercise much control over her in this matter. You should have kept her at home." He should not be blaming Jock when the fault lay with himself. He had known how upset Kate was when he had left, but he had been too filled with worry and rage to think about anything but getting Gavin away from Alec. Christ, but he hadn't expected her to—but he should have expected it. Kate was capable of anything, of confronting any hazard if it meant enough to her. Well, he could not stand here thinking about the danger to her. He would go mad if he did not take action. He turned toward the tent. "I'll go in and see Gavin. Mount up. We'll ride for Kilgranne at once."

"If you like, but I'm not sure she'll be there."

"You believe that Alec will have secreted her somewhere?"

He shook his head. "She asked me to delay you. She clearly didn't want you to lay siege and will see that you don't."

The rage, fear, and frustration within him were mounting more by the second. "For God's sake, she can't manipulate Alec to suit herself. She's only a woman, scarcely more than a child."

"No? I saw her in a different light. The coup at Kilgranne was entirely Kate's, not mine. I believe you may change your mind."

Duncan rode out of the castle toward their forces before they reached the gates.

He was alone.

"They're not here," he said as he reined in before Robert. "She said to tell you they had gone to Edinburgh to join with Mary's sympathizers." He flushed as he glanced uneasily at the clansmen surrounding

Robert before adding, "She said that since she has left you, the marriage is over, and you would be without pride to pursue her when she no longer wants you."

"You see?" Jock murmured. "Another coup. A public rejection to sting your pride before she flits out of reach. It's one thing to rally the clans to avenge an abducted wife—it's quite another to chase down a reluctant spouse." He lowered his voice still more. "And you cannot tell anyone the real reason Alec wants her, if your purpose is to get her back before he announces her claim to the throne."

Robert knew that was true, and he swore beneath his breath. It was not enough he would have to battle Malcolm; he had the damn woman herself with whom to contend. "When did they leave?"

"Before noon," Duncan said. "But you can't hope to catch up with them. My father was in a great hurry, and he planned to set sail from the harbor at Jacklowe by sunset."

It was now close to midnight. With the winter storms over, the northern route around Scotland was both safe and speedy. They would have nearly a two-day head start before Robert could get back to Craighdhu, ready his own ship, and set sail.

"Craighdhu?" Jock asked.

Robert nodded. "It's the quickest way."

"Robert . . . I'm sorry . . . Gavin . . ." Duncan shrugged helplessly. "You know my father. I could not stop him. No one could stop him."

"Aye, I know him." A sickening chill went through him at the memory of Gavin's broken body. Kate thought she could manipulate that bastard to her own designs, but it would take only one false step for Alec to try to subjugate her as he did everyone around him. He could merely hope she did not make that false step until he reached Edinburgh and could deal with Alec himself.

He turned and rode back toward Robbie Mac-Brennan and Jamie Grant to explain why he had brought them here for naught and tell them to go home.

Damn and blast the woman.

13

"*You're not eating. That's* not good. You must keep up your strength." Malcolm nodded at the servant standing at attention at the side of the door of the cabin. "Give the countess a slice of that excellent lamb."

"No, thank you. I'm not hungry." She looked at the table with its fine goblets and polished trenchers without interest. She was unutterably weary, but this interminable meal would soon be over, and she would be permitted to go to her cabin. "It's been a long day."

"I'm sure it's been a longer one for MacDarren," Malcolm said maliciously. "He should be arriving at Kilgranne about now."

"Perhaps." She lifted her glass of wine to her lips. "If he chose to follow me."

"Oh, I believe we both know he'll follow you. MacDarren detests losing anything that belongs to him, and he will particularly dislike the idea of losing to me. Our rivalry has been most bitter over the years." He ate a bit of lamb. "Unfortunately, he has succeeded more often than I in the past. It's been most annoying. I've never understood it, for I never lose to anyone else. That's why I'm very determined not to lose in this endeavor." He chuckled. "This time I've made sure that even if I lose, I'll win."

She was too tired to decipher the cryptic words. "When will we arrived in Edinburgh?"

"Not long. If the winds are with us." Alec smiled. "Are you so eager to start your new life?"

"Aren't you?"

"Aye, but we must go slowly at first."

Kate stifled a sigh of relief. She had been afraid Malcolm would wish to plunge immediately into the conspiracy, and she would be given no opportunity to initiate a plot of her own. Not that she had any idea of what that plot would be. The only certainty was that Alec Malcolm must be destroyed. "You disappoint me. I've waited too long already."

"You're very impatient. Like your mother. I've noticed you have several of her attributes."

"You met my mother?"

"I encountered her several times through the years. I found her very astute."

Astute was not an adjective usually applied to Mary, Kate thought. He was obviously trying to give Kate herself a backhanded compliment. In the past hours she had discovered Jock was right about Malcolm. He was both clever and manipulative and would say anything that would sway her in the way he wanted her to go. She changed the subject. "Where are we staying in Edinburgh?"

"I'm staying at court, but I'm establishing you at my estate, Selwyth, south of the city."

"Why?"

He shrugged. "James will be sure to hear I'm in the city. I prefer that he has no knowledge that you're my companion until the time is right."

"He'll hear soon enough once you start contacting Mary's supporters."

"That's why we will be doing no such thing." He sipped his wine. "I have a few loose ends to tie up, but after I pacify James and give him a plausible reason for my departure, we will be leaving immediately for England."

"England!"

"Aye, it's safer for us to first rally support among the English supporters across the border. We'll go to Kenilworth or perhaps Warwick. Elizabeth is occupied now with the war with Spain and will have no time to worry about a conspiracy that might topple her from the throne." He chuckled with genuine amusement. "And when she does, it will be too late."

"So you intend to take England as well as Scotland?"

"Of course. Didn't I promise to make you the greatest queen the world has ever known?"

"I would have settled for Scotland. It's a dangerous move."

"But one we must take."

But it would be Kate who would be at the center of that risk. Her mother had conspired to seize both crowns and had ended up a prisoner and then a victim of the ax. What did Malcolm care? Kate thought bitterly. She was only a pawn.

"It's not as dangerous as it sounds. You'll find I never act without having the weapons to lay a proper siege. Trust me, I assure you I have no intention of losing my head ... or yours," he added softly. "You have great value to me. I have every intention of guarding you as if you were the crown itself."

A subtle threat lay beneath his words. He wanted her to know he was not fool enough to place trust in her. Suddenly, she'd had enough of this. She was tired and lonely and wanted desperately to run back to Craighdhu. Only months ago she had thought the greatest challenge was defying Sebastian, and now she was matching wits with a man even the vicar would have called an archdemon. She could bear no more tonight. "Then I'm sure I shall be very safe." She pushed back her chair and stood up. "Now, if you will excuse me, I'll retire to my cabin. The hour grows late."

"Certainly." He rose to his feet. "I'll join you shortly."

She looked at him, shocked.

He saw her reaction and raised his brows. "But surely you expected us to seal our pact in the most pleasurable of fashions?"

She had not expected it. Malcolm did not want her body. She knew the signs of desire, and he had displayed none of them.

He smiled. "I can hardly wait."

Then understanding came to her. It was only another way to seek out her weakness and gain an advantage over her. Domination. She restrained a shiver as she realized that this would be no teasing, seductive domination such as Robert had practiced only a few days ago.

She shook her head. "Not yet."

"Tonight," he said firmly. "We will wed as soon as we get to Edinburgh, but I'm too eager to partake of a bridegroom's privilege to wait for the words to be said over us."

If he was eager for anything, it was to be a royal consort and then at some convenient time seize the crown itself. God's blood, she was too tired to face this challenge now.

What was she sniveling about? she told herself in disgust. Challenges did not come when you wished to deal with them, or they would not be challenges. She thought quickly, seeking a way out that would give her the time she needed and still answer his self-interest.

"If we wed in Scotland, James will hear about it. We should wait until we get to England." She met his gaze. "And there's a possibility I may be with child. If you bed me now and I become pregnant, no one will know whether the child is yours or Robert's. Do you wish Robert to have a claim to the throne through your child?"

The thought clearly displeased him. "You know the line of succession must be clear."

"Then you will wait."

His lips tightened. "How long?"

"If I'm not with child, I should have my flux within a month."

"Then I shall be monitoring you closely." He suddenly smiled. "But you're right, under no circumstance should we have MacDarren's child with which to contend. If you prove to be with child, I promise you I'll find a way to rid you of it safely. The ladies of the court use an old woman who has an extensive knowledge of herbs."

She frowned in puzzlement. "I don't know what you mean."

"No? I did not expect you to be this ignorant. You seem so clever, I forgot you were unable to gather much practical knowledge under your vicar's wing. Let me be more clear." He paused and then said, "We will kill the child in your womb."

He was gazing intently at her face, and she knew he was again searching for weakness. She should not let him see the horror the words brought. He had struck too deep, and she could not hide it, so she quickly turned on her heel and moved toward the door. With an effort she managed to keep her voice steady. "Perhaps it won't be necessary. We will see. Good night."

She did not stop walking until she reached her cabin. She leaned back against the door, her stomach heaving, every limb shaking.

He meant to murder her child.

The child she had wanted so desperately, the babe that was to save Robert and Craighdhu for her, would be treated as just another pawn to be removed from the chessboard. She had not even thought such an act possible.

It might be all right—there might be no child.

But what if there was a babe in her womb this very moment?

Why in heaven could she not have just accepted Malcolm into her bed? It would have sickened her, but she could have borne it. This question of succession might never have occurred to him if she had not brought it up.

She had thought she was a match for Malcolm, but her ignorance had already led her to make a mistake that might mean her baby's life.

Edinburgh lay on the southern shores of the Firth of Forth, an arm of the North Sea. Robert chose to anchor the *Irish Princess* at Granton, a sleepy fishing port, rather than the busier Leith.

"You stay here on the ship," Jock said. "I'll go to Bobby MacGrath's and see what he's heard about Malcolm."

"And I'm to sit here and wait?" Robert asked. "Not likely."

"No, you'd probably rather blunder around Edinburgh and let Alec know he has enemies knocking on his front door."

"I wouldn't blunder—" He drew a deep breath. He knew Jock was right, and the safest course was to search out the lay of the land before he showed himself in Edinburgh. He was well known here, and word would instantly be carried to the court of his presence in the town. But dammit, he didn't want to take the safest course. His tension had simmered on this damnable journey until it was a volcano ready to explode. He wanted to *do* something.

But impulsiveness could be fatal for Kate. Alec was walking a thin tightrope, balancing James's influence on one hand and his own ambitions for the throne on the other. If he decided that Robert's presence could sway the balance, he might jettison his plans for the throne and get rid of Kate, the only proof of his treason against James. "Very well. I'll wait here."

Jock nodded approvingly. "Perhaps you have a brain in your head after all." He climbed down the rope ladder and stepped into the longboat. "I'll be back by nightfall."

It was only noon now. Jesus, it was going to be a long day. "Bring MacGrath with you. I want to talk to him."

Robert found talking to Bobby MacGrath a very irritating process. He was turtle slow and as deliberate as a priest giving the last rites.

"I know nothing of any woman," MacGrath said. "Alec Malcolm returned to Edinburgh alone. He's been at court for the last four days."

"Does he have lodgings in town?" Robert asked.

MacGrath shook his head. "He's staying in James's apartments."

Jock asked, "Has he visited anywhere outside the castle since he came?"

"Aye, he visited a cottage at the edge of the city the first day and spent a good four hours there yesterday."

"Whose cottage is it?" Robert asked.

"There's no woman there either."

Robert tried to restrain his impatience and reminded himself that MacGrath was a good, loyal clansman. "Who is there?"

"An old man." MacGrath sipped his ale. "White hair, wild eyes, thin as a string."

"Sebastian Landfield," Robert murmured.

MacGrath shrugged. "I don't know. I never heard his name. I only got close enough to the window to catch one glimpse of him."

The description fit too closely for the man not to be Landfield. Malcolm had mentioned the vicar, but Robert had thought no more about him. This news made no sense. After Alec had wrested the information he had wanted from Sebastian, it was not reasonable he would waste more time on him. "Is this the first time you've seen him?"

MacGrath nodded. "Malcolm paid no visits to him when he was here before. The first I knew of the man was when I followed Alec to the cottage that first day." He paused. "But there was already a guard at the door of the cottage when Alec arrived. It's possible he might have given orders to put him under guard before Alec left Edinburgh."

No matter what Alec's reason for imprisoning him, Sebastian was now Robert's only link to Kate, and there was a slight possibility Alec might have disclosed her whereabouts to the vicar. "Where is he? I want to talk to him."

"Fourteen Greybriar." MacGrath made a face "But I don't know if he'll be able to talk. From the sounds I heard coming from the place yesterday, I'd judge Malcolm's been playing his games with the old man."

"Torture?"

"You didn't say I should interfere with Malcolm," MacGrath said defensively. "And the old man isn't one of ours."

"No, you were right not to interfere. It would have been too dangerous for you." Why would Malcolm think it necessary to torture Sebastian Landfield? He didn't doubt Malcolm derived a feeling of power from tormenting individuals, but he seldom indulged himself without reason. "Is he still alive?"

MacGrath shrugged again. "I don't know. I doubt it. It's been quiet since Malcolm left the cottage yesterday, and there's no longer a guard at the door."

"First, the woman in James's dungeon and now Landfield," Jock murmured. "A connection?"

"Probably," Robert said. "Did you find out who she was, Bobby?"

"English, named Clara Merkert. James had her brought from the town of Bourse. The soldier I spoke to said they were told to make sure no one in the village knew they had taken her."

Bourse was not close to Sheffield, where Kate had spent her life, yet there must be some bond.

"Will you be needing anything else?" MacGrath put down his cup and rose to his feet "I should be getting back."

"Just keep an eye on Malcolm. We'll be in touch with you later to give you our direction. You have my thanks, Bobby, you've been a great help."

Jock watched MacGrath leave the cabin before turning to Robert. "I know it may be of little interest to you, but I heard other news in Edinburgh."

"About Kate?"

Jock smiled sardonically. "No, I told you this news would not overly concern you. It's only the small matter of war. It's growing closer every day. Elizabeth sent Leicester to the Netherlands to seek peace and then promptly commissioned Drake to raid Cadiz. He sank thirty-six Spanish ships. Philip's armada will be ready to strike any time now, and in a sea battle of those proportions it may not be only England that's involved. It would be a miracle if Ireland and Scotland aren't drawn into it."

"I know that," Robert said. "As soon as we get Kate away from Alec, I'm sending you back to protect Craighdhu."

"Sending me back? What of you?"

"I'll make a decision on that later."

"I think you've already made a decision," Jock said softly.

Robert changed the subject "Malcolm has a residence south of the city. If Kate's not in the city, she could be there. We'll ride down tomorrow to Selwyth and see what we can find out." As he saw Jock open his lips to protest, he added, "All right, we'll see what *you* can find out. We'll make camp nearby, and I'll sit meekly and wait for your report."

"It won't be quick. We have no men at Selwyth. I'll have to rely on bribes for information."

"Nothing has been quick yet," Robert said sourly.

Jock's brows lifted. "I've noticed you're a trifle on edge. I'm surprised you don't want to post down there at once."

"Not tonight." He was not about to hurry to Selwyth so he could wait again if there was any other way he could find Kate. "I think we'll go visit Sebastian Landfield."

There was no light glimmering in the windows at 14 Greybriar Street, and as MacGrath had said, no guard at the door.

"I believe MacGrath could be right," Jock said. "It may be too late to talk to the good vicar."

Robert tried the door: It swung open.

The room held the sour odor of sweat and urine, but no death stench fouled the air.

He drew his sword and stepped into the room. "See if you can find a candle and get us some light." His eyes were already becoming accustomed to the darkness, and he could discern that the room was small and almost barren of furniture.

"Serpent . . ."

Robert whirled to the corner of the room from where the weak whisper had come.

"The candle," he said sharply.

"I've found one," said Jock, striking flint behind him. "Be careful."

Light flared, and Robert saw Sebastian Landfield. Or what was left of him.

The old man was tied to a chair in the corner, and Malcolm had been using a knife instead of a whip. So much blood surrounded the chair that Robert wondered that the old man had any left in his body. He had to be near death.

"I will . . . not yield. . . ." Sebastian raised his head

to reveal eyes still burning fanatically in his wreck of a face. "Never . . ."

"Kate," Robert demanded. "Where's Kate?"

"Daughter of the Devil," he whispered. "Not Lilith. Serpent. Writhing, changing . . . like the serpent in Eden. I will . . . not yield. . . ."

"Where's Kate?"

"I will not—" For an instant the hatred vanished from his expression and became pleading. "Kill her . . . kill the serpent."

He was dead.

"Charming of Alec to leave the old man here to slowly bleed to death," Jock said as he came to stand beside Robert. "I'd say he was a trifle annoyed he didn't get what he wanted. I wonder what his purpose was?"

"He wanted Landfield to swear Kate was Mary's daughter." Robert smiled mirthlessly. "But even torture doesn't sway madmen."

"Shall I cut him loose and send for MacGrath to arrange for burial?"

Kill her . . . kill the serpent.

Robert turned away. "Leave the bastard to rot."

"She's here," Jock said as they rode into their camp in the forest a short distance from Selwyth Manor. "For all the good it will do us. Malcolm has an army of guards at Selwyth."

"She's a prisoner?"

Jock shook his head. "Not visibly. I'm sure she would be stopped if she tried to escape, but she's allowed to move freely about the castle and the gardens. She goes for a ride in this very forest every day, suitably accompanied by guards . . . for her protection."

"Then we can take her."

"Not if she doesn't want to go." Jock paused. "It's a hellish task rescuing a woman who doesn't want to be rescued."

His words were unpalatable, but Robert couldn't deny their truth.

"Then I'll have to convince her that she wants to be rescued. Can I get into the castle?"

Jock thought about it. "Possibly. Bribery is always possible with Malcolm's servants. They have no liking for the bastard. I'm sure the guards were warned about an attacking force trying to take Kate away, not one person coming into the castle. The only hazard would be if one of Malcolm's officers recognized you." He stood up. "I'll see what I can do."

"My lady!"

Kate turned at the call to see Kenneth Morrow, Alec's captain of the guard, coming down the garden path toward her. She smothered a twinge of impatience and smiled sweetly. "How nice to see you. Is it not a glorious morning?"

"Glorious. May I say you look just right in this garden," he remarked with clumsy gallantry as he fell into step with her. "Just like a flower yourself."

She was not in the least flowerlike, she thought in disgust. Since she had few weapons in this battle, she had thought to try Jean's tactics and attempt to create a picture of feminine winsomeness. It was not a role that suited her temperament. If she had to shyly lower her eyes one more time, she felt she would vomit. She smiled again instead. "How kind you are. Will you walk with me?"

He shook his head. "I have duties to perform. I've only come with a message. Sir Alec will have the pleasure of joining you for supper tonight."

She tensed. She had known Malcolm would come, but she was still not ready. "How pleasant."

"Will you wish to ride today?"

She turned a corner in the path. "I don't see how I can resist the chance when the day is so bright and the company so—" She inhaled sharply.

Robert!

The man kneeling and digging in the earth of the rose bed was dressed in rough loose trousers and tunic, his head covered by a hat pulled down to shade his eyes, but there was no doubting his identity. She had studied every line of his body, knew every gesture, every texture.

"Is something wrong, my lady?"

"No, of course not," she said quickly. "The sight of the roses took my breath away. I must ask that gardener to gather some for the table tonight."

Good God, what the devil was Robert doing here?

Captain Morrow repeated, "You wish to ride, my lady?"

"Oh, yes, but I'll send a servant to tell you at what hour. I wish to enjoy the garden for a while. It is such a beautiful day."

He continued to walk with her. "It is true. The roses are quite splendid since they opened."

He must not look too closely at those roses, Kate thought. He had accompanied them from Kilgranne, and he would recognize Robert. She directed his attention to a flowering apple tree. "But then all the plants are exquisite here at Selwyth, so different from the Highlands." She sat down on a marble bench. "I believe I'll sit here for a short time."

He stood before her, gazing at her with a foolish grin. What would it take to get the man to leave her? "Really, I'll be quite safe by myself. I'm keeping you from your duties." She smiled sweetly. "You're so good to take such care of me."

"It is my honor and pleasure." He hesitated and bowed. "Until later, my lady." He turned and walked back quickly toward the castle.

She scarcely waited until he was out of sight before she jumped to her feet and flew toward the rose bed. "Are you mad?" she whispered as she stopped beside Robert. "Leave at once!"

Robert didn't look at her as he continued to turn the earth with his spade. "I didn't think your swain was ever going to depart. It appears you've been charming more men than Alec."

"He may be of use to me," she said absently as she gazed at him. Just the sight of him was making her tremble. "And no one charms Alec Malcolm."

"Jock seems to think you capable of leading him around like a tame bear." He stabbed the earth with sudden violence. "But bears have been known to turn and maul their trainers."

"Why are you here?"

"What else would a loving husband do when his wife abandons him?"

She could sense the anger in him. Well, that was what she wanted him to feel toward her. "Have the pride to accept his dismissal and go his own way."

"Oh, no," he said softly. "You won't try that ploy again with me. Though I was most irritated when you humiliated me in front of the clan."

"I'll do it again," she said. "And I'll keep on doing it until you realize I want nothing more to do with you. Didn't Jock tell you I—"

"Jock gave me your message. He did not believe you, and neither did I."

"Then you're a fool. You owe me nothing. You've kept your promise to Elizabeth. I'm the one who left. Go back to Craighdhu."

"And let you stay here on James's doorstep, where any minute Alec may decide to trade you for James's favor?"

"He won't do that."

"How do you know? You're in unknown waters. Ambitions change and waver from day to day here. James smiles at a noble, and it makes ripples throughout the kingdom. Elizabeth sends James a sharp note, and new opportunities present themselves. In the blink of an eye you may prove dispensable to Alec."

"He wants the crown. He needs me to get it," she said. "And we won't be on James's doorstep for very long. We'll be leaving for England as soon as Alec ties up a few loose ends here."

"England," Robert repeated, startled. "Why?"

"He says it will be easier to arouse support below the border."

He shook his head. "Mary's sympathizers are much stronger here in Scotland. Where do you go in England?"

She tried to remember. "Warwick and Kenilworth, I think he said."

"What?" He frowned. "That makes no sense. Both are strongly Protestant."

"It appears Alec disagrees with you." She forced a smile. "Since he wants the English throne as well as Scotland's for me, I'm sure he knows where our best support can be found."

"The throne," Robert repeated. "I'm supposed to believe that's what you covet most in the world."

She lifted her chin. "Why shouldn't I?"

His control suddenly snapped, and he took a step forward and grasped her by the shoulders. "Stop lying to me, Kate. You don't do it well at all. I've come to take you back to Craighdhu."

"That part of my life is over. I won't go back." She wished he would take his hands away. They felt too good, too familiar. "Where is your sense? You've always been so concerned about your Craighdhu. You're endangering it to even suggest I return."

"Let me worry about Craighdhu."

"Then do so." She swallowed. "And let me attend to my own affairs."

"Damn you, listen to me. You can't stay here."

"I *will* stay here. Go away, Robert. This is what I want."

"The hell it is." He jerked her close, his eyes blazing down at her. "*No more lies.*"

She suddenly broke and flared in turn, "Where else do I have to go? I can't go back to Craighdhu. I would destroy it. You were right, and I was wrong. I'll always be a pawn waiting to be used."

"But I'd wager you have no intention of letting Alec use you."

"No." She took a deep breath and then said baldly, "I'm going to kill him."

His grip on her shoulders eased a fraction. "I thought as much."

"I'll kill him and then go away. It's the only way Craighdhu will be safe. The only way I'll be safe." The only way to keep Robert safe.

"Gavin is my friend, Kate. After what happened at Kilgranne, I had every intention of disposing of Alec."

"And then let James use his death to take Craighdhu? No, it has to be me."

"You won't be able to do it. Killing requires a certain innate hardness you don't possess."

"I could learn."

He shook his head.

"You'd be surprised at what I've learned already." She tore away from him and started up the path. "So leave me alone. I don't need you."

"I'll go away for now," he called after her, "but perhaps you'd be interested to know that I stumbled on one of those loose ends Alec was so concerned about tying. Sebastian Landfield is dead."

She halted in shock and turned to face him. "Sebastian?"

"He was tortured to death. It seems he wouldn't be manipulated in the direction Alec wished him to go." He smiled mirthlessly. "For once the vicar is giving you a lesson by example to which you should pay the utmost attention."

Sebastian was dead. She could feel no regret at the passing of her old enemy, but it was difficult to comprehend that he was not alive, no longer a threat to her. "It seems . . . strange."

"That the shark gobbled up the piranha? The meal just makes the shark stronger."

She had never heard of a piranha, but Malcolm was certainly a shark. "He won't gobble me up. I have teeth of my own."

"Aye, but you think before you use them. Hesitation can be fatal with Alec." He paused. "What do you know of a woman named Clara Merkert?"

The change of subject startled her as much as the name she had not heard for years. "Why?"

"James had her brought to Edinburgh from England, and Alec questioned her. There has to be some connection with you."

"She was my nurse. The first memories I have are of Clara." Kate had been so young when she had been taken from the nurse, and those memories were few, only an impression of warmth, a brusque cheerfulness. The import of his words sank home to her. "Question? Do you mean—"

Robert cut through the sentence. "You're coming back with me, Kate. I cannot take you now, but I wish you to be ready."

She shook her head.

"You *will* come, Kate."

She started to turn away when a thought occurred to her. She still was not sure if she was with child. She could not endanger Robert, but she might need help wherever she could find it to save the babe. "If I should change my mind, can I get word to you?"

Robert's gaze searched her face. "Why are you suddenly so uncertain?"

"I'm not uncertain, but it's never wise to close doors."

"You just slammed this one shut most emphatically. What did you remember that frightened you?"

When she didn't answer, he said, "You can't trust anyone here with a message. Jock had to bribe my way in."

She was alone. Well, it was no different than before he had come. She must just forget about his help and solve her own problems.

"Kate."

She looked at him.

"Did you take the bastard to your bed?"

She could sense the raw tension beneath the quiet words. No one was more possessive or passionate than Robert. She should tell him she had bedded Alec. It might infuriate him enough to send him back to Craighdhu.

"Because if you did, I'd understand, but I'd be very unhappy," he said softly. "So unhappy I'd make sure Alec's fate will make Sebastian's seem gentle in comparison."

She stared at him in a mixture of helplessness and shock. He would understand when no other man would have done so. Robert always knew her weaknesses and her strengths; it was one of the things she loved most about him. She could cuddle close and be accepted for what she was, not what she should be. She realized in this moment what a rare treasure that quality was in him, a treasure she had lost.

"Did you take him?" Robert repeated.

She could not lie to him. "Not yet," she whispered. She turned and walked away.

Jock took one look at Robert's expression as he rode into camp and said, "I take it we're going to have trouble."

"What else has the woman ever been to me?" Robert got down from his horse. "She's going to kill him. Surrounded by an army of guards, and she's going to kill the bastard."

"She's not stupid. She'll pick her time."

"Is that all you have to say? What a great help you're being."

"We are bad-tempered, aren't we?"

"Bad-tempered and scared as Hades. Something isn't right. Alec's taking her to England."

"So?"

"To a Protestant stronghold."

Jock gave a low whistle. "Interesting. What's your reading on it?"

"How do I know what the bastard is thinking? It could mean he's decided that it's too much danger and trouble to overthrow the monarchy and intends to get what he wants another way." But what other way? Robert wondered in exasperation. A chilling thought occurred to him. "He could deliver her to Elizabeth to curry favor. Paint Kate as the ambitious conspirator and himself as the loyal subject who entrapped her. Kate's head on the block for an influential post at court."

"Would the queen believe him? She tried to help Kate."

"She doesn't know Kate, and Elizabeth doesn't forgive treason."

"So I've heard," Jock said slowly. "But Elizabeth's favor wouldn't be as attractive to him as a throne."

"He wants power, dammit. A position of influence at Elizabeth's side would give him more power than James possesses."

"True. Then you think he's going for the safe road?"

"I don't know. It's all supposition. But, by God, something's not right."

"And the solution?"

"The same as before. I want you to make sure we know everything that's going on at Selwyth. We watch and wait and try to get her away from him at the earliest opportunity. And try to kill the bastard before she makes the attempt," he added grimly.

• • •

"You look enchanting," Alec said as Kate came down the stairs that evening. "You have a flush of color in your cheeks. Kenneth says you've been spending time in the garden."

She smothered the sudden agitation the casual comment caused. "How could I help it? The roses are in bloom. Selwyth is quite lovely."

"I find it most convenient when I return to Edinburgh. It's sometimes advantageous for me to withdraw from James for short periods." He took her arm and strolled toward the dining hall. "It came to me as a dower gift from my late wife."

The wife Jean had said he had crushed to death with his tyranny, Kate remembered bitterly. "Did you accomplish what you set out to do at court?"

"Partially. James is too flustered about Elizabeth's attack on Cadiz to be insistent about my presence."

"Cadiz?"

"Elizabeth sent Drake to raid the Spanish fleet at Cadiz. Evidently, he was quite successful."

"Why would she do that?"

"It's only a matter of time before Spain is ready to send her armada to invade England. Elizabeth hoped to discourage Philip and deplete his forces at the same time."

"I don't see why that should upset James if he isn't concerned in the battle."

"He cannot decide whether to lick Philip's boots or curry favor with Elizabeth. If Philip succeeds, then he needs to be bosom friends with such a powerful monarch, but if Elizabeth wins, he wants her to declare him heir to her throne." His lips curled contemptuously. "Poor lad, what a predicament. I suppose I'll just have to relieve him of all these diplomatic problems."

"If there's to be a war, perhaps this isn't the time to instigate a conspiracy."

"Nonsense. A world in turmoil offers the most opportunity for change." He paused. "But this war news has altered my plan in one respect. We shall not go to England."

"We'll stay here?"

"No, we sail for the Netherlands tomorrow night."

She looked at him, startled. "Why?"

"We go where we obtain the greatest support."

She could have understood France or Spain, but as far as she knew, the Netherlands held no strong ties to Mary. She shook her head. "It makes no sense."

"Trust me. You'll understand in time." His tone hardened a fraction. "And if you do not, you will still accede to my judgment. We will go to the Netherlands."

"I don't believe we should—" She stopped as she met his gaze. No arguments would sway him from his course this time. For some reason this journey was very important to him.

She felt an instant of panic. She would be sailing to a distant land with no means to escape after she had killed Malcolm.

She should not be such a coward. Robert was only a lad when he had crossed the sea to get back to Craighdhu. The circumstances were much the same. She would merely have to apply herself to find the safest way.

She smiled. "I'm sure the Netherlands will prove most interesting for both of us."

14

"*T*hey leave tonight," Jock said.

"You're sure?" Robert asked.

Jock nodded. "A message went to Leith this morning to ready Alec's ship for sailing on the midnight tide." He paused. "Do we follow them to England or take him now?"

Robert tried to think objectively, but it wasn't possible. His uneasiness had been growing since his meeting with Kate yesterday. He wanted it over and Kate away from that bastard. "Ride to Granton and bring back our men from the ship. We'll take Malcolm on the way to Leith."

"He'll be well guarded."

"He doesn't know we're in Scotland. At least we'll have surprise on our side."

As Jock started for his horse, he said grimly, "Let's hope that's enough."

Robert had the same doubts. They would be outmanned, and a surprise attack might not be sufficient to carry the day.

Unless he could think of a way to render Malcolm's forces helpless, catch them by surprise.

Catch . . .

"Wait," he called to Jock. "I'm going with you to Granton."

"You appear anxious," Kate said lightly as Alec rode back to her for the third time since they had started on their journey. "Are you afraid of highwaymen, my lord?"

"Reivers." Alec smiled at her. "I'm not overly anxious, but I must make sure MacDarren doesn't try to take what's mine."

Kate tried to hide the tension that gripped her. "Has there been any word of him?"

"No, but that doesn't mean he's not in Edinburgh."

"Robert's no fool." Kate looked at the column of armed guards on either side of her in the narrow road. "I'm sure he'd not make an attempt against odds like these."

"I agree, but it never hurts to—"

Huge nets suddenly dropped down from the trees over the heads of the guards riding in front of them!

"What the—" Malcolm turned to see more nets falling down upon the guards to their rear.

"A MacDarren!" The cry rang out as men streamed from the bushes on either side of the road, grabbing the fishing nets holding the soldiers captive. "A MacDarren."

"No!" Kate cried.

Malcolm's guards were fighting the nets, trying to draw their swords even as they were jerked from their horses by the nets and then speared like salmon in a stream.

"Dammit!" Malcolm grabbed the reins of Kate's horse and frantically kicked his own horse, trying to wind his way around the struggle around them.

"Down!" Robert was standing in front of Alec's horse, a sword in his hand.

"Oh, yes," Alec said between his teeth. "By all

means, yes." He drew his sword as he slipped from the saddle.

"Stop it!" Kate cried. "Robert, I don't want this. Why don't you—" She stopped when she realized they were paying no attention to her, and scrambled down from her horse. She could only stand by helplessly as they fought, the steel of their swords gleaming deadly cold in the moonlight. Dear God, she had never realized how big Malcolm was until this moment, how much larger than Robert. His shoulders were massive, and his reach much longer.

Malcolm's expression was set, his lips curled back from his teeth, like that of a savage animal hungry to kill.

Kate's hands clenched. "Robert, can't you see—"

"Stay out of this, Kate." Robert lunged forward, but the tip of his sword was deflected before it reached Malcolm's chest.

He wanted her to stand by meekly while he was killed for her sake. She could not do it.

She looked around wildly for help, then saw one of the guards who had been killed during the first minutes of the attack. She pounced and grabbed the dirk from his belt.

She whirled back to Robert and Malcolm.

Malcolm was cornered against a tree but deftly whirled away and lunged to attack.

She balanced on the balls of her feet, looking for an opportunity.

"I can't deal with both of you, Kate. If you want me to remain alive, you'll stay out of this," Robert said without looking at her. "This is *mine*."

"Your death," Malcolm said. His attitude breathed exultant confidence. "You can't win, MacDarren. I'm stronger and more clever and—" He gasped with pain as Robert's sword shaved his rib.

"And more boastful," Robert said. "First blood, Alec."

"Last blood." Malcolm lunged forward, engaged, and was deflected.

Fear gradually ebbed from Kate as she watched them. Malcolm might have the advantage in sheer physical strength, but Robert was faster and clearly the better swordsman. He was also hard, fierce, and completely ruthless. She had never seen him like this. This was not Robert of Craighdhu but Black Robert the buccaneer, who dealt in blood and death.

"You've grown soft playing games with those courtiers at James's castle, Alec. You should have stayed in the Highlands and honed your skill." Robert parried Alec's thrust, and another streak of blood appeared on Alec's shoulder. "It's harder to best a man when he's not chained to a rack, isn't it?"

Malcolm smiled maliciously. "I knew my toying with Gavin would annoy you."

"I'm not above a little toying myself." The blade of his sword sliced downward at Malcolm's groin.

Malcolm's high squeal of pain sent a shudder through Kate. He staggered backward, looking down at himself.

"Painful?" Robert asked through his teeth. "Try this." His sword entered Alec's stomach, turned in a half-circle, and then withdrew.

To Kate's horror, Malcolm didn't fall. He stood there swaying, his face contorted with incredible pain. "You . . . fool. Can't . . . win."

"A victory wasn't in question. I'm only sorry I don't have more time to play with you as you did Gavin." This time Robert's sword thrust deep into Malcolm's chest and remained there. He released the hilt of the sword and stepped back, waiting for Malcolm to fall.

It was finished.

Malcolm stood gazing at Robert, an expression of incredulity on his face. As Kate watched, Malcolm fell to his knees and then crumpled backward onto the ground.

Alec's hands clutched the sword; blood poured from his palms as the blade bit into them when he tried to pull the sword from his chest. "No," he said in disbelief. "It's not true. I shall ... not die."

"You will die," Robert said coldly. "You're a dead man now."

Alec tried to rise and then fell back with a cry of pain. The disbelief turned to anger, and then incredible malice twisted his features. "You think you've ... won. But you've lost ... too. Confession ..." He coughed, and blood trickled from the corner of his mouth. "James will get ... confession."

Robert stiffened. "What confession?"

"The nurse signed ... it in the dungeon before ... she died. I gave orders ... that it be given to James on my death." His gaze went to Kate in triumph. "I told you ... I wouldn't let ... him win. Craighdhu ... is gone. James will burn down half of Scotland to ... kill her when he reads that confession." He started to laugh. "And you're gone ..." He suddenly arched upward, laughter freezing on his face in a death rictus.

Kate shuddered and glanced away from him.

Robert was cursing beneath his breath. "Christ, why couldn't the woman have died before she signed the damn thing!"

"What did he mean?" she asked dully. "What confession?"

"Proof that you're Mary's daughter. James had your wet nurse brought to Edinburgh, and Alec tortured her to death to obtain information."

"Clara?" Clara was dead. That kind woman she could barely remember had suffered horribly and died because of Kate. The devastation she was spreading was growing, sucking bad and good alike down into a deadly whirlpool. "You didn't tell me he'd killed her too."

"Think about it later." Robert lifted her onto her horse. "At least three of Alec's guard escaped. They'll carry word to Edinburgh."

"I could go after them," Jock suggested.

"It would only buy us a little time. We'd do better to use that time to get to the ship."

Everything was moving too fast for Kate. "I don't wish to—"

"Kate, if you argue with me now, I'll bind you to that horse and gag you," Robert said savagely. "We have to be out to sea before James's soldiers come back and discover Alec's dead."

"We could try to find out who has the confession before he gives it to James," Jock said. "We don't know the timing of Alec's instructions. We could have a day or two before James receives the confession."

"Or we could have an hour. Knowing Alec, I'd wager on the latter." Robert mounted his horse. "I can't take the chance."

The *Irish Princess* sailed out of the port of Granton three hours later, and Robert drew his first relaxed breath since he had killed Malcolm. They were safe for a little while, and he had time to think about their next move.

Kate moved to stand beside Robert at the rail. "I'm not going back to Craighdhu. If you take me there, I'll only run away."

"You'll go where I take you," he said. "There will be no place in all of Scotland that will be safe for you now."

"Then I'll not stay in Scotland either." Her hands clenched on the rail. "Take me to Elizabeth—she helped me before. Perhaps she can find me a haven."

"She helped you because it was convenient and eliminated a potential threat. If James knows who you are, the threat is real, and you're definitely an inconvenience."

"Perhaps you're wrong. I'd rather take my chance with her than have Craighdhu destroyed."

"Kate ..." He drew a deep breath, trying to restrain his frustration. Christ, everything had gone wrong tonight, and her stubbornness was not helping matters. He had seen how the knowledge that another person had died for her had affected her, and he would have liked to give comfort, but there were decisions to make. "Why don't you go to the cabin and go to bed. We'll discuss this in the morning."

"When we'll be well on our way to Craighdhu." Her eyes were glistening in the moonlight. "Why won't you listen to me? All right, don't take me to Elizabeth— take me to the Netherlands as Malcolm was going to do."

"The Netherlands?" he repeated, startled. "I thought you said he was going to take you to England."

"He changed his mind. It had something to do with the war. He said our greatest support would be in the Netherlands." She reached out and grasped his arm. "If you won't take me to Elizabeth, take me to the Netherlands or Italy or ... or Russia. Anywhere but Craighdhu. I can't bear to see— Why are you looking like that? What's wrong?"

He felt as if he had been hit in the stomach. My God, that wily son of a bitch.

"Robert?"

"It's all right. Go to the cabin," he said. "I have to think." He was already thinking, putting the pieces together. "I'll join you in a little while."

"Not tomorrow?"

He shook his head. "In a little while."

He was barely aware of her leaving as he looked blindly out to sea.

Kennilworth.

Our greatest support is in the Netherlands.

The serpent.

Christ.

• • •

Robert did not come to the cabin until after midnight. Kate was in bed but raised herself on one elbow when Robert walked into the room. "You were long enough. Did you think I'd be asleep?"

"I know you better than that," Robert said as he slipped out of his leather vest and threw it on the chair. "With an argument on the horizon you'd stick pins in yourself to keep yourself awake."

"I had no pins," she said. "And I have no desire to argue with you."

"Not if you get your own way." He sat down on the bunk and took off his boots. The scent of him was suddenly there in the darkness: clean linen, salt, and sea. "I have no desire to argue with you either."

There was a note in his quiet voice that made her uneasy. The moonlight streaming through the bank of windows of the forecastle cast a faint blue light over the cabin, but she needed to see more.

"Light the candle."

"The moonlight's good enough."

Her apprehension grew as she realized he did not want her to see him clearly. "What's wrong?" she asked, frowning.

"Because I don't wish to argue with you?"

"No, there's something else. . . ." She sat up and leaned back against the wall, studying him. She was not sure if it was the stark hardness of the moonlight or his expression that made him look so stern. "Are you angry with me?"

"No."

Her hand nervously clutched the cover. "Then you're sad because you think I might destroy Craighdhu. It's not true. I won't let that happen. You just have to let me go away, and it will be the same as if I never set foot on Craighdhu."

"It can never be the same."

"Why not? If I—"

"Because I will love you until the day I die."

The joy that exploded within her was followed immediately by despair. Too late. If he had told her this that afternoon on Craighdhu— No, it had always been impossible. She had just not known it. She smiled tremulously. "That's very pleasant, but it doesn't really matter."

"It matters very much." He turned to face her. "It means I cannot leave you, and I will not let you leave me."

She swallowed and then deliberately hardened her tone. "It does not mean that at all. Why do men always think it is only what they feel that is of any account? I care nothing for you. I only wanted Craighdhu. I plotted and planned—so you must forget about me, and I will forget—"

"Hush." His fingers on her lips stopped the rush of words. "Hush, love."

The tears that had been threatening overflowed and ran down her cheeks. Her head sank against his chest. "Don't let me hurt you. Please, I don't want to hurt you."

He didn't speak. The steady throb of his heart thundered beneath her ear as his hand gently stroked her hair.

"I wanted you to love me, but it's all wrong . . . Maybe if you try, it will go away."

"It won't go away. We'll just have to make the best of it. It can be a very good best, Kate."

"Not if I take Craighdhu from you."

"You won't take it from me. I give it freely."

A gift she could not accept. "Why?" she asked. "I don't deserve it. No woman would deserve it. You can't say it wouldn't hurt."

"No, I can't say that, but it would hurt more to give you up."

"You say that now."

"And I'll say it again fifty years from now. Listen to

me, Kate, this isn't a decision I've made lightly. It's very simple. You are more than Craighdhu. If I have to choose, then I take what is of most value to me."

She knew she couldn't allow it, but perhaps she could steal this moment.

Just once she wanted to say it. Surely, just one time would do no harm. Her halting whisper was scarcely audible in the darkness. "I . . . love you."

His lips feathering her temple were exquisitely tender.

"But I'll get over it," she added quickly. "I do not have a constant nature. So you needn't feel guilt about leaving me."

"I'll keep that in mind. I'm sure it will bring me great comfort."

But he would pay no attention to her words. He knew her too well. He would never leave her, and someday it would destroy him. So she must find a way of leaving him, and she didn't know if she would have the strength if he took her home to Craighdhu.

"I want to go to England."

He stiffened against her. "No."

"Can't you see? It's our only chance. If James knows who I am, then our only hope is if Elizabeth intercedes or finds a haven for me."

"And the chances are that she will do neither."

"We have to try." She could sense his resistance still. "If you love me, take me to Elizabeth." Her arms tightened desperately around him. "Please, Robert."

For a moment she thought he wasn't going to answer. He merely sat holding her, stroking her hair. Finally, he kissed her cheek and said softly, "Very well, lass. We'll go see Elizabeth."

"You're very splendid," Robert said as he helped her into the barge that was to take them to the palace. "I have fond memories of that gown."

So did Kate. She nervously smoothed the crimson

velvet skirt of the gown she had worn on the eve of Jean and Gavin's wedding. "It's the grandest I own. I'm not accustomed to court life, but I thought it would be appropriate."

"More than appropriate." Robert settled on the seat beside her, and the waterman pushed away from the dock. "You look like a flame."

She felt a flicker of surprise. Robert seldom commented on her appearance. Then she understood; he knew she was nervous about the audience with the queen and was trying to give her confidence. "Let's hope Elizabeth approves."

Robert's gaze shifted to the scene passing by on the banks of the river Thames. "Her approval is not a matter of dire necessity. We have other roads we can pursue."

We. On the journey from Scotland she had tried to convince him she would not stay with him whatever the outcome of this audience, but he would not accept it. However, she was too worried about the coming meeting to argue with him now. "What other roads?"

He smiled. "We could sail away and raid Spanish galleons. Would you like to be a pirate, Kate?"

"No, and neither would you. You told me you were done with pirating."

"Circumstances change."

She had changed those circumstances. He was thinking of returning to buccaneering because on the high seas he could fight James with no danger to Craighdhu. Yet such a life would still be exile. She could not permit it. If Elizabeth offered her a haven, she must find a way to claim it without Robert's knowledge of its location. "I will not discuss such foolishness. We will see what Elizabeth says."

He smiled crookedly. "Aye, by all means, we must certainly hear what the queen has to say to your request."

• • •

"Don't bother me, Percy." Elizabeth didn't look up from the letter she was writing. "Can't you see I'm busy?"

"I plead your indulgence, Your Majesty," Percy Montgrave said. "But I thought you'd wish ..." He stopped, searching for words. "The earl of Craighdhu begs an audience with you."

Elizabeth's pen stopped in midmotion. "Begs? That doesn't sound like MacDarren. Your word, Percy?"

Percy scowled. "Demands. I told him you would not see him, but he cares nothing that you're beset by worries about this Spanish—"

"Let him come in," she interrupted.

"And the countess?"

She looked up swiftly. "His countess is here also?"

He nodded. "He wishes an audience for her as well."

She set her pen in the inkwell. "By all means, let her come. I'd be curious to see the woman who would wed a man like MacDarren."

She heard him mutter something in an undertone as he left the chamber. She quickly rose to her feet and moved to the gilt-framed mirror on the wall across the room. She touched the dark circles beneath her eyes. She had not slept well last night, nor many nights before, with all this blasted unrest with Philip. She straightened her ruff and bit her lips to redden them. Did she look old? Good God, why was she concerned with how she looked? It was not her appearance but her spirit and brains that made the world leap at her bidding.

"Your Majesty."

She turned away from the mirror to see Robert MacDarren standing in the doorway, as comely and panther lethal as she remembered.

Her gaze moved to the woman dressed in crimson velvet standing next to him.

Kathryn.

• • •

Elizabeth was not as Kate had pictured her. Her ivory silk gown was magnificent, the ruby locket gracing her throat stunning, but the woman herself was not glorious. She was merely a rouged, aging woman whose tight curls appeared too brilliant a red to be natural.

Then the queen's gaze swept to Kate, and she instantly changed her mind. The woman's gaze was razor sharp, assessing and then summing.

Elizabeth tilted her head. "You're no beauty, but you're not without a certain comeliness." To Robert she said, "You see, I told you the girl would be both meek and presentable."

"Well, at least she's presentable," Robert said as he bowed low. "Your Majesty was right, as usual."

"And you're insolent, as usual. Have the courtesy to halt your mockery and bring your wife closer, so I can get a better look at her."

Kate moved forward and swept the queen a low curtsy. "Your Majesty."

"Rise, rise," the queen said impatiently. "How can I see your features with you looking at my shoes?" Kate lifted her gaze, and Elizabeth's appraisal raked first her face and then the gold-brown hair flowing from beneath the velvet cap. "Good eyes, and your hair has a fine thickness and bright color."

"Did you expect it to be darker?" Robert asked.

Elizabeth turned to Robert. "Of course not. I received reports from the good vicar on the girl."

"And Mary's hair was not dark either," Robert said. "Tell me, do you think she has the same—"

"It's not your place to question but to give answers. Why are you not at Craighdhu, where you're supposed to be?"

"I was at Craighdhu, but circumstances changed, and I was forced to adapt."

Robert was more insolent and mocking than Kate had ever seen him. How the devil was she to ask a favor from Elizabeth if he persisted in antagonizing her? But perhaps that was his purpose. Kate had been aware he had been reluctant to come since the moment she had mentioned it.

Robert continued, "But Your Majesty is also very good at adapting to suit your needs. I remember in the Tower you were—"

"God's blood, Robert, be silent and let me talk to her," Kate snapped in exasperation.

The queen's surprised gaze flew back to Kate. "Ah, not meek at all." She threw back her head and laughed. "It serves you well, MacDarren."

"Aye." Robert smiled. "I've decided I deserve her."

Kate gave him a warning look. "Forgive him, Your Majesty. He's being most discourteous, when we have a favor to ask of you."

"Favor?" Elizabeth repeated warily.

"Haven." Kate quickly related the circumstances that had brought them here. "You've been kind to me in the past. It's my hope you will be equally kind to me now."

"The nurse is dead?" Elizabeth demanded. "What of this confession?"

"We assume James now has it in his hands," Robert answered.

"Damnation." A flush of color darkened Elizabeth's cheeks. "Blunderer. Could you do nothing right, MacDarren?"

"May I remind you that you're the one who chose Sebastian Landfield?" Robert said. "If you'd told me he was mad enough to go to James, I'd have cut his throat before I took Kate to Craighdhu."

"Are you saying the fault is mine?"

"Aye." His smile was a tigerish baring of teeth. "The fault is entirely yours, Your Majesty."

They were like two animals circling each other, about to pounce, Kate thought in frustration. "It does not matter where the fault lies. Will you help me?"

Elizabeth's gaze swung back to her. "I don't know

if I can. If James knows your birth, the risk may be too great. I'm walking a very fine line with him right now."

"So you intend to hand her over to James?" Robert asked.

"I didn't say that," Elizabeth snapped. "It may be possible for me to find her some kind of haven. But not here in England."

"And you will not extend your protection over her?"

"That's not possible. On no account must I appear to have a connection with her."

Robert's expression hardened. "You're wrong," he said. "It's not possible for you to do anything else."

"And why not?"

His gaze met the queen's. "Because we both know what was in that confession signed by Clara Merkert. We know that Mary Stuart was not Kate's mother." He paused. "And that you are."

"Robert!" Kate whispered.

Robert's gaze was fixed on Elizabeth. "It's true, isn't it?"

"Lies," Elizabeth said flatly. "Mad, rambling lies. And such arrant insult, I may have your head for it."

"I don't believe you'd take the risk. You wouldn't want to expose my mad rambling to the light of day. The only safe route would be the assassin's knife, but you'd have grievous problems justifying that to yourself. You do have a conscience."

"Robert, what are you saying?" Kate asked dazedly. "It's not true. You know I'm—"

"How do I know? Because Sebastian told you all your life you were Mary's bastard? Who told him?" He nodded toward Elizabeth. "Her Glorious Majesty. You believed it because he believed it. It was unlikely he would question the queen, whose purity and virginity are legendary, but if he did, she gave him the perfect answer. Wicked Cousin Mary weaving spells in her tower. It was really quite convenient having Mary pris-

oner all those years, wasn't it? You wouldn't have
wanted your child brought up without some deference
shown her station. You robbed her of her birthright,
but you still gave her the myth of being a queen's
child."

"Supposition," Elizabeth said stonily.

"But you once said I was good at supposition,"
Robert replied. "You let me put all the pieces together
that led me where you wanted me to go. Because I
reached those conclusions myself, I never once questioned their truth. Very clever, Your Majesty."

"And why should you doubt those conclusions
now?"

"The confession."

"Which you did not see."

"But whose contents guided Malcolm's every
move."

"Clara Merkert could have told him Kathryn was
Mary's child," Elizabeth said. "It would have instigated
the same actions if this Malcolm was as ambitious as
you say."

"He would have gone after Kate, but not in the
same way. He tortured Sebastian Landfield to get him
to testify to the fact that she was your daughter, not
Mary's, but Sebastian wouldn't yield. Yet in the end he
came to believe it was true. He said, "Not Lilith . . . the
serpent, writhing, changing." The serpent in the garden
of Eden was said to have changed from devil to serpent.
In Sebastian's eyes Kate had changed from Mary's
daughter to Elizabeth's."

"Flimsy," Elizabeth snorted.

Robert nodded. "So flimsy, I didn't even see it. But
then Kate told me Malcolm was taking her to Warwick
and Kenilworth to rouse support."

Kate saw the slightest change in Elizabeth's demeanor.

"I thought it strange, but even then I didn't make
the connection. Until Malcolm suddenly changed his

mind and was taking Kate to the Netherlands instead."
He turned to Kate. "What did he tell you?"

"That my greatest support lay in the Netherlands,"
Kate said haltingly.

"And it did." Robert met Elizabeth's gaze. "Because
this month you sent the earl of Leicester to the Netherlands to try to negotiate peace and shore up foreign defenses in preparation for this war with Spain. He was
no longer in his castle at Kenilworth or at his brother's
estate in Warwick. It was necessary for Malcolm to follow him to the Netherlands to involve him in the conspiracy."

"Robert Dudley is my most loyal servant. The earl
would never enter into a conspiracy against me," Elizabeth said.

"Not even to make his daughter the queen of England, with himself the power behind the throne?"
Robert asked softly.

But her father was the earl of Shrewsbury, Kate
thought in bewilderment. This was all madness. All her
life she had known this to be true, and now she was to
accept not only Elizabeth as her mother, but the earl of
Leicester as her father.

"You're accusing me of fornication with Robin and
then having his child?" Elizabeth asked coldly.

"Who else? There have been rumors about you
two ever since you came to the throne. You refused to
send him away even when your attachment to your
master of horse aroused ridicule among all the nations
of Europe. You heaped honor and riches on him, but
you wouldn't give him what he wanted most. To wed
the queen and gain the power that the position im-
plied." Robert paused. "Because Leicester was always a
very ambitious man. At one time he promised the
Spanish ambassador he would restore the Catholic religion to England if Spain would further his suit with
you."

"He did not mean it," Elizabeth said quickly. "Robin has always been a staunch Protestant."

"But the offer would still have made you uneasy. You could not take the risk of marriage, and you could not give him up. So what course was left when you found yourself with child? Leicester must not know. A man so ambitious would have found the knowledge he had fathered the illegitimate heiress to the throne too tempting to resist."

"I'm surrounded by my ladies of the court at all times. How could I have had a child and escaped notice?"

"It would have been difficult but not impossible. Not for the woman the pope called 'the rarest creature that was in Europe these five hundred years.' "

"You have no proof of this slander," Elizabeth said.

"Except for the confession held by James."

"I'd wager James burned that document two minutes after he received it." Her lips curled. "The young pup would let nothing stand in the way of his pursuit of my throne."

"Which is why you will extend your protection over Kate," Robert said. "And why you will acknowledge her publicly."

"Are you mad? If what you say is true, after striving to keep her from Robin's view all these years, do you think I'd let him know of her existence now?"

"The only way to keep her safe is to acknowledge her."

Elizabeth's gaze narrowed on his face. "So that you may make a move yourself to seize the throne on her behalf. Very clever, but you will not—"

"Stop it!" Kate cut through the queen's words like a white-hot sword. "I will have no more of this. How *dare* you quarrel over me like two mongrel dogs over a bone? This is my *life*." She whirled on Elizabeth. "Are you my mother?"

Elizabeth stared at her without speaking.

"Answer me!"

Robert stepped forward. "Kate, it will be—"

"Be silent." She turned on him. "I'm not pleased with you either. Why didn't you tell me this before? Why let me come here and find out this way?"

"I believe our dear Black Robert was not entirely sure of his ground and was depending on the tactics of surprise to win the battle," Elizabeth said dryly.

"Well, it wasn't kind of him. Neither of you are kind. I will not . . ." She stopped to steady her voice. "Leave us, Robert, I wish to talk to her alone."

"I don't believe that to be a good idea, Kate," Robert said.

"Leave us!"

Robert still stood frowning at her.

"Oh, for God's sake, go," Elizabeth said impatiently. "I will not eat her."

"That was not my concern," Robert said. "I'm afraid she will devour you. That would be a most inconvenient course here in your domain." He smiled ironically as he bowed to Kate. "Be gentle with her, lass. After all, she is your mother."

Elizabeth scowled as she watched him leave the chamber. "Insolent rogue. I should have listened to Percy."

"Are you my mother?" Kate asked again.

"I am the queen of this realm, and you are not treating me with the deference due me."

"I have a right to know," Kate said fiercely. "I've been lied to and used and shuttled to and fro as if I were nothing. If this is true, then you have wronged me, and I *will* have the truth." She met Elizabeth's gaze and asked with measured precision. "Are—you—my—mother?"

Elizabeth did not speak for a moment and then said, "I gave you birth."

Kate felt as if she were going to faint.

Elizabeth lifted her head. "But I will never acknowledge you. Never. It would be far too dangerous."

"To you?"

"To England," Elizabeth said. "If Mary's daughter could be used as a pawn to tear this country apart, how much more hazardous would my daughter be?"

"So you will abandon me again?"

"I did not abandon you. You were given everything I could safely give you."

"You could have given me a father. You could have—"

"Do you think I did not want a child? When Mary gave birth to James, it nearly killed me. I wanted an heir." She shrugged. "It was not possible. I had to make a choice. I do not regret it."

"Because my father had ambitions?"

"Robin was very hungry. There's nothing wrong with ambition as long as it's controlled. I have it in full measure myself." When she saw Kate's expression, she said harshly, "You don't understand. I've loved him all my life. He has been my playmate, my lover, and is now my friend. Do you know how lonely I have been? I *deserved* Robin."

"Then why did you not wed him?"

"You fool, that would have been the fastest way to lose him. I know Robin. The power would have been too heady. . . . He would have tried to grab too much." She shuddered. "And then I would have had to punish him for it."

"By sending him to the block as you did my—" Kate stopped. It was still difficult to realize Mary was not her mother, that it had all been a lie. "Would you have killed him too?"

"You find that hard to believe?" she asked. "Yes, I would have done it. It would have broken my heart, but I would not have been able to do anything else." She smiled cynically. "What do you know? When I was younger than you, my friend Tom Seymour lost his head, and I sat in the Tower waiting to know if I was to die myself. Such circumstances tend to give time for thought and teach hard lessons. It taught me what I valued most in the world and gave me the determination to protect it."

"And the throne is clearly what you value most," Kate said bitterly.

"England is what I value most, and the throne is how I protect it." Her tone hardened. "And not you or Robin or any force on earth will be allowed to destroy it."

"I have no desire to destroy it."

"You can be used to—"

"Stop talking. My head is whirling. I have to think." She walked over to stare blindly out of the mullioned window. She felt Elizabeth's hawklike gaze on her back as she desperately tried to absorb the revelations and emotions that had bombarded her in the last few minutes. She was experiencing resentment, anger, shock, and something else that filled her with fear . . . understanding.

She turned back to face the queen a few minutes later. "You do not have to acknowledge me."

"Perhaps I did not make myself clear: I have no intention of doing so."

Kate ignored the caustic retort. "But you will send a letter to James. In it you will admit that I'm your daughter, but state that as long as James does nothing to harm Robert, myself, or Craighdhu, you will promise to designate James your heir upon your death."

Elizabeth frowned. "I'll do nothing of the sort. I've not yet made that decision."

"No, you prefer to keep James dangling." Kate continued, "You will also tell him that, should he take any overt action against Craighdhu, he will never have the throne of England."

Elizabeth shook her head. "I must have a weapon to bestir James, when Philip sends his armada."

"Then find another," Kate said. "This is *my* weapon."

Elizabeth's lips curled. "You have no weapons against me."

"But I do," Kate paused. "I have my father."

"Robin?"

"Deny me and I will go direct to the Netherlands and rob you of him." Her voice vibrated with intensity. "By God, I'll show you that I'm no pawn. I'll study how to use him, and then I'll tempt him, stir those ambitions you tell me you understand. He'll join with me to overthrow you, and you'll lose your lover and old friend you value so much. In the end you'll have to destroy us both, or we will destroy you."

Elizabeth's lips parted in stunned surprise. "You could not do it."

"Look at me," Kate challenged, passion ringing in every syllable. "I'm your daughter. I can move the world if I choose to do so."

Elizabeth whispered, "I believe you could." She suddenly chuckled. "But not my world."

"We shall see."

Elizabeth shook her head. "It may not be necessary that we have a confrontation. It's possible I can handle James as you suggest and still wrest what I need from him."

Kate was careful not to show either relief or triumph. "I have the utmost confidence you will do so."

"And what assurance do I have that you won't go to Robin, even after I give you these guarantees?"

"The assurance that I have no desire for the throne," Kate said. "I, too, know what I value most in the world, and it's not what you possess."

"Craighdhu and that outrageous scamp in the antechamber? You have no vision."

"That outrageous scamp could rule this kingdom better than you. As for vision, I see a life at Craighdhu with challenges aplenty and a circumstance where I will not have to give my child away to strangers." She moved toward the door. "Send the letter at once. I wish to go home to Craighdhu."

"Are you quite certain that's all you want?" Elizabeth asked silkily.

Kate glanced over her shoulder.

Elizabeth was smiling, and her expression held a mixture of cynicism, sadness, and a touch of malice. "I think not. I see a hunger in you too," she said softly. "After all, you are my daughter."

Robert came to Kate and took her hand as she closed the door of the chamber behind her. "All is well?"

Comfort flowed over her at his touch. She nodded curtly. "Fine."

His gaze searched her features. "You don't look fine."

Because Elizabeth's last remark had shaken her. Her mother had seen something in Kate that she would rather remained buried. "What do you expect when you shock me with—" She stopped as she remembered the guard beside the door. "Let's go back to the ship."

Robert didn't speak again until they were in the barge gliding away from the palace.

"Well, do we go buccaneering?"

She shook her head. "We go back to Craighdhu. It will be safe there as long as my father is alive. My father," she repeated. "Strange. When I believed Shrewsbury was my father, I never really thought about him. And now it's the same with Leicester. They stand in the shadows."

"Understandable. Both Mary and Elizabeth cast a brilliant light."

"I was very angry with her. I told her if she didn't do what I wished, I'd go to my father and together we'd destroy her." She shrugged. "Naturally, I was bluffing."

Robert smiled faintly. "Were you?"

He knew her too well. "No, I meant it. When I was

standing there talking to her, the blood was pounding in my veins. I felt exhilarated, as if I could do anything. And I knew she felt the same way. It was if we were feeding on each other."

"It doesn't surprise me. You're very much alike."

"I don't want to be like her, Robert," she whispered.

"Choose the good and leave the bad."

"You said that about Mary."

"The advice is still sound. Wouldn't you rather be Elizabeth's daughter than Mary's?"

Elizabeth could be devious and selfish, but she was also strong and bold, and something about her struck an answering chord in Kate. "I think ... I could have loved her." Kate grimaced. "But it would have been like loving myself."

"There's nothing wrong with loving, Kate," Robert said. "I make a habit of it."

She shook her head, still remembering that disturbing exhilaration. "I shall not see her again."

"The lure is too strong?"

"I did not say that," she said quickly.

"Would you like to be queen of England? We could do it, you know," he said quietly. "Shall we go to the Netherlands, love?"

She stared at him in shock. "But we're going home."

"Only if that's what you wish. I knew when I brought you to Elizabeth, you might have a decision to make."

"And you brought me anyway?"

"You've been cheated enough in your life. I will not have you cheated again."

He would cheat himself instead. She swallowed to ease the aching tightness in her throat. "You're much too arrogant to be a royal consort."

He lifted her hand to his lips. "I could adapt to the

role as long as you promise to 'consort.' And I would definitely keep Your Majesty entertained."

"I believe you." She laid her head on his shoulder. "But you'll have more time for such activities if we go home to Craighdhu."

"You're sure?"

Suddenly, she was very certain. Elizabeth's path might be challenging, the adulation and power intoxicating, but Kate had no wish to end her life as Elizabeth was going to . . . alone, with only the trappings of glory around her.

"I do not want it," she said firmly as she nestled closer. "And she would not either, if she knew what she was missing. I only want you and Craighdhu."

She could feel the tension he had not let her see ebb out of him. He drew her closer and said lightly, "I'm very gratified you'd give up a throne for me, lass. It's a fine and rare compliment."

"Well, it's not only for you. I did have one other consideration." Her spirits were suddenly lifting as hope soared through her. Why worry that this was only a reprieve? They were going home, and together they would find a way to stay there. She smiled luminously. "Our child should be born by the time the seals return to Craighdhu next year."

"There's Tim MacDougal on the dock." Robert turned to Jock. "Care for Kate. I'll go down to see if there's anything amiss."

Kate watched him hurry down the gangplank and over to the agent. The frown on Robert's face instantly cleared as he spoke to him, she noticed with relief. She had thought Elizabeth would move swiftly to protect Craighdhu, but there was always the possibility that James had instigated trouble.

"All seems to be well," Jock said. "However, I wonder he trusts me to care for you. The last time I handed you over to Alec."

"I handed myself over," Kate said. She turned to look at him. Since they had boarded the *Irish Princess* in Scotland, he had offered her courtesy but had distanced himself. This was the first time she could remember him speaking directly to her. "It was no fault of yours, and Robert knows it."

"I could have prevented it. I chose not to do so." He met her gaze. "I would not make the same decision now."

She tensed. "No?"

A sudden smile lit his face. "You've caused us a great deal of trouble. It would not be sensible to allow you to do so again. I told Robert we would be safer to have you here than on the throne of Scotland, and now that we know you're the heiress to an even greater throne, we must see that you have plenty to do here to keep you out of mischief."

She relaxed. "You know I'm with child?"

"I believe we can keep one small bairn safe—if he's not as self-willed as his mother," he qualified.

"He probably will be."

"Then we'll deal with that problem when it happens." He took her arm. "Robert is hailing us."

"I'll never endanger Craighdhu or Robert," she said in a low voice as he led her toward the gangplank. "You needn't worry about that, Jock."

"I'm not worrying." He didn't look at her as they left the ship. "I knew you'd never allow harm to come to anyone or anything you cared about when we went to Kilgranne, Kate."

Kate. She had a memory of that moment in the courtyard when she had told him never to call her Kate because Kathryn was the name by which she was known to her enemies. She smiled. "I'm glad you've found I know how to do my duty to Craighdhu too, Jock." They had stopped beside Robert and MacDougal, and she looked inquiringly at Robert.

"There's no problem," Robert assured her. "Tim

just wanted to tell me he'd taken care of a matter for me."

"I'm greatly relieved. We've had enough trouble." She smiled at the agent. "I'm very happy to see you, Tim."

MacDougal flushed. "We missed you. You're looking well, my lady."

Robert took Kate's arm and began to walk down the dock. "He also says Gavin is much better and the most foul-tempered invalid on the face of the earth."

"Thank God," she said fervently. "And Jean?"

"She's turned the castle upside down with her demands for Gavin. She and Deirdre are about to come to blows. They both think they know best for him."

Jock and Tim MacDougal fell into step behind them, and Kate was vaguely aware of their voices in low conversation. The sun was shining brightly as they turned into the street that led to the castle, and the entire village seemed to gleam. She could feel tears sting her eyes, and a poignant pang went through her as she realized how close she had come to losing all this. Craighdhu was still in danger, but at least she would have another chance to win this place she loved so dearly.

They had reached the marketplace, and Kate and Robert were suddenly surrounded by men, women, and children.

"It's about time you came back."

She turned to see Deirdre standing in the doorway of the weavers' cottage a few yards down the street.

"Deirdre!" She broke free of the crowd and ran across the street. "How have things been with you?"

"Well enough," the Irishwoman said gruffly. "I'm not the one who ran away after embroiling me with these women and then neglecting her—"

"Hush." Kate dared give her a quick hug. "Say you're glad I returned."

The smallest smile curved Deirdre's lips. "Of

course I'm glad." She added quickly, "I need help with these ninnies who don't know a warp from a shuttle."

Kate grinned. "You'll get it. I hear you and Jean have Gavin almost well."

"He would get well quicker if she would listen to me. She's a willful bit of baggage. But maybe a better woman thän I first thought," she conceded grudgingly.

"Kate." Robert had extracted himself from the crowd and was determinedly drawing her away from Deirdre. "We'll see you later, Deirdre," he told the woman as he whisked Kate away. "We have something to do now."

He was leading her toward the church, she realized with bewilderment. "Why are we going there?"

"Because, as I said, we have a task to perform." Robert took her hand and started up the long flight of steps. "I sent word ahead that the dominie was to be here when we arrived."

"The dominie? Why should ... ?" She stopped as she realized the significance of his words. "You wish to wed me?"

"We are already wed. I merely wish to tighten the bond a bit."

"It would not only tighten it. A wedding in the church would make it irrevocable."

"It's been irrevocable since the moment I saw you, covered with mud, lying on that trail."

She stopped short as they reached the door. "But this is different."

He threw back his head and laughed. "You're going to have my bairn, you defied Elizabeth of England, and you're balking at saying a few words before the dominie?"

"It seems reckless."

His laughter vanished. "It seems reckless to me to risk losing you again. Alec said I was a fool not to wed you before God and man, and I'll not repeat that mistake."

"It means you wouldn't be able to repudiate me, should it become necessary."

"Nor you me," he said. "So if you should change your mind and decide Craighdhu is not enough for you, it would necessitate you taking me with you."

She swallowed. "A hard burden to bear."

"I'll try to make it lighter." He held out his hand. "Will you wed me, Kate?"

She looked down at his outstretched hand. On the night of Gavin and Jean's wedding, almost in this very spot, she had held out her hand to him, asking for trust and commitment. He had given it to her. Now, he was asking her for an even stronger commitment, from which there would be no retreat for either of them. They would rise to triumph or sink to defeat together.

A rare smile lit his face. "Kate?"

She couldn't smile in return. The moment was too solemn, and the joy and fear too overwhelming. That evening of the wedding had been bathed in a haze of mist and magic, but now they were standing in the bold sunlight of reality.

"Come, lass, where is your boldness?"

He was right—their love was great, but they would never survive the challenges ahead unless they faced life with endurance and courage. She reached out and took his hand. "It would be my great honor to wed you, Robert of Craighdhu."

Epilogue

Elizabeth successfully crushed Philip's mighty armada. The victory was attributed to both the strength of the English Navy and Elizabeth's own diplomatic brilliance, as exemplified by her skill in keeping James of Scotland from offering aid to the battered Spanish ships off his coast. Though the earl of Leicester's role in the victory was less than glorious, Elizabeth still showed her esteem for him by making him commander of her army.

Craighdhu
October 30, 1588

"Here's a letter for you, Kate." Gavin came into the hall and started toward the hearth where Kate sat on the floor playing with Patrick before the fire. "The courier is waiting at the dock for an answer."

"From Robert?" she asked eagerly. Robert had been in Ireland for more than two months, protecting their holdings from the ruthlessness of Sir William Fitzwilliam, Elizabeth's lord deputy of Ireland. It was the longest they had been separated since they had returned to Craighdhu. As she rose to her feet, her son immediately gave a howl of outrage and started pulling on the skirt of her gown. She gave him a wooden soldier to distract him as she watched Gavin come toward her.

Disappointment surged through her when Gavin shook his head. "The courier came from the mainland."

"You're limping again," she noticed with a frown. "Is your leg hurting?"

"A wee bit. It always aches when the wind blows from the north. Of course, Jeanie says I only limp to arouse sympathy." He grinned. "She's partially right. With a wife like her a man must use any weapon at hand to get his own way." He pulled a wistful face. "If I limp a little more, will you tell me where you hid my bagpipes?"

"No." She took the letter. "Jock says you must rest those poor wounded fingers."

"It's been more than a year." He wriggled his fingers. "See? No stiffness at all. I could play as well as ever."

"That's what I fear." She opened the envelope and took out the note. The smile that lingered on her lips vanished as she read the two lines scrawled on the parchment.

> *Your father is dead. Come to me.*
> *Elizabeth Regina.*

"What's wrong?" Gavin asked.

Very much could be wrong. If the earl of Leicester was dead, then Kate's hold over Elizabeth was nonexistent.

She handed the letter to Gavin, went over to the desk, and picked up a pen.

"Bad," Gavin murmured as he looked up from the letter. "Are you going?"

"Of course." She scrawled a few lines on the paper, placed it in the envelope, and sealed it. "What else can I do? Give this to the courier and tell Jock we'll be departing immediately."

He took the letter. "I could go with you."

She shook her head. "I'll take Jock. I want you to be here when Robert returns and keep him from following me."

"It won't be easy."

"You'll do the task better than Jock. Both of their instincts would be to attack instead of waiting to see if there's another way."

He puffed up his chest. "While I, on the other hand, am the virtual soul of diplomacy."

"Well . . ." She decided not to deflate him. "Will you ask Jean if she will take care of Patrick?"

"I promise we'll devote our full attention to the lad. It will be good practice for when we have our own bairn." He smiled beguilingly. "Now I know Patrick's a little young, but this would be a fine time to further his musical appreciation. If you'd only tell me where my bagpipes are?"

When Kate was shown into Elizabeth's chamber, she found the queen sitting by the window, idly toying with the strings of the lute on her lap. Elizabeth appeared smaller, almost shrunken, her skin parchment pale and her eyes swollen with weeping.

"You look well," she said listlessly. Then she snapped, "No, you look disgustingly radiant. It offends me."

"My apologies," Kate said. "I did not know my father, so I cannot feel distressed at his passing."

Elizabeth scowled. "You should at least have the grace to look anxious now that you no longer have a weapon against me."

"I'm concerned, but it's never wise to reveal weakness. We both know that."

"Yes." For an instant a fleeting smile crossed Elizabeth's face. "We do." She sat up straighter in the chair. "I will make this short. I have taken pity on your plight. I will extend the protection I have given you."

"Indeed?" Kate asked warily.

"However, you must pay the price. You must come here to London."

"Impossible."

"You say impossible to me?"

"Impossible," Kate repeated. "I will not leave Robert, and I will not ask him to leave Craighdhu." She paused. "And I now have a son."

"I'm aware of that. A boy."

Kate nodded. "Patrick's a fine healthy lad."

"Bring them with you." Elizabeth held up her hand. "Don't protest until you hear me out. I have no liking for handing this land over to that sniveling boy on the Scottish throne. I've not labored all my life to enrich this realm to have him squander it." She lifted her chin. "But, with proper guidance, you might prove adequate to the task."

Kate could see where the conversation was leading, and relief rushed through her. It was going to be all right. Elizabeth was handing her another weapon. She smiled. "I'd be more than adequate. I'd make the things you've accomplished during your reign seem trifling in comparison."

"Arrogance," Elizabeth snorted. "Living with that insolent pirate has not improved you."

"But it has infinitely enriched me."

"At any rate, I've decided I will name you my heir. It will cause a great deal of trouble, but between us we can—" She stopped as she saw Kate shaking her head. "You *refuse* me?"

"I don't want the throne."

"Nonsense. You want it. Everyone wants it."

"I have all I need at Craighdhu."

Elizabeth studied her expression. "You do mean it," she said wonderingly.

"But there's always the possibility I could change my mind." Kate grinned. "You'll never know, so you must keep your protection in place to guard the future queen of England."

"Oh, must I?"

Kate nodded. "It would not be to your advantage to do anything else."

Elizabeth's outrage gave way to a reluctant smile. "I should have taken you the last time I saw you. There's nothing like that first taste of power. You were wavering—I could have swayed you."

Looking back on that day, Kate knew she might be right. "It's possible."

"I could have had you." Elizabeth leaned back wearily in her chair, her forefinger plucking at the strings of the lute. Her fire was suddenly gone, and she was once more only an aging, sorrowing woman. She whispered, "Robin loved music. He gave me this lovely instrument. He gave me many wonderful gifts."

"I'm sure he did."

"But do you know the most valuable gift he gave me?"

Kate shook her head.

"He made me laugh. What a rare—" Her eyes glistened with tears, and she drew a deep breath. "Well, why are you standing there? The audience is over. You're dismissed."

Kate curtsied and started to leave.

"I named you after my father's last wife," Elizabeth abruptly called after her. "Kathryn Parr was very kind to me when I was a child."

It seemed an odd thing for her mother to say to end this interview, but perhaps no stranger than the audience itself.

Kate opened the door.

"I loved her very much ... Kathryn."

It was the closest Elizabeth would ever come to admitting regret for giving up her child. Well, surrender was not easy for Kate either. Time might have lessened her hurt and resentment, but they were still present. Yet in this instant of parting she found she did not wish to leave without matching Elizabeth's compromise with one of her own.

"I've never liked to be called Kathryn." A smile lit her face as she looked over her shoulder. "Call me Kate."

April 29, 1603
Craighdhu

Kate and Robert watched Percy Montgrave slip and slide on the wet hillside as he struggled up to the cliff where they were standing. He was carrying a large shawl-wrapped bundle in his arms, and the burden only made his climb more difficult.

"Should we go down and help him?" Kate asked.

"Not unless you mean me to help him off the cliff," Robert murmured. "I have no kind memories of Montgrave."

"God's blood, this is an inhospitable place," Montgrave said as he reached the crest of the hill. He looked down with revulsion at the seals below. "Blustery winds and wild beasts. It suits you well, MacDarren."

"Aye, it does." Robert drew a protective step closer to Kate. "What are you doing here?"

"I brought your wife a gift from the queen." He handed the wrapped object to Robert as he reached beneath his cloak. "You heard she died on March twenty-fourth of this year?"

"Yes." The word of Elizabeth's death had filled Kate

with a confusion of emotions, foremost of which had
been sadness and regret.

He brought out the envelope for which he had
been fumbling and handed it to Kate. "She gave me this
letter and the gift to bring to you a week after she took
to her bed. She told me to tell you there are great riches
to be found in music."

"And that was her only message?" What had she
expected? Kate thought ruefully. Certainly not a tender
farewell or an admission from the queen that she had
been wrong in her treatment of her daughter.

"You're fortunate she made this much effort,"
Percy said sharply. "She was not herself. She was tired
... so tired...." He shook his head as if trying to rid
himself of the memory. "She was a very difficult
woman but ... I shall miss her. It seems very ...
empty." He turned and started down the hill. "I must
get back to court. James set out immediately for London when he heard of her death. It was not wise of me
to leave before I welcomed him, but my duty to her
came first."

Robert watched him leave as Kate opened the envelope. "He's right, it wasn't wise. They'll all be vying
for position at court now that James is king. Maybe
Montgrave isn't as bad as I thought."

The letter from Elizabeth was brief and written in
a weak, spidery hand.

> Kate,
>   I seldom give second chances, but perhaps
> reparation is due you. I have implied to all that
> James is my choice to succeed me, but I will state
> it neither verbally nor in writing. One copy of
> the document in the casing of this lute will go to
> James, another will be sent to the bishop of Can-
> terbury for safekeeping with instructions to the
> bishop that it not be opened unless he is ordered
> to do so by you.

*If you are wise, you will use this document
as I would have done. If you are as foolish as I
think you are, you will keep it only as a safe-
guard to use over James should he attack you.*
　　　　　　　　　　　　Elizabeth Regina

Robert unwrapped the shawl covering the lute,
parted the strings, and drew out the document inside
the cavity. He unfolded and quickly scanned it. "It's
Elizabeth's will, naming you the successor to the
throne."

Kate had thought that was what it would be. Elizabeth was too determined not to make one final attempt to get what she wanted. But maybe Kate was
being too harsh. Perhaps this was another gesture of
reconciliation like the one Elizabeth had made at their
last meeting.

"What shall we do with it?" Robert asked quietly.

She looked down at the seals and the sea, the pan-
orama of life and birth on the black rocks below.

A second chance to shift the balance. Power and
glory against Robert and the children and a happiness
that had shone like a brilliant sun these many years.
The fact that those years had been spent under the
shadow of the sword, with not one moment taken for
granted, had only made them more precious.

There was no contest.

She took Elizabeth's will and tucked the document
back into the hidden depths of the lute. "I do believe
we should give this lute to Patrick." She kissed Robert
lovingly on the cheek before linking her arm with his.
"A distraction is definitely needed. That rascal Gavin
has been teaching our son the bagpipes, and I believe
the lad's going to be even worse at it than Gavin himself."

About the Author

IRIS JOHANSEN has won every major romance writing award for her achievements in the genre since the publication of her very first novel, which earned her the Best New Category Romance Author Award from *Romantic Times*. She has won the *Affaire de Coeur* Silver Pen Award as their readers' favorite author, and most recently was honored with *Romantic Times*'s Lifetime Achievement Award.

*If you loved THE MAGNIFICENT ROGUE,
don't miss*

THE BELOVED SCOUNDREL

*Iris Johansen's next thrilling tale of abduction,
seduction, and surrender that sweeps from the
shimmering halls of Regency England to the
decadent haunts of a notorious rogue . . .*

Marianna Sanders realized she could not trust the
dark and savagely seductive stranger who had come
to spirit her away across the sea. She possessed a secret that could topple an empire, a secret Jordan
Draken, the duke of Cambaron, was determined to
wrest from her. In the eyes of the world the arrogant
duke was her guardian, but they both knew she was
to be a prisoner in his sinister plot—or a slave of his
exquisite pleasure.

In the following exerpt Marianna meets Jordan for
the first time. Read on for a tantalizing taste of Iris
Johansen's *The Beloved Scoundrel*, available in early
1994.

The Window to Heaven was shattered.

Only moonlight and cold wind streamed through the huge circular cavity where splendor and beauty had once reigned.

Marianna's fingers dug into the door to keep herself upright as she stared at the devastation. The journey had taken too long. She had failed Mama. The pattern was smashed, the *Jedalar* was gone. Then she forgot everything but her deep sense of loss at the sheer desecration of the act. She knew the *Jedalar* should be more important to her than the window, but—Dear God, all that wonder and beauty gone forever.

Why was she so stunned? They had destroyed everything else in her life. Perhaps it was even fitting that this last beautiful remnant had been destroyed along with those she loved.

"Marianna." Alex, her four-year-old brother, tugged at her arm. "I think I hear them!"

She went rigid, listening. She heard nothing, just the wind whistling through the shelled and deserted housed of the town. She looked out the doors of the church, her gaze searching the ruins that had once been the town of Casimar. She still heard nothing, but Alex had always possessed sharper hearing than she did. "Are you sure?"

"No, but I think . . . " He tilted his head. "Yes!"

She should never have come back. She should have

taken the road to the south. Mama would have forgiven her. They had not taken quite everything from her. She still had Alex, and by God in heaven she *would not* let him die.

She shut the heavy brass-studded door and pulled Alex behind her as she ran down the long aisle toward the altar, stumbling over a broken iron candelabra and several fat white candles scattered on the marble floor. The soldiers had wreaked their usual havoc here, she thought grimly. Everything of value had either been stolen or destroyed in this church that she had visited all her life. The gold crucifix that had once adorned the wall beneath the Window to Heaven had been stolen, the statue of Mary and the Child to the left of the altar had been toppled from the pedestal.

"Horses," Alex whispered.

She heard them now, too. The sharp clip-clop of hooves on the cobblestoned street outside.

"They won't find us," she whispered back. "They didn't see us come in, and those pigs can have no traffic with either churches or God." She pulled Alex behind a column near the altar and crouched down beside him. "We will stay here awhile and wait for them to go away."

Alex shivered and drew closer to her. "What if they do come?"

"They won't." She slid her arm around his shoulders. He was thinner than he had been last week, she realized in concern, and he had been coughing all day. The scraps of food she had managed to salvage from the deserted farmhouses outside the town had barely been enough to keep them alive.

"What if they do?" Alex repeated with a child's persistence.

"I said they—" She stopped. She didn't know the duke's soldiers wouldn't come, she thought wearily. She could not be sure of anything or anyone. She doubted if those monsters would come to worship, but they might come to loot and burn again. "If they come, we will hide here in the shadows and be very quiet until they leave. Can you do that?"

He nodded, his weight heavier against her. "I'm cold, Marianna."

"I know. As soon as we hear them leave, we'll find somewhere to shelter for the night."

"Can we light a fire?"

She shook her head. "But maybe we can find a blanket for you."

"And for you." The faint smile he gave her was enough to light his face with the cherubic radiance that had led her mother to use him as a model in her last work. It was the first time she had seen him smile since the night they had—

Mama . . .

She quickly blocked the thought. She must not think of that night or anything that had happened. She found that it weakened her, and she must stay strong for Alex.

"A blanket for me, too." She wanted to lean forward and kiss him, but Alex had reached the advanced age of four and regarded himself as too old to be kissed. "Just as soon as they leave the village."

But they weren't leaving. They were coming closer. She could hear the horses just outside the church and men's voices laughing and talking.

Her heart pounded as she drew Alex closer.

Let them go away, she prayed frantically. Please let them pass by the church.

Footsteps on the stone stairs.

The muscles of her stomach tightened painfully.

"Marianna?"

"Shhh." Her hand clamped over Alex's mouth.

The door creaked as it swung open. So much for prayers. Now she must do as she had been taught—rely only on herself.

Mama.

A tide of grief overwhelmed her, tears stung her eyes until she could barely see the man standing in the doorway.

She blinked them back. She had not cried since it had happened and she would not cry now. Tears were for the weak, and she must be strong.

She watched the man start down the aisle. He was tall, very tall, his stride long and purposeful, his dark cloak billowing behind him like the wings of a vulture. He was not in the duke's livery, but that didn't mean he wasn't the enemy. No one followed him, she noticed in relief. He had left those other pigs outside. She had a better chance of besting one man.

He stumbled in the darkness and muttered a curse.

She heard Alex's gasp beneath her hand that covered his lips. There had been many curses that night, curses and laughter and screams. She had held Alex to her breast so he would not see, but she had not been able to keep him from hearing. Her hand kneaded his thin shoulders in silent comfort.

The man stumbled again, then stooped to pick up something from the floor. A few minutes later a tiny flame of light pierced the darkness as he lit the stub of a broken candle he had retrieved.

She shrank further back into the shadows even as her gaze raked the enemy to search out weakness.

Dark hair tied back in a queue, a long face, a glimmer of green eyes.

He lifted the candle high, his gaze searching the darkness until he found the gaping hole that had once been the Window to Heaven. His hand tightened on the candle, his face contorted in an expression of demonic fury. "Damnation!" His booted foot kicked out at the shards of glass on the marble floor. "Damn it to hell!"

It was an English curse. He must be English like Papa, but she had never seen Papa in a fury like this.

Alex whimpered.

The man stiffened. "Who's there?"

He was turning toward them! She tried to think quickly through the sick terror tightening her chest. If he saw them, they would be helpless prey. Their only weapon was surprise.

"Stay here," she whispered. "Wait!" She pushed Alex further into the shadows, then charged toward the man.

"What the dev— Oof." Her head connected with his stomach and knocked the breath out of him. She grabbed the broken iron candelabra from the floor and brought it up between his legs. He gasped and doubled over in agony.

"Alex! Come!" she called.

Alex was behind her in seconds. She grabbed his hand and ran up the aisle toward the door.

She hit the floor, hard. The man had tackled her! He flipped her over and leaped astride her. Helpless. She was helpless as Mama had been helpless.

"No!" She struggled wildly.

"Lie still, damn you."

Alex leaped onto the man's back, his thin arms encircling his neck.

"Run, Alex," Marianna cried. "Run!"

She felt the man tense above her. "My God!" he muttered, and then in disgust, "Children!" He leaped to his feet, throwing off Alex's hold. Marianna scrambled to her knees and reached for the candelabra she had dropped in the struggle.

"Marianna!"

She looked up to see her brother struggling in the arms of the man. She lunged up at him, wielding the iron candelabra, but Alex was immediately lifted as a shield between them.

"Oh no, not again," he said grimly, this time in Montavian. "I will not permit a second assault on my person. I have other plans for my manhood."

As all men did. She wished he had a sword to cut it off. "Let him down," she said fiercely.

"Presently." He must be very strong; he was holding Alex as if he were weightless. "But only if you promise not to attack me."

"Put him down."

"Or?"

"I'll find a way to hurt you again."

"Ah, another threat. You're a little young to deal in threats."

She took a step closer.

He stiffened, his wary gaze on the iron pole in her hands. "Keep your distance." As she stopped, he relaxed a little. "One of the first things you should learn is that the man who possesses the prize dictates the terms. Now, I seem to have captured an object you value." He backed away from her a few paces. "He's very small, isn't he? Small children are so easy to hurt."

Fear ripped through her. "I'll kill you if you—"

"I have no intention of harming him," he interrupted. "Not if you don't force me to defend myself."

She studied him. His thick, dark hair had come loose from its queue in their struggle, and it framed a long face that was all planes and hollows. His brows slashed black and straight over startling green eyes, and his nose reminded her of the beak of an eagle. It was a hard face, a face as inflexible as stone, the face of a man who could be cruel.

"Answer my questions and I'll set this young man down," he said. "I assure you I don't usually make war on children."

She did not trust him, but she had little choice. "What do you want to know?"

"What are you doing here?"

She floundered for a convincing answer. "It was cold and we needed shelter for the night."

"There's not much shelter here with that window broken." His gaze was on her face, reading her expression. He didn't believe her, she realized in despair. She had never been good at lying. He continued. "Perhaps you're a thief. Perhaps you came in here to see what you could steal. It wouldn't be—"

"Marianna wouldn't steal," Alex said belligerently. "She only wanted to see the window, but it was gone. She would never—"

"Hush, Alex," she said sharply. It wasn't Alex's fault. He was only defending her and didn't know the importance of the *Jedalar.*

"The window?" He glanced over his shoulder. "Hell yes, it's gone." That terrible anger twisted his face again. "Bastards! I *wanted* that window."

He wanted the Window to Heaven. Then he must be one of them! "Who . . . who . . . are you?"

His gaze narrowed on her face. "Not Mephistopheles, as you seem to think. Who do you think I am?"

She moistened her lips. "I think you belong to the Duke of Nebrov."

"I belong to no one." His lips tightened. "Certainly not to that whoreson bastard. I don't— Ouch!"

Alex's teeth had sunk into his hand.

Marianna tensed, preparing to spring if he retaliated against the boy.

But he merely shook the boy's teeth off his hand as if he were a troublesome puppy. "It seems the cub is also fierce."

"He's afraid. Let him down."

"I'll strike a bargain with you. I'll put him down if you promise not to run away."

He had seemed sincere in his dislike of the duke, but that didn't mean he was not the enemy. He wanted the window. "You put him down and let him leave us and I'll not run away."

"But then I'll not have my shield."

She smiled with fierce satisfaction. "No."

His lips quirked but he did not smile in turn. "Done. I think I can protect myself from one small girl. Drop your weapon."

She hesitated, then dropped the iron pole.

"Good. Your promise?"

She had hoped he would not demand the words. "I promise," she said grudgingly and then quickly added, "If I see no danger to Alex."

He set the little boy on his feet. "There's no danger here for the boy."

There was danger everywhere and she must be prepared to face it. She turned to Alex. "Go to the garden and wait for me there."

"I don't want to go."

She didn't want Alex to go, either. The night was cold and he was ill and she did not know how long this Englishman would keep her here. She took off her wool shawl and wrapped it around him. "But you must." She gave him a gentle push. "I'll be with you soon."

He started to protest but stopped when he met her gaze. Then he turned and ran toward the small door to the left of the altar.

She was alone with the stranger. What if he hurt her the way they had hurt her mother? Fear closed around her heart, robbing her of breath, freezing her blood as she turned to face him.

• • •

"You sent away my hostage," he said mockingly. He set one of the candelabras upright, found the candle he had dropped and relit it. "It makes me feel exceptionally insecure. I don't know if I can tolerate— Good God you're shaking."

"I'm not." Her eyes shimmered with defiance. "I'm not afraid."

He could see that she was more than afraid, she was terrified. It was probably good that she feared him—fear would produce answers. But for some inexplicable reason he wanted to save her pride. "I didn't say you were. It must be the cold. You gave the boy your shawl." He took off his cloak. "Come here and let me put this around you."

She looked at the cloak as if it were a sword pointed at her. She took a deep breath. "I will not fight you, but you must make me a promise. You must not kill me afterward. Alex needs me."

"After what?" he asked. His gaze narrowed on her face and he understood. "Christ! You think I intend to rape you?"

"It's what men do to women."

"How old are you?"

"I've almost reached my sixteenth year."

"You look younger." In the loose, ragged blouse and skirt she wore her body appeared to be as straight and without womanly form as that of a child. She was small boned, delicate, almost painfully thin, and a smudge darkened one cheek. Her pale hair was pulled back in a long braid and added to the effect of extreme and vulnerable youth.

She stared at him scornfully. "What difference does it make how old I am? I'm female and that's all men care about."

Her tone was so certain, he felt a surge of pity for the waif. "Has this happened to you before?"

"Not to me." Her tone was suddenly reserved. He could almost see her withdraw inside herself, sidling away from some pain she would not discuss.

"And it won't happen now," he said grimly. "I'm not known to be above debauchery, but I don't rape children."

But she wasn't a child. Her clear blue eyes gazed at him with a worldliness far beyond her years, and her lips were set tight to prevent their trembling. The delicate beauty of her features should have reflected wonder instead of the raw wariness he saw there. He had seen the same look on the faces of the children in the towns and villages along Kazan's border, and it made him as angry now as it had then. "Where are your parents?"

She did not answer at once and when she did, it was in such a low voice that he had to strain to hear. "Dead."

"How?"

She did not answer at all this time.

"Who?"

"The duke."

He remembered her earlier accusation. "The Duke of Nebrov?"

She nodded.

It was no surprise to him. The powerful Duke of Nebrov had launched an insurrection against his brother, King Josef, over a year ago. It had been a bitter struggle and both armies had almost been destroyed before the duke had been forced to acknowledge defeat. The king's forces had been too scattered and weak to pursue Nebrov to his own lands, where he was now licking his wounds and undoubtedly building a new army. As the duke retreated, he made sure that Montavia suffered as much as possible and had given his men free rein to rape and pillage as they pleased. "One of the duke's troops killed your parents?"

She shook her head. "The duke," she whispered. She stared straight ahead as if the scene was there before her. "He did it. He did it."

"The duke himself?" That was unusual. Zarek Nebrov was a brutal bastard, but his rage was usually cold and controlled and he seldom indulged in blood spilling without reason. "Are you sure?"

"He came to our cottage and he ... I'm sure." She shuddered. "Mama told me ... She had seen him before. He hurt ... them and then he killed them."

"Why?"

He received no reply.

"Did you hear me?"

"I heard you." She said haltingly, "If you do not wish to hurt me, may I go now?"

Christ, he felt as brutal a bastard as Nebrov. The girl was helpless and in pain. He should just call Gregor and have him send one of his men to find the girl's nearest relations and take her to them. But he knew he had to find out more. The coincidence was too blatant. She had come to see the window, and according to her few agonized words the girl's mother had been tortured before she was killed. Nebrov never did anything without reason. "No, you may not go." He held out his cloak to her again. "You will put on this cloak." He deliberately kept his tone hard, but he sat down in a pew so that he would appear less threatening to her. He felt like a giant looming over her fragile form. "Sit down."

"I won't talk about that anymore," she said unsteadily. "No matter what you do to me."

That painful memory was probably her weakest link, but he found he couldn't strike at it. "Stay," he said wearily. "I promise I'll never ask you to talk about that night again."

She hesitated, her gaze searching his face. Then she took his cloak and slipped it on but did not sit down. "Why do you want me to stay?"

"I'm not sure." God knows, he had done all he could. Now that he knew the window was destroyed, his only course was to meet with Janos so that he could carry the word to Kazan and then board his ship and leave this damn country. Even if this waif knew something she wasn't telling, the window was broken, damn it. Yet he couldn't let it rest until he was certain Nebrov hadn't discovered something he had not. His gaze returned to the cavity surrounded by jagged glass. "It seems strange that we were both brought together at this place and time. Do you believe in fate?"

"No."

"I do. My mother was a Tartar and she instilled a belief in the fates along with mother's milk." His stare never left the empty window. "The town is sacked and deserted. You and your brother are ragged and in want and you couldn't be sure the duke's forces wouldn't return, yet you picked this time to come to see the window. Why?"

"Why did you?" she countered.

"I wished to acquire it. I heard it was magnificent and I wished to take it back to my home."

"You wished to steal it."

"You don't understand."

"You wished to steal it," she repeated, her tone uncompromising.

"All right, have it your way. I wished to steal it." He met her gaze. "Now, why did you come?"

Those clear, fierce eyes slid away from his own. "I had to see if it was still there."

"Why?"

She didn't reply.

"You would be wise to answer me."

Her defiant gaze shifted back to him and her tone was scornful as she echoed his own lie, "Why, I heard it was magnificent and I wanted it for my home."

The girl had courage. She was still frightened and yet she refused to yield. He was careful not to show the flicker of admiration he felt. "Shall I go to the garden and fetch your brother? I'm sure he would tell me why you're here."

"Leave him alone!"

"Then tell me the truth."

She burst out, "Because it was mine!"

He hid the excitement that jolted through him. "The Pope would not agree. Everything in his churches belongs to God and so to him."

"It *is* mine," she said fiercely. "My grandmother gave it to me before she died last year."

"How kind of her. And what right did she have to bestow such a gift?"

"She created it. She said the church did not pay us for the work, so it was still ours."

"I fear she told you a falsehood. The window was created by Anton Pragini, a great craftsman."

She shook her head. "That was my grandfather, but it wasn't he who was the craftsman, it was my grandmother."

His brows lifted. "A woman?"

"That's why she had to let him lay claim to the work.

They would not have accepted the work of a woman. It is always our women who do the work."

"Always?"

She nodded. "For over five hundred years the women in my family have worked in glass. We're trained from the time we leave the cradle. My mother said I have a special gift and when I'm grown I will be as great a craftsman as my grandmother."

A flare of hope shot through him. "And just how familiar are you with the Window to Heaven?"

He had carefully kept his tone offhand, but she went rigid. Clearly she knew more than she was telling. He retreated quickly and changed the subject. "What do the men of your family do while you're creating these glorious works?"

A little of her tension eased. "Whatever they wish. They are well taken care of."

"Then it's the women who work to provide the living and care for the men of the family?"

She frowned at him. "Of course. It is our duty. We always— Why are you looking at me like that?"

"Forgive me if I find the idea extraordinary."

She shifted uneasily. "I must go. Alex is waiting."

"And where will you go? I assume your home is in ruins like the rest of Talenka."

"We don't live here. Our cottage is just outside Samda."

Samda was over seventy miles to the west, a rough, hard trek even for a man on horseback, and yet this young girl had been driven to forge her way to this church on foot. "Do you have relatives in Samda?"

"I have no one anywhere," she said matter-of-factly, but desolation echoed beneath the words.

He had a sense of everything coming together. After all the hell and blood that had gone before, fate had finally got it right. "Then I'll take you with me."

She stared at him.

"Come with me," he said. His eyes glinted with recklessness. "It's clear you were sent to me as a gift, and I never refuse a gift from the gods."

She started backing away from him.

She was looking at him as if he had gone mad. Well, he felt a little mad at the moment. Despair and anger had changed to hope, and that could be a heady brew.

"How can you take care of your Alex without help? He needs hot food and warm clothing. I can give these to you."

She hesitated. "Why . . . would you do this?"

"Perhaps I wish to do my kind Christian duty and aid two orphans," he said mockingly.

Those clear blue eyes searched his expression. "But I think you're not a kind man."

"How clever of you to realize that fact, but you're not entirely correct. I do practice kindness . . . when it's convenient. It is convenient now. Isn't that fortunate for you and your Alex?"

She shook her head, her gaze clinging to his.

He could see she wanted desparately to be convinced. All he had to do was say the words she wanted to hear. He tried to decide the best way to proceed. Persuading women to do as he wanted had never been a problem. He had learned to charm and beguile before he left the nursery. Yet he was curiously reluctant to lie to this big-eyed waif. "You're quite right. I've never been known to follow the path of duty. I've always found it an abysmal bore." He continued crisply. "Very well, I do have a reason for wanting to help you, but I have no intention of divulging it. If you want to come with me, then you'll do so on my terms. You'll agree to obey me without question and in return I'll promise that there will be food and shelter and protection for both of you as long as you're under my care. If you choose not to come, then you can stay here in these ruins and let your brother starve to death."

He turned and started back up the aisle. He had no intention of leaving her here even if it meant abducting her, but it would be simpler if she made the decision.

"Wait."

He stopped but didn't turn around. "You're coming with me?"

"Yes." She moved brusquely forward. "I'll go with you." She added quickly, "For now. But Alex stays in the garden until I'm sure it's safe. I'll take food and blankets to him."

"As you like. But you'd better make up your mind quickly. I intend to leave this town by sunrise."

"That's too soon," she said, panic-stricken.

"Sunrise," he repeated. "What did the boy call you? Marianna?"

"Marianna Sanders."

"Sanders." He opened the heavy door for her. "That's not a Montavian name."

"My father was English." She slanted him a glance. "Like you."

He recalled his outburst of profanity when he had seen the broken window. "And your mother?"

She looked away from him and he was again aware of that wall of reserve. "Montavian." She asked quickly, "Why is an Englishman in Montavia?"

"Because he wants to be," he said mockingly. "You've not asked me my name. I'm hurt you have so little interest when we're to be fast companions."

"Well, what is it?" she said impatiently.

He bowed. "Jordan Draken. At your service."

IRIS JOHANSEN
Bantam's Mistress of Romantic Fantasy

The Tiger Prince
———— 29968-9 $5.50/6.50 In Canada

Last Bridge Home
———— 29871-2 $4.50/5.50 In Canada

The Golden Barbarian
———— 29604-3 $4.99/5.99 In Canada

The Wind Dancer Trilogy

"Destined to be a classic series." —*Affaire de Coeur*

The Wind Dancer
———— 28855-5 $4.95/5.95 In Canada

Storm Winds
———— 29032-0 $4.99/5.99 In Canada

Reap the Wind
———— 29244-7 $4.99/5.99 In Canada

Look for these titles at your local bookstore or use this page to order.

❏ Please send me the books I have checked above. I am enclosing $ _____ (add $2.50 to cover postage and handling). Send check or money order, no cash or C. O. D.'s please.

Mr./ Ms. _____

Address _____

City/ State/ Zip _____

Send order to: Bantam Books, Dept. FN37, 2451 S. Wolf Road, Des Plaines, IL 60018

Allow four to six weeks for delivery.

Prices and availability subject to change without notice.   FN37 - 9/93

THE LATEST IN BOOKS
AND AUDIO CASSETTES

Paperbacks

❏	28412-6	A SEASON OF SWANS	Celeste de Blasis	$5.95
❏	28354-5	SEDUCTION	Amanda Quick	$5.99
❏	28594-7	SURRENDER	Amanda Quick	$5.99
❏	29316-8	RAVISHED	Amanda Quick	$4.99
❏	28435-5	A WORLD OF DIFFERENCE	Leona Blair	$5.95
❏	28416-9	RIGHTFULLY MINE	Doris Mortman	$5.95
❏	27032-X	FIRST BORN	Doris Mortman	$5.99
❏	27283-7	BRAZEN VIRTUE	Nora Roberts	$4.99
❏	27891-6	PEOPLE LIKE US	Dominick Dunne	$5.99
❏	27260-8	WILD SWAN	Celeste De Blasis	$5.95
❏	25692-0	SWAN'S CHANCE	Celeste De Blasis	$5.95
❏	27790-1	A WOMAN OF SUBSTANCE		
		Barbara Taylor Bradford		$5.95
❏	29761-9	THE WILD ROSE	Doris Mortman	$5.99
❏	28734-6	WELL-SCHOOLED IN MURDER		
		Elizabeth George		$5.99

Audio

❏ SEPTEMBER by Rosamunde Pilcher
Performance by Lynn Redgrave
180 Mins. Double Cassette   45241-X $15.99
❏ THE SHELL SEEKERS by Rosamunde Pilcher
Performance by Lynn Redgrave
180 Mins. Double Cassette   45183-9 $15.99
❏ COLD SASSY TREE by Olive Ann Burns
Performance by Richard Thomas
180 Mins. Double Cassette   45166-9 $15.99
❏ WELL-SCHOOLED IN MURDER by Elizabeth George
Performance by Derek Jacobi
180 Mins. Double Cassette   45278-9 $15.99

Available at your local bookstore or use this page to order.

Send to: Bantam Books, Dept. FBS
2451 S. Wolf Road
Des Plaines, IL 60018

Please send me the items I have checked above. I am enclosing
$_____ (please add $2.50 to cover postage and handling). Send
check or money order, no cash or C.O.D.'s, please.

Mr./Ms._____

Address_____

City/State_____Zip_____

Please allow four to six weeks for delivery.
Prices and availability subject to change without notice.   FBS 6/93